About the Author

Since her first novel, *From Doon with Death*, published in 1964, Ruth Rendell has won many awards, including the Crime Writer's Association Gold Dagger for 1976's best crime novel with *A Demon In My View*, and the Arts Council National Book Award, genre fiction, for *The Lake of Darkness* in 1980.

In 1985 Ruth Rendell received the Silver Dagger for *The Tree of Hands*, and in 1987, writing as Barbara Vine, won her third Edgar from the Mystery Writers of America for *A Dark-Adapted Eye*.

She won the Gold Dagger for *Live Flesh* in 1986, for *King Solomon's Carpet* in 1991 and, as Barbara Vine, a Gold Dagger in 1987 for *A Fatal Inversion*.

Ruth Rendell won the *Sunday Times* Literary Award in 1990, and in 1991 she was awarded the Crime Writer's Association Cartier Diamond Dagger for outstanding contributions to the genre. In 1996 she was awarded the CBE, and in 1997 was made a Life Peer.

Her books have been translated into twenty-five languages and are also published to great acclaim in the United States.

Ruth Rendell has a son and two grandsons, and lives in London

By Ruth Rendell

OMNIBUSES

Collected Short Stories
Wexford: An Omnibus
The Second Wexford Omnibus
The Third Wexford Omnibus
The Fourth Wexford Omnibus
The Fifth Wexford Omnibus
The Ruth Rendell Omnibus
The Second Ruth Rendell Omnibus
The Third Ruth Rendell Omnibus

SHORT STORIES

The Fallen Curtain
Means of Evil
The Fever Tree
The New Girl Friend
The Copper Peacock
Blood Lines
Piranha to Scurfy

NOVELLA

Heartstones

NON FICTION

Ruth Rendell's Suffolk
Ruth Rendell's Anthology
  Of the Murderous Mind

CHIEF INSPECTOR WEXFORD NOVELS

From Doon with Death
A New Lease of Death
Wolf to the Slaughter
The Best Man to Die
A Guilty Thing Surprised
No More Dying Then
Murder Being Once Done
Some Lie and Some Die
Shake Hands For Ever
A Sleeping Life
Put On by Cunning
The Speaker of Mandarin
An Unkindness of Ravens
The Veiled One
Kissing the Gunner's Daughter
Simisola
Road Rage
Harm Done
Babes in the Wood

NOVELS

To Fear a Painted Devil
Vanity Dies Hard
The Secret House of Death
The Face of Trespass
A Demon in My View
A Judgment in Stone
Make Death Love Me
The Lake of Darkness
Master of the Moor
The Killing Doll
The Tree of Hands
Live Flesh
Talking to Strange Men
The Bridesmaid
Going Wrong
The Crocodile Bird
The Keys to the Street
A Sight for Sore Eyes
Adam & Eve and Pinch Me
The Rottweiler
Thirteen Steps Down

RUTH RENDELL

NO MORE DYING THEN

SOME LIE AND
SOME DIE

arrow books

This edition published by Arrow Books in 2005

Arrow Books
The Random House Group Ltd
20 Vauxhall Bridge Road, London SW1V 2SA

Random House Australia (Pty) Limited
20 Alfred Street, Milsons Point, Sydney,
New South Wales 2061, Australia

Random House New Zealand Limited
18 Poland Road, Glenfield
Auckland 10, New Zealand

Random House (Pty) Limited
Endulini, 5a Jubilee Road
Parktown 2193, South Africa

The Random House Group Limited Reg. No. 954009

www.randomhouse.co.uk

A CIP catalogue record for this book
is available from the British Library

Papers used by Random House are natural,
recyclable products made from wood grown in sustainable
forests. The manufacturing processes conform to the
environmental regulations of the country of origin.

ISBN 0 09 190745 4

Printed and bound in Great Britain by
Cox & Wyman Ltd, Reading, Berkshire

RUTH RENDELL

NO MORE DYING THEN

arrow books

For Gerald Austin

So shalt thou feed on death that feeds on men,
And death, once dead, there's no more dying then.

Shakespeare, Sonnet 146

Chapter 1

The spell of fine weather which so often occurs in the middle of October is known as St Luke's Little Summer. The 'little summer' part needs no explanation; the St Luke bit derives from its coincidence with the eighteenth, which is that saint's day. Basking in the warm autumn sunlight, Station Sergeant Camb delivered this piece of interesting but useless information to Harry Wild and smiled sententiously.

'Is that so? Maybe I'll do a diary note on it.' Wild sucked at his smelly old pipe and rested leather-patched elbows on the counter top. He yawned. 'Haven't you got anything more exciting for me?'

Camb caught the yawn and yawned himself. He remarked for the third time on the closeness of the weather and then he opened his book.

'Two vehicles in collision at the junction of Kingsmarkham High Street and Queen Street,' he read. 'Nobody hurt. That was Sunday. Nothing in that for the *Courier*, is there? Girl of seventeen missing, but we know where she is all right. Oh, and there's a baboon got lost from the pet shop ...' Wild looked up, lazily enquiring. '... Only they found it up on their balcony, tucking in to the waste bin.'

'What a dump,' said Wild. He put away his notebook. 'Still, I opted for the quiet life. I could be up in Fleet Street tomorrow if I fancied it. Only got to say the word and I'd be up there where it's all happening.'

1

'Sure you would.' Camb knew very well that Wild remained as chief reporter of the *Kingsmarkham Courier* because idleness and general ineptitude, as well now as his advancing years, made him unfit for any more illustrious newspaper. Wild had been coming into the police station for more years than Camb cared to remember and every time he came he talked about Fleet Street as if he had rejected it and not it him. But they sustained the fiction for the sake of peace and pleasantness. 'Much the same for me,' he said. 'Many a time in the old days Mr Wexford begged me to consider the C.I.D. but I wouldn't. I'm not ambitious. I don't say I wouldn't have had the ability, mind.'

'Of course you would've.' Playing fair, Wild returned praise for praise. 'Where does it get you, though, ambition? Look at Inspector Burden, just to take an example. Worn out, and not forty yet, I daresay.'

'Well, he's had a lot of trouble, hasn't he? Losing his wife like that and two kids to bring up.'

Wild gave a heavy lugubrious sigh. 'That,' he said, 'was a tragic business. Cancer, wasn't it?'

'That's right. Fit as a fiddle this time last year and dead by Christmas. Only thirty-five. It makes you think.'

'In the midst of life. Looks to me as if he's taken it hard. I suppose they were a devoted couple?'

'More like sweethearts than man and wife.' Camb cleared his throat and stood up straighter as the lift opened and Chief Inspector Wexford marched out.

'Gossiping again, Sergeant? Good afternoon, Harry.' Wexford just glanced at the two empty teacups on the counter. 'This place,' he said, 'gets more like a Mothers' Union bun fight every week.'

'I was just telling Mr Wild,' said Camb with dignity, 'about our escaped baboon.'

'My God, that's hot news. There's a story in that, Harry. Terrorising the populace, mothers afraid to let their kids out of their sight. Is any woman safe while this wild beast roams our meadows?'

'It's been found, sir. In a dustbin.'

'Sergeant, if I didn't know you to be incapable of it, I should say you were mocking me.' Wexford quivered with silent laughter. 'When Inspector Burden comes in, tell him I've gone, will you? I want a few hours to enjoy our Indian Summer.'

'St Luke's Little Summer, sir.'

'Indeed? I stand corrected. I wish I had the time to devote to digging up these fascinating pieces of meteorological lore. I'll give you a lift, Harry, if you've finished your monkey business.'

Camb sniggered. 'Thanks very much,' said Wild.

It was gone five but still very warm. The sergeant stretched and wished Constable Peach would appear so that he could send him to the canteen for another cup of tea. Half an hour and he would knock off.

Presently the phone rang.

A woman's voice, low and rich. Actressy. Camb thought. 'I'm sorry to trouble you, but my little boy ... He's – well, he was out playing and he's – he's disappeared. I don't ... Am I making a fuss over nothing?'

'Not at all, madam,' said Camb soothingly. 'That's what we're here for, to be troubled. What name is it?'

'Lawrence. I live at 61 Fontaine Road, Stowerton.'

Camb hesitated for a second. Then he remembered Wexford had told him all cases of missing children must be reported to C.I.D. They didn't want another Stella Rivers ...

'Don't worry, Mrs Lawrence. I'm going to put you through to someone who will help you.' He got the switchboard and heard Sergeant Martin's voice, put down the receiver.

3

Sergeant Camb sighed. It was a pity Harry had gone like that, just when the only piece of news had come in for weeks. He could give poor old Harry a ring ... Tomorrow would do. The kid would be found, come to that, like that monkey had been. Missing people and things usually were found in Kingsmarkham and in more or less good order. Camb turned his head in the sunlight like someone turning a piece of toast in the red light of a fire. It was twenty past five. By six he'd be sitting down to his dinner in Severn Court, Station Road; then a little jaunt out with the wife to the Dragon, then telly ...

'Having a nice little kip, Sergeant?' said a cold voice with an edge to it like a freshly unwrapped razor blade. Camb nearly jumped out of his skin.

'Sorry, Mr Burden. It's the heat, makes you sleepy. St Luke's Little Summer, they call it, on account of ...'

'Are you off your bloody head?' Burden had never sworn in the old days. It had been quite a joke in the police station the way he never took the name of the Lord in vain or said bloody or any of the things everyone else said. Camb liked the old days better. He felt his face reddening and it wasn't the sun. 'Any messages for me?' Burden snapped.

Camb looked at him sadly. He was terribly sorry for Inspector Burden, his heart ached for his bereaved colleague, and that was why he forgave Burden for humiliating him and showing him up in front of Martin and Gates and even Peach. Camb couldn't imagine what it must be like to lose one's wife, the mother of one's children, and be alone and desolate. Burden was so thin. The sharp high cheekbones jutted out of his taut skin and his eyes glittered nastily when you glanced at them but they were unbearable when you looked deeper. Once he had been rather a handsome man, English-looking, blond

4

and ruddy, but now all the colour and life had gone out of him and he was a sort of grey. He still wore a black tie, pulled so tight you thought it would choke him.

Once, when it had first happened, the sergeant had expressed his sympathy along with everyone else, and that was all right, that was expected. And then, later, he had tried to say something more sincere and more personal, and Burden had swung on him like a man drawing a sword. He had said terrible things. It was more terrible to hear them coming from those mild cool lips than from the mouths of the Kingsmarkham roughs who used them habitually. It was like opening a nice book written by someone whose books you liked and asked the library to keep for you, opening it and reading a word that used to be printed with an f and a dash.

So, although Camb wanted at this moment to say something kind – wasn't he old enough to be this man's father? – he only sighed and replied in a blank official voice, 'Mr Wexford went home, sir. He said he ...'

'That's all?'

'No, sir. There's a child missing and ...'

'Why the hell didn't you say so before?'

'It's all taken care of,' Camb stammered. 'Martin knows and he's bound to have phoned Mr Wexford. Look, sir, it's not for me to interfere, but – well, why don't you just go home, sir?'

'When I require your instructions, Sergeant, I'll ask for them. The last child that went missing here was never found. *I am not going home.*' I have nothing to go home for. He didn't say it, but the words were there and the sergeant heard them. 'Get me an outside line, will you?'

Camb did so and Burden said, 'My home.' When Grace Woodville answered, Camb gave the phone to

5

her brother-in-law. 'Grace? Mike. Don't wait dinner for me. There's a child missing. I should be in by ten.'

Burden crashed down the receiver and made for the lift. Camb watched the doors blankly for ten minutes and then Sergeant Mathers came down to take over the desk.

The bungalow in Tabard Road looked exactly as it had done in Jean Burden's lifetime. The floors gleamed, the windows shone and there were flowers – chrysanthemums at this season – in the Poole pottery vases. Plain English food was served at regular times and the children had the cared-for look of children who have a loving mother. The beds were made by eight-thirty, the washing was on the line by nine and a pleasant cheerful voice sounded a greeting to those who came home.

Grace Woodville had seen to all this. It had seemed to her the only way, to keep the house as her sister had done, to act with the children as her sister had done. She already looked as much like her sister as is possible for two women who are not twins. And it had worked. Sometimes she thought John and Pat almost forgot. They came to her when they were hurt or in trouble or had something interesting to tell just as they had gone to Jean. They seemed happy, recovered from the wound of Christmas. It had worked for them and the house and the practical business of running things, but it hadn't worked for Mike. Of course it hadn't. Had she really thought it would?

She put down the phone and looked into the glass where she saw Jean's face looking back at her. Her own face had never seemed like Jean's while Jean was alive, but quite different, squarer and stronger and more fulfilled and – well, why not say it? – more intelligent. It was like Jean's now. The liveliness had

6

gone out of it, the sharp wit, and that wasn't surprising when she thought how she spent her days, cooking and cleaning and comforting and waiting at home for a man who took it all for granted.

She called out, 'John? That was your father. He won't be home till ten. I think we'll eat, shall we?' His sister was in the garden, gathering caterpillars for the collection she kept in the garage. Grace was more afraid of caterpillars than most women are of mice or spiders, but she had to pretend to like them, even to gloat over them, because she was all Pat had for a mother. 'Pat! Food, darling. Don't be long.'

The little girl was eleven. She came in and opened the matchbox she was holding. Grace's heart squeezed and chilled at the sight of the fat green thing inside. 'Lovely,' she said faintly. 'A lime hawk?' She had done her homework, and Pat, like all children, valued adults who bothered.

'Look at his sweet face.'

'Yes, I am. I hope he'll grow into a chrysalis before the leaves die off. Daddy won't be home for dinner.'

Pat gave an indifferent shrug. She didn't love her father much at present. He had loved her mother more than her, she knew that now, and she also knew that he ought to love her to make up for what she had lost. One of the teachers at school had told her that he would, that all fathers did that. She had waited and he hadn't. He had always stayed out late working but now he stayed out nearly all the time. She transferred her simple animal-like love to her Aunt Grace. Privately she thought it would be nice if John and her father went away and left her with her aunt and then the two of them would have a lovely time collecting better and rarer caterpillars and reading books on natural history and science and the Bolshoi Ballet.

She sat down at the table next to her aunt and then began to eat the chicken-and-ham pie which was just like the ones Jean used to make.

Her brother said, 'We had a debate at school today on the equality of the sexes.'

'That was interesting,' said Grace. 'What did you have to say?'

'I left most of the talking to the others. One thing I did say, women's brains don't weigh as much as men's.'

'They do,' said Pat.

'No, they don't. They don't, do they, Auntie Grace?'

'I'm afraid they don't,' said Grace, who had been a nurse. 'But that doesn't mean they aren't as good.'

'I bet,' said Pat with a vindictive look at her brother, 'I bet mine weighs more than yours. My head's bigger. Anyway, it's all boring, discussions and stuff. A lot of talk.'

'Come along, darling, eat your pie.'

'When I am grown up,' said Pat, beginning on a perennial theme, 'I'm not going to talk and argue and do boring things. I'm going to get my degree – no, maybe I'll wait till I've got my doctorate – and then I'm going to go to Scotland and make a big investigation of the lochs, all the very deep lochs, and discover the monsters that live in them, and then I'm ...'

'There aren't any monsters. They looked and they never found one.'

Pat ignored her brother. 'I'll have divers and a special boat and a whole staff and Auntie Grace will be at the station looking after us and cooking for us.'

They began to argue fiercely. It could happen, Grace thought. That was the horrible thing, it could just happen. Sometimes she could see herself staying here until they were grown up and she was old and then tagging along after Pat, being her housekeeper. What else would she be fit for then? And what did it matter whether her brain weighed less than a man's or more or the same when it was stuck in a little house in the depths of Sussex, atrophying away?

She had been a sister in a big London teaching hospital when Jean died and she had taken the six weeks' leave that was owing to her to come here and care for Mike and Mike's children. Just six weeks she was going to stay. You didn't spend years of your life studying, taking cuts in salary, to study for more qualifications, going to the States for two years to learn the latest obstetric methods at a Boston clinic, and then just give it all up. The hospital board had told her not to and she had laughed at the very idea. But the six weeks had lengthened into six months, into nine, ten, and now her post at the hospital had been filled by someone else.

She looked thoughtfully at the children. How could she leave them now? How could she even think of leaving them for five years? And then Pat would be only sixteen.

It was all Mike's fault. A hard thing to think, but true. Other men lost their wives. Other men adjusted. On Mike's salary and with his allowances he could afford a housekeeper. And it wasn't only that. A man as intelligent as Mike ought to realise what he was doing to her and the children. She had come at his invitation, his passionate plea, thinking that she would have his support in her task, certain that he would make an effort to be home in the evenings, take the children out at weekends, compensate them in some measure for the loss of their mother. He had done none of this. How long was it now since he'd spent one evening at home? Three weeks? Four? And he wasn't always working. One night when she could no longer stand the sight of John's bitter rebellious face she had phoned Wexford and the chief inspector had told her Mike went off duty at five. A neighbour had told her later where Mike went. She had seen him sitting in his car on one of the paths in Cheriton Forest, just sitting still and staring at the straight, parallel, endless trees.

'Shall we have some television?' she said, trying to keep the weariness out of her voice. 'There's quite a good film on, I believe.'

'Too much homework,' John said, 'and I can't do the maths till my father comes. Did you say he'd be back at ten?'

'He said about ten.'

'I think I'll go into my room, then.'

Grace and Pat sat on the sofa and watched the film. It was all about the domestic lives of policemen and bore little relation to reality.

Burden drove to Stowerton, through the new part and into the old High Street. Fontaine Road was parallel with Wincanton Road, and there, years and years ago when they were first married, he and Jean had for six months rented a flat. Wherever he went in Kingsmarkham and its environs he kept coming on places that he and Jean had been to or visited on some special occasion. He couldn't avoid them, but the sight of them brought fresh hurt every time and the pain did not diminish. Since her death he had avoided Wincanton Road, for there they had been especially happy, young lovers learning what love was. Today had been a bad day, bad in that for some reason he was ultra-sensitive and prickly, and he felt that the sight of the house where their flat had been would be the last straw. Control might go utterly and he would stand at the gate and weep.

He didn't even look at the street name as he passed it but kept his eyes fixed straight ahead. He turned left into Fontaine Road and stopped outside number 61.

It was a very ugly house, built about eighty years ago, and surrounded by a wild untended garden full of old fruit trees whose leaves lay in drifts on the grass. The house itself was built of khaki-coloured bricks with a shallow, almost flat, slate roof. Its windows were the sash kind and very small, but the front door was enormous, quite out of proportion, a great heavy thing with inset panels of red and blue stained glass. It was slightly ajar.

Burden didn't go into the house at once. Wexford's car, among other police cars, was parked against the fence which divided the end of the street from the field Stowerton Council had turned into a children's playground. Beyond this came more fields, woods, the rolling countryside.

Wexford was sitting in his car, studying an ordnance survey map. He looked up as Burden approached and said:

'Good of you to get here so fast. I've only just arrived myself. Will you talk to the mother or shall I?'

'I will,' said Burden.

There was a heavy knocker on the front door of number 61, shaped like a lion's head with a ring in its mouth. Burden touched it lightly and then he pushed open the door.

Chapter 2

A young woman was standing in the hall, holding her hands clasped in front of her. The first thing Burden noticed about her was her hair which was the same colour as the dead apple leaves that had blown in on to the tiled passage floor. It was fiery copper hair, neither straight nor curly but massy and glittering like fine wire or thread spun on a distaff, and it stood out from her small white face and fell to the middle of her back.

'Mrs Lawrence?'

She nodded.

'My name is Burden, Inspector Burden, C.I.D. Before we talk about this I'd like a photograph of your son and some article of clothing he's recently worn.'

She looked at him, wide-eyed, as if he were a clairvoyant who could sense the missing boy's whereabouts from handling his garments.

'For the dogs,' he said gently.

She went upstairs and he heard her banging about feverishly, opening drawers. Yes, he thought, it would be an untidy house with nothing in its place, nothing to hand. She came back, running, with a dark green school blazer and an enlarged snapshot. Burden looked at the photograph as he hurried up the road. It was of a big sturdy child, neither very clean nor very tidy, but undeniably beautiful, with thick light hair and large dark eyes.

The men who had come to search for him stood about in groups, some in the swings field, some clustered around the police cars. There were sixty or seventy of them, neighbours, friends and relatives of neighbours, and others who had arrived on bicycles from further afield. The speed with which news of this kind travels always amazed Burden. It was scarcely six o'clock. The police themselves had only been alerted half an hour before.

He approached Sergeant Martin, who seemed to be involved in some kind of altercation with one of the men, and handed him the photograph.

'What was all that about?' said Wexford.

'Chap told me to mind my own business because I advised him he'd need thicker shoes. That's the trouble with getting the public in, sir. They always think they know best.'

'We can't do without them, Sergeant,' Wexford snapped. 'We need every available man at a time like this, police and public.'

The two most efficient and experienced searchers belonged, properly speaking, in neither category. They sat a little apart from the men and viewed them with wary scorn. The labrador bitch's coat gleamed like satin in the last of the sun, but the alsatian's thick pelt was dull and rough and wolflike. With a quick word to the man Sergeant Martin had admonished not to go near the dogs – he appeared to be about to caress the alsatian – Wexford passed the blazer over to the labrador's handler.

While the dogs explored the blazer with expert noses, Martin formed the men into parties, a dozen or so in each and each with its leader. There were too few torches to go round and Wexford cursed the season with its deceptive daytime heat and its cold nights that rushed in early. Already dark fingers of cloud were creeping across the redness of the sky and a sharp bite of frost threatened. It would be dark before the search parties reached the wood that crouched like a black and furry bear over the edges of the fields.

Burden watched the small armies enter the wide swings field and begin the long hunt that would take them to Forby and beyond. A frosty oval moon, just beginning to wane from the full, showed above the woods. If only it would shine bright, unobscured by that blue-black floating cloud, it would be a greater asset than all their torches.

The women of Fontaine Road who had hung over their gates to see the men go now strayed lingeringly back into their houses. Each one of them would have to be questioned. Had she seen anything? Anyone? Had anything at all out of the way happened that day? On Wexford's orders, Loring and Gates were beginning a house-to-house investigation. Burden went back to Mrs Lawrence and followed her into the front room, a big room full of ugly Victorian furniture to match the house. Toys and books and magazines were scattered everywhere and there were clothes about, shawls and scarves draped over the furniture. A long patchwork dress on a hanger hung from a picture rail.

The place looked even dirtier and frowstier when she switched on the standard lamp, and she looked stranger. She wore jeans, a satin shirt and strings of tarnished chains around her neck. He didn't need to admire her, but he would have liked to be able to feel sympathy. This woman with her wild hair and her strange clothes made him immediately feel that she was no fit person to be in charge of a child and even that her appearance and all he associated with it had perhaps contributed to that child's disappearance. He told himself not to jump to conclusions, not yet.

'Now, what is the boy's name and how old is he?'

'John. He's five.'

'Not at school today?'

'It's half-term for the primary schools,' she said. 'I'll tell you about this afternoon, shall I?'

'Please.'

'Well, we had our lunch, John and I, and after lunch at about two his friend from next door came to call for him. He's called Gary Dean and he's five too.' She was very composed, but now she swallowed and cleared her throat. 'They were going to play in the street on their tricycles. It's quite safe. They know they have to stay on the pavement.

'When John goes out to play I look out of the window every half-hour or so to see he's all right and I did that today. You can see all the street and the field where the swings are from my landing window. Well, for a bit they played on the pavement with the other boys, all boys from around here, but when I looked out at half past three they'd gone into the swings field.'

'You could make out your son from this distance?'

'He's wearing a dark blue sweater and he's got fair hair.'

'Go on, Mrs Lawrence.'

She took a deep breath and clasped the fingers of one hand tightly in the other.

'They'd left their tricycles in a sort of huddle on the pavement. The next time I looked they were all on the swings and I could pick out John by his hair and his sweater. Or – or I thought I could. There were six boys there, you see. Anyway, when I looked out again they'd all gone and I went down to open the front door for John. I thought he must be coming in for his tea.'

'But he wasn't?'

'No, his tricycle was on the pavement by itself.' She bit her lip, her face very white now. 'There

15

weren't any children in the street. I thought John must have gone into someone else's house – he does that sometimes although he's not supposed to without telling me so I waited – oh, five minutes, not more – and then I went into the Deans to see if he was there. It gave me a shock,' she said, half-whispering. 'That was when I first started getting frightened. Gary was there, having his tea, and there was a boy with him in a blue sweater and with fair hair, but it wasn't John. It was his cousin who'd come over for the afternoon. You see, I realised then that the boy I'd been thinking was John ever since half past three was this cousin.'

'What did you do next?'

'I asked Gary where John was and he said he didn't know. He'd gone some hours ago, he said – that was how he put it, hours ago – and they thought he was with me. Well, I went to another boy's house then, a boy called Julian Crantock at 59, and Mrs Crantock and I, we got it out of Julian. He said Gary and the cousin had started on John, just silly children's teasing, but you know what they're like, how they hurt each other and get hurt. They picked on John about his sweater, said it was a girl's because of the way the buttons do up at the neck, and John – well, Julian said he sat on the roundabout by himself for a bit and then he just walked off towards the road.'

'This road? Fontaine Road?'

'No. The lane that runs between the swings field and the farm fields. It goes from Stowerton to Forby.'

'I know it,' Burden said, 'Mill Lane. There's a drop into it from those fields, down a bank, and there are trees all along the top of the bank.'

She nodded. 'But why would he go there? Why? He's been told again and again he's never to leave the street or the swings field.'

'Little boys don't always do as they are told, Mrs Lawrence. Was it after this that you phoned us?'

'Not at once,' she said. She lifted her eyes and met Burden's. They were greenish-grey eyes and they held a terrified bewilderment, but she kept her voice low and even. 'I went to the houses of all the boys. Mrs Crantock came with me and when they all said the same, about the quarrel and John going off, Mrs Crantock got out her car and we drove along Mill Lane all the way to Forby and back, looking for John. We met a man with cows and we asked him, and a postman and someone delivering vegetables, but nobody had seen him. And then I phoned you.'

'So John has been missing since about three-thirty?'

She nodded. 'Nearly three hours. It's getting dark. He's afraid of the dark.'

Her composure remained and yet Burden felt that the wrong word or gesture from him, perhaps even a sudden sound, would puncture it and release a scream of terror. He didn't quite know what to make of her. She looked peculiar, the kind of woman who belonged to a world he knew of only through newspapers. He had seen pictures of her, or of women who closely resembled her, leaving London courts after being found guilty of possessing cannabis. Such as she were found dead in furnished rooms after an overdose of barbiturates and drink. Such as she? The face was the same, pinched and pale, and the wild hair and the repellent clothes. It was her control which puzzled him and the sweet soft voice which didn't fit the image he had made for her of eccentric conduct and an unsound life.

'Mrs Lawrence,' he began, 'we get dozens of cases of missing children in the course of our work and more than ninety per cent of them are found safe and sound.' He wasn't going to mention the girl who hadn't been found at all. Someone else probably would, some interfering neighbour, but perhaps by then the boy would be back with his mother. 'Do you know what happens to most of them? They wander away out of pique or bravado and get lost and exhausted, so they lie down in some warm hole and – sleep.'

Her eyes dismayed him. They were so large and staring and she hardly seemed to blink at all. Now he saw in them a faint gleam of hope. 'You are very kind to me,' she said gravely. 'I trust you.'

Burden said awkwardly, 'That's good. You trust us and let us do the worrying, eh? Now what time does your husband get home?'

'I'm divorced. I live alone.'

He wasn't surprised. She would be divorced. She couldn't be more than twenty-eight and by the time she was thirty-eight she would probably have been married and divorced twice more. God knew what combination of circumstances had brought her to the depths of Sussex from London where she rightly belonged, to live in squalour and cause untold trouble to the police by her negligence.

Her quiet voice, grown rather shaky, broke into his harsh and perhaps unjust reverie. 'John's all I've got. I've no one in the world but John.'

And whose fault was that? 'We'll find him,' said Burden firmly. 'I'll find a woman to be with you. Perhaps this Mrs Crantock?'

'Would you? She's very nice. Most of the people around here are nice, although they're not . . .' She paused and considered. 'They're not quite like any people I've known before.'

I'll bet they're not, thought Burden. He glanced at the patchwork dress. For what respectable social occasion would any woman choose to wear a thing like that?

18

She didn't come to the door with him. He left her staring into space, playing with the long chain of beads that hung round her neck. But when he was outside he looked back and saw her white face at the window, a smeared dirty window that those thin hands had never polished. Their eyes met for a moment and convention forced him to grin uneasily. She gave no answering smile but only stared, her face as pale and wan as the moon between clouds of heavy hair.

Mrs Crantock was a neat and cheerful woman who wore her greying black hair in crisp curls and a string of cultured pearls against her pink twinset. At Burden's request she left immediately to keep Mrs Lawrence company. Her husband had already gone off with the search parties and only Julian and his fourteen-year-old sister remained in the house.

'Julian, when you saw John walk off towards Mill Lane, did you see anything else? Did anyone speak to him?'

The boy shook his head. 'He just went off.'

'And then what did he do? Did he stand under the trees or go down the lane?'

'Don't know.' Julian fidgeted and looked down. 'I was on the swings.'

'Did you look over towards the lane? Didn't you look to see where he was?'

'He'd gone,' said Julian. 'Gary said he'd gone and a jolly good thing because we didn't want babies.'

'I see.'

'Honestly, he doesn't know,' said the sister. 'We've been on and on at him but he really doesn't know.'

Burden gave up and went to the Deans at 63.

'I'm not having Gary hounded,' said Mrs Dean, a hard-looking young woman with an aggressive manner. 'Children quarrel all the time. Gary's not to

19

be blamed because John Lawrence is so sensitive that a bit of teasing makes him run off. The child's disturbed. That's what's at the root of the trouble. He comes from a broken home, so what can you expect?'

These were Burden's own sentiments. 'I'm not blaming Gary,' he said. 'I just want to ask him some questions.'

'I'm not having him bullied.'

These days the least bit of opposition was liable to set him off.

'You're at liberty,' he said sharply, 'to report me to the Chief Constable, madam, if I bully him.'

The boy was in bed but not asleep. He came down in his dressing-gown, his eyes sulky and his lip stuck out.

'Now, Gary, I'm not angry with you. No one's angry. We just want to find John. You understand that, don't you?'

The boy didn't answer.

'He's tired,' said his mother. 'He's told you he didn't see anyone and that ought to be enough.'

Burden ignored her. He leant towards the boy. 'Look at me, Gary.' The eyes which met his were full of tears. 'Don't cry. You could help us, Gary. Wouldn't you like everyone to think of you as the boy who helped the police to find John? All I want you to tell me is if you saw anyone at all, any grown-up, by the lane when John went away.'

'I didn't see them today,' said Gary. He screamed and threw himself on his mother. 'I didn't see them, I didn't!'

'I hope you're satisfied,' said Mrs Dean. 'I'm warning you, I shall take this further.'

'I didn't see that person,' Gary sobbed.

'Well, Mike?' said Wexford.

'It looks as if a man's been hanging about that

playing field. I thought I might have a go at the people in the end houses overlooking the swings field.'

'All right, and I'll try the two end ones in Wincanton.'

Did Wexford remember that he and Jean had once lived there? Burden wondered if he was attributing an excess of sensitivity to the chief inspector. Probably. A policeman has no private life when on a case. He made his way to the bottom of Fontaine Road. The fields were dark now but occasionally in the far distance, he could make out the gleam from a torch.

The last two houses faced each other. One was a detached bungalow, vintage 1935, the other a tall narrow Victorian place. Both had side windows facing the field. Burden knocked at the bungalow and a girl came to the door.

'I'm out at work all day,' she said. 'I've only just got in and my husband isn't home yet. What's happened? Has something awful happened?'

Burden told her.

'You can see the field from my window,' she said, 'but I'm never here.'

'I won't waste your time, then.'

'I hope you find him,' the girl said.

The door of the Victorian house was opened before he reached it. As soon as he saw the face of the woman who was waiting for him he knew she had something to tell him. She was elderly, sharp-eyed and spry.

'It wasn't that man, was it? I'll never forgive myself if it was him and I . . .'

'Perhaps I could come in a minute? And may I have your name?'

'Mrs Mitchell.' She took him into a neat, newly decorated room. 'I ought to have gone to the police before but you know how it is. He never did

21

anything, he never even spoke to any of the children. I did mention it to young Mrs Rushworth because her Andrew plays there, but she's always so busy, out at work all day, and I expect she forgot to tell the other mothers. And then when he didn't come back and the children went back to school . . .'

'Let's begin at the beginning, shall we, Mrs Mitchell? You saw a man hanging about the swings field. When did you first see him?'

Mrs Mitchell sat down and took a deep breath. 'It was in August, during the school holidays. I always clean my upstairs windows on a Wednesday afternoon and one Wednesday I was doing the landing window and I saw this man.'

'Where did you see him?'

'Over by the Forby road, Mill Lane, under the trees. He was standing there, looking at the children. Let me see, there was Julian Crantock and Gary Dean and poor little John Lawrence and Andrew Rushworth and the McDowell twins, and they were all playing on the swings and this man was looking at them. Oh, I should have gone to the police!'

'You spoke to one of the mothers, Mrs Mitchell. You mustn't reproach yourself. I take it you saw this man again?'

'Oh, yes, the next Wednesday, and I made a point of looking the next day, the Thursday, and he was there again, and it was then I spoke to Mrs Rushworth.'

'So, in fact, you saw him often throughout the August holiday?'

'We had a spell of bad weather after that and the children couldn't go into the field, and then it was time to go back to school. I forgot all about the man after that. Until yesterday.'

'You saw him *yesterday*?'

Mrs Mitchell nodded. 'It was Wednesday and I was doing the landing window. I saw the children come into the field and then this man appeared. It gave me a shock, seeing him again after two months. I thought to myself, I'm going to stand at this window and watch you and see what you do. But he didn't do anything. He walked around the field and he picked some leaves, branches of autumn leaves, you know, and then he stood still for a bit, looking at the boys. He was there for about half an hour and when I was just thinking, I'll have to get a chair because my legs won't hold me up, he went down over the bank.'

'Had he a car?' Burden asked quickly. 'In the lane?'

'I couldn't see. I *think* I heard a car start up but it mightn't have been his, might it?'

'Did you see him today, Mrs Mitchell?'

'I should have looked, I know that. But I *had* told Mrs Rushworth and it was her responsibility. Besides, I'd never seen this man do anything.' She sighed. 'I went out at two today,' she said. 'I went to see my married daughter in Kingsmarkham.'

'Describe this man to me, Mrs Mitchell.'

'I can do that,' she said, pleased. 'He was young, hardly more than a boy himself. Very slim, you know, and sort of slight. Not as tall as you, not nearly. About five feet six. He always wore the same clothes, one of those – what d'you call them? – duffel coats, black or very dark grey, and those jeans they all wear. Dark hair, not long for these days, but a lot longer than yours. I couldn't see his face, not from this distance, but he had very little hands. And he limps.'

'*Limps?*'

'When he was walking round the field,' said Mrs Mitchell earnestly, 'I noticed that he dragged one of his feet. Just slightly. Just a slight little limp.'

Chapter 3

The next parallel street was called Chiltern Avenue and access to it was by a footpath which ran along the side of Mrs Mitchell's house between her garden and the field. Burden went down Chiltern Avenue, calling at every house. The McDowell family lived at number 38 and the twins, Stewart and Ian, were still up.

Stewart had never seen the man, for during most of August he had been confined indoors with tonsillitis and today he had been with his mother to the dentist. But Ian had seen him and had even discussed him with Gary Dean, his special friend.

'He kept right under the trees all the time,' said Ian. 'Gary said he was a spy. Gary went to talk to him one day but he ran into Mill Lane.'

Burden asked the boy to describe him, but Ian lacked Mrs Mitchell's powers of observation.

'Just a man,' he said. 'About as big as my brother.' The brother in question was fifteen. Burden asked about the limp.

'What's limp?'

Burden explained. 'Dunno,' said Ian.

Further down, in a house of the same vintage as Mrs Lawrence's, he encountered the Rushworth family. Rushworth, it appeared, was an estate agent in Kingsmarkham, and he had gone off with the search parties, but his wife was at home with her four unruly children, all of whom were still up. Why hadn't she come to the police when Mrs Mitchell had first warned her back in August?

A little blonde woman whose stilt heels and long fingernails combined with a bouncing crest of hair gave her the look of a delicate game bird, Mrs Rushworth burst into tears.

'I meant to.' She choked. 'I had every intention. I work so hard. I work in my husband's office, you know. There's never a moment to do *anything*!'

It was almost eight and John Lawrence had been missing for four and a half hours. Burden shivered a little less from the frosty chill of the night than from the sense of impending tragedy, of coming events casting a long cold shadow before them. He went over to the car and got in beside Wexford.

The chief inspector's driver had left him alone and he sat in the back of the black official car, not making notes, no longer studying his map, but pondering deeply. There was very little light – he hadn't switched on the interior light – and in the shadows he might have been a figure of stone. From head to foot he was grey – grey sparse hair, old grey raincoat, shoes that were always a little dusty. His face was deeply lined and in the half-dark it too looked grey. He turned slightly as Burden came in and fixed on him a pair of grey eyes which were the only brilliant sharp thing about him. Burden said nothing and for a few moments the two men were silent. Then Wexford said:

'A penny for them, Mike.'

'I was thinking of Stella Rivers.'

'Of course you were. Aren't we all?'

'It was her half-term holiday too,' Burden said. 'She was an only child of divorced parents. She also disappeared in Mill Lane. There are a good many similarities.'

'And a good many dissimilarities too. For one thing, she was a girl and older. You don't know much about the Stella Rivers case. You were off sick when it happened.'

They had thought he was going to have a breakdown. Back in February it had been when the first shock of Jean's death had abated, leaving grief and panic and the horror of his situation to pour in. He had lain in bed, sleeping when Dr Crocker drugged him, shouting out when he was conscious that it was only the flu he had, that he must get up and go back to work. But he had been off work for three weeks and when at last he was better he had lost nearly two stone. Still, he had been alive, while Stella Rivers was dead or vanished from the face of her small earth.

'She also lived with her mother,' said Wexford, 'and her stepfather. On Thursday, February 25th, she had a riding lesson at Equita, the riding school in Mill Lane near Forby. She had her regular lessons on Saturdays, but this was an extra one, arranged to take advantage of her half-term holiday. The stepfather, Ivor Swan, drove her to Equita from their home at Hall Farm in Kingsmarkham, but there was some doubt as to how she was to get home again.'

'What d'you mean, doubt?'

'After she disappeared both Ivor and Rosalind Swan said Stella had told them she would get a lift home in a friend's car, as she sometimes did as far as Kingsmarkham, but it appeared that Stella had had no such idea and expected Swan to pick her up. When it got to six o'clock – the lesson ended at four-fifteen – Rosalind Swan, having checked with the friend, phoned us.

'We went first to Equita, saw Miss Williams who runs the school and her assistant, a Mrs Fenn, and were told that Stella had left alone at four-thirty. By now it was raining hard and the rain had begun at about four-forty. Eventually we made contact with a man who had passed Stella at four-forty and offered her a lift to Stowerton. At this time she was walking along Mill Lane towards Stowerton. She refused his offer which made us think she was a sensible girl who wouldn't take lifts from strangers.'

'She was twelve, wasn't she?' Burden put in.

'Twelve, slight and fair-haired. The man who offered her the lift is called Walter Hill and he's the manager of that little branch of the Midland Bank in Forby. If misguided, he's perfectly respectable and had nothing to do with her disappearance. We checked and double-checked him. No one else ever came forward to say he had seen Stella. She walked out of Equita, apparently believing she would meet her stepfather, and vanished into thin air.

'I can't go into all the details now, but of course we investigated Ivor Swan with the utmost care. Apart from the fact that he had no real alibi for that afternoon, we had no real reason to believe he wished harm to Stella. She liked Swan, she even seemed to have had a sort of crush on him. Not one relative or friend of the Swans could tell of any trouble whatsoever in their household. And yet . . .'

'And yet what?'

Wexford hesitated. 'You know those feelings I get, Mike, those almost supernatural sensations that something isn't, well – well, quite right?'

Burden nodded. He did.

'I felt it there. But it was only a feeling. People boast of their intuition because they only care to remember the times they've been proved right. I never let myself forget the numberless times my premonitions have been wrong. We never found the least thing to pin on Swan. We shall have to resurrect the case tomorrow. Where are you going?'

'Back to Mrs Lawrence,' said Burden.

An anxious-looking Mrs Crantock admitted him to the house.

'I don't think I've been much help,' she whispered to him in the hall. 'We aren't very close, you see, just neighbours whose children play with each other. I didn't know what to say to her. I mean, normally we'd discuss our little boys, but now – well, I didn't feel ...' She gave a helpless shrug. 'And you can't talk to her about ordinary things, you know. You never can. Not about the house or what goes on in the neighbourhood.' Her forehead wrinkled as she made a mammoth effort to explain the inexplicable. 'Perhaps if I could talk about books or – or something. She just isn't like anyone else I know.'

'I'm sure you've done very well,' said Burden. He thought he knew very well what Mrs Lawrence would like to talk about. Her idea of conversation would be an endless analysis of the emotions.

'Well, I tried.' Mrs Crantock raised her voice. 'I'm going now, Gemma, but I'll come back later if you want me.'

Gemma. A curious name. He didn't think he had ever come across it before. She *would* have an outlandish name, either because her equally eccentric parents had labelled her with it or – more likely – she had adopted it herself on the grounds of its originality. Suddenly impatient with himself, he wondered why he kept speculating about her in this irritating way, why every new piece of knowledge of her he acquired gave immediate rise to enquiry. Because she is, or soon will be, involved in a murder case, he told himself. He pushed open the living-room door, his mind full of the flamboyant, wild and outrageous image he had made, and stopped, taken aback at what he saw. Yet it was only what he had left behind, a white-faced frightened girl, crouched in a chair, waiting, waiting ...

She had switched on an electric fire, but it had done little to warm the room and she had wrapped herself in one of the shawls he had seen, a heavy black-and-gold thing with a long fringe. He found he couldn't picture her with a child or imagine her reading bedtime stories or pouring out cornflakes. Sitting in some club, yes, singing and playing a guitar.

'Would you like some tea?' she said, turning to him. 'Some sandwiches? I can easily make sandwiches.'

'Don't bother for me.'

'Will your wife have something for you when you get home?'

'My sister-in-law,' he said. 'My wife's dead.'

He didn't like having to say it. People immediately became embarrassed, blushing or even recoiling slightly as if he had some infectious disease. Then came the rush of awkward insincere sympathy, meaningless words to be gabbled through and then as soon forgotten. No one ever looked as if they really cared, or no one had until now.

Gemma Lawrence said quietly and slowly, 'I am so sorry. She must have been quite young. That was a great tragedy for you. Now I can see what has taught you to be kind to other people who are in trouble.'

He felt ashamed of himself and shame made him stammer. 'I – well ... I think I would like those sandwiches if it isn't any trouble.'

'How could it be?' she asked wonderingly, as if the polite conventional phrase was new to her. 'Naturally I want to do something in return for all you're doing for me.'

She brought the sandwiches in a very short time. It was evident they hadn't taken long to make. Ham had been roughly placed between two doorsteps of bread and the tea was in mugs without saucers.

Women had been spoiling Burden all his life, serving him food on dainty china from trays covered with lace cloths, and he took a sandwich without much enthusiasm, but when he bit into it he found that the ham was tasty and not too salty and the bread fresh.

She sat on the floor and rested her back against the armchair opposite to him. He had told Wexford there were many more questions he wanted to ask her and he hazarded a few of them, routine enquiries as to John's adult acquaintances, the parents of his school friends, her own friends. She responded calmly and intelligently and the policeman's part of his mind registered her answers automatically. But something strange had happened to him. He was absorbing with a curious unease a fact which the average man would have observed as soon as he laid eyes on her. She was beautiful. Thinking the word made him look away, yet carry with him, as if imprinted on his retina, a brilliant impression of that white face with its good bones and, more disturbingly, her long legs and full firm breasts.

Her hair was vermilion in the red firelight, her eyes the clear water-washed green of jewels that are found under the sea. The shawl gave her an exotic look as if she were set within the frame of a Pre-Raphaelite portrait, posed, unreal, unfitted for any ordinary daily task. And yet there was about her something entirely natural and impulsive. Too natural, he thought, suddenly alarmed, too real. She is more real and more aware and more natural than any woman has a right to be.

Quickly he said, 'Mrs Lawrence, I'm sure you told John never to speak to strange men.'

The face whitened. 'Oh, yes.'

'But did he ever tell you that a man had spoken to him?'

30

'No, never. I take him to school and fetch him home. He's only alone when he goes out to play and then the other boys are with him.' She lifted her face and now there was no guard on it. 'What do you mean?'

Why did she have to ask so directly? 'No one has told me they saw any stranger speak to John,' he said truthfully, 'but I have to check.'

She said in the same uncompromising level voice, 'Mrs Dean told me a child was lost in Kingsmarkham last February and never found. She came in to tell me while Mrs Crantock was here.'

Burden forgot that he had ever allied himself with Mrs Dean. In savage, unpoliceman-like tones he burst out before he could stop himself, 'Why the hell don't these busybodies keep their mouths shut?' He bit his lip, wondering why what she had said brought out so much violence in him and the desire to go next door and strike the Dean woman. 'That child was a girl,' he said, 'and much older. The kind of – er – pervert who needs to attack girls isn't likely to be interested in a small boy.' But was that true? Who could yet understand the mysteries of a sane mind, let alone a diseased one?

She drew the shawl more closely about her and said, 'How shall I get through the night?'

'I shall get you a doctor.' Burden finished his tea and got up. 'Didn't I see a doctor's plate in Chiltern Avenue?'

'Yes. Dr Lomax.'

'Well, we'll get some sleeping pills out of this Lomax, and a woman to stay the night with you. I'll see you're not left alone.'

'I don't know how to thank you.' She bowed her head and he saw that at last she began to cry. 'You'll say it's only your job and your duty, but it's more

31

than that. I – I do thank you. When I look at you I think, Nothing can happen to John while he's there.'

She was looking at him as a child should look at its father but as he could never remember his own children looking at him. Such trust was a terrible responsibility and he knew he shouldn't foster it. There was more than a fifty-fifty chance now that the child was dead and he wasn't God to bring the dead to life. He ought to say that she mustn't worry, mustn't think about it – how cruel and stupid and insensitive! – but all he could say in the face of those eyes was, 'I'll go for the doctor now and he'll see you get a good night.' There was no need to add anything but he added, 'Don't sleep too long. I'll be back with you by nine.'

Then he said good night. He didn't mean to look back. Something impelled him. She was standing in the doorway, framed in yellow light, a curious outlandish figure in that gypsy gilded shawl, her hair so bright that it seemed on fire. She waved to him tentatively, rather shyly, her other hand smoothing away the tears from under her eyes. He had seen pictures of women like her but never known them, never spoken to them. Briefly he wondered if he wanted the child found, wanted it so passionately, because that would mean he need never see her again. He turned sharply towards the street and went to summon Dr Lomax.

A great moon drifted above the fields, pale and misty as if it drifted in a pool of water. Burden waited until the searchers got back at midnight. They had found nothing.

Grace had left a note for him: 'John waited up till eleven for you to help him with his maths. Could you just glance at it? He was in quite a state. G.'

It took Burden a couple of seconds to adjust to the

fact that his own son was also called John. He glanced at the homework and, as far as he could see, the algebra was correct. A lot of fuss about nothing. These little nagging notes of Grace's were getting a bit much. He opened the door of his son's room and saw that he was fast asleep. Grace and Pat slept in the room that had been his and Jean's – impossible as his bedroom after her death – and he couldn't very well open that door. In his own room, once Pat's, a little room with ballet dancers cavorting on the walls as appropriate for an eleven-year-old, he sat on the bed and felt the tiredness ebb away, leaving him as alert as at eight in the morning. He could be weary to the point of collapse, but let him come in here, be alone with himself, and immediately he would be filled with this frightful, degrading urgency.

He put his head in his hands. They all thought he missed Jean as a companion, as someone to talk to and share trouble with. And so he did, terribly. But what assailed him most every day and every night, without respite, was sexual desire, which, because it had had no release in ten months, had become sealed-up, tormented sexual madness.

He knew very well how they all thought of him. To them he was a cold fish, stern when confronted by license, mourning Jean only because he had become used to marriage and was what Wexford called uxorious. Probably, if they had ever thought of it, they imagined him and Jean making love once a fortnight with the light out. It was the way people did think about you if you were the sort of man who shied away from dirty jokes and found this permissive society foul.

They never seemed to dream that you could hate promiscuity and adultery because you knew what marriage could be and had experienced it to such a degree of excellence that anything else was a mockery, a poor imitation. You were lucky but ... Ah, God, you were unlucky too! – cast adrift and sick when it was over. Jean had been a virgin when he married her and so had he. People said – stupid people and the stupid things they said – that it made it hard when you married, but it hadn't for him and Jean. They had been patient and giving and full of love and they had been so fulsomely rewarded that, looking back as from a desert, Burden could hardly believe it had been so good almost from the start with no failures, no disappointments. But he could believe it because he knew and remembered and suffered.

And if they knew? He was aware what their advice would be. Get yourself a girl friend, Mike. Nothing serious. Just a nice easy girl to have a bit of fun with. Perhaps you could do that if you'd been used to kicking over the traces. He had never been any woman's lover but Jean's. Sex for him had been Jean. They didn't realise that telling him to get another woman would be like telling Gemma Lawrence to get another child.

He took off his clothes and lay face downwards, his fists carefully clenched and pushed under the pillow. There was no doubt in his mind how the night would be passed. All nights were the same. First the lying awake and the longing, the actual physical pain, as if his body was a great scream with no outlet for the scream to escape through; then at last sleep with the full, rich and orgiastic dream that would come to him just before the dawn.

Chapter 4

If Mike made the slightest effort at an apology, Grace decided, she wouldn't say a word. Of course, he had to work and many times he couldn't get away without putting his job in jeopardy. She knew what that meant. Before she came to be his housekeeper she had had men friends, some who were just friends and some, a few, who were lovers, and often she had had to break a date because there was an emergency on at the hospital. But the next day she had always phoned or written a note to explain why.

Mike wasn't her lover but only her brother-in-law. Did that mean he owed her nothing, not even common politeness? And had you the right to stand up your children without a word, even when your son was trembling with nerves at nearly midnight because he couldn't believe he'd got his algebra right and old Parminter, the maths man, would put him in detention if he hadn't?

She cooked eggs and bacon for the lot of them and laid the dining table with a clean cloth. Not for the first time she wished her sister hadn't been such an excellent housekeeper, so correct and near-perfect in everything she did, but at least slackened to the extent of serving breakfast in the kitchen. Living up to Jean made life a bit of a burden.

She hadn't meant to make a pun and she didn't laugh. Her face hardened when Mike came down, grunted to the children and took his place at the table without a word. He wasn't going to mention last night. Well, she would.

'That algebra was perfectly O.K., John.'

The boy's face lit as it always did when Burden spoke to him.

'I reckoned it was. I don't really care about it, only old Mint Face will keep me in if it's not. I don't suppose you'd give me a lift to school.'

'Too busy,' said Burden. 'The walk does you good.' He smiled, but not too kindly, at his daughter. 'And you too, miss,' he said. 'Right, get going. It's nearly half past.'

Grace didn't usually see them to the door but she did today to make up for their father's hardness. When she came back Burden was on his second cup of tea and before she could stop herself she had burst into a long tirade all about John's nerves and Pat's bewilderment and the way he left them all alone.

He heard her out and then he said, 'Why is it that women' – he corrected himself, making the inevitable exception – 'most women – can't realise men have to work? If I didn't work God knows what would happen to the lot of you.'

'Were you working when Mrs Finch saw you sitting in the car in Cheriton Forest?'

'Mrs Finch,' he flared, 'can mind her own bloody business!'

Grace turned her back. She found she was slowly counting to ten. Then she said, 'Mike, I do understand. I can imagine how you feel.'

'I doubt that.'

'Well, I think I can. But John and Pat can't. John needs you and he needs you cheerful and matter-of-fact and – and like you used to be. Mike, couldn't you get home early tonight? There's a film they'd both like to see. It doesn't start till seven thirty, so you wouldn't have to be home till seven. We could all go. It would mean so much to them.'

'All right,' he said. 'I'll do my best. Don't look like that, Grace. I'll be home by seven.'

Her face lit up. She did something she hadn't done since his wedding. She bent over and kissed his cheek. Then she began quickly to clear the table. Her back was to him so that she didn't see the shiver he gave and the way he put his hand up to his face like a man who has been stung.

Gemma Lawrence had put on clean jeans and a clean thick sweater. Her hair was tied back in a bunch with a piece of ribbon and she smelt of soap like a good clean child.

'I slept all night.'

He smiled at her. 'Cheers for Dr Lomax,' he said.

'Are they still searching?'

'Of course. Didn't I promise you? We've borrowed a whole army of coppers from all the surrounding districts.'

'Dr Lomax was very kind. D'you know, he said that when he was living in Scotland before he came here his own little boy was missing and they found him in a shepherd's hut lying asleep, cuddling the sheep-dog. He'd wandered for miles and this dog had found him and looked after him like a lost lamb. It reminded me of Romulus and Remus and the wolf.'

Burden didn't know who Romulus and Remus were, but he laughed and said, 'Well, what did I tell you?' He wasn't going to spoil her hopes now by pointing out that this wasn't Scotland, a place of lonely mountains and friendly dogs. 'What are you going to do today? I don't want you to be alone.'

'Mrs Crantock's asked me to lunch and the neighbours keep coming in. People are very kind. I

37

wish I had some closer friends here. All my friends are in London.'

'The best thing for worry,' he said, 'is work. Take your mind off things.'

'I don't have any work to do, unfortunately.'

He had meant housework, cleaning, tidying, sewing, tasks which he thought of as naturally a woman's work, and there was plenty of that to be done. But he could hardly tell her that.

'I expect I'll just sit and play records,' she said, shifting a dirty cup from the record player to the floor. 'Or read or something.'

'As soon as we have any news. I'll come to you. I won't phone, I'll come.'

Her eyes shone. 'If I were the Prime Minister,' she said, 'I'd make you a superintendent.'

He drove to Cheriton Forest where the search was now centred and found Wexford sitting on a log. It was misty this morning and the chief inspector was wrapped in an old raincoat, a battered felt hat pulled down over his eyes.

'We've got a lead on the car, Mike.'

'What car?'

'Last night when they were out in the fields one of the search party told Martin he'd seen a car parked in Mill Lane. Apparently, he had a week off in August and he took his dog walking regularly up Mill Lane and three times he noticed a car parked near the spot where Mrs Mitchell saw the man. He noticed it because it was obstructing the lane, only leaving room for single-line traffic. A red Jaguar. Needless to say, he didn't get the number.'

'Did he see the man?'

'He didn't see anyone. What we want now is to find someone who regularly uses that road. A baker, for instance.'

'I'll see to that,' said Burden.

In the course of the morning he found a baker's roundsman who used the road every day and the driver of a van delivering soft drinks who used it only on Wednesdays and Fridays. The baker had seen the car because, coming round a corner one afternoon, he had almost hit it. A red Jaguar, he confirmed, but he hadn't taken the number either. And although he had been on the road the day before, he had passed the swings-field hedge at two and the car wasn't there then. At half-past four two women in a car had asked him if he had seen a little boy, but he was almost into Forby by then. The red Jaguar might have passed him, might have contained a child, but he couldn't remember.

The soft-drinks man was less observant. He had never noticed anything out of the way on that road, either recently or in August.

Burden went back to the station and had a quick lunch in Wexford's office. They spent the afternoon interviewing a sad little stream of men, all shifty and most undersized, who at some time or other had made overtures to children. There was the retarded nineteen-year-old whose speciality was waiting outside school gates; the middle-aged primary-school teacher, sacked by the authority years ago; the draper's assistant who got into train compartments that contained a solitary child; the schizophrenic who had raped his own little daughter and since been discharged from mental hospital.

'Lovely job, ours,' said Burden. 'I feel slimy all over.'

'There but for the grace of God ...' said Wexford. 'You might have been one of them if your parents had rejected you. I might if I'd responded to the advances made to me in the school cloakroom. They sit in darkness, they're born, as Blake or some clever sod said, to endless night. Pity doesn't cost anything,

Mike, and it's a damn sight more edifying than shouting about flogging and hanging and castrating and what you will.'

'I'm not shouting, sir. I just happen to believe in the cultivation of self-control. And my pity is for the mother and that poor kid.'

'Yes, but the quality of mercy is not strained. The trouble with you is you're a blocked-up colander and your mercy strains through a couple of miserable little holes. Still, none of those wretched drop-outs was near Mill Lane yesterday and I don't see any of them living it up in a red Jaguar.'

If you haven't been out in the evening once in ten months the prospect of a trip to the cinema in the company of your brother-in-law and two children can seem like high living. Grace Woodville went to the hairdresser's at three and when she came out she felt more elated than she had the first day Pat came to kiss her of her own accord. There was a nice golden-brown sweater in Moran's window, and Grace, who hadn't bought a garment in months, decided on an impulse to have it.

Mike should have a special dinner tonight, curried chicken. Jean had never cooked that because she didn't like it, but Mike and the children did. She bought a chicken and by the time John and Pat came home the bungalow was filled with the rich scents of curry sauce and sweet-sour pineapple.

She had laid the table by six and changed into the new sweater. By five to seven they were all sitting in the living room, all dressed-up and rather self-conscious, more like people waiting to be taken to a party than a family off to the local cinema.

The telephone calls had begun. They came in to Kingsmarkham police station not only from people in the district, not only in Sussex, but from Birmingham and Newcastle and the north of Scotland. All the callers claimed to have seen John Lawrence alone or with a man or with two men or two women. A woman in Carlisle had seen him, she averred, with Stella Rivers; a shopkeeper in Cardiff had sold him an ice-cream. A lorry-driver had given him and his companion, a middle-aged man, a lift to Grantham. All these stories had to be checked, though all seemed to be without foundation.

People poured into the station with tales of suspicious persons and cars seen in Mill Lane. By now not only red Jaguars were suspect but black ones and green ones, black vans, three-wheelers. And meanwhile the arduous search went on. Working without a break, Wexford's force continued a systematic house-to-house investigation, questioning most particularly every male person over sixteen.

Five to seven found Burden outside the Olive and Dove Hotel in Kingsmarkham High Street, facing the cinema, and he remembered his date with Grace and the children, remembered, too, that he must see Gemma Lawrence before he went off duty.

The phone box outside the hotel was occupied and a small queue of people waited. By the time they had all finished, Burden judged, a good ten minutes would have passed. He glanced again at the cinema and saw that whereas the last programme began at seven-thirty, the big picture didn't start until an hour later. No need to phone Grace when he could easily drive to Stowerton, find out how things were with Mrs Lawrence and be home by a quarter to eight. Grace wouldn't expect him on time. She knew better than that. And surely even his two wouldn't want to sit through a film about touring in East Anglia, the news and all the trailers.

For once the front door wasn't open. The street

was empty, almost every house well-lit. It seemed for all the world as if nothing had happened yesterday to disturb the peace of this quiet country street. Time passed, men and women laughed and talked and worked and watched television and said, What can you do? That's life.

There were no lights on in her house. He knocked on the door and no one came. She must have gone out. When her only child was missing, perhaps murdered? He remembered the way she dressed, the state of her house. A good-time girl, he thought, not much of a mother. Very likely one of those London friends had come and she'd gone out with him.

He knocked again and then he heard something, a kind of shuffling. Footsteps dragged to the door, hesitated.

He called, 'Mrs Lawrence, are you all right?'

A little answering sound came to him, half a sob and half a moan. The door quivered, then swung inwards.

Her face was ravaged and swollen and sodden with crying. She was crying now, sobbing, the tears streaming down her face. He shut the door behind him and switched on a light.

'What's happened?'

She twisted away from him, threw herself against the wall and beat on it with her fists. 'Oh God, what shall I do?'

'I know it's hard,' he said helplessly, 'but we're doing everything that's humanly possible. We're . . .'

'Your people,' she sobbed, 'they've been in and out all day, searching and – and asking me things. They searched this house! And people kept phoning, awful people. There was a woman – a *woman* . . . Oh my God! She said John was dead and she – she described how he died and she said it was my fault! I can't bear it, I can't bear it, I shall gas myself, I shall cut my wrists . . .'

'You must stop this,' he shouted. She turned to him and screamed into his face. He raised his hand and slapped her stingingly on the cheek. She gagged, gulped and crumpled, collapsing against him. To stop her falling, he put his arms round her and for a moment she clung to him, as in a lover's embrace, her wet face buried in his neck. Then she stepped back, the red hair flying as she shook herself.

'Forgive me,' she said. Her voice was hoarse with crying. 'I'm mad. I think I'm going mad.'

'Come in here and tell me. You were optimistic earlier.'

'That was this morning.' She spoke quietly now in a thin broken voice. Gradually and not very coherently she told him about the policeman who had searched her cupboards and tramped through the attics, how they had torn away the undergrowth that swamped the roots of old trees in that wild garden. She told him, gasping, of the obscene phone calls and of the letters, inspired by last night's evening-paper story, the second post had brought.

'You are not to open any letters unless you recognise the handwriting,' he said. 'Everything else we'll look at first. As to the phone calls . . .'

'Your sergeant said you'd have an arrangement to get my phone monitored.' She sighed deeply, calmer now, but the tears were still falling.

'Have you got any brandy in this – er – place?'

'In the dining room.' She managed a damp, weak smile. 'It belonged to my great-aunt. This – er – place, as you call it, was hers. Brandy keeps for years and years, doesn't it?'

'Years and years make it all the better,' said Burden.

The dining room was cavernous, cold and smelling

of dust. He wondered what combination of circumstances had brought her to this house and why she stayed. The brandy was in a sideboard that looked more like a wooden mansion than a piece of furniture, it was so ornamented with carved pillars and arches and niches and balconies.

'You have some too,' she said.

He hesitated. 'All right. Thank you.' He made his way back to the armchair he had occupied before going to the dining room, but she sat down on the floor, curling her legs under her and staring up at him with a curious blind trust. Only one lamp was alight, making a little golden glow behind her head.

She drank her brandy and for a long time they sat without talking. Then, warmed and calmed, she began to speak about the lost boy, the things he liked doing, the things he said, his little precocious cleverness. She spoke of London and of the strangeness of Stowerton to herself and her son. At last she fell silent, her eyes fixed on his face, but he had lost the embarrassment which this trusting childlike stare had at first occasioned in him and it didn't return even when, leaning forward with quick impulsiveness, she reached for his hand and held it tightly.

He wasn't embarrassed, but the touch of her hand electrified him. It brought him such a shock and such sudden turbulence that instead of the normal reactions of a normal man enclosing the hand of a pretty woman in his own he had the illusion that his whole body was holding her body. The effect of this was to make him tremble. He loosened his fingers and said abruptly, breaking the now heavy and languorous silence, 'You're a Londoner. You like London. Why do you live here?'

'It is rather ghastly, isn't it?' All the harshness and terror had gone from her voice and once more it was soft and rich. Although he had known she was bound to speak in answer to his question, the sound of her beautiful voice, quite normal now, disturbed him almost as much as the touch of her hand. 'A dreadful old white elephant of a house,' she said.

'It's no business of mine,' he muttered.

'But it's no secret either. I didn't even know I had this great-aunt. She died three years ago and left this house to my father, but he was dying himself of cancer.' With a peculiarly graceful but unstudied movement she raised her hand and pushed away the mass of hair from her face. The full embroidered sleeve of the strange tunic she wore fell away from her arm and the skin glowed whitely, faint golden down gleaming in the lamplight. 'I tried to sell it for my father, but no one wanted it, and then he died and Matthew – my husband – left me. Where else could I go but here? I couldn't afford the rent of our flat and Matthew's money had run out.' It seemed like hours since those eyes had first begun staring at him, but now at last she turned them away. 'The police,' she said very softly, 'thought Matthew might have taken John.'

'I know. It's something we always have to check on when the child of – er – estranged or divorced parents is missing.'

'They went to see him, or they tried to. He's in hospital, having his appendix out. I believe they talked to his wife. He married again, you see.'

Burden nodded. With more than a policeman's natural curiosity he passionately wanted to know whether this Matthew had divorced her or she him, what he did for a living, how it had all come about. He couldn't ask her. His voice felt strangled.

She edged a little closer towards him, not reaching out for his hand this time. Her hair curtained her face. 'I want you to know,' she said, 'how you've helped me. What a comfort you've been. I should have broken down completely tonight if you hadn't come. I should have done something dreadful.'

'You mustn't be alone.'

'I've got my sleeping tablets,' she said, 'and Mrs Crantock is coming in at ten.' Slowly she got to her feet, reached out and switched on the standard lamp. 'She'll be here in a minute. It's five to now.'

Her words and the sudden brightness brought Burden sharply back to reality. He blinked and shook himself.

'Five to ten? I've just remembered, I'm supposed to be taking my family to the pictures.'

'And I've stopped you? Would you like to phone? Please do. Use my phone.'

'Too late, I'm afraid.'

'I'm dreadfully sorry.'

'I think my being here was more important, don't you?'

'It was important to me. But you must go now. Will you come again tomorrow? I mean you yourself.'

He was standing in the doorway as she spoke. She put her hand lightly on his arm and they were close together, their faces only a foot apart. 'I – yes . . . Yes, of course.' He was stammering badly. 'Of course I'll come.'

'Inspector Burden . . . No, I can't keep calling you that. What's your first name?'

'I think it will be best if you . . .' he began, and then, almost desperately, 'It's Michael. People call me Mike.'

'Mike,' she said, and at that moment, as she dwelt on the name, repeating it softly, Mrs Crantock rang the bell.

Grace was curled up on the sofa and he could see that she had been crying. The enormity of what he

46

had done for a moment overcame that other enormity, the urgency of his body.

'I'm terribly sorry,' he said, going over to her. 'The phone box was full and later ...'

She lifted her head and faced him. 'We sat here and we waited for you. When you hadn't come by eight we had our meal, though it was ruined. I said, "Let's go just the same," and John said, "We can't go without Dad. We can't let him come home and find us gone."'

'I said I'm sorry,' said Burden.

'You could have phoned!' Grace said passionately. 'I wouldn't say a word if you'd phoned. Don't you realise, if you go on like this, you'll – you'll destroy those children!'

She went out and the door closed behind her, leaving Burden to thoughts that were neither of her nor his children.

Chapter 5

Burden looked at the sheet of paper Wexford had handed him. Written on it in a bold, large but childlike hand were the names of every man, woman and child Gemma Lawrence had known during the past ten years.

'When did she write all that out?'

Wexford eyed him briefly and narrowly. 'This morning with Loring's help. You aren't her exclusive private eye, you know.'

Burden flushed. What hundreds of people she knew and what extraordinary names they had! Artists and models and theatre folk, he supposed, suddenly bad-tempered. 'Have we got to interview all this lot?'

'The Met are going to help us there. I asked Mrs Lawrence to write down every name because I want to show the list to the Swans.'

'You are connecting the two cases, then?'

Wexford didn't answer directly. He took the list from Burden, gave him another piece of paper and said, 'This came. It's been gone over for fingerprints, so you needn't worry about touching it. Of course there weren't any prints.'

'John Lawrence is safe and well with me,' Burden read. 'He is happy playing with my rabbits on the farm. To show you this is not a hoax, I am enclosing a lock of his hair.' The note, written in block capitals on a sheet of lined paper, was correctly spelt and punctuated. 'His mother can have him back on Monday. I will bring him to the southern end of Myfleet Ride in Cheriton Forest at 9 a.m. If anyone tries to collect him before nine-thirty, I will know and I will shoot John dead. This is a serious warning. I will not break my promise if you co-operate.'

Burden dropped it in disgust. Used as he was to such things, he could still not read them without a shudder. 'Was there a lock of hair?' he asked.

'Here.'

It had been twisted into a smooth neat circle like a woman's pin curl. Burden lifted it in tweezers, noting the delicacy of each red-gold strand, the absence of those kinks and ridges which occur in adult hair.

'It's human,' said Wexford. 'I got Crocker on to it at once. He says it's the child's hair, but, of course, we shall have to have more expert tests.'

'Has Mrs Lawrence been told?'

'Thank God he's safe,' she said when she had read the first lines. She held the letter momentarily to her breast but she didn't cry. 'He's safe and well on a farm somewhere. Oh my God, and what agonies I've been through! Imagine, all that for nothing and he'll be back with me on Monday.'

Burden was appalled. He had already told her not to bank on the letter at all, that in ninety-nine cases out of a hundred such letters are cruel hoaxes. For all the notice she took, he might not have spoken.

'Let me see the hair,' she said.

Reluctantly he took the envelope which contained it from his briefcase. She gasped when she saw the small golden curl. So far it had been handled carefully with tweezers, but she took it, stroked it and pressed it to her mouth. 'Come upstairs.'

He followed her into John's bedroom, noticing that

49

the child's bed hadn't been made since his disappearance. It was a nice bedroom, though, full of toys and with a beautiful expensive wallpaper of Dürer animals reproduced in line and wash. However much she might neglect the rest of the house, she had cared for this room and probably done the papering herself. Burden's opinion of her as a mother rose.

She went over to a small blue-painted chest of drawers and picked up John's hairbrush. A few fine blond hairs were caught in its bristles and, with an earnest concentrated expression, she compared them with the lock in her hand. Then she turned and smiled radiantly.

Burden had never seen her really smile before. Until then her smiles had been brief and watery, reminding him, he thought suddenly, of a faint sun coming out after rain. Such metaphors were very unusual with him, fanciful and not in his line. But he thought it now as he received the full force of her brilliant happy smile and saw again how beautiful she was.

'It is the same, isn't it?' she said, the smile fading as she almost pleaded, '*Isn't it?*'

'I don't know.' There was certainly a strong similarity, but Burden didn't know whether he wanted the hairs to be the same or not. If this man really had John and if he had really cut that lock from John's head, was it likely that he would let the boy go otherwise unharmed? Would he risk the boy's identifying him? On the other hand, he had demanded no money ... 'You're his mother,' he murmured. 'I wouldn't like to say.'

'I know he's safe,' she said. 'I feel it. I've only got to get through two more days.'

He hadn't the heart to say any more then. Only a brute, he thought, would destroy such shining happiness. So that she shouldn't read the last lines he wanted to take the letter from her, but she read it to the end.

'I've heard about cases like this,' she said, a little fear returning to her voice as she gazed at him, 'and what the police do. You wouldn't – you wouldn't do – do what he says you're not to do? You wouldn't try to trap him? Because then John . . .'

'I promise you,' he said, 'that we shall do nothing which might in any way endanger John's life.' She had said nothing vindictive about the writer of the letter, he noticed. Other women in her position would have raged and screamed for revenge. She had merely been filled with joy. 'We shall go there on Monday morning, at nine-thirty, and if he is there we shall bring him back to you.'

'He'll be there,' she said. 'I trust this man. I've got a feeling he's genuine. Really, I have, Mike.' Her use of his Christian name brought colour into his face. He felt his cheeks burn. 'He's probably dreadfully lonely,' she said gently. 'I know what it is to be lonely. If John has given him a few days' respite from his loneliness I don't grudge John to him.'

It was incredible and Burden couldn't understand. If it had been his child, his John, he would have wanted to kill the man, to see him die a lingering death. As it was, his feelings towards the letter-writer were so violent that they frightened him. Let me get at him, he thought, give me five minutes alone in the cell with him and, by God, if I lose my job for it . . . He pulled himself up with a jerk and saw that her eyes were on him, kind, sweet and compassionate.

In his haste to see Gemma, Burden had forgotten the Swans, but now he remembered Wexford saying the note helped to establish a connection between the two cases. The chief inspector was still in his office.

'Swan lives on a farm,' he said. 'I phoned but he's out till three.'

'Does he keep rabbits?'

'Don't mention rabbits to me. I've only just got over an hour with the secretary of the local rabbit club. Rabbits! The place is crawling with them, Old English, Blue Beverens, you name 'em, we've got 'em. I tell you, Mike, it's like the Apocrypha says, "The coneys are a feeble folk, but they make their houses in the rocks"!'

'And every fancier being checked?' said Burden, unsmiling.

Wexford nodded. 'And I know the bloody thing's a hoax,' he said. 'I shall spend the best part of my weekend – and so will dozens of other policemen – chasing rabbits and farmers and checking shot-gun licences and being polite to human hair experts, but I know very well it's a hoax and what I'm doing is an utter waste of time.'

'But it has to be done.'

'Of course it has to be done. Let's go to lunch.'

At the Carousel Café only ham and salad was left on the menu. Wexford picked without enthusiasm at the salad in which lettuce leaves were economically eked out with shreds of cabbage and carrot. 'Can't get away from rabbits,' he muttered. 'Want me to tell you about Swan and his wife?'

'I suppose I ought to have a bit of background.'

'Usually,' Wexford began, 'you feel too much sympathy with the parents of a lost child. You find your emotions getting involved.' He shifted his gaze from his plate to Burden's face and pursed his lips. 'Which doesn't help,' he said. 'I didn't feel particularly sorry for them. You'll see why not in a minute.' Clearing his throat, he went on, 'After Stella disappeared, we did more research into the life and background of Ivor Swan than I can ever remember doing with anyone. I could write his biography.

'He was born in India, the son of one General Sir Rodney Swan, and he was sent home to school and then to Oxford. Being in possession of what he calls small private means, he never took up any particular career but dabbled at various things. At one time he managed an estate for someone, but he soon got the sack. He wrote a novel which sold three hundred copies, so he never repeated that experiment. Instead he had a spell in P.R. and in three months lost his firm an account worth twenty thousand a year. Utter ingrained laziness is what characterises Ivor Swan. He is indolence incarnate. Oh, and he's good-looking, staggeringly so, in fact. Wait till you see.'

Burden poured himself a glass of water but said nothing. He was watching Wexford's expression warm and liven as he pursued his theme. Once he too had been able to involve himself as raptly in the characters of suspects.

'Swan rarely had any settled home,' Wexford said. 'Sometimes he lived with his widowed mother at her house in Bedfordshire, sometimes with an uncle who had been some sort of big brass in the Air Force. And now I come to an interesting point about him. Wherever he goes he seems to leave disaster behind him. Not because of what he does but because of what he *doesn't* do. There was a bad fire at his mother's house while he was staying there. Swan had fallen asleep with a cigarette burning in his fingers. Then there was the loss of the P.R. account because of what he didn't do; the sacking from the estate management job – he left a pretty mess behind him there – on account of his laziness.

'About two years ago he found himself in Karachi. At that time he was calling himself a free-lance journalist and the purpose of his visit was to enquire into the alleged smuggling of gold by airline staff. Any story he concocted would probably have been libellous, but, as it happened, it was never written or, at any rate, no newspaper printed it.

'Peter Rivers worked for an airline in Karachi, not as a pilot but among the ground staff, meeting aircraft, weighing baggage, that sort of thing, and he lived with his wife and daughter in a company house. In the course of his snooping Swan made friends with Rivers. It would be more to the point to say he made friends with Rivers' wife.'

'You mean he took her away from him?' Burden hazarded.

'If you can imagine Swan doing anything as active as taking anyone or anything away from anyone else. I should rather say that the fair Rosalind – "From the East to Western Ind, no jewel is like Rosalind" – fastened herself to Swan and held on tight. The upshot was that Swan returned to England plus Rosalind and Stella and about a year later Rivers got his decree.

'The three of them all lived in a poky flat Swan took in Maida Vale, but after they were married Swan, or more likely Rosalind, decided the place wasn't big enough and they came out here to Hall Farm.'

'Where did he get the money to buy a farm?'

'Well, in the first place it isn't a farm any more but a chichi tarted-up farm*house* with all the land let off. Secondly, he didn't buy it. It was part of the property held under a family trust. Swan put out feelers to his uncle and he let him have Hall Farm at a nominal rent.'

'Life's very easy for some people, isn't it?' said Burden, thinking of mortgages and hire purchase and grudgingly granted bank loans. 'No money worries, no housing problems.'

'They came here last October, a year ago. Stella was sent to the convent at Sewingbury – uncle paid the fees – and Swan let her have these riding lessons. He rides himself and hunts a bit. Nothing in a big way, but then he doesn't do anything in a big way.

'As to Rivers, he'd been having it off on the quiet with some air hostess and he also has married again. Swan, Rosalind and Stella plus an *au pair* girl settled down quite comfortably at Hall Farm, and then, bang in the middle of all this bliss, Stella disappears. Beyond a doubt, Stella is dead, murdered.'

'It seems clear,' said Burden, 'that Swan can have had nothing to do with it.'

Wexford said obstinately, 'He had no alibi. And there was something else, something less tangible, something in the personality of the man himself.'

'He sounds too lazy ever to commit an aggressive act.'

'I know, I know.' Wexford almost groaned the words. 'And he had led, in the eyes of the law, a blameless life. No history of violence, mental disturbance or even bad temper. He hadn't even the reputation of a philanderer. Casual girl friends, yes, but until he met Rosalind he had never been married or engaged to be married or even lived with a woman. But he had a history of a sort, a history of disaster. There's a line in rather a sinister sonnet – "They that have power to hurt and will do none". I don't think that means they don't do any hurt but that they do *nothing*. That's Swan. If he didn't do this killing it happened because of him or through him or because he is what he is. D'you think that's all airyfairy moonshine?'

'Yes,' said Burden firmly.

St Luke's Little Summer maintained its glory, at least by day. The hedges were a delicate green-gold and

frost had not yet bitten into blackness the chrysanthemums and michaelmas daisies in cottage gardens.
The year was growing old gracefully.

The farm was approached by a narrow lane
scattered with fallen leaves and overhung by hedges
of Old Man's Beard, the vapourish, thistledown seed
heads of the wild clematis, and here and there,
behind the fluffy masses, rose Scotch pines, their
trunks a rich coral pink where the sun caught them.
A long low building of stone and slate stood at the
end of this lane, but most of its stonework was
obscured by the flame and scarlet virginia creeper
which covered it.

'*Du coté de chez Swan,*' said Wexford softly.

Proustian references were lost on Burden. He was
looking at the man who had come round from the
back of the house, leading a big chestnut gelding.

Wexford left the car and went up to him. 'We're a
little early, Mr Swan. I hope we're not putting you
out?'

'No,' said Swan. 'We got back sooner than we
expected. I was going to exercise Sherry but that can
wait.'

'This is Inspector Burden.'

'How do you do?' said Swan, extending a hand.
'Very pleasant, all this sunshine, isn't it? D'you mind
coming round the back way?'

He was certainly an extremely handsome man.
Burden decided this without being able to say in
what his handsomeness lay, for Ivor Swan was
neither tall nor short, dark nor fair, and his eyes were
of that indeterminate colour men call grey for want
of a more accurate term. His features had no special
regularity, his figure, though lean, no sign of athletic
muscular development. But he moved with an
entirely masculine grace, exuded a vague lazy charm

and had about him an air of attractiveness, of making himself immediately noticed.

His voice was soft and beautiful, the words he used slowly enunciated. He seemed to have all the time in the world, a procrastinator who would always put off till tomorrow what he couldn't bring himself to do today. About thirty-three or thirty-four, Burden thought, but he could easily pass for twenty-five to a less discerning observer.

The two policemen followed him into a kind of lobby or back kitchen where a couple of guns and an assortment of fishing tackle hung above neat rows of riding boots and wellingtons.

'Don't keep rabbits, do you, Mr Swan?' Wexford asked.

Swan shook his head. 'I shoot them, or try to, if they come on my land.'

In the kitchen proper two women were engaged on feminine tasks. The younger, an ungainly dark girl, was preparing – if the heaps of vegetables, tins of dried herbs, eggs and mincemeat spread on the counter in front of her were anything to go by – what Burden chauvinistically thought of as a continental mess. Well away from the chopping and splashing, a minute doll-like blonde was ironing shirts. Five or six had already been ironed. There were at least that number remaining. Burden noticed that she was taking extreme care not to cause a horizontal crease to appear under the yoke of the shirt she was at present attending to, an error into which hasty or careless women often fall and which makes the removal of a jacket by its wearer an embarrassment.

'Good afternoon, Mrs Swan. I wonder if I may trouble you for a few minutes?'

Rosalind Swan had a girlish air, a featherlight 'bovver' haircut and nothing in her face or manner to show that eight months before she had been deprived of her only child. She wore white tights and pink buckled shoes, but Burden thought she was as old as he.

'I like to see personally to all my husband's laundry,' she declared in a manner Burden could only describe as merry, 'and Gudrun can't be expected to give his shirts that little extra wifely touch, can she?'

From long experience Burden had learnt that if a man is having an affair with another woman and, in that woman's presence, his wife makes a more than usually coquettish and absurd remark, he will instinctively exchange a glance of disgust with his mistress. He had no reason to suppose Gudrun was anything more than an employee to Swan – she was no beauty, that was certain – but, as Mrs Swan spoke, he watched the other two. Gudrun didn't look up and Swan's eyes were on his wife. It was an appreciative, affectionate glance he gave her and he seemed to find nothing ridiculous in what she had said.

'You can leave my shirts till later, Rozzy.'

Burden felt that Swan often made remarks of this nature. Everything could be put off till another day, another time. Idleness or chat took precedence over activity always with him. He nearly jumped out of his skin when Mrs Swan said gaily:

'Shall we go into the lounge, my lover?'

Wexford just looked at him, his face impassive.

The 'lounge' was furnished with chintzy chairs, doubtful antiques, and, hanging here and there, brass utensils of no apparent use to a modern or, come to that, ancient household. It reflected no particular taste, had no individuality, and Burden remembered that Hall Farm, doubtless with all its contents, had been supplied to Swan by an uncle because he had nowhere else to live.

Linking her arm into her husband's, Mrs Swan led him to a sofa where she perched beside him, disengaged arms and took his hand. Swan allowed himself to be thus manipulated in a passive fashion and seemed to admire his wife.

'None of these names mean anything to me, Chief Inspector,' he said when he had looked at the list. 'What about you, Roz?'

'I don't think so, my lover.'

Her lover said, 'I saw in the paper about the missing boy. You think the cases have some connection?'

'Very possibly, Mr Swan. You say you don't know any of the people on this list. Do you know Mrs Gemma Lawrence?'

'We hardly know anyone around here,' said Rosalind Swan. 'You might say we're still on our honeymoon, really.'

Burden thought this a tasteless remark. The woman was all of thirty-eight and married a year. He waited for her to say something about the child who had never been found, to show some feeling for her, but Mrs Swan was looking with voracious pride at her husband. He thought it time to put his own spoke in and he said flatly:

'Can you account for your movements on Thursday afternoon, sir?'

The man wasn't very tall, had small hands, and anyone could fake a limp. Besides, Wexford had said he hadn't had an alibi for that other Thursday afternoon . . .

'You've quite cast me for the role of kidnapper, haven't you?' Swan said to Wexford.

'It was Mr Burden who asked you,' Wexford said imperturbably.

'I shall never forget the way you hounded me when we lost poor little Stella.'

'Poor little Stella,' Mrs Swan echoed comfortably.

'Don't get upset, Rozzy. You know I don't like it when you're upset. All right, what was I doing on Thursday afternoon? Every time you add anyone to your missing persons list I suppose I must expect this sort of inquisition. I was here last Thursday. My wife was in London and Gudrun had the afternoon off. I was here all alone. I read for a bit and had a nap.' A flicker of temper crossed his face. 'Oh, and at about four I rode over to Stowerton and murdered a couple of tots that were making the streets look untidy.'

'Oh, Ivor, darling!'

'That sort of thing isn't amusing, Mr Swan.'

'No, and it's not amusing for me to be suspected of making away with two children, one of them my own wife's.'

No more could be got out of him. 'I've been meaning to ask,' said Burden as they drove back, 'did she go on calling herself Rivers after her mother re-married?'

'Sometimes she was one, sometimes the other, as far as I could gather. When she became a missing person she was Stella Rivers to us because that was her real name. Swan said he intended to have the name changed by deed poll, but he hadn't taken any steps towards it. Typical of him.'

'Tell me about this non-existent alibi,' said Burden.

Chapter 6

Martin, Loring and their helpers were still interviewing rabbit-keepers, Bryant, Gates and half a dozen others continuing a house-to-house search of Stowerton. During the chief inspector's absence Constable Peach had brought in a child's plimsoll which he had found in a field near Flagford, but it was the wrong size, and, anyway, John Lawrence hadn't been wearing plimsolls.

Wexford read the messages which had been left on his desk, but most were negative and none needed immediate attention. He scanned the anonymous note again, then put it back in its envelope with a sigh.

'We had enough letters in the Stella Rivers case to paper the walls of this office,' he said, 'and we followed them all up. We had five hundred and twenty-three phone calls. The fantasies that go on in people's minds, Mike, the power of their imaginations! They were nearly all well intentioned. Ninety per cent of them really thought they had seen Stella and . . .'

Burden interrupted him. 'I want to hear about Swan's alibi.'

'Swan drove Stella to Equita at two-thirty. Silly sort of name, isn't it? Whether it's supposed to mean all the pupils are equal or the only thing they teach is horse-riding, I wouldn't know.'

Burden was always impatient with these

digressions. 'What kind of a car does he drive?'

'Not a red Jag. An oldish Ford shooting brake. He left Stella at the gates, believing, he said, that friends would bring her home, and went back home himself. At three-thirty he also got on a horse, that Sherry thing, and rode to Myfleet to see, believe it or not, a man about a dog.'

'You're joking.'

'Would I, about a thing like this? There's a fellow in Myfleet called Blain who breeds pointers. Swan went to look at some puppies with an eye to buying one for Stella. Of course, he didn't buy one, any more than he ever got her the pony he promised or got her name changed. Swan's always "just going to do something". One of the Four Just Men, he is.'

'But he did call on this man?'

'Blain told us Swan was with him from ten to four until four-fifteen, but he didn't get back to Hall Farm until five-thirty.'

'Where did he say he had been in that hour and a quarter?'

'Just riding round. The horse, he said, needed exercise. Maybe it also needed a wash, for both rider and mount must have been wet through when Swan got home. But odd though this sounds, it is the kind of thing Swan would do. He *would* moon about on horseback in the rain. His ride, he said, took him through Cheriton Forest, but he couldn't produce a single person to corroborate this. On the other hand, he could have got to Mill Lane in the time and killed Stella. But if he did, why did he? And what did he do with her body? His wife hasn't an alibi either. She says she was at Hall Farm and she can't drive. At any rate, she hasn't a driving licence.'

Burden digested all this carefully. Then, he decided, he wanted to know more about Stella's departure from Equita. He wanted the details Wexford hadn't had time to give him when they had sat together in the car in Fontaine Road.

'The children,' said Wexford, 'had an hour's riding lesson and a further hour they spent messing about with the horses. Miss Williams, the owner of Equita, who lives in that house adjoining the stables, saw Stella that afternoon but says she didn't speak to her and we have no reason to doubt her word. It was Mrs Margaret Fenn who took the children out for their ride. She's a widow of about forty and she lives in what used to be the lodge to Saltram House. Know it?'

Burden knew it. Ruined Saltram House and its grounds, now turned to wilderness, had been a favourite resort of his and Jean's. For them it had been a place of romance, a lost domain, where they had gone for evening walks in the early days of their marriage and where they had later returned many times to bring their children on picnics.

All that day he had hardly thought about Jean and his happy past with her. His misery had been suspended by the present tumultuous events. But now again he saw her face before him and heard her call his name as they explored the gardens that time had laid waste and, hand in hand, entered the dark cold shell of the house. He shivered.

'You all right, Mike?' Wexford gave him a brief anxious glance and then he went on. 'Stella said good-bye to Mrs Fenn and said that as her step-father – incidentally, she always referred to him as her father – hadn't yet arrived, she would walk along Mill Lane to meet him. Mrs Fenn didn't much like letting the girl go alone, but it was still light and she couldn't go with her as she still had another hour and a half at Equita in which to clear up. She watched Stella go through the gates of Equita, thus becoming the last person but one to see her before she disappeared.'

'The last but one?'

'Don't forget the man who offered her a lift. Now for the houses in Mill Lane. There are only three between Equita and Stowerton, all widely separated, Saltram Lodge and two cottages. Before Hill offered her the lift she had passed one of these cottages, the one that is occupied only at week-ends, and, this being a Thursday, it was empty. We know no more of what happened to her after she was seen by Hill, but if she walked on unmolested she would next have come to the second cottage which has a tenant, not an owner occupier. This tenant, a single man, was out at work and didn't return until six. Again this was carefully checked because both this cottage and Saltram Lodge have telephones and one of the possibilities which occurred to me was that Stella might have called at a house and asked to phone Hall Farm. The third and last house, Saltram Lodge, was also empty until Mrs Fenn got home at six. She had had some relatives staying with her, but they had left for London by the three-forty-five train from Stowerton. A taxi-driver confirmed that he had picked them up at the lodge at twenty past three.'

'And was that all?' Burden said. 'No more leads?'

Wexford shook his head. 'Not what you'd call leads. The usual flock of people came forward with unhelpful evidence. A woman had picked up a child's glove outside one of the cottages but it wasn't Stella's. There was another of those free-lift merchants who said he had picked up an elderly man near Saltram Lodge at five-thirty and driven him into Stowerton, but this driver was a shifty sort of fellow and he impressed me as a sensation-monger rather than someone whose word you could rely on.

'A van-driver claimed to have seen a boy come out

of the back door of the rented cottage and perhaps he did. They all leave their back doors unlocked in this part of the world. They think there's no crime in the country. But the van-driver also said he heard screams coming from behind the hedge just outside Equita, and we *know* Stella was alive and unharmed until she had refused Hill's offer. I doubt if we shall ever find out any more.'

Wexford looked tired, his jowly face heavier and more drooping than usual. 'I shall take a couple of hours off tomorrow morning, Mike, and I advise you to do the same. We're both dead-beat. Have a lie-in.'

Burden nodded abstractedly. He didn't say that there is no point in lying-in when there is no one to lie in with, but he thought it. Wearily he found himself recalling as he went out to his car those rare but delightful Sunday mornings when Jean, usually an early riser, consented to remain in bed with him until nine. Lying in each other's arms, they had listened to the sound of Pat making tea for them in the kitchen, and had sat bolt upright, jerking away from each other when she came in with the tray. Those had been the days, but he hadn't known it at the time, hadn't appreciated and treasured each moment as he should have done. And now he would have given ten years of his life for one of those mornings back again.

His memories brought him a dull misery, his only consolation that soon he would be in the company of someone as wretched as himself, but when he walked up to the always open door he heard her call out to him gaily and as intimately as if they were old friends, 'I'm on the phone, Mike. Go in and sit down. Make yourself at home.'

The telephone must be in the dining room, he thought. He sat down in the other room, feeling uncomfortable because untidiness always made him ill-at-ease. He wondered how anyone as beautiful and as charming as she could bear to live in such disorder and wondered more when she came in, for she was a changed woman, brilliantly smiling, almost elegant.

'You needn't have rung off on my account,' he said, trying not to stare too hard at the short kingfisher-blue dress she wore, the long silver chains, the silver comb in her high-piled hair.

'That was Matthew,' she said. 'They brought him a phone and he phoned me from his bed. He's terribly worried about John, but I told him it was all right. I told him everything would be all right on Monday. He has so many worries, poor boy. He's ill and his wife's expecting a baby and he's out of work and now this.'

'Out of work? What sort of work does he do?'

She sat down opposite him and crossed the best pair of legs Burden thought he had ever seen. He stared at a patch of floor some inches from her feet.

'He's a television actor, or he is when he can get work. He so terribly wants to be a household word. The trouble is his face is wrong. Oh, I don't mean he isn't good-looking. He was born too late. He looks just like Valentino and that won't do these days. John's going to be just like him. He's very like him now.'

Matthew Lawrence ... it rang some sort of bell. 'I think I may have seen his picture in the papers,' said Burden.

She nodded earnestly. 'Squiring Leonie West about, I expect. She used to be photographed wherever she went.'

'I know her. She's a ballet dancer. My daughter's crazy about ballet. As a matter of fact, I think that's where I've seen your ex-husband, in pictures with Leonie West.'

'Matthew and Leonie were lovers for years. Then he met me. I was a drama student and I had a small part in a television series he was in. When we got married he said he wouldn't see Leonie any more, but he really only married me because he wanted a child. Leonie couldn't have children, otherwise he'd have married her.'

She had been speaking in a very cool practical voice, but now she sighed and fell silent. Burden waited, no longer tired, even more interested than usual in other people's life stories, although this one perturbed him strangly.

After a while she went on. 'I tried to keep our marriage going and when John was born I thought we had a chance. Then I found out Matthew was still seeing Leonie. At last he asked me to divorce him and I did. The judge expedited the decree because there was a child on the way.'

'But you said Leonie West couldn't ...'

'Oh, not Leonie. He didn't marry her. She was years older than he was. She must be well into her forties by now. He married a girl of nineteen he met at a party.'

'Good God,' said Burden.

'She had the baby, but it only lived two days. That's why I'm keeping my fingers crossed for them now. This one just must be all right.'

Burden couldn't keep his feelings to himself any longer. 'Don't you bear any malice?' he said. 'I should have thought you'd hate him and his wife and that West woman.'

She shrugged. 'Poor Leonie. She's too pathetic now to hate. Besides, I always rather liked her. I don't hate Matthew or his wife. They couldn't help themselves. They did what they had to do. You couldn't expect them all to spoil their lives for me.'

'I'm afraid I'm rather old-fashioned in these

things,' said Burden. 'I believe in self-discipline. They spoiled your life, didn't they?'

'Oh, *no*! I've got John and he makes me very very happy.'

'Mrs Lawrence . . .'

'Gemma!'

'Gemma,' he said awkwardly. 'I must warn you not to bank too much on Monday. I don't think you should bank on it at all. My chief – Chief Inspector Wexford – has absolutely no faith in the veracity of this letter. He's sure it's a hoax.'

She paled a little and clasped her hands. 'No one would write a letter like that,' she said innocently, 'if it wasn't true. Nobody could be so cruel.'

'But people are cruel. Surely you must know that?'

'I won't believe it. I know John is going to be there on Monday. Please – please don't spoil it for me. I'm holding on to it, it's made me so happy.'

He shook his head helplessly. Her eyes were beseeching. imploring him to give her one word of encouragement. And then, to his horror, she fell on her knees in front of him, seizing both his hands in hers.

'Please, Mike, tell me you think it'll be all right. Just say there's a chance. There could be, couldn't there? Please, Mike!'

Her nails dug into his wrists. 'There's always a chance . . .'

'More than that, more than that! Smile at me, show me there's a chance.' He smiled, almost desperately. She sprang up. 'Stay there. I'm going to make coffee.'

The evening was dying away. Soon it would be quite dark. He knew that he should go away now, follow her outside and say briskly, 'Well, if you're all right, I must be on my way.' Staying here was wrong, entirely overstepping the bounds of his duty.

If she needed company it ought to be Mrs Crantock or one of those strange friends of hers.

He couldn't go. It was impossible. What a hypocrite he was with his talk of self-discipline. Jean? he said, savouring her name experimentally. If Jean had been at home there would have been no staying, no need for control.

She came back with the coffee and they drank it in the dusk. Soon he could hardly see her and yet somehow he felt her presence more forcefully. In one way he wanted her to turn on the light, but at the same time he prayed that she wouldn't and thus destroy the atmosphere, warm, dark and scented with her scent, a tension and yet a peace.

She poured him more coffee and their hands touched. 'Tell me about your wife,' she said.

He had never told anyone. He wasn't the kind of man to open his heart and relieve his soul. Grace had tried to draw him out. That idiot Camb had tried and, in a more subtle and tactful way, Wexford himself. And yet he would have liked to tell someone, if only the right listener could be found. This beautiful kind woman wasn't the right listener. What would she with her strange past, her peculiar permissiveness, understand of his notions of monogamy, his one-woman life? How could he talk to her of his simple gentle Jean, her quiet existence and her abominable death?

'It's all over now,' he said shortly. 'Best forgotten.' Too late he realised the impression his words had made.

'Even if you haven't been too happy,' she said, 'you don't just miss the person, you miss love.'

He saw the truth of it. Even for him it was true. But love wasn't quite the word. There was no love in those dreams of his and Jean never entered them. As

69

if to deny his own thoughts, he said harshly, 'They say you can find a substitute, but you can't. I can't.'

'Not a substitute. That's the wrong word. But someone else for another way of love perhaps.'

'I don't know. I have to go now. Don't put on the light.' Light would show her too much, his face after suppressed pain had worked on it, and, worse than that, the hunger for her he could no longer hide. 'Don't put on the light!'

'I wasn't going to,' she said softly. 'Come here.'

It was a little light kiss on the cheek she gave him, such as a woman may give a man she has known for years, the husband of a friend perhaps, and, returning it, touching her cheek, he still meant to kiss her in the same way with a comradely reassurance. But he felt his heart beating and hers beside it as if he had two hearts of his own. Their mouths met and his long control broke.

He kissed her with everything he had, crushing her in his arms and forcing her back against the wall, his tongue thrusting down into her mouth.

When he let her go and moved away shivering, she stood still with her head bowed, saying nothing. He opened the front door and ran from her, not looking back.

Chapter 7

Sunday, the morning of his lie-in. He had passed a horrible night, filled with dreams so disgusting that if he had read them in some work on psychology – the kind that Grace was always on about – he would have had no difficulty in believing they were the product of a diseased and perverted mind. Even thinking of them made him shudder with shame.

If you lie wakeful in bed when it is already light you have to think. But of what? Jean who was gone for ever? Dreams that made you wonder if inside you were as bad as all those local deviates? Gemma Lawrence? What a fool he had been to kiss her, to stay sitting there with her in the dark, to get involved!

He got up quickly. It was only seven-thirty when he came into the kitchen and no one else was about. He made a pot of tea and took a cup in to each of the others. It was another beautiful clear day.

Grace sat up in bed and took the teacup. She wore a night-gown just like Jean's. Her morning face was a little puffy with sleep, dreamy and vague just as Jean's had always been. He hated her.

'I have to go out,' he said. 'Work.'

'I didn't hear the phone,' said Grace.

'You were asleep.'

His children didn't stir when he put their teacups beside them. They were heavy sleepers and it was only natural. Burden knew all that, but it seemed to him that they no longer cared for him. Their mother was dead but they had a mother substitute, a mother facsimile. It was all one to them, he thought, whether their father was there or not.

He got out his car and drove off, but with no clear picture of where he was going. Perhaps to Cheriton Forest to sit and think and torture himself. But instead of taking the Pomfret road he found himself heading towards Stowerton. All the control he had left was needed to stop him going towards Fontaine Road, but he kept his control and turned instead into Mill Lane.

It was here that the red Jaguar had been seen. Behind those trees the young duffel-coated man with the small hands had strolled picking leaves. Were they connected, the car and the youth? And was it possible in this wicked and cynical world that the leaf-picker kept rabbits – perhaps he had been picking leaves for his rabbits – and needed a child only for the pleasure of that child's company and the sight of its happy face when a small eager hand stroked thick smooth fur?

On such a morning even this improbable and Peter Panlike notion seemed feasible. In the distance, ahead of him, he could hear the bells of St Jude, Forby, ringing for early Communion. He knew now where he was going. He rounded a bend in the road and Saltram House came suddenly and gloriously into view.

Who would have supposed, looking at it from this distance as it proudly crowned the hill, that those windows were not glazed, those rooms not inhabited, but that the great stone edifice was merely a shell, the skeleton, so to speak, of a palace? It was golden-grey in the morning sun, a palladian house, late eighteenth century, and in its splendid proportions it seemed both to smile and to frown on the valley below.

Fifty years old now, the tale of its destruction was known to everyone in Kingsmarkham. During the First World War it had been. Whoever had owned the house, and this was now forgotten, had given a house party and his guests had gone out on to a flat area of the roof to watch a Zeppelin pass over. One of them had dropped a cigar butt over the parapet and the butt had set fire to the shrubs below. There was nothing now behind those blank exquisite windows, nothing but trees and bushes which had grown up out of the burnt foundations to thrust their branches where once women in Paris gowns had walked, looking at pictures and trailing their fans.

He started the car again and drove slowly up to the iron gates where the drive to Saltram House began. On the left of the gates stood a small one-storey white house with a thatched roof. A woman was in the garden, picking mushrooms from the lawn. Mrs Fenn, he supposed. She hadn't lived there in the days when he and Jean used to come picnicking in the grounds. The lodge had stood empty for years.

Of course, these grounds would have been thoroughly searched back in February and then again by the search parties on Thursday night and Friday. But did the searchers know the place as he knew it? Would they know the secret places as he knew them?

Burden opened the gates and they creaked dully on their hinges.

Wexford and his friend Dr Crocker, the police doctor, sometimes played golf together on Sunday mornings. They had been friends since boyhood, these two, although Wexford was the senior by seven years and the doctor was a spry lean fellow who looked quite young when seen from a distance, whereas Wexford was a huge man, gone to seed and stout, with dangerously high blood pressure.

It was on account of this hypertension that Crocker had suggested the Sunday golf sessions and prescribed a rigorous diet. Wexford lapsed from his diet twice a week on average, but he didn't greatly object to the golf, although his handicap was disgracefully around thirty-six. It got him out of going to church with his wife.

'You wouldn't fancy a little drop of something?' he asked wistfully in the club bar.

'At this hour?' said Crocker, the disciplinarian.

'It's the effect that counts, not the hour.'

'If my sphyg wasn't about the best you can buy,' said the doctor, 'it would have busted last time I took your blood pressure. I kid you not, it would have snapped in sheer despair. You wouldn't put a thermometer under the hot tap now, would you? What you need isn't alcohol but a few brisk swings under the pro's eagle eye.'

'Not that,' Wexford pleaded. 'Anything but that.'

They went on to the first tee. His expression inscrutable, Crocker watched his friend fumbling in his golf bag and then he handed him a five iron without a word.

Wexford drove. The ball disappeared, but nowhere in the direction of the first hole. 'It's so bloody unfair,' he said. 'You've been at this ridiculous pastime all your life and I'm a mere novice. It's giving me a hell of an inferiority complex. Now if we were to fetch someone else in on this, Mike Burden, for instance ...'

'Do Mike good, I daresay.'

'I worry about him,' said Wexford, glad of a respite before having to witness one of the doctor's perfect drives. 'I wonder sometimes if he isn't heading for a nervous breakdown.'

'Men lose their wives. They get over it. D'you know what? Mike will marry his sister-in-law. It's right on the cards. She looks like Jean, she acts like Jean. Mike can marry her and almost stay monogamous. Enough of this nonsense. We're here to play golf, remember.'

'I mustn't go too far from the club-house. They may want to reach me at any time if anything comes up about that missing boy.'

It was a genuine anxiety on Wexford's part and not an excuse, but he had cried wolf on the golf course too often. The doctor grinned nastily. 'Then they can come and fetch you. Some members of this club can actually *run*, you know. Now watch me carefully.' He took his own well-seasoned five and drove with beautiful precision. 'On the green, I fancy,' he said complacently.

Wexford picked up his bag, sighed, and then strode manfully up the fairway. He murmured under his breath and with feeling towards the doctor's back, '"Thou shalt not kill but needs't not strive, officiously to keep alive."'

The aspect of the house which faced the road and in front of which Burden now parked his car was the back or, more properly, the garden front. There could be no doubt from this distance that Saltram House was a shell. He went up to one of the stone-faced windows and stared through it into the still, dim and silent depths. Elder trees and young oaks – for how old is a mature oak? – thrust their way up out of sand and rubble. The scars of the fire had long faded, their blackness washed away by fifty winters of rain. The leaves were golden now and rattling yellow, lying in their thousands on broken stone and massed rubble. The house had been like this when he and Jean had first come here and the only change was that the trees were taller, nature more rampant and more arrogant in her conquest, and yet it seemed to him that the ruin was personal, symbolic of his own.

He never read poetry. He seldom read anything. But like that of most people who don't read, his memory was good and sometimes he remembered the things Wexford had quoted to him. Under his breath, wonderingly, he whispered:

'Ruin hath taught me thus to ruminate
That time will come and take my love away . . .'

He didn't know who had said it, but whoever it was knew all right. He swung away from the back of the house. There was no entering it this way. You entered by the front, clambering through what had once been an Italian garden.

To the right and left of him neglected parkland fell away. Whom did it belong to? Why did no one farm it? He didn't know the answers, only that this was a still and beautiful desert where grass grew long and wild and trees that man, not nature, had planted, cedars and ilexes and the tall slender *gingko biloba*, the Chinese maidenhair tree, raised proud trunks and prouder branches from an alien soil. It was a wilderness, desperately sad in that it should have been tended, was designed to be tended, but those who loved to tend it had been removed by ruining time. He thrust aside branches and brambles and came to the incomparably more beautiful front of Saltram House.

There was a great pediment crowning it with a frieze of classical figures and beneath this, above the front door, a vertical sun-dial, sky blue with figures of gold, which the wind and rain had scarred but not spoiled. From where he stood Burden could see the sky through the bones, as it were, of the house, pieces of sky as blue as the sun-dial.

It was no longer possible, and hadn't been for years, to walk into the Italian garden or up to the house without climbing. Burden scrambled over a five-foot-high wall of broken stone, through the cracks of which brambles and bryony had thrust their tendrils.

He had never seen the fountains playing, but he knew there had once been fountains here. Twelve years ago, when he and Jean had first penetrated as far as this, two bronze figures holding vases aloft had stood on either side of the overgrown drive. But vandals had come since then and torn the statues from their plinths, greedy perhaps for the lead from which the fountain pipes were made.

One figure had been that of a boy, the other of a girl in delicate drapery. The boy had disappeared, but the girl lay among the weeds, and the long-leaved grey mullion with its yellow flowers pushed its stalks between her arm and the curve of her body. Burden bent down and lifted the statue. It was broken and half-eaten away by verdigris and underneath it the ground was quite bare, a blank area of earth oddly and unpleasantly in the shape of a small human body.

He replaced the mass of metal which had once been a fountain and climbed the broken steps that led up to the door. But as soon as he stood on the threshold, at the point where in the past guests had entered and given their cloaks to a servant, he saw that there was no concealing a body here, not even the small body of a five-year-old.

For everything in Saltram House, cupboards, doors, staircase, even to a great extent dividing walls, was gone. There remained scarcely anything of the works of man. True, the towering and somewhat sinister walls of the house soared above him, but even these, which had once been painted and adorned with frescoes, were now hung everywhere with ivy, and they sheltered from the wind a young forest of rich growth. Elders and oaks, birch and beech saplings had forced their way from the rich burnt soil and some of them now rivalled the walls themselves in height. Burden was looking down into a copse which the breeze, entering by the window holes, ruffled gently. He could see the roots of these trees and see too that nothing lay amongst them.

He gazed and then he turned away. Down the steps he went and back into the Italian garden, remembering with a sudden pang how they had once eaten their tea on this very spot, and Pat, a little girl or so, had asked him why he couldn't make the fountains play. Because they were broken, because there was no water, he had said. He had never thought of it again, never wondered about it till now.

But those fountains had played once. Where had the water come from? Not directly from the main, surely, even if main water had ever reached Saltram House. For things like this, fountains and any ornamental water gadgets, you always had tanks. And whether there was main water or not at the time the house was burnt, there certainly wouldn't have been when the fountains were set up in seventeen something or other.

Therefore the water must have been stored somewhere. Burden felt a little thrill of dread. It was a stupid idea, he told himself. Fantastic. The searchers had been all over these grounds twice. Surely a notion like this would have occurred to one of them? Not if they didn't know the place like I do, he thought, not if they didn't know that statue was once a fountain.

He knew he wouldn't rest or have a moment's peace if he went now. He dropped down off the steps and stood knee-deep in weeds and brambles. The cisterns, if cisterns there were, wouldn't be up here by the house but as near as possible to the fountain plinths.

In the first place, these plinths were hard to find. Burden cut himself an elder branch with his penknife and pruned off its twigs. Then he began lifting away the dead and dying growth. In places the tangle seemed immovable and he had almost decided this was an impossible task when his stick struck something metallic and gave off a dull ring. Using his bare hands now, he tore away first ivy and under it a tenacious heathy plant to reveal a bronze disc with a hole in its centre. He closed his eyes, thought back and remembered that the boy had stood here, the girl in a similar position on the other side of the drive.

Now where would the cistern be? Not surely between the plinth and the drive, but on the other side. Again he used his stick. It hadn't rained for two or three weeks and the ground beneath the jungle of weeds was as hard as stone. No use going by feel, unless he felt with his feet. Accordingly, he shuffled slowly along the not very clear passage his stick was making.

He was looking down all the time, but still he stumbled when his left toe struck what felt like a stone ridge or step. Probing with the stick, he found the ridge and then traced a rectangular outline. He squatted down and worked with his hands until he had cleared away all the growth and revealed a slate slab the size and shape of a gravestone. Just as he had thought, the fountain cistern. Would it be possible to raise that slab? He tried and it came up easily before he had time to brace himself against the shock of what he might find inside.

The cistern was quite empty. Dry, he thought, for half a century. Not even a spider or a woodlouse had penetrated its stone fastness.

Well, there was another one, wasn't there? Another cistern to feed the fountain on the opposite side? No difficulty, at any rate, about finding it. He paced out the distance and cleared the second slab. Was it his imagination or did the growth seem newer here? There were no dense brambles, anyway, only the soft sappy weeds that die away entirely in winter. The slab looked just like its fellow, silvery black and here and there greened with lichen.

Burden's fingers were torn and bleeding. He wiped them on his handkerchief, raised the slab and, with a rasping intake of breath, looked down at the body in the cistern.

Chapter 8

Harry Wild knocked out his pipe into the ashtray on Camb's counter. 'Well, are you going to tell me?'

'I don't know anything, Harry, and that's a fact. They sent for Mr Wexford off the golf course and he just about tore in here. You'll have to wait till he's got a moment to spare. We're all at sixes and sevens. I don't remember a Sunday like it all my time in the force.'

The phone rang. Camb lifted the receiver and said, 'You've seen John Lawrence in Brighton, madam? One moment while I put you through to the officers who are dealing with this information.' He sighed. 'That,' he said to Wild, 'makes thirty-two calls today from people who claim to have seen that kid.'

'He's dead. My informant who's very reliable says he's dead. Burden found his body this morning and that's why I'm working on a Sunday.' Wild watched to see how this affected Camb, and then added, 'I just want confirmation from Wexford and then I'm off to interview the mother.'

'Rather you than me,' said Camb. 'By gum, I wouldn't have your job for all the tea in China.'

Not at all abashed, Wild re-lit his pipe. 'Talking of tea, I don't suppose there's any going?'

Camb didn't answer him. His phone was ringing again. When he had dealt with a man who claimed to have found a blue sweater answering to the description of the one John Lawrence had been wearing he looked up and saw the lift doors open. 'Here's Mr Wexford now,' he said, 'and Mr Burden. On their way to the mortuary to see what Dr Crocker's come up with, I daresay.'

'Ah, Mr Burden,' Wild said, 'the very man I want to see. What's all this about finding the body of the lost kid?'

Burden gave him an icy stare, then turned on his heel, but Wexford snapped, 'What d'you want to know for, anyway? That rag of yours doesn't go to press till Thursday.'

'Excuse me, sir,' said Camb, 'but Mr Wild wants to send the stories to the London papers.'

'Oh, linage. I see. Well, far be it from me to keep a journalist from earning an honest penny on the Sabbath. Mr Burden did find a body this morning, in one of the fountain cisterns at Saltram House. You can say foul play is suspected. The body is that ...' He paused and then went on more quickly, 'of a female child, aged about twelve, so far unidentified.'

'It's Stella Rivers, isn't it?' said Wild greedily. 'Come on, give a working man a break. This could be the biggest story of my career. Missing child found dead in ruins. No clue yet to lost boy. Is Kingsmarkham another Cannock Chase? I can see it all, I can ...'

Wexford had great self-control. He also had two daughters and a grandson. He loved children with a passionate tenderness and his self-control broke down.

'Get out of here!' he roared. 'You back-street death reporter! You revolting ghoulish hack! Get out!'

Wild got out.

A gloom settles on policemen and on their police station when the body of a child has been found. Later they hunt for a child's killer with zeal, but at first, when the crime is discovered, they are aghast and sick at heart. For this is the crime most against nature, most life-denying and least forgivable.

Not at all ashamed of his castigation of Harry Wild, Wexford made his way to the mortuary where Dr Crocker and Burden stood on either side of the sheeted body.

'I've sent Loring to fetch Ivor Swan, sir,' said Burden. 'Better have him do it than the mother.'

Wexford nodded. 'How did she die?'

'The body's been there for God knows how many months,' said Crocker. 'The path experts will have to get working on it. I'd say, at a guess, asphyxiation. Violent pressure on the windpipe. There are no wounds or anything like that and she wasn't strangled. No sexual interference.'

'We knew,' said Wexford quietly, 'that she must have been dead. It oughtn't to seem so horrible. It oughtn't to be such a shock. I hope she wasn't too frightened, that's all.' He turned away. 'I hope it was quick,' he said.

'That,' said Crocker, 'is the kind of thing you'd expect her parents to say, not a tough old nut like you, Reg.'

'Oh, shut up. Maybe it's because I know her parents won't say it that I'm saying it. Look at you, you bloody half-baked quack, you don't even *care*.'

'Now, steady on . . .'

'Here's Mr Swan,' said Burden.

He came in with Loring. Dr Crocker lifted the sheet. Swan looked and went white. 'That's Stella,' he said. 'The hair, the clothes . . . God, how horrible!'

'You're sure.'

'Oh, yes. I'd like to sit down. I've never seen a dead person before.'

Wexford took him into one of the interview rooms on the ground floor.

Swan asked for a glass of water and didn't speak again until he had drunk it.

'What a ghastly sight! I'm glad Roz didn't see it. I thought I was going to pass out in there.' He wiped his face with his handkerchief and sat staring at nothing but as if he were still seeing the child's body. Wexford thought his horror was occasioned only by the sight of what eight months underground had done to Stella Rivers and not by personal grief, an impression that wasn't much weakened when Swan said, 'I was fond of her, you know. I mean, it wasn't as if she was my own but I'd got quite attached to her.'

'We've been into all that before, Mr Swan. How well do you know the grounds of Saltram House?'

'That's where she was found, isn't it? I don't even know where it is.'

'And yet you must have passed the house every time you drove Stella to Equita.'

'D'you mean that ruin you can see from the road?'

Wexford nodded, watching the other man carefully. Swan looked at the walls, the floor, anywhere but at the chief inspector. Then he said in the tone a man uses when his car keeps breaking down, 'I don't know why this sort of thing has to happen to me.'

'What d'you mean, "this sort of thing"?'

'Oh, nothing. Can I go now?'

'Nobody's detaining you, Mr Swan,' said Wexford.

Half an hour later he and Burden were sitting on the crumbling wall watching half a dozen men at work in the cistern, photographing, measuring, examining. The sun was still hot and its brilliance gave to the place an air of classical antiquity. Broken columns showed here and there among the long grass and the investigations had turned up fragments of pottery.

It might have been an archaeological dig they were

supervising rather than a hunt for clues in a murder case. They had failed to find any trace of the male statue, but the figure of the girl lay as Burden had left her, lay like a dead thing, her face buried in ivy, her sculpted metal hair gleaming in the sun as gold as the hair of Stella Rivers in life.

'You'll think me a fanciful old fool,' said Wexford musingly, 'but I can't help seeing the analogy. It's like an omen.' He pointed to the statue and looked quizzically at Burden. 'The girl's dead. The boy has disappeared, someone has taken him away.' He shrugged. 'In life,' he said. 'In bronze. And somewhere maybe the thief has set the boy up in pleasant surroundings, taken care of him. I mean the statue, of course.'

'Well, sure, what else? More likely used what was useful and chucked the rest out.'

'Christ . . .' Wexford saw that the inspector had no idea what he had meant and gave up. He ought to have known, he reflected, that it was no use going into flights of fancy with Mike. 'Whoever put her in there,' he said more practically, 'knew the place better than you do. You didn't even know there were any cisterns.'

'I've only been here in summer. The slabs wouldn't be so overgrown in wintertime.'

'I wonder?' Wexford called Peach over. 'You were with the search parties in February, Peach. Did you notice the cisterns?'

'We covered this ground the day after Stella went missing, sir. The Friday, it was. It poured with rain all the previous night and it was raining hard when we were here. The whole of this area was a sea of mud. I don't reckon you could have guessed the cistern slabs were there.'

'I think we'll go and have a word with Mrs Fenn.'

She was a small fair woman, anxious to help,

appalled at the discovery which had been made less than a quarter of a mile from her home.

'She was the most promising pupil I had,' she said in a quiet voice with an edge of horror to it. 'I used to boast about her to my friends. Stella Rivers, I used to say – or Stella Swan, you never knew which was her right name – Stella Rivers will be a first-class show jumper one day. She won't, will she? God, it's so *awful*. I'll never forgive myself for letting her go off on her own that day. I should have phoned Mr Swan. I knew he was a bit absent-minded. That wasn't the first time he'd let her down and forgotten to come.'

'You mustn't blame yourself,' said Wexford. 'Tell me, did you know those fountains had cisterns? If you knew, it means other local people would know.'

'Of course I knew.' Mrs Fenn looked puzzled. 'Oh you mean they get overgrown in summer?' Her brow cleared. 'I often ride up there in dry weather and take my guests for walks or on picnics. I know I've pointed out the fountains to people because the statues are so pretty, aren't they?' With a little tremor in her voice she said, 'I shan't feel like going there ever again.' She shook her head with a kind of shudder. 'After heavy rain the slabs might get covered, especially if a lot of earth got washed down from the side of the house.'

They were carrying the slab out to the waiting van now. It would go to the lab for extensive tests.

'If he left any prints,' said Wexford, 'all the mud and water will have got rid of them. The weather was on his side, wasn't it? What's the matter? Had an idea?'

'I'm afraid not.' Burden contemplated the quiet lane and the surrounding meadows. He didn't look back at the house but he felt its blind empty eyes on him. 'I was wondering about Mrs Lawrence,' he said. 'I mean, ought I to go and . . .'

Wexford snapped off the sentence in his scissors voice. 'Martin's been. I sent him to Fontaine Road as soon as we heard what you'd found. It wouldn't do for her to hear we'd found a body and not know whose.'

'That's what I thought.'

'So you needn't bother with her tonight. She won't want coppers hanging around her place all the time. Let her have a bit of peace. Besides, she said she'd got a friend coming down from London.'

He needn't bother with her tonight ... Burden wondered who the friend was. Man or woman? Actress? Artist? Maybe someone who would listen avidly while Gemma told her about the kiss she had received from a sex-starved policeman. No, he needn't go there again tonight or any other night, come to that. The Stella Rivers case would take up all his time and it would be better that way. Far better, said Burden firmly to himself.

The national press had arrived in force on Sunday evening, and Wexford, most unwillingly, had held a conference. He didn't like reporters, but they had their uses. On the whole, he supposed, the publicity they gave to pain and horror did more good than harm. Their stories would be inaccurate, with most of the names spelt wrong – a national daily had once repeatedly referred to him as Police Chief Waterford – but the public would be alerted, someone might come up with something helpful. Certainly there would be hundreds of phone calls and, no doubt, more anonymous letters of the kind that this morning had sent Martin, Gates and Loring to keep a date in Cheriton Forest.

Wexford had left home before his morning paper arrived, and now, at nine, he entered Braddon's to buy all the dailies. The shop had only just opened, but there was someone ahead of him. Wexford sighed. He knew that round grizzled head, that short spare figure. Even now, when innocently purchasing sixty Number Six, the man had an air of lurking. 'Good morning, Monkey,' said Wexford softly.

Monkey Matthews didn't jump. He froze briefly and then turned round. It was easy to see when you regarded him full-face how he had acquired his nickname. He stuck out his prognathous jaw, wrinkled up his nose and said glumly, 'Small world. I come in here with Rube, just for the bus ride, minding my own business, and before I get me first fag on I've got the fuzz on me tail.'

'Don't be like that,' said Wexford pleasantly. He bought his papers and shepherded Monkey out on to the pavement.

'I haven't done nothing.'

Monkey always made this remark to policemen, even when he encountered one by chance, as on this present occasion. And Burden had once replied, Two negatives make an affirmative, so we know where we are, don't we?

'Long time no see.' Wexford abhorred the expression, but Monkey would understand it and find it irritating.

He did. To cover a slight confusion he lit a cigarette and inhaled voraciously. 'Been up north,' he said vaguely. 'Had a spell in the rag trade. Liverpool.'

Later, Wexford decided, he would check. For the present he made an inspired guess. 'You've been in Walton.'

At the name of the prison, Monkey removed the cigarette from his lip and spat. 'Me and my partner,' he said, 'as straight a feller as you'd wish to meet, we had this stall like and a dirty little bastard of a fuzz cadet planted fifty dozen pair of fishnet tights on us.

Seconds, they was supposed to be, but half of them hadn't got no crotch. Bleeding little agent provoker.'

'I don't want to hear that sort of talk,' said Wexford, and then less severely, 'Back with Ruby, are you? Isn't it about time you made an honest woman of her?'

'Me with a wife living?' Unconsciously, Monkey echoed the Lear Limerick. 'Bigamy, sir, is a crime,' he said. 'Pardon me, but that's my bus coming. I can't stand about nattering all day.'

Grinning broadly, Wexford watched him scuttle off to the bus stop on the Kingsbrook bridge. He scanned the front page of the first of his papers, saw that Stella had been found by a Sergeant Burton in a cave not far from the tiny hamlet of Stowerton, and changed his grin to a scowl.

Chapter 9

Monkey Matthews had been born during the First War in the East End of London and had been educated for the most past in Borstal institutions. His marriage at the age of twenty to a Kingsmarkham girl had brought him to her home town where he had lived – when not in gaol – with his wife in her parents' house. Violence was foreign to him, but only perhaps because he was a coward, not from principle. He stole mostly. He stole from private houses, from his own wife and her aged parents and from those few people who were foolish enough to employ him.

The second war absorbed him into the Army, where he stole stores, officers' uniforms and small electrical equipment. He went to Germany with the army of occupation; he became an expert in the black market and, on his return home, was probably Kingsmarkham's first spiv. Patiently, his wife took him back each time he came out of prison.

In spite of his looks, he was attractive to women. He met Ruby Branch in Kingsmarkham magistrates' court as she was leaving it after being put on probation and he entering between two policemen. They didn't, of course, speak. But Monkey sought her out when he was free again and became a frequent visitor to her house in Charteris Road, Stowerton, especially when Mr Branch was on night work. He suggested to her that she wasn't getting the most out of her job at the underwear factory and soon, on his advice, she was clocking out most Fridays wearing three bras, six slips and six suspender belts under her dress. An ardent lover, Monkey was waiting for her when she came back from Holloway.

Since those days Wexford had put Monkey away for shop-breaking, larceny as a servant, attempting to blow up one of Ruby's rivals with a home-made bomb, and stealing by finding. Monkey was nearly as old as Wexford, but there was as much life left in him as in the chief inspector, although he smoked sixty cigarettes a day, had no legitimate means of support and, since his wife had finally thrown him out, no fixed abode.

Returning to his office, Wexford wondered about him. Monkey could never be free for long without getting into trouble. Busy as he was, Wexford decided to do the checking he had resolved on outside the newsagent's.

His notion that Monkey had been in Walton was soon confirmed. He had been released in September. The conviction had been for receiving, knowing it to have been stolen, so huge a quantity of tights, nylon briefs, body stockings and other frippery which, had it ever been sold, would surely have supplied the entire female teenage population of Liverpool for months to come.

Shaking his head, but smiling rather wryly, Wexford dismissed Monkey from his mind and concentrated on the pile of reports that awaited his attention. He had read through three of them when Sergeant Martin came in.

'No one turned up, of course?' he said, looking up.

'I'm afraid not, sir. We separated, according to instructions. It's out of the question we could have been spotted, the forest's so thick there. The only person to come along the road was the receptionist at the Cheriton Forest Hotel. No one came down the ride. We stayed there till ten.'

'I knew it would be a dead loss,' said Wexford.

Burden shared his chief's antipathy to Ivor and Rosalind Swan but he found it impossible to view them with Wexford's cynicism. They had something, those two, the special relationship of two people who love each other almost exclusively and who mean their love to survive until death parts them. Would he ever again find a love like that for himself? Or was to have it once all that any man could expect, knowing that few ever found it at all? Rosalind Swan had lost her only child in a hideous way but she could bear that loss without too much pain while she had her husband. He felt that she would have sacrificed a dozen children to keep Swan. How had Stella fitted into this honeymoon life? Had either or both of them felt her a hindrance, a shadowy and undesired third?

Wexford had been questioning them for half an hour and Mrs Swan looked tired and pale, but she seemed to feel the enormity of her husband's interrogation more keenly than its cause. 'Ivor loved Stella,' she kept saying, 'and Stella loved him.'

'Come, Mr Swan,' Wexford said, ignoring this, 'you must often since then have thought about that ride of yours and yet you can't name to me a single person, apart from Mr Blain, who might have seen you.'

'I haven't thought about it much,' Swan said, holding his wife's hand closely in both his own. 'I wanted to forget it. Anyway, I do remember people, only not what they looked like or their car numbers. Why should I go about taking car numbers? I didn't know I'd have to give anyone an alibi.'

'I'll get you a drink, my lover.' She took as much trouble over it as another woman might over the preparation of her baby's feed. The glass was polished on a table napkin, Gudrun was applied to for ice. 'There. Have I put too much soda in?'

'You're good to me, Rozzy. I ought to be looking after you.'

Burden saw her grow pink with pleasure. She lifted Swan's hand and kissed it as if there was no one there to see. 'We'll go away somewhere,' she said. 'We'll go away tomorrow and forget all this beastliness.'

The little scene which had brought a pang of envy to Burden's heart had no softening effect on Wexford. 'I'd rather you didn't go anywhere until we've got a much clearer picture of this case,' he said. 'Besides, there will be an inquest which you must attend and, presumably,' he added with stiff sarcasm, 'a funeral.'

'An inquest?' Swan looked aghast.

'Naturally. What did you expect?'

'An inquest,' Swan said again. 'Will I have to attend it?'

Wexford shrugged impatiently. 'That's a matter for the coroner, but I should say, yes, certainly you will.'

'Drink up your drink, my lover. It won't be so bad if we're together, will it?'

'There's a mother for you!' Wexford exploded.

Burden said nothing for a moment. He was wondering if most of the ideas he held on mother love were perhaps fallacious. Until now he had supposed that to a woman the death of her child would be an insupportable grief. But maybe it wouldn't. People were very resilient. They recovered fast from tragedy, especially when they had someone to love, especially when they were young. Rosalind Swan had her husband. Whom would Gemma Lawrence have when she was fetched away to view a body in a mortuary?

It was three days since he had seen her, but hardly an hour had passed without his thinking of her. He relived that kiss and each time he experienced it again in retrospect he felt a shivering thrill of excitement. Telling himself to stop dwelling on it and on her was useless, and there was no question for him of out of sight, out of mind. She was almost more vivid to him in her absence than her presence, her body softer and fuller, her hair more thick and brilliant, her childlike sweetness sweeter. But while he kept away he felt that he was safe. Time would dull the memory if only he had the strength to stay away.

In the back of the car Wexford's probing eyes were on him. He had to say something.

'What about the father, Rivers?' he managed at last. 'You must have got on to him way back in February.'

'We did. Immediately after the divorce he married again and his airline sent him to San Francisco. We did more than get on to him. We checked him very closely. There was always the chance that he had popped over and smuggled the child into the States.'

'What, just like that? Hopped on a plane, grabbed her and flown off again? He can't be a rich man.'

'Of course he isn't,' Wexford retorted, 'but he could have done it just as easily as if he were a millionaire with a private aircraft. Don't forget he works for an airline and like any of their employees travels at about a tenth of the usual rate. The same applies within reason to any dependent he might take with him. Also he'd have access to any aircraft, provided there was a vacant seat. Gatwick's only about thirty miles from here, Mike. If he had found out the girl's movement, fiddled a passport and a ticket, he could have done it all right.'

'Only he didn't.'

'No, he didn't. He was at work in San Francisco all day on February 25th. Naturally, he came over when he was told Stella had disappeared and, no doubt, he'll be over again now.'

Detailed reports from forensics had come in during Wexford's absence. They confirmed Crocker's diagnosis and, for all the expertise of those who had compiled them, added little to it. Eight months had elapsed since the child's death, but the conclusion was that she had died from manual pressure on her throat and mouth. Her mildewed and tattered clothes afforded no clues and neither did the slab which had covered the cistern.

More phone calls had come in from people who claimed to have seen John, to have seen Stella alive and well in September, to have seen them alive and well and together. A woman holidaying in the Isle of Mull wrote to say a girl answering Stella's description had spoken to her on a beach and asked to be shown the road to Tobermory. The little boy with her had fair hair and the girl said his name was John.

'I wish they wouldn't waste our time,' said Wexford, knowing it would have to be followed up, picking up the next envelope. 'What's this, then? Another communication from our rabbit-keeper, I think.'

'I warned you not to wait for me. Did you think I would not know what was in your minds? I know everything. Your men are not very skilful at hiding. John was disappointed at not going home on Monday. He cried all night. I will return him only to his mother. She must be waiting *alone* on Friday at twelve noon in the same place. Remember what I did to Stella Rivers and do not try any more tricks. I am sending a copy of this letter to John's mother.'

'She won't see it, that's one blessing. Martin's collecting all her mail unopened. If we don't catch this joker before Friday we'll have to dress one of the policewomen up in a red wig.'

The idea of this travesty of Gemma waiting for a boy who wouldn't come made Burden feel rather sick. 'I don't like that bit about Stella Rivers,' he muttered.

'Doesn't mean a thing. He's just read the papers, that's all. My God, don't say you're going to fall for his line. He's just a hoaxer. Here's Martin now with Mrs Lawrence's mail. I'll take those, thank you, Sergeant. Ah, here's our joker's effusion in duplicate.'

Burden couldn't stop himself. 'How is she?' he said quickly.

'Mrs Lawrence, sir? She was a bit the worse for wear.'

Blood came into Burden's cheeks. 'What d'you mean, worse for wear?'

'Well, she'd been drinking, sir.' Martin hesitated, letting his face show as much exasperation as he dared. The inspector's eyes were cold, his face set, a prudish blush on his cheeks. Why did he always have to be so darned strait-laced? Surely a bit of sorrow-drowning was permitted in a woman as mad with anxiety as Mrs Lawrence? 'You can understand it. I mean to say ...'

'I often wonder what you do mean to say, Martin,' Burden snapped. 'Believe me, it's not clear from your words.'

'I'm sorry, sir.'

'I suppose she's got someone with her?' Wexford raised his eyes from the letter and its copy which he had been perusing.

'The friend didn't turn up,' said Martin. 'Apparently, she took offence because the Met had been on to her, asking if she or some boy friend of hers had seen John lately. I gather they weren't too tactful, sir. The boy friend's got a record and he's out of work. This girl who was coming to stay with Mrs Lawrence teaches at drama school and acts a bit. She said that if it got about, the police questioning her, it wouldn't do her any good in her profession. I did offer to fetch a neighbour to be with Mrs Lawrence but she wouldn't have any. Shall I pop back and . . . ?'

'Pop anywhere as long as you get out of here!'

'Break it up,' said Wexford mildly. 'Thank you, Sergeant.' He turned to Burden when Martin had gone. 'You've been in a state, Mike, ever since we left Hall Farm. Why bite his head off? What's he done?'

If Burden had realised how haggard his own face was, how it mirrored all his pain and his turbulent feelings, he wouldn't have lifted it numbly to stare at the chief inspector. Thoughtfully, Wexford returned his gaze, but for a moment neither man spoke. Why don't you get yourself a woman? Wexford was thinking. D'you want to drive yourself into a nervous collapse? He couldn't say those things aloud, not to Mike Burden.

'I'm going out,' Burden muttered. 'See if they need any help searching the forest.'

Wexford let him go. He shook his head gloomily. Burden knew as well as he did that they had completed their search of Cheriton Forest on Monday afternoon.

Chapter 10

The inquest on Stella Rivers was opened and adjourned until further evidence should come to light. Swan and his wife were there and Swan stumbled brokenly through his evidence, impressing the coroner as a shattered parent. This was the first sign Wexford had seen of any real grief in Stella's stepfather and he wondered why it had taken the inquest to bring it out. Swan had heard the news of Burden's discovery stoically and had identified Stella's body with no more than physical nausea. Why break down now? For he had broken down. Leaving the court, Wexford saw that Swan was weeping, a lost soul, clinging to his wife's arm.

Now, if ever, was the time to verify Rosalind Swan's statement that she couldn't drive. Wexford watched eagerly as they got into the shooting brake. And it was she, he saw, who got into the driving seat. But after a while, when they had whispered together and Rosalind had briefly laid her cheek against her husband's, they changed places. Odd that, Wexford thought.

Swan took the wheel wearily and they drove off in the direction of the Myfleet road.

She would get him home and comfort him with her drinks and her kisses and her love, Wexford thought. 'Come, come, come, come, give me your hand,' he said to himself. 'What's done cannot be undone. To bed, to bed, to bed.' But Rosalind Swan was no Lady Macbeth to counsel murder or even connive at it. As far as he knew. Certainly she would cover up any crime Swan might commit, even the killing of her own child, for the sake of keeping him with her.

The fine weather had broken. It was raining now, a fine drizzle dispersing the fog which had settled on Kingsmarkham since early morning. Pulling up his raincoat collar, Wexford walked the few yards that separated the court from the police station. No one at the inquest had mentioned John Lawrence, but the knowledge that a second child was missing had underlain, he felt, everything that was said. There was not a soul in Kingsmarkham or Stowerton who didn't connect the two cases, not a parent who doubted that a child killer stalked their countryside. Even the policemen who stood about the entrances to the court wore the grave aspect of men who believed a madman, a pathological criminal who killed children simply because they were children, went free and might attack again. He couldn't recall any inquest at which these hardened men had looked so dour and so downcast.

He stopped in his tracks and viewed the length of the High Street. The primary school's half-term was over and all the younger children back at work. The big ones hadn't yet broken up. But was it imagination or fact that he could hardly see a single four-year-old out with its mother this morning, scarcely a toddler or a baby in its pram? Then he spotted a pram which its owner was parking outside the supermarket. He watched her lift out the baby and its older sister, take the one in her arms and propel the other, who could only just walk, ahead of her into the shop. That such care should have to be exercised in the town whose guardian he was brought him a deep depression.

Why not Ivor Swan? Why not? It meant nothing that the man had no record. He had no record perhaps because no one had ever found him out. Wexford decided that he would again review Swan's life with particular reference to the districts he had lived in since he left Oxford. He would find out if any children had disappeared while Swan was in their vicinity. If Swan had done this, he swore to himself, he would get Swan.

But before making further investigations into the antecedents of her stepfather he had to see Stella's father. Their appointment was for twelve and when Wexford reached his office Peter Rivers had already been shown in.

A woman is often attracted by the same type of man and Rivers was not unlike his supplanter. Here was the same dapper quality, the same groomed look, neat small head, finely cut, almost polished, features and womanish tapering hands. But Rivers lacked Ivor Swan's indolent air, the impression he gave that sexually he would be far from indolent. There was something bustling about him, a fussy restiveness combined with a nervous manner, that might not endear itself to a silly romantic woman like Rosalind Swan.

He jumped up when Wexford came into the room and embarked on a long explanation of why he hadn't attended the inquest followed by an account of the tiresomeness of his journey from America. Wexford cut him short.

'Will you be seeing your former wife while you are here?'

'I guess so.' Sponge-like, Rivers, although domiciled for less than a year in America, had already picked up a transatlantic phraseology. 'I guess I'll have to. Needless to say, I can't stand that Swan. I should never have let Stell go to him.'

'Surely you had no choice, Mr Rivers?'

'Where did you get that idea? I never opposed her mother's application for custody, that's all, on account of Lois – that's the present Mrs Rivers – not wanting to be lumbered with a big kid like that. Rosie wasn't keen on getting custody either, come to that. Swan egged her on. I can tell you why, if you want to know.'

Sickened by all this, Wexford merely looked his assent.

'Swan knew he wouldn't have a bean after he'd paid the costs, nowhere to live, nothing. The three of them were pigging it in a crumby furnished place in Paddington. His uncle told him he'd let him have that Hall Farm place if Rosie kept Stell. I know it for a fact. Rosie told me.'

'But why? Why should his uncle care?'

'He wanted Swan to settle down, raise a family and do a bit of good for himself. Some hopes! Swan was supposed to take an agricultural course at the college here so that he could farm the land. As soon as he got here he let the whole lot off to a farmer who had his eye on it. I don't know why the uncle doesn't kick them both out. He's got pots of money and no one to leave it to but Swan.'

'You seem to know a lot about it, Mr Rivers.'

'I made it my business to. Yes, sir! Rosie and me have corresponded regularly since Stell went missing. I'll tell you another thing. Before he came out to Karachi and messed up my married life Mr Ivor Swan was living with this uncle *and* the aunt. Only she died while he was there. You'll know what I mean when I say she died very suddenly.'

'Will I?'

'You're a detective. I'd have thought that'd make you sit up. Swan thought he was coming in for some money, but it all went to uncle.'

'I don't think I need detain you any longer, Mr Rivers,' said Wexford, who was beginning to think Rosalind Swan had decidedly bad taste in men. The dislike he felt for Swan was nothing to the loathing this man aroused in him. He watched Rivers buttoning his raincoat and waited for him to say something to the effect that he mourned the child whom nobody seemed to have wanted. The words came at last and in curious form.

'It was a bit of a shock hearing she was dead,' Rivers said briskly, 'but she'd been dead to me for a couple of years, anyway, in a manner of speaking. I guess I'd never have seen her again.' He made for the door, not at all abashed by Wexford's scowl. 'A newspaper's offered me two thousand for my exclusive story.'

'Oh, I should take it,' said Wexford in a level voice. 'It will be some recompense for your tragic loss.'

He went to the window. It was still raining. The children who went home to lunch were issuing from Queen Street where the primary school was. Usually on wet days they managed the journey as best they could. Today, the first day of the second half of term, not one went unaccompanied, not one lacked the shelter of an umbrella, which seemed to Wexford to have a deeper significance than that of protecting small heads from the drizzle.

Routine checking occupied Burden's afternoon. It was only just after six when he got home. For almost the first time since Jean's death he was anxious to be at home and with his children, particularly with his daughter. All day long he had been thinking of her, her image driving away Gemma's, and as he made himself more and more familiar with the circumstances of Stella's life and death, he kept seeing Pat alone and frightened and cruelly overpowered and – dead.

It was she who rushed to let him in almost before his key was in the lock. And Burden, thinking he saw in her eyes some special alarm, some unusual need for comfort, bent swiftly and put his arms round her. Had he only known it, Pat had quarrelled with her aunt and natural ally and was turning for support to the only other available grown-up.

'What is it, darling?' He saw a car stopping, a hand beckoning, a figure stepping out into the wet dusk. 'Tell me what's happened?'

'You've got to tell Auntie Grace she's not to meet me from school. I'm at the high school, I'm not an infant. I was *humiliated*.'

'Oh, is that all?' With relief came gratitude. He laughed at Pat's rebelliously pouting lower lip, tugged at her ponytail, and went out to the kitchen to thank Grace for her forethought. What a fool he had been to worry when he had such a guardian!

But he felt a need to stay close by his daughter that evening. All through their meal and afterwards, while he was helping John with his geometry – Pythagoras' theorem which 'old Mint-face' insisted on the third form knowing by the next day – his thoughts and his eyes wandered to Pat. He had failed in his duty to her, failed, through the indulgence of selfish grief, to watch over her and interest himself in her activities as he should have done. Suppose she were taken from him as Stella Rivers, her contemporary, had been taken?

'In a right-angled triangle,' he said mechanically, 'the square on the hypoteneuse is equal to the sum of the squares on the other two sides.'

Grace hadn't failed. He watched her covertly while John drew his diagram. She was sitting in a dark corner of the room, a table lamp throwing a small pool of light on to the letter she was writing. Suddenly it occurred to him that she must thousands

of times have sat in just that attitude, at a lamplit
desk in a long quiet hospital ward, writing the
night's report and, while all the time aware that she
was surrounded by people who depended on her,
yet at the same time detached from them and
contained. She wrot – indeed she did everything –
with a beautiful economy of movement, an absence
of fuss or flutter. Her training had taught her this
efficiency, this almost awe-inspiring reliability, but
instead of spoiling her delicate feminine quality, had
somehow enhanced it. They had had wisdom and
prevision, he thought, those parents-in-law of his,
when they named her Grace.

And now his gaze encompassed both his daughter
and his sister-in-law, the child moving up to her aunt
and standing beside her within the same circle of
light. They were very alike, he saw, with the same
strong gentle face and the same light gauzy hair.
They were both like Jean. The image of Gemma
Lawrence coarsened beside them, became harsh-
coloured, red and white and strained. Then it
dwindled away, leaving a vacant space for his
daughter and her aunt to fill with the wholesome
beauty he understood.

Grace, he realised, was just the type of woman he
most admired. There was the delicate prettiness he
loved combined with the competence he needed.
Couldn't she, he asked himself, be Jean all over
again? Why not? Couldn't she be his Rosalind Swan,
as loving, as devoted, as all-in-all to him, without the
other woman's silly affectations? Usually, when they
parted for the night, Grace simply got up out of her
chair, picked up her book and said, 'Well, good
night, Mike. Sleep well,' and he said, 'Good night,
Grace. I'll see that everything's locked up.' That was
all. They never even touched hands, never stood
close beside each other or let their eyes meet.

But tonight, when the time came for them to separate, why shouldn't he take her hand and, saying something of what her goodness had meant to him, take her gently in his arms and kiss her? He glanced at her again and this time both Grace and Pat turned to him and smiled. His heart seemed to swell with an easy warm happiness, very different from the storm of feelings Gemma Lawrence aroused in him. That had been a kind of madness, nothing more than lust brought about by frustration. How unimportant it seemed now!

Pat loved her aunt. If he married Grace she would return to him entirely. He put out his hand to his daughter and she, her earlier annoyance with him forgotten, skipped over to the sofa where he was sitting and snuggled close against him, her arms hard around his neck.

'Shall I show you my scrapbook?'

'What have you got in it?' said John, his eyes on the proof of his theorem. 'Pictures of caterpillars?'

'Caterpillars are my summer hobby.' Pat spoke with great dignity. 'You're so ignorant you wouldn't know, but in the winter they go into their chrysalises.'

'And even you couldn't collect pictures of chrysalises. Here, let's see.'

'You shan't! You're not to! It's mine!'

'Leave her alone, John. Put that book down.'

John said in disgust, 'It's only dancers, old ballet dancers.'

'Come and show me, love.'

Pat resumed her semi-suffocation of her father. 'Can I have ballet lessons, Daddy? I do want to. It's the great ambition of my life.'

'I don't see why not.'

Grace was smiling at him, her letter completed. They smiled at each other like fond parents, happy in conspiracy, in contemplation of what they would do for their children.

'You see,' said Pat, 'it'll be too late if I don't start now. I know I should have to work and work, but I don't mind that because it's my great ambition, and perhaps I could get a scholarship and be in the Bolshoi and be a *prima ballerina assoluta* like Leonie West.'

'I thought,' said her brother, 'you were going to be a research scientist.'

'Oh, *that*. That was ages ago, when I was a child.'

A cold shadow had touched Burden. 'Who did you say?'

'Leonie West. She's gone to live in *absolute retirement* in her flat and her house at the seaside. She broke her leg ski-ing and couldn't dance any more, but she was the most wonderful dancer *in the world*.' Pat considered. 'Anyway, I think so,' she said. 'I've got masses and masses of pictures of her. Shall I show you?'

'Yes, darling, if you like.'

There were indeed masses and masses of pictures. Pat had cut them out of magazines and newspapers. Not all of them were of Leonie West, but most were.

In the distant shots she was a beautiful woman, but time and perhaps too the exigencies of continual strenuous dancing showed the toll they had taken in close-ups. For Burden that heavily painted heart-shaped face with its smoothly parted black hair held no magic, but he made appreciative comments to please his daughter as he turned the pages.

There were stills of ballet films, shots of the star at home, at social functions, dancing all the great classical roles. He was nearly at the end now.

He said, 'They're very nicely arranged, dear,' to Pat, and turned to the last photograph.

A fan of Leonie West would have seen only her, a magnificent figure in a floor-length cloak stiff with gold enbroidery. Burden hardly noticed her. He was looking, his heart knocking dully, at the crowd of friends from which she had emerged. Just behind the dancer, holding a man's arm and smiling listlessly with a kind of shy anxiety, was a red-haired woman swathed in a black-and-gold shawl.

He didn't need the caption to tell him anything, but he read it. 'Pictured at the first night of *La Fille Mal Gardée* at Covent Garden is Miss Leonie West with (right) actor Matthew Lawrence and his wife Gemma, 23.' He said nothing, but closed the book quickly and leaned back, shutting his eyes, as if he had felt a sudden pain.

No one took any notice of him. John was repeating the proof of his theorem, learning it by heart. Pat had taken her book away to restore it to some secret treasure chest. It was nine o'clock.

Grace said, 'Come along, my dears. Bed.'

The usual argument ensued. Burden put in the stern words which were expected of him, but he felt no enthusiasm, no real care whether his children got the required amount of sleep or not. He picked up the evening paper which he hadn't yet read. The words were just a black-and-white pattern, hieroglyphics as meaningless as they would be to someone who has never learned to read.

Grace came back from kissing Pat good night. She had combed her hair and put on fresh lipstick. He noticed and he felt a shrinking distaste. This was the same woman that, half an hour before, he had considered wooing with a view to making her his second wife. He must have been mad. Suddenly he saw clearly that all his imaginings of the evening had been madness, a fantasy of his own conjuring, and what they had made to appear as madness was his reality.

He could never marry Grace, for in gazing at her, studying and admiring her, he had forgotten what any happy marriage must have, what Rosalind Swan so evidently had. He liked Grace, was at ease with her. She was his ideal of what a woman should be, but he hadn't a particle of desire for her. The thought of attempting to kiss her, of going further than a kiss, caused a shrivelling in his flesh.

She had brought her chair closer to the sofa where he sat and, laying aside her book, looked expectantly at him, waiting for the conversation, the adult exchange of views, which all day long she was denied. His feeling for her was so slight, his acceptance of her as someone content with the world he had provided for her so great, that it hardly occurred to him she would be hurt by anything he did.

'I'm going out,' he said.

'What, *now*?'

'I've got to go out, Grace.'

He saw it now. Am I so boring? her eyes said. I have done everything for you, kept your house, cared for your children, borne with your moods. Am I so boring that you can't sit quietly with me for one single evening?

'Please yourself,' she said aloud.

Chapter 11

The rain had stopped and a thick mist settled on the countryside. Water clung to the trees in heavy drops and fell dully and regularly so that it seemed as if it were still raining. Burden swung the car into Fontaine Road and immediately made a U-turn out again. He was suddenly loth to let his car be seen outside her house at night. All the street would be on watch, ready to spread rumours and tell tales.

Finally he parked at the bottom of Chiltern Avenue. A footpath, skirting the swings field, joined this cul-de-sac with its neighbour, Fontaine Road. Burden left the car under a street lamp whose light the fog had dimmed to a faintly glowing nimbus and walked slowly towards the path. Tonight its entrance looked like the opening to a black tunnel. There were no lights on in the adjacent houses, no sound in the darkness but that of water dripping.

He walked along between bushes whose branches with their wet dying leaves splashed his face and dragged softly at his clothes. Half-way through he found the torch he always carried and switched it on. Then, just as he reached the point where a gate in Mrs Mitchell's fence opened into the path, he heard pounding feet behind him. He swung round, directing his torch beam back the way he had come and on to a white face framed in flying wet hair.

'What is it? What's the matter?'

The girl must have recognised him, for she almost

threw herself into his arms. He recognised her too. It was Mrs Crantock's daughter, a child of about fourteen.

'Did something frighten you?' he asked.

'A man,' she said breathlessly. 'Standing by a car. He spoke to me. I got in a panic.'

'You shouldn't be out alone at night.' He shepherded her into Fontaine Road, then thought better of it. 'Come with me,' he said. She hesitated. 'You're all right with me.'

Back through the black tunnel. Her teeth were chattering. He raised his torch and brought it like a searchlight on to the figure of a man who stood beside the bonnet of Burden's parked car. The duffel coat he wore with its raised hood gave him enough of a sinister air to alarm any child.

'Oh, it's Mr Rushworth.' She sounded shamefaced.

Burden had already recognised the man and saw he was recognised too. Frowning a little, he walked towards the husband of the woman who had failed to notify the police after Mrs Mitchell's warning.

'You gave this young lady a bit of a scare.'

Rushworth blinked in the glare of the torch. 'I said hallo to her and something about it being an awful night. She scooted off like all the devils in hell were after her. God knows why. She knows me by sight, at any rate.'

'Everyone round here is a bit nervous at present, sir,' said Burden. 'It's wiser not to speak to people you don't really know. Good night.'

'I suppose he was taking his dog out,' the girl said as they came into Fontaine Road. 'I didn't see his dog, though. Did you?'

Burden hadn't seen a dog. 'You shouldn't be out alone at this time of night.'

'I've been round to my friends. We were playing records. My friend's father said he'd see me home, but I wouldn't let him. It's only a couple of minutes' walk. Nothing could happen to me.'

'But something did, or you thought it did.'

She digested this in silence. Then she said, 'Are you going to see Mrs Lawrence?'

Burden nodded, and, realising she couldn't see his nod, said a bald, 'Yes.'

'She's in an awful state. My father says he wouldn't be surprised if she did something silly.'

'What does that mean?'

'Well, *you* know. Committed suicide. I saw her after school in the supermarket. She was just standing in the middle of the shop, crying.' A true daughter of the *bourgeoisie*, she added with some disapproval, 'Everyone was looking at her.'

Burden opened the gate to the Crantocks' garden. 'Good night,' he said. 'Don't go out alone after dark any more.'

There were no lights in Gemma's house and for once the front door was shut. Very likely she had taken one of Lomax's sleeping tablets and gone to bed. He peered through the stained glass and made out a faint gleam of light coming from the kitchen. She was still up, then. He rang the bell.

When the gleam grew no brighter and still she didn't come, he rang the bell again and banged the lion's-head door knocker. Behind him, from the branches of the untended trees, came the incessant drip drip of water. He remembered what Martin had said about her drinking and then what the Crantock girl had said and, having rung the bell once more in vain, he made for the side entrance.

The path was nearly as overgrown as the gardens of Saltram House. He pushed away wet holly and slimy creeper, soaking his hair and his raincoat. His hands were so wet that he could hardly turn the handle on the back door, but the door wasn't locked and at last he got it open.

She was slumped at the kitchen table, her head on her outflung arms, and in front of her was an unopened bottle, labelled: 'Chianti-type wine, produce of Spain. This week's offer, 7p off.' He went up to her slowly and laid his hand on her shoulder.

'Gemma . . .'

She said nothing. She didn't move. He pulled up another chair, pulled it close to her, and took her gently in his arms. She rested against him, not resisting, breathing shallowly and fast, and Burden forgot all his agony of the past week, his battling against temptation, in an overwhelming selfish happiness. He could hold her like this for ever, he thought, warmly and wordlessly, without passion or desire or the need for any change.

She lifted her head. Her face was almost unrecognisable, it was so swollen with crying. 'You didn't come,' she said. 'For days and days I waited for you and you didn't come.' Her voice was thick and strange. 'Why didn't you?'

'I don't know.' It was true. He didn't know, for now his resistance seemed the height of pointless folly.

'Your hair's all wet.' She touched his hair and the raindrops on his face. 'I'm not drunk,' she said, 'but I have been. That stuff is very nasty but it deadens you for a bit. I went out this afternoon to buy some food – I haven't eaten for days – but I didn't buy any, I couldn't. When I came to the sweet counter I kept thinking of how John used to beg me to buy chocolate and I wouldn't because it was bad for his teeth. And I wished I'd let him have it, all he wanted, because it wouldn't have made any difference now, would it?'

112

She stared at him blankly, the tears pouring down her face.

'You mustn't say that.'

'Why not? He's dead. You know he's dead. I keep thinking that sometimes I got cross with him and I smacked him and I wouldn't let him have the sweets he wanted ... Oh, Mike! What shall I do? Shall I drink that wine and take all Dr Lomax's tablets? Or shall I go out in the rain and just walk and walk till I die? What's the use of living? I've got no one, no one.'

'You've got me,' said Burden.

For answer she clung to him again, but this time more tightly. 'Don't leave me. Promise you won't leave me.'

'You ought to go to bed,' he said. There was, he thought, a sickening irony here. Wasn't that what he had intended when he left the car in the next street? That he and she should go to bed? He had really imagined that this demented grief-stricken woman would welcome his love-making. You fool, he whispered harshly to himself. But he managed to say calmly, 'Go to bed. I'll make you a hot drink and you can take a tablet and I'll sit with you till you go to sleep.'

She nodded. He wiped her eyes on a handkerchief Grace had ironed as carefully as Rosalind Swan ironed her husband's shirts. 'Don't leave me,' she said again, and then she went, dragging her feet a little.

The kitchen was in a hideous mess. Nothing had been washed up or put away for days and there was a stale sweetish smell. He found some cocoa and some dried milk and did his best with these unsatisfactory ingredients, mixing them and heating them on a cooker that was black with burned-on fat.

She was sitting up in bed, the black-and-gold

113

shawl around her shoulders, and that magic exotic quality, compounded of colour and strangeness and lack of inhibition, had to some extent returned to her. Her face was calm again, the large still eyes staring. The room was untidy, chaotic even, but its chaos was powerfully feminine, the scattered clothes giving off mingled sweet scents.

He tipped a sleeping pill out of the bottle and handed it to her with her drink. She gave him a wan smile and took his hand, lifting it first to her lips and then holding it tight.

'You won't ever stay away from me like that again?'

'I am a poor substitute, Gemma,' he said.

'I need,' she said softly, 'another kind of loving to make me forget.'

He guessed at what she meant but didn't know what reply to make, so he sat silently with her, holding her hand, until at last her hand grew limp and she sank back against the pillows. He switched off the bed lamp and stretched himself beside her but on top of the covers. Presently her steady regular breathing told him that she was asleep.

The luminous dial of his watch showed half past ten. It seemed much later, as if a lifetime had passed since he left Grace and drove out here through the damp, rain-filled mist. The room was cold, perfumed and thick-aired and cold. Her hand lay loosely in his. He slid his hand away and edged across the bed to get up and leave.

Wary, even in sleep, she murmured, 'Don't leave me, Mike.' Thick with sleep, her voice held a note of terror, of dread that she might again be abandoned.

'I won't leave you.' He made up his mind quickly and decisively. 'I'll stay all night.'

Shivering, he stripped off his clothes and got into bed beside her. It seemed quite natural to lie as he

114

had lain beside Jean, his body curled about hers, his left arm around her waist, clasping the hand which again had grown possessive and demanding. Although cold to him, his body must have felt warm to her, for she sighed with a kind of happiness and relaxed against him.

He thought he would never sleep or, if he did, that he would fall immediately into one of those dreams of his. But the way they were lying, side by side, was what he had been used to in his happy years and had missed bitterly in the last wretched one. It brought him desire, but at the same time it lulled him. While wondering how he could bear this continuing continence, he fell asleep.

It was just beginning to get light when he awoke to find the other half of the bed empty but still warm. She was sitting by the window, wrapped in her shawl, a big album with gilt clasps open on her lap. He guessed that she was looking, in the first light of dawn, at pictures of her son, and he felt a powerful black jealousy.

For what seemed a long time he watched her, almost hating the child who came between them and drew his mother away with a ghostly subtle hand. She was slowly turning the pages, pausing sometimes to stare downwards with a passionate intensity. A resentment which he knew was totally unjust made him will her to look at him, to forget the child and remember the man who longed to be her lover.

At last she lifted her head and their eyes met. She said nothing and Burden didn't speak, for he knew that if he did it would be to say cruel indefensible things. They gazed at each other in the pale grey morning light, and then, getting up silently, she drew the curtains. They were of brocade, old and frayed but still retaining their rich plum colour and, filtering through them, the light in the room looked purplish. She dropped the shawl and stood still in this coloured shadow-light so that he might look at her.

Her red hair seemed to have grown purple, but the colour hardly touched her body, which was dazzling white. He gazed at her in a kind of wonder, content for the moment to do nothing but gaze. This ivory woman, still and smiling now, was nothing like his lascivious dream woman, nor did she resemble the distraught and weary creature he had comforted to sleep. The child had almost vanished from his jealousy and, he believed, from her thoughts. It was hardly possible to imagine that this exquisite firm body had ever borne a child.

Only a little stabbing doubt remained.

'Not out of gratitude, Gemma,' he said. 'Not to reward me.'

She moved then and came close to him. 'I never even thought of that. That would be to cheat.'

'To forget, then? Is that what you want?'

'Isn't all love about forgetting?' she said. 'Isn't it always a lovely escape from – from hatefulness?'

'I don't know.' He put out his arms to her. 'I don't care.' Gasping at the feel of her, here the slenderness and there the swell of flesh, he said breathlessly, 'I shall hurt you. I can't help it, it's been so long for me.'

'And for me,' she said. 'It will be like the first time. Oh, Mike, kiss me, make me happy. Make me happy for a little while. . . .'

Chapter 12

'Not bad news?' said Dr Crocker. 'About the Lawrence boy, I mean?'

Morosely eyeing the pile of papers on his desk, Wexford said, 'I don't know what you're on about.'

'You haven't got a lead, then? I was sure there must be something when I passed Mike driving out of Chiltern Avenue at seven-thirty this morning.' He breathed heavily on one of Wexford's window-panes and began drawing one of his recurrent diagrams. 'I wonder what he was doing?' he said thoughtfully.

'Why ask me? I'm not his keeper.' Wexford glared at the doctor and at his drawing of a human pancreas. 'I might ask you what you were doing, come to that.'

'A patient. Doctors always have an excuse.'

'So do policemen,' Wexford retorted.

'I doubt if Mike was ministering to a fellow who'd been struck down with stroke. Worst case I've come across since they called me out to that poor old boy who collapsed on Stowerton station platform back in February. Did I ever tell you about that? Chap had been staying here on holiday, got to the station and then found he'd left one of his cases behind in this hotel or whatever it was. Went back for it, got in a bit of a flutter and the next thing . . .'

Wexford let out an angry bellow. 'So what? Why tell me? I thought you were supposed to treat your patients in confidence. I'll have a stroke myself if you go on like that.'

'It was just that possibility,' said Crocker sweetly, 'that inspired my little narrative.' He dotted in the Islets of Langerhans with his little finger. 'Want a fresh prescription for those tablets of yours?'

'No, I don't. I've got hundreds of the damned things left.'

'Well, you shouldn't have,' said Crocker, pointing a damp finger at him. 'You can't have been taking them regularly.'

'Go away. Get lost. Haven't you anything better to do than deface my windows with your nasty anatomical studies?'

'Just going.' The doctor made a dancing exit, pausing in the doorway to favour the chief inspector with what seemed to Wexford a meaningless wink.

'Silly fool,' Wexford remarked to the empty room. But Crocker's visit had left him with an uneasy feeling. To rid himself of it, he began to read the reports the Metropolitan Police had sent him on Gemma Lawrence's friends.

For the most part they appeared to be in the theatrical profession or on its fringes, but hardly a name was familiar to him. His younger daughter had just left drama school and through her Wexford had heard of many actors and actresses whose names had never been in lights or the print of the *Radio Times*. None of them appeared in this list and he was aware of what they did only because 'actor' or 'assistant stage manager' or 'model' was written after almost every name.

They were an itinerant crowd, mostly – in Wexford's own official terminology – of no fixed abode. Half a dozen had been convicted on charges of possessing drugs or of allowing cannabis to be smoked on their premises; a further two or three fined for conduct likely to lead to a breach of the peace. Demonstrating or taking their clothes off in the Albert Hall, Wexford supposed. None were harbouring John Lawrence; none showed by their past histories or their present tendencies a propensity to violence or perverted inclination. From reading between the lines, he gathered that, rather than desire the company of a child, they would go to almost any lengths to avoid having one.

Only two names on the list meant anything to him. One was a ballet dancer, her name at one time a household word, the other a television character actor whose face appeared so monotonously on Wexford's screen that he was sick of the sight of him. He was called Gregory Devaux and he had been a friend of Gemma Lawrence's parents. Particular interest had been taken in him because once, five years ago, he had attempted to smuggle out of the country, and the care of his estranged wife, their six-year-old son. The report promised that a watch would be kept on Gregory Devaux.

According to the porter of the Kensington block where she had a flat, Leonie West, the dancer, had been in the South of France since August.

Nothing there. No hint of any of them taking more than a casual friendly interest in Mrs Lawrence and her son; no hint of a connection between any of them and Ivor Swan.

At ten Martin came in with Policewoman Polly Davies whom Wexford scarcely recognised under the red wig she wore.

'You look terrible,' he said. 'Where in God's name did you dig that up? A jumble sale?'

'Woolworth's, sir,' said Martin, rather offended. 'You're always telling us to go easy on expenses.'

'No doubt it would look better if Polly hadn't got black eyes and such a – well, Welsh complexion.

119

Never mind. You'll have to cover it, anyway. It's pouring with rain.'

Sergeant Martin always took an old-womanish interest in the weather and its vagaries. Having first wiped off the doctor's pancreas diagram, he opened the window and stuck out one hand. 'I think it'll stop, sir. I see a gleam of light.'

'I only wish you did,' said Wexford. 'Pray cover your dismay as best you can. I've decided to come with you. I get sick of all this vicarious living.'

They went down the corridor in single file, to be stopped by Burden who opened the door of his own office. Wexford looked him up and down, looked him all over, hard.

'What's got into you? Your Ernie bonds come up?'
Burden smiled.

'I am glad,' said Wexford sarcastically, 'that some-one sees fit to spread a little sunshine in this deluge, in this – er – town of terror. What d'you want, anyway?'

'I thought you might not have seen today's paper. There's an interesting story on the front page.'

Wexford took the paper from him and read the story as he went down in the lift. Under the headline, *Landowner Offers £2,000 reward. New Move in Stella Hunt*, he read: 'Group Captain Percival Swan, wealthy landowner and uncle of Mr Ivor Swan, Stella Rivers' stepfather, told me last night that he was offering a reward of £2,000 for information leading to the discovery of Stella's killer. "This is a devilish thing," he said as we chatted in the drawing room of his centuries-old mansion near Tunbridge Wells. "I was fond of Stella, though I had seen little of her. Two thousand pounds is a large sum, but not too large to sacrifice for the sake of seeing justice done." '

There was a good deal more in the same vein. Not

so very interesting, Wexford thought, as he got into his car.

True to Sergeant Martin's prediction, the rain soon left off. Cheriton Forest was shrouded in thick white mist.

'You may as well take that thing off,' said Wexford to Polly Davies. 'He won't be able to see you if he does come.'

But nobody came. No car passed along the road and no one came down the Myfleet Ride which joined it. Only the mist moved sluggishly and the water which dripped from the boughs of the closely planted fir trees. Wexford sat on a damp log among the trees, thinking of Ivor Swan who rode in this forest and knew it well, who had ridden here on the day his stepdaughter died. Did he really suppose Swan would appear, walking on the wet sandy ride or mounted on the chestnut horse? With the child perched beside him or holding his hand? A hoax, a hoax, a cruel nonsense, he kept saying to himself, and at one, when the appointed time was an hour behind him and he was shivering with cold, he came out of his hiding place and whistled up the other two.

If Burden remained in his early mood he would, at any rate, have a cheerful lunch companion. There was no one behind the desk in the police-station foyer, an unheard-of dereliction of duty. With mounting rage Wexford stared at the empty stool on which Sergeant Camb should have been perched and was about to press a bell that had never, in all its years of existence, needed to be pressed before, when the Sergeant appeared, scuttling from the lift, the inevitable tea-cup in his hand.

'Sorry, sir. We're so short-handed what with all these crazy calls coming in that I had to fetch my own tea. I've only been away half a tick. You know me, sir, I perish without my tea.'

'Next time,' said Wexford, 'you perish. Remember, Sergeant, that the guard dies but it never surrenders.'

He went upstairs and looked for Burden.

'Mr Burden went to lunch ten minutes ago, sir,' said Loring.

Wexford cursed. He badly wanted to engage with Burden in one of those acrimonious but rewarding conferences which both cemented their friendship and contributed to their work. Lunch alone at the Carousel would be a dismal affair. He opened the door of his own office and stopped dead on the threshold.

Seated in the chief inspector's swivel chair at the chief inspector's rosewood desk, the cigarette in his fingers scattering ash all over the lemon-coloured carpet, was Monkey Matthews.

'They might have told me,' said Wexford distantly, 'that I'd been deposed. This kind of thing smacks of goings-on behind the Iron Curtain. What am I to do? Manage a power station?'

Monkey grinned. He had the grace to get up out of Wexford's chair. 'I'd never have believed,' he said, 'it was so easy to get into a nick. I reckon that old geezer Camb must have dropped dead at last and they've all gone off to bury him. Got in without a soul the wiser, I did. Bloody sight easier,' he added, 'to get in this nick than get out of it.'

'You won't find it hard today. You can get out now. And fast, before I do you for being found on enclosed premises for an unlawful purpose.'

'Ah, but my purpose *is* lawful.' Monkey surveyed the room with a pleased expression. 'This is the first time I've ever been in a nick of what you might call my own accord.' A dreamy smile spread across his face and was abruptly quenched by a fit of coughing.

Wexford stood half in the office, half in the corridor, waiting unsympathetically.

'You may as well shut the door,' said Monkey when he had recovered. 'We don't want the whole place to hear, do we? I've got some info. The Lawrence case.'

Wexford closed the door but gave no other sign that Monkey's remark had interested him. '*You* have?' he said.

'Friend of mine has.'

'I didn't know you had any friends, Monkey, bar poor old Ruby.'

'You don't want to judge everybody by yourself,' said Monkey, stung. He coughed and stubbed out his cigarette, immediately lighting another and regarding the discarded stub with resentment, as if some peculiarity of its construction or fault in its make-up were responsible for his choking attack, rather than the tobacco it contained. 'I've got a lot of friends, picked up in me travels.'

'Picked up in cells, you mean,' said Wexford.

Monkey had long ago forgotten how to blush, but the wary look which crossed his face told Wexford the shot had gone home. 'My friend,' he said, 'come down here yesterday for a bit of a holiday with me and Rube. A bit of a rest, like. He's an old feller and his health's not what it was.'

'All those damp exercise yards, I daresay.'

'Oh, give over, will you? My friend has got some info as'll open your eyes all right, re the antecedents of Mr Ivor Bloody Swan.'

If Wexford was surprised, he didn't show it. 'He has no antecedents,' he said coldly, 'or not what you mean by the term.'

'Not wrote down, I daresay. Not all our misdemeanours is recorded, Mr Wexford, not by a long chalk. I've heard it said there's more murderers

123

walking the streets free as ever got topped on account of them as they murdered being thought to have died natural.'

Wexford rubbed his chin and looked thoughtfully at Monkey. 'Let's see your friend,' he said, 'and hear what he's got to say. It might be worth a few bob.'

'He would want paying.'

'I'm sure he would.'

'He made a point of that,' said Monkey conversationally.

Wexford got up and opened a window to let some of the smoke out. 'I'm a busy man, Monkey. I can't hang about fencing with you all day. How much?'

'A monkey,' said Monkey succinctly.

In a pleasant but distant voice, tinged with incredulous outrage, Wexford said, 'You must be off your nut if you seriously think the government is going to pay five hundred pounds to a clapped-out old lag for information it can get for nothing out of a file.'

'Five hundred,' Monkey repeated, 'and if it all works out nice, the two thou reward the uncle's putting up.' He coughed thickly but with no sign of distress. 'If you don't want nothing to do with it,' he said sweetly, 'my friend can always go to the chief constable. He's called Griswold, isn't he?'

'Don't you bloody threaten me!' said Wexford.

'Threaten? Who's threatening? This info's in the public interest, that's what it is.'

Wexford said firmly, 'You can bring your friend along here and then we'll see. Might be worth a couple of nicker.'

'He won't come here. He wouldn't go voluntary like into a fuzz box. Different to me, he is. But him and me, we'll be in the Pony six sharp tonight and I daresay he'd accept a friendly overture in the form of liquor.'

Was it possible that there was something in this

story? Wexford wondered after Monkey had gone. And immediately he recalled Rivers' hints as to the death of Swan's aunt. Suppose, after all, that Swan *had* hastened the old lady's departure? Poison, maybe. That would be in Swan's line, a lazy, slow way of killing. And suppose this friend of Monkey's had been in service in the house, an odd-job man or even a butler? He might have seen something, extracted something, kept it hidden for years in his bosom . . .

Wexford came down to earth and, laughing, quoted to himself a favourite passage from Jane Austen: 'Consult your own understanding, your own sense of the probable, your own observation of what is passing around you. Does our education prepare us for such atrocities? Do our laws connive at them? Could they be perpetrated without being known in a country like this where social and literary intercourse is on such a footing; where every man is surrounded by a neighbourhood of voluntary spies and where roads and newspapers lay everything open?'

Long ago he had learned these lines by heart. They had been of constant service to him and, when inclined to sail away on flights of fancy, kept his feet firmly on the ground.

It was much too late now to go out for lunch. The staff of the Carousel looked askance at you if you arrived for your midday meal after one-thirty. Wexford sent to the canteen for sandwiches and had eaten the first half-round when the report on the lock of hair came in from the lab. The hair, Wexford read, was a child's but not John Lawrence's. Comparison had been made with the strands taken from John's hairbrush. Understanding only about twenty-five per cent of the technical jargon, Wexford did his best to follow just how they could be so certain the hairs in the brush differed from the hairs in the cut lock, and finally had to be content to know that they did differ.

His phone rang. It was Loring from the room where all the calls connected with the Lawrence and Rivers cases were received and checked.

'I think you'll want to take this one, sir.'

Immediately Wexford thought of Monkey Matthews and just as quickly dismissed the thought. Monkey had never been known to use a telephone.

'Record it, Loring,' he said, and then, 'Is it from a call box?'

'I'm afraid not, sir. We can't trace it.'

'Put him on,' said Wexford.

As soon as he heard the voice he knew an attempt was being made to disguise it. A couple of pebbles in the man's mouth, he decided. But some quality, the pitch perhaps, couldn't be disguised. Wexford recognised the voice. Not its owner, nor could he recall where he had seen the speaker, what he had said or anything about him. But he was sure he recognised the voice.

'I'm not prepared to give my name,' it said. 'I've written to you twice.'

'Your letters were received.' Wexford had stood up to take the call and from where he stood he could see the High Street and see a woman tenderly lifting a baby from a pram to take it with her into a shop. His anger was immense and he could feel the dangerous blood pounding in his head.

'You played around with me this morning. That's not going to happen tomorrow.'

'Tomorrow?' Wexford said evenly.

'I shall be in the grounds of Saltram House tomorrow by the fountains. I'll be there at six p.m. with John. And I want the mother to come for him. *Alone.*'

'Where are you speaking from?'

126

'My farm,' said the voice, growing squeaky. 'I've got a three-hundred-acre farm not so far from here. It's a fur farm, mink, rabbits, chinchillas, the lot. John doesn't know I keep them for their fur. That would only upset him, wouldn't it?'

Wexford caught the authentic note of derangement. He didn't know whether this comforted or distressed him. He was thinking about the voice which he had heard before, a thin high voice, its possessor quick to take offence, looking for insult where none existed.

'You haven't got John,' he said. 'That hair you sent me wasn't John's.' Scorn and rage made him forget caution. 'You are an ignorant man. Hair can be as precisely identified as blood these days.'

Heavy breathing at the other end of the line succeeded this statement. Wexford felt that he had scored. He drew breath to let loose vituperation, but before he could speak the voice said coldly:

'D'you think I don't know that? I cut that hair from Stella Rivers.'

Chapter 13

The Piebald Pony is not the kind of pub connoisseurs
of rural England normally associate with her countryside. Indeed, if you approach it from the direction
of Sparta Grove, and if you keep your eyes down so
that you cannot see the green surrounding hills, you
would not suppose yourself in the country at all.
Sparta Grove and Charteris Road which it joins at a
right angle – on this corner stands the Piebald Pony –
resemble the back streets of an industrial city. A few
of the houses have narrow front gardens, but most
doors open directly on to the pavement, as do the
entrances to the Pony's public and saloon bars.

One of these rooms fronts Sparta Grove, the other
Charteris Road. They are the same shape and size
and the saloon bar is distinguished from the public
only in that drinks cost more in the former, about a
third of its stone floor is covered with a square of
brown Axminster and its seating includes a couple of
settees, upholstered in battered black, of the kind
that used to be seen in railway waiting rooms.

On one of the settees, under a poster recommend-
ing the Costa del Sol and displaying a photograph of
a girl in a wet-look bikini leering at a bull in its death
throes, sat Monkey Matthews with an old man. He
looked, Wexford thought, very much by time's fell
hand defaced and in nearly as bad case as the bull. It
wasn't that he was thin or pale – in fact his squarish
toad's face was purple – but there was an air about

him of one who has been physically ruined by years of bad feeding, damp dwellings and nasty indulgences whose nature Wexford preferred not to dwell on.

Each man had an almost empty half-pint glass of the cheapest obtainable bitter and Monkey was smoking a minuscule cigarette.

"Evening,' said Wexford.

Monkey didn't get up but indicated his companion with an airy wave. 'This is Mr Casaubon.'

Wexford gave a tiny sigh, the outward and audible sign of an inward and outraged scream. 'I don't believe it,' he said thinly. 'Just enlighten me as to which one of you two intellectuals is acquainted with George Eliot.'

Far from living up to Monkey's image of a man intimidated by the police, Mr Casaubon had brightened as soon as Wexford spoke and now rejoined in thick hideous cockney, 'I see him once. Strangeways it was, 1929. They done him for a big bullion job.'

'I fear,' Wexford said distantly, 'that we cannot be thinking of the same person. Now what are you gentlemen drinking?'

'Port and brandy,' said Mr Casaubon almost before the words were out, but Monkey, to whom what could be inhaled always took priority over what could merely be imbibed, pushed forward his empty bitter glass and remarked that he would appreciate twenty Dunhill International.

Wexford bought the drinks and tossed the crimson and gold package into Monkey's lap. 'I may as well open the proceedings,' he said, 'by telling you two jokers you can forget about five hundred pounds or anything like it. Is that clear?'

Mr Casaubon received this in the manner of one used to frequent disappointment. The liveliness which had briefly appeared in his watery eyes died away and, making a low humming sound that might have been a long-drawn murmur of assent or just an attempt at a tune, he reached for his port and brandy. Monkey said, 'When all's said and done, me and my friend would settle for the reward.'

'That's very handsome of you,' said Wexford sarcastically. 'I suppose you realise that money will be paid only for information leading directly to the arrest of the murderer of Stella Rivers?'

'We wasn't born yesterday,' said Monkey. This remark was so obviously true, particularly in the case of Mr Casaubon, who looked as if he had been born in 1890, that the old man broke off from his humming to emit a cackle of laughter, showing Wexford the most hideous, dilapidated and rotting set of teeth he had ever seen in a human mouth. 'We can read what's in the papers as well as you,' Monkey went on. 'Now then, cards on the table. If my friend tells you what he knows and what he's got papers to *prove*, are you going to do fair by us and see we get what's our right when Swan's under lock and key?'

'I can get a witness, if that's what you want. Mr Burden perhaps?'

Monkey puffed smoke out through his nostrils. 'I can't stomach that sarcastic devil,' he said. 'No, your word's good enough for me. When folks run down the fuzz I always say, Mr Wexford's hounded me, God knows, but he . . .'

'Monkey,' Wexford interrupted, 'are you going to tell me or aren't you?'

'Not here,' said Monkey, shocked. 'What, give you a load of info that'll put a man away for life here in what you might call the market place?'

'I'll drive you back to the station, then.'

'Mr Casaubon wouldn't like that.' Monkey stared at the old man, perhaps willing him to show some

sign of terror, but Mr Casaubon, his eyelids drooping, simply continued to hum monotonously. 'We'll
go to Rube's place. She's out baby-sitting.'

Wexford shrugged his agreement. Pleased, Monkey gave Mr Casaubon a poke. 'Come on, mate,
wakey-wakey.'

It took Mr Casaubon quite a long time to get on to
his legs. Wexford walked impatiently to the door,
but Monkey, not usually renowned for his considerate manners, hovered with some solicitude at his
friend's side, and then, giving him an arm, helped
him tenderly out into the street.

Burden had never phoned her before. His heart
palpitated lightly and fast as he listened to the
ringing tone and imagined her running to answer,
her heart beating quickly too because she would
guess who it was.

The steadiness of her voice took the edge off his
excitement. He spoke her name softly, on a note of
enquiry.

'Yes, speaking,' she said. 'Who is it?'

'Mike.' She hadn't recognised his voice and his
disappointment was profound.

But immediately he had identified himself she
gasped and said quickly, 'You've got some news for
me? Something's happened at last?'

He closed his eyes momentarily. She could only
think of that child. Even his voice, her lover's voice,
was to her just the voice of someone who might have
found her child. 'No, Gemma, no, there's nothing.'

'It was the first time you ever phoned me, you see,'
she said quietly.

'Last night was a first time too.'

She said nothing. Burden felt that he had never
known so long a silence, aeons of silence, time for
twenty cars to drone past the phone box, time for the

131

lights to change to green and back again to red, time for a dozen people to enter the Olive and leave the door swinging, swinging, behind them until it lapsed into stillness. Then at last she said, 'Come to me now, Mike. I need you so.'

There was another woman he had to have speech with first.

'I'm just going out on a job, Grace,' said Burden, too strait-laced, too innocent perhaps, to see a *double entendre* which would have had Wexford in stitches. 'I may be hours.'

They were given to pregnant, throbbing silences, his women. Grace broke the one she had created with a sharp ward sister's snap. 'Don't lie to me, Mike. I just phoned the station and they said you had a free evening.'

'You had no business to do that,' Burden flared. 'Even Jean never did that and she had the right, she was my wife.'

'I'm sorry, but the children asked and I thought . . . As a matter of fact, there's something special I want to discuss with you.'

'Can't it wait till tomorrow?' Burden thought he knew these discussions of Grace's. They were always about the children, more precisely about the children's psychological problems or what Grace imagined those problems to be: Pat's supposedly butterfly mind and John's mental block over his mathematics. As if all children didn't have their difficulties which were a part of growing up and which he in his day, and surely Grace in hers, had faced satisfactorily without daily analysis. 'I'll try to be in tomorrow night,' he said weakly.

'That,' said Grace, 'is what you always say.'

His conscience troubled him for about five minutes. It had long ceased to do so before he reached the outskirts of Stowerton. Burden had yet to learn that the anticipation of sexual pleasure is the most powerful of all the crushers of conscience. He wondered why he felt so little guilt, why Grace's reproach had only momentarily stung him. Her words – or what he could recall of them – had become like the meaningless and automatic admonition of some school-teacher spoken years ago. Grace was no longer anything to him but an impediment, an irritating force which conspired with work and other useless time-wasters to keep him from Gemma.

Tonight she came to the door to meet him. He was prepared for her to speak of the child and her anxieties and her loneliness, and he was ready with the gentle words and the tenderness which would come so easily to him after an hour in bed with her but which now his excitement must make strained and abrupt. She said nothing. He kissed her experimentally, unable to guess her mood from those large blank eyes.

She took his hands and put them against her waist which was naked when she lifted the shirt she wore. Her skin was hot and dry, quivering against his own trembling hands. Then he knew that the need she had spoken of on the phone was not for words or reassurance or searching of the heart but the same need as his own.

If Mr Casaubon had been capable of inspiring the slightest sentimentality, Wexford reflected, it would have been impossible to witness Monkey's extravagant care of him without disgust. But the old man – his real name would have to be ferreted out from some file or other – was so obviously a villain and a parasite who took every advantage of his age and an infirmity that was probably assumed that Wexford could only chuckle sardonically to himself as he watched Monkey settle him into one of Ruby Branch's armchairs and place a cushion behind his head. No doubt it was obvious to the receiver of these attentions as it was to the chief inspector that Monkey was merely cosseting the goose that would lay a golden egg. Presumably Mr Casaubon had already come to some financial agreement with his partner or impresario and knew there was no question of affection or reverence for old age in all this fussing with cushions. Humming with contentment in the fashion of an aged purring cat, he allowed Monkey to pour him a treble whisky, but when the water jug appeared the hum rose a semitone and a gnarled purple hand was placed over the glass.

Monkey drew the curtains and placed a table lamp on the end of the mantelpiece so that its radiance fell like a spotlight on the bunchy rag-bag figure of Mr Casaubon, and Wexford was aware of the dramatic effect. It was almost as if Monkey's protégé was one of those character actors who delight to appear solo on the London stage and for two hours or more entertain an audience to a monologue or to readings from some great novelist or diarist. And Mr Casaubon's repetitive nodding and humming rather enhanced this impression. Wexford felt that at any moment the play would begin, a witticism would issue from those claret-coloured lips or the humming would give place to a speech from *Our Mutual Friend*. But because he knew that this was all fantasy, deliberately achieved by that crafty little con-man Monkey Matthews, he said sharply: 'Get in with it, can't you?'

Mr Casaubon broke the silence he had maintained since leaving the Piebald Pony. 'Monk can do the talking,' he said. 'He's got more the gift of the gab than me.'

Monkey smiled appreciatively at this flattery and lit a cigarette. 'Me and Mr Casaubon,' he began, 'made each other's acquaintance up north about twelve months back.' In Walton gaol, Wexford thought, but he didn't say it aloud. 'So when Mr Casaubon was glancing through his morning paper the other day and saw about Mr Ivor Swan and him living in Kingsmarkham and all that, his thoughts naturally flew to me.'

'Yes, yes, I get all that. In plain English he saw the chance to make a little packet and thought you could help him to it. God knows why he didn't come straight to us instead of getting involved with a shark like you. Your gift of the gab, I suppose.' A thought struck Wexford. 'Knowing you, I wonder you didn't try putting the black on Swan first.'

'If you're going to insult me,' said Monkey, snorting out smoke indignantly, 'we may as well have done, and me and my friend'll go to Mr Griswold. I'm doing this as a favour to you, like to advance you in your profession.'

Mr Casaubon nodded sagely and made a noise like a bluebottle drowsing over a joint of beef. But Monkey was seriously put out. Temporarily forgetting the respect due to age and golden geese, he snapped in the tone usually reserved for Mrs Branch, 'Give over that buzzing, will you? You're getting senile. Now you can see,' he said to Wexford, 'why the silly old git needs me to prop him up.'

'Go on, Monkey. I won't interrupt again.'

'To get to the guts of the business,' said Monkey, 'Mr Casaubon told me – and showed me his paper to prove it – that fourteen years back your Ivor Bloody Swan – listening, are you? Ready for a shock? – your Ivor Swan killed a kid. Or, to put it more accurate,

135

caused her death by drowning her in a lake. There, I thought that'd make you sit up.'

Rather than sitting up, Wexford had slumped into his chair. 'Sorry, Monkey,' he said, 'but that's not possible. Mr Swan hasn't a stain on his character.'

'Hasn't paid the penalty, you mean. I'm telling you, this is fact, it's gospel. Mr Casaubon's own niece, his sister's girl, was a witness. Swan drowned the kid and he was up in court, but the judge acquitted him for lack of evidence.'

'He can't have been more than nineteen or twenty,' Wexford said ruminatively. 'Look here, I'll have to know more than that. What's this paper you keep on about?'

'Give it here, mate,' said Monkey.

Mr Casaubon fumbled among his layers of clothing, finally bringing out from some deep recess beneath mackintosh, coat and matted wool a very dirty envelope inside which was a single sheet of paper. He held it lovingly for a moment and then handed it to his go-between who passed it on to Wexford.

The paper was a letter with neither address nor date.

'Before you read it,' said Monkey, 'you'd best know that this young lady as wrote it was chambermaid in this hotel in the Lake District. She had a very good position, lot of girls under her. I don't know exactly what she was but she was the head one.'

'You make her sound like the madame in a brothel,' said Wexford nastily, and cut short Monkey's expostulation with a quick, 'Shut up and let me read.'

The letter had been written by a semi-literate person. It was ill-spelt, almost totally lacking in punctuation. While Mr Casaubon hummed with the

136

complacency of a man showing off to an acquaintance the prize-winning essay of some young relative, Wexford read the following.

'Dear Uncle Charly.

'We have had a fine old fuss up hear that you will want to know of there is a young Colledge feller staying in the Hotel and what do you think he as done he as drowned a little girl swimmin in the Lake in the morning befor her Mum and Dad was up and they have had him up in Court for it Lily that you have herd me speak of had to go to the Court and tell what she new and she tell me the Judge give it to him hot and strong but could not put him away on account of Nobody saw him do the deed the young fellers name is IVOR LIONEL FAIRFAX SWAN i got it down on paper when Lily said it gettin it from the Judge on account i new you would wish to know it in ful.

'Well Uncle that it all for now i will keep in touch as ever hoping the news may be of use and that your Leg is better
Your Affect. Neice

'Elsie'

The pair of them were staring eagerly at him now. Wexford read the letter again – the lack of commas and stops made it difficult to follow – and then he said to Mr Casaubon, 'What made you keep this for fourteen years? You didn't know Swan, did you? Why keep this letter in particular?'

Mr Casaubon made no reply. He smiled vaguely as people do when addressed in a foreign language and then he held out his glass to Monkey, who promptly refilled it and, once more taking on the task of interpreter, said, 'He kept all her letters. Very devoted to Elsie is Mr Casaubon, being as he never had no kiddies of his own.'

'I see,' said Wexford, and suddenly he did. He felt his features mould themselves into a scowl of rage as the whole racket worked by Mr Casaubon and his niece grew clear to him. Without looking again at the letter he recalled certain significant phrases. 'A fine old fuss that you will want to know of' and 'hoping the news may be of use' sprang to mind. A chambermaid, he thought, a chiel among us taking notes ... How many adulterous wives had Elsie spotted? Into how many bedrooms had she blundered by the merest chance? How many homosexual intrigues had she discovered when homosexual practice was still a crime? Not to mention the other secrets to which she would have had access, the papers and letters left in drawers, the whispered confidences between women, freely given at night after one gin too many. The information about Swan, Wexford was sure, was just one of many such pieces of news retailed to Uncle Charly in the knowledge that he would use them for the extortion of money of which Elsie, in due course, would claim her share. A clever racket, though one which, to look at him now, had not finally worked to Mr Casaubon's advantage.

'Where was this Elsie working at the time?' he snapped.

'He don't remember that,' said Monkey. 'Somewhere up in the Lakes. She had a lot of jobs one way and another.'

'Oh, no. It was all one way and a dirty way at that. Where is she now?'

'South Africa,' mumbled Mr Casaubon, showing his first sign of nervousness. 'Married a rich yid and went out to the Cape.'

'You can hang on to the letter.' Monkey smiled ingratiatingly. 'You'll want to do a bit of checking up. I mean, when all's said and done, we're only a couple of ignorant fellers, let's face it, and we wouldn't know how to go about getting hold of this judge and all that.' He edged his chair towards Wexford's. 'All we want is our rightful dues for setting you on the track. We don't ask for no more than the reward, we don't want no thanks nor nothing . . .' His voice faltered and Wexford's baleful face finally silenced him. He drew in a deep lungful of smoke and appeared to decide that at last it was time to offer hospitality to his other guest. 'Have a drop of Scotch before you go?'

'I wouldn't dream of it,' Wexford said pleasantly. He eyed Mr Casaubon. 'When I drink I'm choosey about my company.'

Chapter 14

Nervous bliss, Wexford decided, best described Inspector Burden's current state of mind. He was preoccupied, often to be found idle and staring distantly into space, jumping out of his skin over nothing, but at least it was a change from that bleak irritable misery everyone had come to associate with him. Very likely the cause of the change was a woman, and Wexford, encountering his friend and assistant in the lift on the following morning, remembered Dr Crocker's words.

'How's Miss Woodville these days?'

He was rewarded, and somewhat gratified, by the uneven burning blush that spread across Burden's face. It confirmed his suspicion that recently there had been something going on between those two and something a good deal more exciting than discussions about whether young Pat ought to have a new blazer for the autumn term.

'My wife,' he went on, pressing his point home, 'was only saying yesterday what a tower of strength Miss Woodville has been to you.' When this evoked no response, he added, 'All the better when the tower of strength has an uncommonly pretty face, eh?'

Burden looked through him so intensely that Wexford suddenly felt quite transparent. The lift halted.

'I'll be in my office if you want me.'

Wexford shrugged. Two can play at that game, he thought. You won't get any more friendly overtures from me, my lad. Stiff-necked prude. What did he care about Burden's dreary love life, anyway? He had other things on his mind and because of them he hadn't slept much. Most of the night he had lain awake thinking about that letter and Monkey Matthews and the old villain who was Monkey's guest, and he had pondered on what it all meant.

Elsie was as sharp as a needle but bone ignorant. To a woman like her any J.P. was a judge and she wouldn't know the difference between assizes and a magistrates' court. Was it possible that all those years ago the young Swan had appeared before a *magistrate*, charged with murder or manslaughter, and the case been dismissed? And if that was so had the facts of that hearing somehow escaped being included in Wexford's dossier of Swan?

Night is a time for conjecture, dreams, mad conclusions; morning a time for action. The hotel had been somewhere in the Lake District and as soon as he was inside his office Wexford put through calls to the Cumberland and Westmorland police. Next he did a little research into the antecedents of Mr Casaubon, working on the assumption that he had been in Walton at the same time as Monkey, and this conclusion and the investigations it led to proved fruitful.

His name was Charles Albert Catch and he had been born in Limehouse in 1897. Pleased to discover that all his guesswork had been correct, Wexford learned that Catch had served three terms of imprisonment for demanding money with menaces but since reaching the age of sixty-five had fallen on evil days. His last conviction was for throwing a brick through the window of a police station, a ploy to secure – as it had done – a bed and shelter for the blackmailer who had become an impoverished vagrant.

Wexford wasted no sympathy on Charly Catch but he did wonder why Elsie's information had led her uncle to take no steps against Swan at the time. Because there really was no evidence? Because Swan had been innocent with nothing to hide or be ashamed of? Time would show. There was no point in further conjecture, no point in taking any steps in the matter until something came in from the Lakes.

With Martin and Bryant to keep watch from a discreet distance, he sent Polly Davis, red-wigged, off to her assignation at Saltram House. It was raining again and Polly got soaked to the skin, but nobody brought John Lawrence to the park of Saltram House or to the Italian garden. Determined not to speculate any further on the subject of Swan, Wexford racked his brains instead about the caller with the shrill voice, but still he was unable to identify that voice or to remember any more about it but that he had heard it somewhere before.

Holding her in his arms in the dark, Burden said, 'I want you to tell me that I've made you happier, that things aren't so bad because I love you.'

Perhaps she was giving one of her wan smiles. He could see nothing of her face but a pale glow. The room smelt of the scent which she used to use when she was married and had, at any rate, a little money. Her clothes were impregnated with it, a stale musty sweetness. He thought that tomorrow he would buy her a bottle of scent.

'Gemma, you know I can't stay the night. I only wish to God I could, but I promised and . . .'

'Of course you must go,' she said. 'If I were going to my — to my children, nothing would keep me.

142

Dear kind Mike, I won't keep you from your *children*.'

'You'll sleep?'

'I shall take a couple of those things Dr Lomax gave me.'

A little chill touched his warm body. Wasn't satisfied love the best soporific? How happy it would have made him to know that his love-making alone could send her into sweet sleep, that thoughts of him would drive away every dread. Always the child, he thought, always the boy who had secured for himself all his mother's care and passion. And he imagined the miracle happening and the lost dead boy, restored to life and to home, running into the darkened bedroom now, bringing his own light with him, throwing himself into his mother's arms. He saw how she would forget her lover, forget that he had ever existed, in a little world made just for a woman and a child.

He got up and dressed. He kissed her in a way that was meant to be tender only but became passionate because he couldn't help himself. And he was rewarded with a kiss from her as long and desirous as his own. With that he had to be satisfied; with that and with the crumpled chiffon scarf he picked up as he left the room.

If only he would find his bungalow empty, he mused as he drove towards it. Just for tonight, he told himself guiltily. If only he could go into emptiness and solicitude, free of Grace's gentle brisk demands and Pat's castles in the air and John's mathematics. But if he were going home to an empty house he wouldn't be going home at all.

Grace had said she wanted to discuss something with him. The prospect was so dreary and so tedious that he forebore speculating about it. Why endure an agony twice over? He held the scented chiffon against his face for comfort before entering the house but instead of comfort it brought him only longing.

His son was hunched over the table, ineptly grasping a compass. 'Old Mint Face,' he said when he saw his father, 'told us that "mathema" means knowledge and "pathema" means suffering, so I said they ought to call it pathematics.'

Grace laughed a little too shrilly. She was flushed, Burden noticed, as if with excitement or perhaps trepidation. He sat down at the table, neatly drew the diagram for John and sent him off to bed. 'May as well have an early night myself,' he said hopefully.

'Spare me just ten minutes, Mike. I want – there's something I want to say to you. I've had a letter from a friend of mine, a girl – a woman – I trained with.' Grace sounded extremely nervous now, so unlike herself that Burden felt a small disquiet. She was holding the letter and seemed about to show it to him, but she changed her mind and stood clutching it. 'She's come into some money and she wants to start a nursing home and she . . .' The words tumbled out in a rush, '. . . she wants me to come in with her.'

Burden was beginning on a bored, 'Oh, yes, that's nice,' when suddenly he did a double-take and what she was actually saying came home to him. The shock was too great for thought or politeness or caution. 'What about the children?' he said.

She didn't answer that directly. She sat down heavily like a tired old woman. 'How long did you think I would stay with them?'

'I don't know.' He made a helpless gesture with his hands. 'Till they're able to look after themselves, I suppose.'

'And when will that be?' She was hot now and angry, her nervousness swamped by indignation. 'When Pat's seventeen, eighteen? I'll be forty.'

'Forty's not old,' said her brother-in-law feebly.

'Maybe not for a woman with a profession, a career she's always worked at. If I stay here for another six years I won't have any career, I'd be lucky to get a job as a staff nurse in a country hospital.'

'But the children,' he said again.

'Send them to boarding school,' she said in a hard voice. 'Physically, they'll be just as well looked after there as here, and as for the other side of their lives – what good do I do them alone? Pat's coming to an age when she'll turn against her mother or any mother substitute. John's never cared much for me. If you don't like the idea of boarding school, get a transfer and go to Eastbourne. You could all live there with Mother.'

'You've sprung this on me, all right, haven't you, Grace?'

She was almost in tears. 'I only had Mary's letter yesterday. I wanted to talk to you yesterday, I begged you to come home.'

'My God,' he said, 'what a thing to happen. I thought you liked it here, I thought you loved the kids.'

'No, you didn't,' she said fiercely, and her face was suddenly Jean's, passionate and indignant, during one of their rare quarrels. 'You never thought about me at all. You – you asked me to come and help you and when I came you turned me into a sort of house-mother and you were the lofty superintendent who condescended to visit the poor orphans a couple of times a week.'

He wasn't going to answer that. He knew it was true. 'You must do as you please, of course,' he said.

'It isn't what I please, it's what you've driven me to. Oh, Mike, it could have been so different! Don't you see? If you'd been with us and pulled your weight and made me feel we were doing something worth while *together*. Even now if you ... I'm trying to say ... Mike, this is very hard for me. If I thought you might come in time to ... Mike, won't you help me?'

She had turned to him and put out her hands, not impulsively and yearningly as Gemma did, but with a kind of modest diffidence, as if she were ashamed. He remembered what Wexford had said to him that morning in the lift and he recoiled away from her. That it was almost Jean's face looking at him, Jean's voice pleading with him, about to say things which to his old-fashioned mind no woman should ever say to a man, only made things worse.

'No, no, no!' he said, not shouting but whispering the words with a kind of hiss.

He had never seen a woman blush so fierily. Her face was crimson, and then the colour receded, leaving it chalk white. She got up and walked away, scuttling rather, for on a sudden she had lost all her precise controlled gracefulness. She left him and closed the door without another word.

That night he slept very badly. Three hundred nights had been insufficient to teach him how to sleep without a woman and, after them, two of bliss had brought back with savagery all the loneliness of a single bed. Like a green adolescent he held, pressed against his face so that he could smell it, the scarf of the woman he loved. He lay like that for hours, listening through the wall to the muffled crying of the woman he had rejected.

Chapter 15

The lock of hair did not belong to Stella Rivers either. Enough of her own blonde curls remained on what remained of her for them to make comparison. 'A bracelet of bright hair about the bone,' Wexford thought, shuddering.

That proved nothing, of course. It was only to be expected, it was known, that the fur man – Wexford thought of his correspondent and his caller as the 'fur man' now – was a liar. There was nothing for him to do but wait for news from the Lakes, and his temper grew sour. Burden had been unbearable for the last couple of days, hardly answering when you spoke to him and not to be found when most he was wanted. The rain fell unceasingly too. Everyone in the police station was irritable and the men, depressed by the weather, snapped at each other like wet, ill-tempered dogs. The black-and-white foyer floor was blotched all day by muddy foot-marks and trickles from sodden raincapes.

Marching briskly past the desk to avoid an encounter with Harry Wild, Wexford almost crashed into a red-faced Sergeant Martin who was waiting for the lift.

'I don't know what the world's coming to, sir, I really don't. That young Peach, usually won't say boo to a goose, flares up at me because I tell him he should be wearing a stouter pair of boots. Mind your own business, he has the nerve to say to me. What's up, sir? What have I said?'

'You've solved something for me,' Wexford said, and then more soberly, because this was only the beginning of an investigation, not a solution: 'Sergeant, the night we were searching for John Lawrence you told a man in the search party to put on thicker shoes – you must have a thing about it – and he too told you to mind your own business. Remember?'

'I can't say I do, sir.'

'I spoke to him too,' Wexford said wonderingly. 'He tried to stroke the dogs.' Fur, he thought, fur and rabbits. He had tried to stroke the alsatian, his hand seemingly impelled towards that soft thick coat. 'God, I can't remember what he looked like! But I remember that voice. That voice! Sergeant, the man you spoke to, the man who tried to stroke the dogs, is the writer of those letters.'

'I just don't recall him, sir.'

'Never mind. It should be easy to find him now.'

But it wasn't.

Wexford went first to Mr Crantock, the husband of Gemma Lawrence's neighbour, who was head cashier at the Kingsmarkham branch of Lloyd's Bank. Certain that this man would know every member of the search parties by sight if not by name, Wexford was disappointed to learn that not every searcher had been drawn from the three streets, Fontaine Road, Wincanton Road and Chiltern Avenue.

'There were a lot of chaps I'd never seen before,' said Crantock. 'Heaven knows where they came from or how they got to know the kid was missing that early. But we were glad of anyone we could get, weren't we? I remember there was one character came on a bike.'

'News of that kind travels fast,' Wexford said. 'It's

a mystery how it does, but people get to know of things before there's time for them to be on television or radio or in the papers.'

'You could try Dr Lomax. He led one of the parties until he had to go back on a call. Doctors always know everybody, don't they?'

The supplier of Gemma Lawrence's sleeping pills practised from his own home, a Victorian Gothic house of considerable dimensions that was superior to its neighbours in Chiltern Avenue. Wexford arrived in time to catch the doctor at the end of his afternoon surgery.

Lomax was a busy harassed little man who spoke with a shrill voice, but it wasn't the shrillness Wexford was listening for and, besides, the doctor had a faint Scottish accent. It seemed that he too was unlikely to be of much help.

'Mr Crantock, Mr Rushworth, Mr Dean . . .' He enumerated a long list of men, counting them on his fingers, though of what use this was Wexford didn't know, as the search parties had never been counted. Lomax, however, seemed certain when he reached the end of his list that there had been three strangers, one the cyclist.

'How they even knew about it beats me,' he said, echoing Crantock. 'I only knew myself because my wife came in and told me while I was holding surgery. She acts as my nurse, you see, and she'd overheard someone talking in the street while she was helping an elderly patient out of a car. She came straight in here and told me and when my last patient had gone I went outside to see what I could do and saw all your cars.'

'What time would that have been?'

'When my wife told me or when I went outside? It would have been something after six when I went out, but my wife told me at twenty past five. I can be sure of that because the old lady she helped from the car always comes at five twenty on the dot on Thursdays. Why?'

'Were you alone when your wife told you?'

'No, of course not. I had a patient with me.'

Wexford's interest quickened. 'Did your wife come up to you and whisper the news? Or did she say it aloud so that the patient could have heard?'

'She said it aloud,' said Lomax rather stiffly. 'Why not? I told you she acts as my nurse.'

'You will remember who the patient was, naturally, Doctor?'

'I don't know about naturally. I have a great many patients.' Lomax reflected in silence for a moment. 'It wasn't Mrs Ross, the old lady. She was still in the waiting room. It must have been either Mrs Foster or Miss Garrett. My wife will know, she has a better memory than I.'

Mrs Lomax was called in.

'It was Mrs Foster. She's got four children of her own and I remember she was very upset.'

'But her husband didn't come in the search party,' said Lomax, who seemed now to be following Wexford's own line of reasoning. 'I don't know him, he's not my patient, but he couldn't have. Mrs Foster had just been telling me he'd broken one of his big toes.'

Except to say in an embarrassed low tone, 'Of course, I'll stay till you've made other arrangements,' Grace had scarcely spoken to Burden since telling him of her plans. At table – the only time they were together – they kept up a thin polite pretence of conversation for the sake of the children. Burden spent his evenings and his nights with Gemma.

He had told her, but no one else, that Grace was deserting him, and wondered, not understanding at

150

all, when her great wistful eyes widened and she said how lucky he was to have his children all to himself with no one to come between or try to share their love. Then she fell into one of her terrible storms of weeping, beating with her hands on the dusty old furniture, sobbing until her eyes were swollen and half-closed.

Afterwards she let him make love to her, but 'let' was the wrong word. In bed with him she seemed briefly to forget that she was a mother and bereaved and became a young sensual girl. He knew that sex was a forgetting for her, a therapy – she had said as much – but he told himself that no woman could show so much passion if her involvement was solely physical. Women, he had always believed, were not made that way. And when she told him sweetly and almost shyly that she loved him, when she hadn't mentioned John for two hours, his happiness was boundless, all his load of cares nothing.

He had had a wonderful idea. He thought he had found the solution to the sorrows of both of them. She wanted a child and he a mother for his children. Why shouldn't he marry her? He could give her another child, he thought, proud in his virility, in the potency that gave her so much pleasure. She might even be pregnant already, he had done nothing to avoid it. Had she? He was afraid to ask her, afraid to speak of any of this yet. But he turned to her, made strong and urgent by his dreams, anxious for quick possession. Even now they might be making a child, the two of them. He hoped for it, for then she would have to marry him. . . .

The Fosters lived in Sparta Grove, a stone's throw from the Piebald Pony, in a little house that was one of a row of twelve.

'I didn't tell a soul about that poor kid,' said Mrs

151

Foster to Wexford, 'except my husband. He was sitting in a deck-chair, resting his poor toe, and I rushed out to tell him the good news.'

'The *good* news?'

'Oh dear, what must you think of me! I don't mean the poor little boy. I did mention that, but only in passing. No, I wanted to tell him what the doctor said. Poor man, he'd been going up the wall and so had I, for that matter. My husband, I mean, not the doctor. We thought we was going to have another one you see, thought I'd fallen again and me with four already. But the doctor said it was the onset of the change. The relief! You've no idea. I give the kids their tea and then my husband took me up the Pony to celebrate. I did mention the poor little boy when we was in there. I mean, you like to have a bit of a natter, don't you, especially when you're on top of the world. But it was well gone seven before we got there, that I do know.'

It had looked like a promising lead, had proved a dead end.

It was still half-light and Sparta Grove full of children, playing on the pavements. No one seemed to be supervising them, no one peeping from behind a curtain to keep an eye on that angelic-looking boy with the golden curls or guarding the coffee-skinned, sloe-eyed girl on her tricycle. No doubt the mothers were there, though, observing while themselves remaining unobserved.

The Pony was opening and, as sure as the sun rises, Monkey Matthews, supporting Charly Catch alias Mr Casaubon, appeared from the direction of Charteris Road. Wexford hurried off before they spotted him.

Find the three strangers in the search party was next morning's order of the day, made the more urgent by the printed letter which awaited Wexford among his mail. It was repetitious and Wexford hardly glanced at it, for awaiting him also was a report compiled and signed by an Inspector Daneforth of the Westmorland Constabulary.

Strict orders having been given that he was not to be disturbed, Wexford read:

'On August 5th, 1957, the body of a child, Bridget Melinda Scott, aged 11, was recovered from Fieldenwater lake, Westmorland. The child was found to have met her death by drowning and on August 9th an inquest was held by the Mid-Westmorland Coroner, Dr Augustine Forbes.'

An inquest. Of course! Why hadn't he thought of that? Elsie would call an inquest a court and a coroner a judge. Vaguely disheartened, Wexford read on.

'Evidence was given by:

'1) Lilian Potts, chambermaid, employed at the Lakeside Hotel where Bridget Scott with her parents, Mr and Mrs Ralph Scott, was a guest. Miss Potts told the coroner that she had met Bridget in one of the first floor passages of the hotel at 8 a.m. on the morning of August 5th. Bridget had said she was going swimming in the lake and was wearing a bathing costume with a beach robe over it. She was alone. Miss Potts advised her not to go out of her depth. Bridget made no reply and Miss Potts saw her go down the stairs.

'2) Ralph Edward Scott, plumbing engineer, of 28 Barrington Gardens, Colchester, Essex. Mr Scott said he was the father of Bridget Scott. He and his wife and daughter had been spending a fortnight's holiday at the Lakeside Hotel, Fieldenwater. By August 5th they had been there for ten days. Bridget was a keen swimmer and used to swim in the lake regularly before breakfast. On August 5th, before he and his wife were up, Bridget came into their bedroom to say she was going for a swim. He warned her to stay close to the shore. He never saw her alive again.

'3) Ada Margaret Patten, widow, aged 72, of 4 Blenheim Cottages, Water Street, Fieldenwater Village. She said she had been exercising her dog, as was her habit, at 8.15 a.m. on the north shore of Fieldenwater, the opposite shore to that on which the hotel is situated. She heard a cry for help and noticed that there was a bather in difficulties. Herself unable to swim, Mrs Patten observed two men bathing at the eastern end of the lake and another man fishing from a rowing boat a short distance from the bather who had called for help. Asked by the coroner to explain what she meant by a short distance, Mrs Patten said she would calculate the distance was about twenty yards. Mrs Patten was carrying a walking stick which she waved in the direction of the boat. She also tried to attract the attention of the other two bathers. The men at the eastern end of the lake eventually heard her and began to swim northwards. Her shouts had no apparent effect on the fisherman in the boat. Finally, she saw the boat moving towards the distressed swimmer but before it reached that part of the lake the swimmer had disappeared. She did not understand how the boatman could have failed to hear her as sound carries over water. She had often been in boats on the lake herself and knew that sounds from the shore were clearly audible in its centre.

'4) George Baleham, agricultural worker, of 7, Bulmer Way, New Estate, Fieldenwater Village. Mr Baleham told the coroner that he and his brother had gone for a swim in Fieldenwater at 7.30 a.m. on August 5th. He saw a child enter the lake from the Lakeside Hotel towards 8.10. Five minutes later he heard cries from across the water and heard Mrs

154

Patten shouting. Immediately he and his brother began swimming towards the child who was two hundred yards from them. There was a boat in the vicinity of the child and he saw a man fishing from it. He shouted to the man in the boat, "There's a kid drowning. You are nearer than us," but the boat did not move. Mr Baleham said the boat did not begin to move until he was ten yards from it. By this time the child had disappeared. In his opinion, the man in the boat could easily have reached the child before she sank. From where he was he could not have failed to see the child or hear her cries.

'5) Ivor Lionel Fairfax Swan . . .'

Here it was then, what he had been waiting for. The name in cold type gave Wexford a strange little cold thrill. He felt like a man who for months has stalked a particular stag and now, groping through the brush and undergrowth of a bleak moor, sees his quarry standing aloof and unsuspecting, near him, oh, so near! on a crag. Stealthily and silently he reaches for his gun.

'5) Ivor Lionel Fairfax Swan, student, aged 19, of Carien Hall, Carien Magna, Bedfordshire, and Christ's College, Oxford. Mr Swan said he was on holiday at the Lakeside Hotel with two friends. Bridget Scott had occasionally spoken to him in the hotel lounge and on the lake beach. Apart from that he did not know her and had never spoken to her parents. He enjoyed fishing and sometimes hired a boat to take out on to the lake in the early morning.

'On August 5th he took the boat out at 7 a.m. He was alone on the lake. He noticed two men swimming from the eastern shore at about 7.40, then, soon after eight, Bridget Scott came down the steps from the hotel and entered the water. He did not know whether she was a strong swimmer or not. He knew very little about her.

155

'She called something out to him but he did not answer. He thought she would make a nuisance of herself and disturb the fish. Some minutes later he heard her call again and again he took no notice. Several times in the previous week she had done things to draw his attention to herself and he thought it wiser not to encourage her. He heard Mrs Patten shouting, but thought she was calling her dog.

'Very soon after that two swimmers attracted his attention and then he saw that Bridget was in genuine difficulty. At once he began to draw in his line and make towards where he had last seen her. By then she had disappeared.

'In answer to the coroner's questions, Mr Swan said he had not thought of diving overboard and swimming. His line was an expensive one and he did not wish to spoil it. He could not dive and was not a strong swimmer. Up until the moment Bridget sank he had never believed her to be in genuine distress. No, he would not say he disliked the child. He had hardly known her. It was true he had not liked her attempts to intrude on himself and his friends. He was sorry she was dead and wished now that he had made efforts to save her. He was, however, sure in his own mind, that under the circumstances, he had acted as would any other man in his position.

'6) Bernard Varney Frensham, aged 19, student, of 16 Paisley Court, London, S.W.7 and Christ's College, Oxford. Mr Frensham said he was a friend of Mr Swan and had been on holiday with him and his (Mr Frensham's) fianceé at the Lakeside Hotel. Bridget Scott had taken an immediate liking to Mr Swan, a "crush" he supposed it would be called, and had tended to pester him. He said he had never been in a boat on Fieldenwater. Fishing did not interest him. When asked by the coroner if Mr Swan was a good swimmer, Mr Frensham said, "Must I answer that?" Dr Forbes insisted and Mr Frensham said he did not know anything about Mr Swan's style as a swimmer. He had never swum for his college. Pressed further, Mr Frensham said that he had once been shown a life-saving certificate with Mr Swan's name on it.

At this point there was a note explaining that medical and police evidence had been omitted. The report ended:

'The coroner commended Mr George Baleham and Mr Arthur Baleham for their prompt action in attempting to save the child.

'He then reprimanded Mr Swan. He said this was the worst case of callousness towards a child who was obviously drowning that he had ever come across. He took a serious view of what he could only call deliberate and cowardly lying on Mr Swan's part. Far from being an indifferent swimmer, he was an expert at life-saving. There was no doubt in his mind that Mr Swan had refused to listen to the child because he believed, or said he believed, she was pestering him. If he had jumped overboard when he first heard her cry out, Bridget Scott would be alive today. He could not be excused on the ground of his youth as he was a man of intelligence, an Oxford undergraduate and a man of privileged background. The coroner said he was only sorry the law permitted him to take no further steps. He then expressed sympathy for Mr and Mrs Scott.

'A verdict was returned of death by misadventure.'

Chapter 16

When giving Burden a résumé of Swan's life, Wexford had remarked on the series of disasters he had left in his wake. Here, then, was another instance of that catastrophe-causing faculty of his, that gift, or propensity, of leaving a trail of trouble and distress and disturbance. A true catalyst was Swan, Wexford reflected, a possessor of the power to hurt who yet did – nothing.

It wasn't difficult to picture that morning on the lake, Swan's line cast, the sun shining on the flat brown water, and Swan off in one of his daydreams that nothing must be allowed to disturb. Had he even caught a fish? Did he ever actually *do* anything? Shoot a rabbit? Choose a dog? Buy a pony?

And that was the crux of it. Clearly, Swan had let a child die. But the operative word there was 'let'. Would he actively force death on a child? Had he the nerve, the impulse, the *energy*?

Wexford would have liked to chew the whole thing over with Burden. They were illuminating and fruitful, those long discussions of theirs, examining motive, analysing character. But Burden was no longer fit to participate in such conversations. As soon expect percipience and intelligent speculation from Martin as from him. Each day he seemed to go a little more downhill, to grow more irritable and more distracted until Wexford began to wonder with dread how long it could go on. At present he daily covered up for Burden, did his work, smoothed his path. There was a limit to that, for soon the crack-up would come, the error that couldn't be overlooked or the hysterical scene in public. And then what? The embarrassed request for Burden's resignation before he was forced out?

Wexford shook himself out of these miserable reflections to concentrate on the report. One mystery, at any rate, was cleared up. He need no longer wonder why Swan had baulked at attending an inquest, particularly an inquest on another dead little girl.

The next step was to find Frensham, and this proved easy. Fourteen years had changed him from an undergraduate into a stock jobber, moved him from his parents' flat but not from Kensington, and maintained him in his bachelor state. What had happened to that fiancée who had accompanied him on that Lake holiday?

Hardly a question which need concern him, Wexford decided. He made the requisite polite phone call to the Metropolitan Police and then prepared to set off for London. In the foyer he met Burden.

'Any lead on the missing men from the search party?'

Burden lifted troubled eyes and muttered, 'Martin's got it in hand, hasn't he?'

Wexford went out into the rain, not looking back.

He alighted at Gloucester Road Tube station, got lost, and had to ask a policeman the way to Veronica Grove. At last he found it, a narrow little tree-lined lane which threaded its way from Stanhope Gardens down behind Queen's Gate. Water dripped softly from the branches overhead, and, except that the trees were planes and not oaks, he felt that he might have been at home in Kingsmarkham. The environs of the Piebald Pony were much more his idea of what London should be.

Meditating on such anomalies, he came within a few minutes to Bernard Frensham's house. It was tiny, a mews cottage, with neat but empty window boxes, and it looked very modest unless you happened to know that such properties were sold for twenty-five thousand pounds.

A manservant, small, lithe and dark, admitted him and showed him into the single living room the house contained. It was, however, a large room on three different levels and the furnishing gave an impression of varying textures, satiny polish, smooth velvet, delicate filigree work and highlighted china, rather than of solid masses. Much money had been spent on it. The years Swan has wasted had been turned to good account by his friend.

Frensham, who had risen from his chair at the far end of the room when Wexford entered it, had received prior warning of his coming. And 'warning' rather than 'notice' seemed the appropriate word, for it was very apparent that he had been drinking. Because the coming interview caused him disquiet? Wexford was forced to suppose so. A stock jobber could hardly be so successful as Frensham surely was if seven o'clock always saw him as drunk as he was tonight.

Not that he didn't hold it well. It was only the brandy smell and the strangeness of Frensham's eyes that told Wexford of his condition.

He was thirty-three and he looked forty, the black hair already thinning and the face marked with dark patches. On the other hand, Swan, his contemporary, looked twenty-seven. Slothfulness and placidity preserve youth; hard work and anxiety accelerate its passing.

Frensham wore a beautiful suit of charcoal grey

with a coppery sheen to it, a black-and-copper tie, and, on the little finger of his left hand, an opal ring. What an impression of civilised distinction the man would have made, Wexford thought, but for the brandy on his breath which struck you full-blast in the face.

'Let me give you a drink, Chief Inspector.'

Wexford would have refused, was on the point of refusing, but there was so much subdued urgency in Frensham's added, 'Please do,' that he felt bound to consent.

Frensham opened the door and called a name that sounded like 'Haysus'. Brandy was brought and various other bottles and decanters. When the man-servant had gone, Frensham said, 'Odd, aren't they, the Spanish? Calling a boy Jesus.' He gave a short disconcerting giggle. 'Most inappropriate, I can tell you. His parents are Maria and Joseph, or so he says.'

Taking a gulp of his drink, he pursued this theme, but Wexford decided he wouldn't be sidetracked by Iberian nomenclature. It was impossible not to feel that Frensham was trying to postpone their discussion for as long as possible.

'May we talk about Mr Ivor Swan, sir?'

Frensham left the subject of Spanish names abruptly and said in a clipped voice, 'I haven't seen Ivor for years, not since we both came down from Oxford.'

'That doesn't matter. I have. Perhaps you can't remember much about him?'

'I remember all right,' said Frensham. 'I shall never forget.' He got up and walked across the room. At first Wexford thought he had gone to fetch a photograph or some document and then he realised that Frensham was in the grip of a powerful emotion. His back was towards the chief inspector and for some minutes he didn't move. Wexford sat watching

161

him in silence. He wasn't easily embarrassed, but he wasn't prepared for Frensham's next words either. Wheeling round suddenly, staring oddly at Wexford, he said, 'Has he vine leaves in his hair?'

'I beg your pardon?'

'You have never seen or read *Hedda Gabler*? It doesn't matter. It's the kind of question I feel natural to ask about Ivor.' The man was very drunk, with the intoxication that rids the tongue of inhibition without slurring speech. He came back to his chair and rested his elbows against the back of it. 'Ivor was remarkably beautiful then, a pale golden-brown Antinous. I was very fond of him. No, that isn't true. I loved him with – with all my heart. He was very lazy and – well, tranquil. He never seemed to know what the time was or to take any account of time at all.' Frensham spoke as if he had forgotten Wexford was there or forgotten what he was. He reached for his brandy standing up. 'That kind of indifference to time, that sublime idleness, is very attractive. I often think it was this quality in her, rather than her religious zeal, that made Christ praise Mary and condemn Martha, the bustling busy worker.'

Wexford had not come to hear about the character of Ivor Swan, which he thought he already understood, but he was no more willing to interrupt Frensham in the midst of his discourse than a spiritualist would have been to cut short the outpourings of a medium in a trance. He felt somehow, as might the spiritualist also, that it would be dangerous to do so.

'He was always pursued by droves of girls,' Frensham went on. 'Some of them were beautiful and all of them were intelligent. I am speaking, of course, of Oxford girls. He slept with some of them but he never took them out, not even for a drink. He couldn't be bothered. He used to say he didn't like clever women because they tried to make him talk.

'Once I told him the sort of woman he would marry, a feather-brained idiot who would adore him and fuss about him and demand only his presence. He wouldn't marry her, she would marry him, drag him to the altar against all odds. I saw in the paper he is married. Is she like that?'

'Yes, she is,' said Wexford. 'Exactly like that.'

Frensham sat down heavily. He looked ravaged now, as if overcome by painful memories. Wexford wondered if he and Swan had really been lovers, but decided against it. The willingness would have been there on Frensham's part all right, but Swan just wouldn't have been 'bothered'.

'I never married,' said Frensham. 'I was engaged to that girl, Adelaide Turner, but it never came to anything. I remember Ivor didn't want her to go on holiday with us and I didn't either, not really, not by then. He said she would get in the way.' He refilled his glass and said, 'I can't stop drinking. I'm afraid. I don't drink much usually but once I start I can't stop. I promise you I won't make a fool of myself.'

Some would say he was doing that already. Wexford was less harsh. He felt sorry for Frensham, sorrier when he said suddenly:

'I don't know whether I'm giving you a true picture of Ivor's character or not. You see, although I haven't seen him for twelve years, I dream about him a great deal, as much as three times a week. It must sound very silly, I haven't ever told anyone before. I mention it now because I don't know any more what is the real Ivor and the Ivor my own dreams have created. The two images are so confused they have run into each other and become one.'

Wexford said gently, 'Tell me about the holiday. Tell me about Bridget Scott.'

'She was only eleven,' Frensham said, and his voice was saner and more even when he wasn't speaking of Swan. 'But she looked much older, at least fourteen. It sounds very absurd to say she fell in love with him at first sight, but she did. And, of course, at that age she hadn't learned to hide her feelings. She used to pester Ivor all the time, ask him to go swimming with her, wanted him to sit next to her in the lounge. She even asked her mother in our hearing if he could go up and say good night to her when she was in bed.'

'And how did Swan deal with all that?'

'Simply by taking no notice. He treated Adelaide in the same way. He used to answer Adelaide if she spoke to him, but most of the time he didn't speak to Bridget at all. He said she got in the way, and once, I remember, he told her so.'

Frensham leaned back and gave a heavy sigh. His eyes closed momentarily and he opened them as if with a great effort. 'The coroner,' he said, 'was an old man like a vulture. I didn't want to betray Ivor. They made me tell them about his swimming. I hadn't any choice.' The heavy lids fell again. 'I felt like Judas,' he said.

'What happened that morning when Bridget was drowned?'

Still Frensham kept his eyes closed and now his speech had begun to thicken. 'I never went out fishing with Ivor. I've never been an early riser. Ivor was. You'd think a man like – a man like him, would go to bed late and get up late. Ivor always used to be up by six. He'd sleep in the day, of course, if he got the chance. He could sleep anywhere. It was the early morning he liked and the countryside, the peace of it and the light.' Frensham made a funny little noise like a sob. 'He used to quote those lines of

W. H. Davies. "What is this life, if full of care, we have no time to stand and stare?"'

'Go on about that morning.'

Frensham sat up, and half-toppled forward, resting his elbows on his knees, his chin in his hands. 'I don't know. I wasn't there. I woke up to hear people shouting in the corridor outside my room, running up and down and shouting. You can imagine. I went outside. The mother was there, screaming, and that poor old man, Scott.'

'Old? Bridget's father?'

'Not really old, I suppose. About sixty. The mother was younger. They had older children, someone told me. Does it matter? I found Ivor in the dining room, drinking coffee. He was very white. He said, "It was nothing to do with me. Why involve me?" and that was all he ever said about it.'

'You mean he never again mentioned the subject of Bridget Scott's drowning to you? Not when you both had to attend the inquest?'

'He didn't like it because we had to stay on over the end of our holiday,' remembered Frensham, and now a glaze had come across his eyes. Weariness? Tears? Or only the effect of the drink? 'After – after the inquest he wouldn't let me speak of it. I don't know what he felt.' Very softly now, Frensham said, 'It may have been callousness or that he was upset or just wanted to forget. There wasn't much about the inquest in the daily papers and when we went up no one knew until – until Adelaide told them.'

'Why do you think he let her drown?' said Wexford.

'She got in his way,' said Frensham, and then he began to cry weakly. 'When people annoyed him or began to – to bore him he just – just – just . . .' There was a sob between each word. '. . . Just – ignored – them – pretended – they – weren't – there – didn't –

165

talk – didn't – see – them – did that – to – me – after – later . . .' He threw out a hand and the brandy glass went over, spreading a stain across the thick pale carpet.

Wexford opened the door and called, 'Here, Jesus, or whatever your name is, your master wants you. You'd better get him to bed.'

The man came in, sidling and smiling. He put his arms under Frensham's shoulders and whispered to him. Frensham lifted his head and said to Wexford in a normal clear tone, 'Vine leaves in his hair . . .' Then he closed his eyes and slid into unconsciousness.

Chapter 17

Friday's edition of the *Kingsmarkham Courier* carried on its front page a double-column spread asking for the three missing men from the search party to come forward. Much good that would do, Wexford thought, as he read it. Hadn't it occurred to Martin, when he asked Harry Wild for publicity, that an appeal of this kind would fetch forth only the innocents? And where was Burden in all this, Burden who was supposed to rule the place in Wexford's absence, yet who seemed as much surprised by the newspaper appeal as he was?

When he got back from London he had phoned Burden's house. He needed to discuss that interview with someone and he thought too that this might be a way of reawakening Burden's interest. But Grace Woodville had told him her brother-in-law was out, she didn't know where.

'I think he may just be sitting somewhere in his car, brooding about Jean and – and everything.'

'He's supposed to leave a number where he can be found.'

'Cheriton Forest doesn't have a number,' said Grace.

On Saturday afternoon two men walked into Kingsmarkham police station to say that they had read the *Courier* and believed they were two of the three missing men. They were brothers, Thomas and William Thetford, who lived in adjoining houses in

Bury Lane, a half-slum, half-country road on the far side of Stowerton, not far from Sparta Grove. News of John Lawrence's disappearance had been brought to them by William's wife who cleaned for Mrs Dean and who had reached home at five-thirty. The Thetford brothers were on shift work, had both finished for that day. Guessing a search party might be got up – hoping for a bit of excitement to brighten up their day, Wexford thought – they had got into William's car and driven to Fontaine Road.

Neither man had a squeaky voice or even a voice Wexford could remember hearing before. They denied having passed the news on to anyone and said they had discussed it only with each other. Wexford supposed that routine demanded an interview with Mrs Thetford. Monday would be time enough for that.

'Golf in the morning?' said Dr Crocker, bouncing in after the Thetfords had gone.

'Can't. I'm going to Colchester.'

'Whatever for?' Crocker said crossly, and then, without waiting for an answer, 'I wanted to have a little chat with you about Mike.'

'I'd really rather you didn't. I'd rather you saw him. You're his doctor.'

'I think he's found a better doctor than I,' said Crocker slyly. 'I saw his car again last night.'

'Don't tell me. In Cheriton Forest. And he was in it, brooding.'

'It wasn't and he wasn't. It was parked at the bottom of Chiltern Avenue at midnight.'

'You're ubiquitous, you are,' Wexford grumbled. 'You're like the Holy Ghost.'

'It was at the bottom of *Chiltern Avenue*, next to *Fontaine Road* at *midnight*. Come on, Reg. I knew you were thick round the middle but not . . .' The doctor tapped his head, '. . . not up here.'

'That's not possible,' said Wexford sharply. His voice faltered. 'I mean ... Mike wouldn't ... I don't want to talk about it.' And he cast upon the doctor a fierce glare. 'If I don't know about it,' he said with none of his usual logic, 'it isn't happening.'

'I know it would be like a miracle,' said Gemma, 'but if – if John is ever found and comes back to me, I shall sell this house, even if I only get what the land's worth, and go back to London. I could live in one room, I shouldn't mind. I hate it here. I hate being in here and I hate going out and seeing them all look at me.'

'You talk like a child,' said Burden. 'Why talk about what you know can't happen? I asked you to marry me.'

She got up, still without answering, and began to dress, but not in the clothes she had taken off when she and Burden had come into the bedroom. He watched her hungrily, but puzzled as he always was by nearly every facet of her behaviour. She had pulled over her head a long black dress, very sleek and tight. Burden didn't know whether it was old, a garment of her aunt's, or the latest fashion. You couldn't tell these days. Over her shoulders and around her waist she wrapped a long scarf of orange and blue and green, so stiff and encrusted with embroidery that it crackled as she handled it.

'We used to dress up a lot, John and I,' she said, 'dress up and be characters from the *Red Fairy Book*. He would have grown up to be a great actor.' Now she was hanging jewellery all over herself, long strings of beads draped from her neck and wound about her arms. 'That sometimes happens when one of your parents, or both of them, has been a second-rate artist. Mozart's father was a minor musician.' She swayed in the soft red light, extending her arms.

There was a ring on every finger to weigh down her thin hands. She shook down her hair and it fell in a flood of fire, the light catching it as it caught all the stones in the cheap rings and made them flash.

Burden was dazzled and fascinated and appalled. She danced across the room, drawing out the scarf and holding it above her head. The jewels rang like little bells. Then she stopped, gave a short abrupt laugh, and ran to him, kneeling at his feet.

'"I will dance for you, Tetrarch,"' she said. '"I am awaiting until my slaves bring perfumes to me and the seven veils and take off my sandals."'

Wexford would have recognised the words of Salome. To Burden they were just another instance of her eccentricity. Very distressed and embarrassed, he said, 'Oh, Gemma . . . !'

In the same voice she said, 'I will marry you if . . . if life is to go on like this with nothing, I'll marry you.'

'Stop play-acting.'

She got up. 'I wasn't acting.'

'I wish you'd take those things off,' he said.

'You take them off.'

Her huge staring eyes made him shiver. He reached out both hands and lifted the bunch of chains from her neck, not speaking, hardly breathing. She lifted her right arm, curving it in a slow sweep and then holding it poised. Very slowly he slid the bracelets down over her wrist and let them fall, pulled the rings from her fingers one by one. All the time they stared into each other's eyes. He thought that he had never in his life done anything as exciting, as overpoweringly erotic, as this stripping a woman of cheap glittering jewellery, although in doing so he had not once touched her skin.

Never . . . He hadn't even dreamed that such a thing might be possible for him. She stretched out her left arm and he made no other move towards her until the last ring had joined the others in a heap on the floor.

It wasn't until he awoke in the night that he realised fully what had happened, that he had proposed and been accepted. He told himself that he ought to be elated, in a seventh heaven of happiness, for he had got what he wanted and there would be no more agony or struggling or loneliness or dying small daily deaths.

The room was too dark for him to see anything at all, but he knew exactly what the first light would show him here and downstairs. Yesterday it hadn't mattered much, the mess and the chaos, but it mattered now. He tried to see her installed in his own house as its mistress, caring for his children and cooking meals, tending on them all as Grace did, but it was impossible to conjure up such a picture, he hadn't enough imagination. What if Wexford were to call one night for a chat and a drink as he sometimes did and Gemma appear in her strange dress and her shawl and her long beads? And would she expect him to have her friends there, those itinerant sub-actors with their drugs? And his children, his Pat ... !

But all that would change, he told himself, once they were married. She would settle down and be a housewife. Perhaps he could persuade her to have that mane of hair cut, that hair which, at one and the same time, was so beautiful and so evocative of desire and yet so unbecoming in a policeman's wife. They would have a child of their own, she would make new suitable friends, she would change ...

He did not allow himself to dwell on the notion that such changes as he envisaged would destroy her personality and dull all the strangeness that had first attracted him, but it touched the edges of his mind. He pushed it away almost angrily. Why make difficulties where none existed? Why seek always to find flaws in perfect happiness?

Gemma and he would have love, a nightly orgy for two, an endless honeymoon. He turned towards her, pressing his lips against the mass of hair of which he planned to deprive her. Within minutes he was asleep and dreaming that he had found her child, restoring him to her and seeing her, by that gift, transformed into everything he wanted her to be.

'Kingsmarkham?' said Mrs Scott, smiling comfortably at Wexford. 'Oh, yes, we know Kingsmarkham, don't we, dear?' Expressionless, her husband gave a tiny nod. 'We've got a niece lives in ever such a nice little house near Kingsmarkham, built back in the seventeen hundreds, it was, and we used to go there regularly for our holidays right up till this year. But now ...'

Wexford, who while she was speaking had been taking stock of the room and looking particularly at the framed photographs of those older Scott children who had survived, middle-aged now and with teenage children of their own, followed her gaze towards their progenitor.

No need to ask why they wouldn't go back to Kingsmarkham or to question the implication that they would take no more holidays. Scott was a little old man, nearing eighty, whose face was badly twisted, especially about the mouth. Two sticks hung from the wings of his chair. Wexford supposed that he was unable to walk without their aid and, from his silence, was beginning to suppose that Ralph Scott had also lost the power of speech. It was something of a shock when the distorted mouth opened and a harsh voice said:

'What about a cup of tea, Ena?'

'I'll have it ready in a jiffy, dear.'

Mrs Scott jumped up and mouthed something to Wexford, indicating that he should join her in the kitchen. This was a sterile-looking place full of gadgets, and it was modern enough to gladden the heart of any house-proud woman, but Mrs Scott seemed to think it needed apology.

'Mr Scott had a stroke back in the winter,' she said as she plugged in an electric kettle, 'and it's really aged him. He's not at all the man he was. That's why we moved out here from Colchester. But if he was himself I'd have had everything automatic here, he'd have done the lot himself, not left it to those builders. I wish you could have seen my house in the town. The central heating was *too* hot. You had to have the windows open night and day. Mr Scott did all that himself. Of course, him being in the trade all his life, there's nothing he doesn't know about heating and pipes and all that.' She stopped, stared at the kettle which was making whining noises, and said in a voice that seemed to be suppressing something explosive, 'We saw in the papers about that man Swan and you digging all that up again about his little girl. It made Mr Scott ill, just seeing his name.'

'The child died back in the winter.'

'Mr Scott never saw the papers then. He was too ill. We never knew Swan lived near our niece. We wouldn't have gone if we had. Well, he was living there the last time we went but we didn't know.' She sat down on a plastic-upholstered contemporary version of a settle and sighed. 'It's preyed on Mr Scott's mind all these years, poor little Bridget. I reckon it would have killed him to have come face to face with that Swan.'

'Mrs Scott, I'm sorry to have to ask you, but in your opinion, is it possible he let your daughter drown? I mean, is it possible he knew she was drowning and let it happen?'

She was silent. Wexford saw an old grief cross her face, travel into her eyes and pass away. The kettle boiled with a blast and switched itself off.

Mrs Scott got up and began making the tea. She was quite collected, sorrowful but with an old dry sadness. The fingers on the kettle handle, the hand on the teapot, were quite steady. A great grief had come to her, the only grief, Aristotle says, which is insupportable, but she had borne it, had gone on making tea, gone on exulting in central heating. So would it be one day for Mrs Lawrence, Wexford mused. Aristotle didn't know everything, didn't know perhaps that time heals all pain, grinds all things to dust and leaves only a little occasional melancholy.

'Mr Scott loved her best,' Bridget's mother said at last. 'It's been different for me. I had my sons. You know how it is for a man and his little girl, his youngest.'

Wexford nodded, thinking of his Sheila, his ewe lamb, the apple of his eye.

'I never took on about it like he did. Women are stronger, I always say. They get to accept things. But I was in a bad way at the time. She was my only girl, you see, and I had her late in life. In fact, we never would have had another one, only Mr Scott was mad on getting a girl.' She looked as if she were trying to remember, not the facts, but the emotions of the time, trying and failing. 'It was a mistake going to that hotel,' she said. 'Boarding houses were more in our line. But Mr Scott was doing so well and it wasn't for me to argue when he said he was as good as the next man and why not a hotel when we could afford it? It made me feel uncomfortable, I can tell you, when I saw the class of people we had to mix with, Oxford boys and a barrister and a Sir. Of course, Bridget didn't know any different, they were just people to her and she took a fancy to that Swan. If I've wished it once I've wished it a thousand times that she'd never set eyes on him.

'Once we were in the lounge and she was hanging about him – I couldn't stop her. I did try – and he gave her such a push, not saying anything, you know, not talking to her, that she fell over and hurt her arm. Mr Scott went right over and had a go at him, told him he was a snob and Bridget was as good as him any day. I'll never forget what he said. "I don't care whose daughter she is," he said. "I don't care if her father's a duke or a dustman. I don't want her around. She gets in my way." But that didn't stop Bridget. She wouldn't leave him alone. I've often thought since then that Bridget swam out to that boat so as she could be alone with him and no one else there.'

Mrs Scott picked up her tray, but made no other move to return to the sitting room. She seemed to be listening and then she said:

'She couldn't swim very far. We'd told her over and over again not to go out too far. Swan knew, he'd heard us. He let her drown because he just didn't *care*, and if that's killing, he killed her. She was only a child. Of course he killed her.'

'A strong accusation to make, Mrs Scott.'

'It's no more than the coroner said. When I saw in the paper about his own little girl I didn't feel sorry for him, I didn't think he'd got his deserts. He's done the same to her, I thought.'

'The circumstances were hardly the same,' said Wexford. 'Stella Rivers died from suffocation.'

'I know. I read about it. I'm not saying he did it

deliberately any more than I'm saying he actually pushed Bridget under the water. It's my belief she got in his way too – stands to reason she would, a stepdaughter and him newly married – and maybe she said something he didn't like or got too fond of him like Bridget, so he got hold of her, squeezed her neck or something and – and she died. We'd better go back to Mr Scott now.'

He was sitting as they had left him, his almost sightless eyes still staring. His wife put a teacup into his hands and stirred the tea for him.

'There you are, dear. Sorry I was so long. Would you like a bit of cake if I cut it up small?'

Mr Scott made no reply. He was concentrating on Wexford and the chief inspector realised that no explanation of his visit had been given to the old man. True, there had been a passing reference to Kingsmarkham and a niece, but Wexford had not been identified by name or rank.

Perhaps it was the look in his wife's eyes or perhaps something that he had overheard while they were in the kitchen that made him say suddenly in his harsh monotone:

'You a policeman?'

Wexford hesitated. Scott was a very sick man. It was possible that the only real contact he had ever had with the police was when his beloved daughter died. Would it be wise or kind or even necessary to bring memories back to that exhausted, fuddled brain?

Before he could make up his mind, Mrs Scott said brightly, 'Oh, no dear. Whatever gave you that idea? This gentleman's just a friend of Eileen's from over Kingsmarkham way.'

'That's right,' said Wexford heartily.

The old man's hand trembled and the cup rattled

in its saucer. 'Shan't go there any more, not in my state. Shan't last much longer.'

'What a way to talk!' Mrs Scott's brisk manner did little to cover her distress. 'Why, you're almost your old self again.' She mouthed incomprehensible things to Wexford and followed them up with a louder, 'You should have seen him last March, a couple of weeks after he had that stroke. More dead than alive he was, worse than a new-born baby. And look at him now.'

But Wexford could hardly bear to look. As he left them, he reflected that the interview hadn't been entirely fruitless. At least it would spur him on to take Crocker's tablets with renewed zeal.

Chapter 18

The impressions Swan made on other people had subtly altered Wexford's own image of him, investing him with a callous coldness and a magnetic beauty, making him god-like in appearance and power, so that when he came face to face with the man himself once more he felt a sense of let-down and almost of shock. For Swan was just Swan, still the idle good-looking young man leading his slow aimless existence. It was strange to reflect that the mere mention of his name might be enough to kill Mr Scott and that, incubus-like, he lived a separate life as the haunter of Frensham's dreams.

'Does Roz have to know about this?' he asked, and went on when Wexford looked surprised, 'I'd more or less forgotten it myself, except that going to that inquest brought it back. Do we have to talk about it?'

'I'm afraid we do.'

Swan shrugged. 'We won't be overheard. Roz is out and I got rid of Gudrun.' Wexford's face showed the absurd effect this had on him and Swan gave a low ironical laugh. 'Told her to go, sacked her, I mean. What did you think I'd done? Made away with her? In your eyes my path is strewn with corpses, isn't it? Roz and I love to be alone and Gudrun got in our way, that's all.'

That phrase again. 'She got in his way ...' Wexford was beginning to get the shivers every time he heard it.

'D'you want a drink? It'll have to be something out of a bottle. Making tea and coffee is Roz's province and, anyway, I don't know where she keeps the things.'

'I don't want a drink. I want to hear about Bridget Scott.'

'Oh God, it was such a hell of a long time ago, ancient history. I suppose you've already had a splendid selection of biased accounts.' Swan sat down and rested his chin in his hands. 'I don't know what you want me to say. I went to this hotel with another man and a girl. If you'll give me a minute I'll try and remember their names.'

'Bernard Frensham and Adelaide Turner.' Poor Frensham, Wexford thought. Swan lived on in his dreams but he had no reciprocal place in Swan's memory.

'Why ask me if you've already talked to them?'

'I want your version.'

'Of what happened on the lake? All right. I did let her drown, but I didn't know she was drowning.' Swan's face was petulant. In the November light, fitful and fading, he might have been nineteen again, but Wexford could see no shadow of vine leaves in his hair. 'She plagued the life out of me,' he said, the sullen look deepening. 'She hung about me and tried to get me to go swimming and walking with me and she staged scenes to attract my attention.'

'What sort of scenes?'

'Once she was out in a rowing boat and I was swimming and she started shouting she'd dropped her purse overboard and would I dive for it. I didn't but what's-his-name – Frensham – did and after we'd all been messing about for about ten minutes she produced it from the bottom of the boat. It was all a ploy. Then she came into my room once in the afternoon when I was trying to sleep and said if I

179

wouldn't speak to her she'd scream and when people came she'd tell them I'd done something to her. A kid of eleven!'

'So that when you heard her cry for help you thought it was another ruse to attract your attention?'

'Of course I did. That other time when she'd threatened to scream, I said, "Scream away". I can't be taken in by that kind of thing. Out in the boat, I *knew* she was putting on an act. I couldn't believe it when they said she'd drowned.'

'Were you sorry?'

'I was a bit shattered,' said Swan. 'It made an impression on me, but it wasn't my fault. For quite a long time after that I didn't like having kids of that age around me. I don't now, come to that.'

Had he realised what he had said? 'Stella was just that age when you first saw her, Mr Swan,' said Wexford.

But Swan seemed unaware of the innuendo. He went on to make matters worse. 'She used to try the same things on, as a matter of fact, always trying to get attention.' The petulance returned, making him almost ugly. 'Could she have a dog? Could she have a horse? Always trying to involve me. I sometimes think . . .' He directed at Wexford a gaze full of fierce dislike. 'I sometimes think the whole world is trying to get between me and what I want.'

'And that is?'

'To be left alone with Rosalind,' said Swan simply. 'I don't want children. All this has made me loathe children. I want to be in the country with Roz, just the two of us, in peace. She's the only person I've ever known who wants me for what I am. She hasn't made an image of me that's got to be lived up to, she doesn't want to jolly me along and encourage me. She loves *me*, she really knows me and I'm first with

180

her, the centre of her universe. Once she'd seen me she didn't even care about Stella any more. We only kept her with us because I said we ought, that Roz might regret it later if she didn't. And she's jealous. Some men wouldn't like that, but I do. It gives me a wonderful feeling of happiness and security when Roz says if I so much as looked at another woman she'd do that woman the worst injury in her power. You don't know what that means to me.'

I wonder what it means to me? Wexford thought. He said nothing but continued to keep his eyes fixed on Swan who suddenly flushed. 'I haven't talked so much to anyone for years,' he said, 'except to Roz. That's her coming in now. You won't say anything about . . .? If she began suspecting me I don't know what I'd do.'

It was the sound of a car Swan had heard, the Ford shooting brake crunching on the gravel outside Hall Farm.

'I was under the impression you couldn't drive a car, Mrs Swan,' he said as she came in.

'Were you? I let my licence lapse while I was out in the East but I took a new test last month.'

She had been shopping. In London perhaps, at any rate in some more sophisticated place than Kingsmarkham. Her packages were wrapped in black paper lettered with white, scarlet printed with gold. But she hadn't been buying for herself.

'A tie for you, my lover. Look at the label.' Swan looked and so did Wexford. The label said Jacques Fath. 'And some Russian cigarettes and a book and . . . It doesn't look very much now I've got it all home. Oh, how I wish we were rich!'

'So that you could spend it all on me?' said Swan.

'Who else? Did you remember to ring the electric people, darling?'

'I never got around to it,' said Swan. 'It went right out of my head.'

'Never mind, my lover. I'll see to it. Now I'm going to make you some nice tea. Were you lonely without me?'

'Yes, I was. Very.'

She had hardly noticed Wexford. He was investigating the murder of her only child but she had hardly noticed him. Her eyes, her attention, were solely for her husband. It was he who, now there was someone to prepare it, rather grudgingly suggested that Wexford might care to stay and share their tea.

'No, thank you,' said the chief inspector. 'I wouldn't want to be in your way.'

The lock of hair had belonged neither to John Lawrence nor to Stella Rivers, but it was a child's hair. Someone had cut it from a child's head. That meant whoever had written the letters had access to a golden-headed child. And more than just access. No one could go up to a child in the street and chop off a piece of his or her hair without getting into trouble. Technically, it would be assault. Therefore, the letter-writer, the 'fur man', must be in such close association with a golden-headed child as to be able to cut off a lock of its hair either while it was asleep or with its permission.

But how far did that get him? Wexford pondered. He couldn't interview every golden-haired child in Sussex. He couldn't even ask for such children to come forward, for the person 'in close association' – father? uncle? – would prevent the one significant child from answering his appeal.

Although it wasn't the prescribed time, Wexford swallowed two of his blood-pressure tablets, washing them down with the dregs of his coffee. He'd need them if he was going to spend the rest of the day scouring Stowerton. Mrs Thetford first, to see if there was any chance she had broadcast the news of John's disappearance around the town. Then perhaps Rushworth. Sit down with Rushworth for hours if necessary, make him remember, make him describe his fellow searchers, get to the bottom of it *today*.

The climate in which Burden and his sister-in-law now lived wasn't conducive to confidences. It was nearly a week since she had smiled at him or said any more than 'Colder today' or 'Pass the butter, please'. But he would have to tell her about his forthcoming marriage, and tell the children too, perhaps even ask their permission.

He thought his opportunity had come when, thawing a little, Grace said, 'Aren't you having next weekend off?'

Guardedly, he said, 'Supposed to be. We're very busy.'

'Mother's asked all four of us down for the weekend.'

'I don't think . . .' Burden began. 'I mean, I couldn't manage it. Look here, Grace, there's something . . .'

Grace jumped up. 'There's always something. Don't bother to make excuses. I'll go alone with the children, if you've no objection.'

'Of course I've no objection,' said Burden, and he went off to work, or what would have been work if he had been able to concentrate.

He had half-promised to have his lunch in Fontaine Road. Bread and cheese, he supposed it would be, in that loathsome kitchen. Much as he longed to be with Gemma in the night, the meals she prepared had no attraction for him. The police-station canteen was almost preferable. And suddenly it occurred to him that soon every meal he ate at home would be prepared by Gemma.

Wexford had gone out somewhere. Time was when the chief inspector would never have gone out without leaving a message for him, but all that was changed now. He had changed it and the change in him had lost him Wexford's esteem.

Descending in the lift, he hoped he wouldn't encounter Wexford, and when the door opened he saw that there was no one in the foyer but Camb and Harry Wild, who these days had become almost a fixture, as much a part of the furnishings as the counter and the little red chairs. Burden treated him like a chair, accepting his presence but otherwise ignoring him. He was nearly at the swing doors when they burst open and Wexford appeared.

Except when he was with Gemma, muttering had become Burden's normal mode of speech. He muttered a greeting and would have gone on his way. Wexford stopped him with the 'Mr Burden!' he habitually used in the presence of such as Camb and Wild.

'Sir?' said Burden with equal formality.

Speaking in a lower tone, Wexford said, 'I've spent the morning with that fellow Rushworth, but I couldn't get a thing out of him. Strikes me as a bit of a fool.'

With an effort, Burden tried to fix his mind on Rushworth. 'I don't know,' he said. 'I wouldn't have considered him as a possible suspect myself, but he does wear a duffel coat and there was that business when he nearly frightened the wits out of the Crantock girl.'

'*He did what?*'

The words had been spoken in a sharp hiss. 'I told you,' Burden said. 'It was in my report.' Hesitating, muttering again, he recounted to the chief inspector his experience of the encounter in Chiltern Avenue. 'I must have told you,' he faltered. 'I'm sure I . . .'

Wexford forgot about Wild and Camb. 'You never did!' he shouted. 'You never made any bloody report. D'you mean to tell me now – *now* – that Rushworth molested a child?'

Burden had no words. He felt his face grow crimson. It was true – he remembered now – he had made no report, the whole thing had vanished from his mind. Love and involvement had driven it away, for that night, while Stowerton was wrapped in mist, had been his first night with Gemma.

Things might have come to a head then between him and Wexford but for the intervention of Harry Wild. Insensitive to atmosphere, quite incapable of ever supposing himself to be *de trop*, Wild turned round and said loudly:

'D'you mean to tell me you've got Bob Rushworth lined up for this job?'

'I don't mean to tell you anything,' Wexford snapped.

'There's no need to be like that. Don't you want any help in your enquiries?'

'What do you know about it?'

'Well, I do know Rushworth,' said Wild, pushing himself between the two policemen. 'And I know he's a nasty customer. Friend of mine rents a cottage from him down in Mill Lane, but Rushworth keeps a key to it and pops in and out just whenever the fancy takes him. He went through all my friend's private papers one day without so much as by your leave and his boy goes in and takes apples out of the garden, pinched a pint of milk once. I could tell you things about Bob Rushworth as'd make . . .'

'I think you've told me enough, Harry,' said Wexford. Without extending the usual invitation to lunch, without even looking at Burden again, he swung out of the police station the way he had come.

Because he was sure that if he went to the Carousel

Burden would only follow him and ruin his lunch with mealy-mouthed excuses, Wexford drove home and surprised his wife, who seldom saw him between nine and six, with a peremptory demand for food. He couldn't remember when he had last been in such a bad temper. Angry-looking black veins were standing out on his temples and this alarmed him so that he took two anti-coagulant tablets with the beer Mrs Wexford produced off the ice. Burden ought to know better than to upset him like that. Fine thing if he ended up like poor old Scott.

Somewhat calmer by three o'clock, he drove off to see Mrs Thetford. According to a neighbour, she was out at her job of cleaning for Mrs Dean. Wexford hung about till she got back and saw no reason to refuse her offer of a cup of tea and a piece of fruit cake. The Rushworths were both out all day, anyway, and he wanted to see them together rather than endure another interview with Rushworth in his estate agent's office, their conversation constantly interrupted by phone calls from clients.

But tea and cake were all he got out of Mrs Thetford. She repeated the story he had already heard from her husband. Mrs Dean had given her the news about John Lawrence at five o'clock but she declared she had passed it on to no one except her husband and her brother-in-law.

He drove slowly up the lane and entered Sparta Grove. Lomax's patient, Mrs Foster, was his only hope now. She must have told someone what she had overheard at the doctor's. Or been overheard herself? It was a possibility, perhaps the only one remaining. Number 14 was her house. Wexford parked outside it and then he saw the boy. He was swinging on the gate of the house next door, number 16, and his rather long hair was bright gold.

By now all the children were home from school

and Sparta Grove was full of them. Wexford beckoned to a girl of about twelve and she approached the car suspiciously.

'I'm not supposed to talk to strange men.'

'Very proper,' said Wexford. 'I'm a policeman.'

'You don't look like one. Show me your warrant card.'

'By gum, you'll go far if you don't come to a bad end.' He produced his card and the child scrutinised it with huge delight. 'Satisfied?'

'Mmm.' She grinned. 'I learnt how to do that off the telly.'

'Very educational, the telly. I wonder they bother to keep the schools open. You see that boy with the fair hair? Where does he live?'

'Where he is. That house he's on the gate of.'

Ungrammatical but explanatory. 'You needn't tell him I was asking.' Wexford produced a coin which he knew he wouldn't get back out of expenses.

'What shall I say, then?'

'Come, come. You're a resourceful girl. Say I was a strange man.'

Now was not the time. He must wait until all the children were in bed. When the Piebald Pony opened he went into the saloon bar and ordered sandwiches and half a bitter. Any minute now, he thought, Monkey and Mr Casaubon would come in. Delighted to see him in their local, they would try to ascertain how near they were to getting their hands on that two thousand, and it would give him much pleasure to tell them they had never been farther from it. He would even be indiscreet and reveal his innermost conviction, that Swan was guiltless of any crime but that of indifference.

But nobody came. It was seven when Wexford left the Piebald Pony and walked three-quarters of the length of quiet, dimly-lit Sparta Grove.

He tapped on the door of number 16. No lights showed. Every one of those children must now be safely in bed. In this house the golden-headed boy would be sleeping. From the look of the place – no blue-white glow of a television screen showed behind the drawn curtains – his parents had gone out and left him alone. Wexford had a low opinion of parents who did that, especially now, especially here. He knocked again, harder this time.

To a sensitive astute person an empty house has a different feel from a house which simply appears to be empty but which, in reality, contains someone who is unwilling to answer a door. Wexford sensed that there was life somewhere in that darkness, conscious tingling life, not just a sleeping child. Someone was there, a tense someone, listening to the sound of the knocker and hoping the knocks would cease and the caller go away. He made his way carefully through the side entrance and round to the back. The Fosters' house next door was well lit but all the doors and windows were shut. A yellow radiance from Mrs Foster's kitchen showed him that number 16 was a well-kept house, its path swept and its back doorstep polished red. The little boy's tricycle and a man's bike leaned against the wall and both were covered by a sheet of transparent plastic.

He hammered on the back door with his fist. Silence. Then he tried the handle very stealthily, but the door was locked. No getting in here without a warrant, he thought, and there was no hope of getting one on the meagre evidence he had.

Treading softly, he began to move round to the back of the house, feeling moist turf under his feet. Then, suddenly, a flare of light caught him from behind and he heard Mrs Foster say, as audibly as if she were standing beside his ear, 'You won't forget to put the bin out, will you, dear? We don't want to miss the dustmen two weeks running.'

Just as he thought. Every word spoken in the garden of number 14 could be heard in this garden. Mrs Foster hadn't seen him. He waited until she had retreated into her kitchen before moving on.

Then he saw it, a thin shaft of light, narrower than the beam from a pencil torch stretching across the grass from a french window. Tiptoeing, he approached the source of this light, a tiny gap between drawn curtains.

It was difficult to see anything at all. Then he saw that right in the middle of the window the edge of the curtain had been caught up on a bolt. He squatted down but still he couldn't see in. There was nothing for it but to lie down flat. Thank God there was no one to see him or observe how hard he found it to perform what should have been one of man's most natural actions.

Flat on his belly now, he got one eye up against the uncurtained triangle. The room unfolded itself before him. It was small and neat and conventionally furnished by a house-proud wife with a red three-piece suite, a nest of tables, wax gladioli and carnations whose petals were wiped each day with a damp cloth.

The man who sat writing at a desk was quite relaxed now and intent on his task. The importunate caller had gone away at last and left him to the special peace and privacy he demanded. It would show in his face, Wexford thought, that concentration, that terrible solitary egotism, but he couldn't see his face, only the bare legs and feet, and sense the man's rapt absorption. He suspected that under the fur coat he wore he was quite naked.

Wexford watched him for some minutes, watched him pause occasionally in his writing and pass the

189

thick furry sleeve across nose and mouth. It made him shiver, for he knew he was eavesdropping on something more private than secret speech or love-making or the confessional. This man was not alone with himself, but alone with his other self, a separate personality which perhaps no one else had ever seen until now.

To witness this phenomenon, this intense private fantasising in a room which epitomised conformity, seemed to Wexford an outrageous intrusion. Then he remembered those fruitless trysts in the forest and Gemma Lawrence's hope and despair. Anger drove out shame. He pulled himself on to his feet and rapped hard on the glass.

Chapter 19

In his anxiety to reach the lift, Burden shoved Harry Wild out of the way.

'Manners,' said the reporter. 'There's no need to push. I've a right to come in here and ask questions if I . . .'

The sliding door cut off the rest of his remarks which would perhaps have been to the effect that, but for his modesty and fondness for the quiet life, he would have been exercising his rights in loftier portals than those of Kingsmarkham police station. Burden didn't want to hear. He only wanted Harry's statement, that they had found the boy, confirmed or denied.

'What's this about a special court?' he demanded, bursting into Wexford's office.

The chief inspector looked tired this morning. When he was tired his skin took on a grey mattness and his eyes looked smaller than ever, but still steel-bright, under the puffy lids.

'Last night,' he said. 'I found our letter-writer, a certain Arnold Charles Bishop.'

'But not the boy?' Burden said breathlessly.

'Of course not the boy.' Burden didn't like it when Wexford sneered like that. His eyes seemed to be drilling two neat holes into the inspector's already aching head. 'He's never even seen the boy. I found him at his home in Sparta Grove where he was occupied in writing another letter to me. His wife was out at her evening class, his children were in bed. Oh, yes, he has children, two boys. It was from the head of one of them that he cut the hair while the kid was asleep.'

'Oh God,' said Burden.

'He's a fur fetishist. Want me to read his statement?'

Burden nodded.

'"I have never seen John Lawrence or his mother. I did not take him away from the care of his mother, his legal guardian. On October 16, at about 6 p.m., I overheard my neighbour, Mrs Foster, tell her husband that John Lawrence was missing and that search parties would probably be arranged. I went to Fontaine Road on my bicycle and joined one of these search parties.

'"On three subsequent occasions in October and November I wrote three letters to Chief Inspector Wexford. I did not sign them. I made one telephone call to him. I do not know why I did these things. Something came over me and I had to do them. I am a happily married man with two children of my own. I would never harm a child and I do not own a car. When I wrote about the rabbits I did this because I like fur. I have three fur coats but my wife does not know this. She knows nothing of what I have done. When she goes out and the children are asleep I often put one of my coats on and feel the fur.

'"I read in the paper that Mrs Lawrence had red hair and John Lawrence fair hair. I cut a piece of hair from the head of my son Raymond and sent it to the police. I cannot explain why I did this or any of it except by saying that I had to do it."'

Burden said hoarsely, 'The maximum he can get is six months for obstructing the police.'

'Well, what would you charge him with? Mental torture? The man's sick. I was angry too last night, but not any more. Unless you're a brute or a moron you can't be angry with a man who's going through life with a sickness as grotesque as Bishop's.'

Burden muttered something about it being all right for those who weren't personally involved, but Wexford ignored it. 'Coming over to the court in about half an hour?'

'To go through all that muck again?'

'A great deal of our work consists of muck, as you call it. Clearing muck, cleaning up, learning what muck is and where it lives.' Wexford rose and leaned heavily on his desk. 'If you don't come, what are you going to do? Sit here mooning all day? Delegating? Passing the buck? Mike, I have to say this. It's time I said it. I'm tired. I'm trying to solve this case all on my own because I can't count on you any more. I can't talk to you. We used to thrash things out together, sift the muck, if you like. Talking to you now – well, it's like trying to have a rational conversation with a zombie.'

Burden looked up at him. For a moment Wexford thought he wasn't going to answer or defend himself. He just stared, a dead empty stare, as if he had been interrogated for many days and many sleepless nights and could no longer sort out the painful twisted threads that contributed to his unhappiness. But he knew, for all that, that the time for fobbing Wexford off was long gone by, and he brought it all out in a series of clipped sentences.

'Grace is leaving me. I don't know what to do about the kids. My personal life's a mess. I can't do my job.' A cry he hadn't meant to utter broke out. 'Why did she have to die?' And then, because he couldn't help himself, because tears which no one must see were burning his eyelids, he sank his head into his hands.

The room was very still. Soon I must lift my head,

Burden thought, and take away my hands and see his derision. He didn't move except to press his fingers harder against his eyes. Then he felt Wexford's heavy hand on his shoulder.

'Mike, my dear old friend . . .'

An emotional scene between two normally unemotional men usually has its aftermath of deep miserable embarrassment. When Burden had recovered he felt very embarrassed, but Wexford neither blustered heartily nor made one of those maladroit efforts to change the subject.

'You're due to be off this weekend, aren't you, Mike?'

'How can I take time off now?'

'Don't be a bloody fool. You're worse than useless the state you're in. Make it a long weekend, starting on Thursday.'

'Grace is taking the children down to Eastbourne . . .'

'Go with them. See if you can't make her change her mind about leaving. There are ways, Mike, aren't there? And now – my God, look at the time! – I'll be late for the court if I don't get cracking.'

Burden opened the window and stood by it, letting the thin morning mist cool his face. It seemed to him that with the arrest of Bishop their last hope – or his last fear? – of finding John Lawrence had gone. He wouldn't disturb Gemma with it and she had never read the local papers. The mist, floating white and translucent, washed him gently and calmed him. He thought of the mist by the seaside and the long bare beaches, deserted in November. Once there, he would tell the children and Grace and his mother-in-law about Gemma, that he was to be married again.

He wondered why the idea of this chilled him more than the cold touch of the autumnal air.

Because she was the strangest successor to Jean he could have picked in all his world? In the past he had marvelled at men who, in their selflessness or their temporary infatuation, marry crippled or blind women. Wasn't he contemplating doing just that, marrying a woman who was crippled in her heart and her personality? And that was the only way he knew her. How would she be if her deformity were healed?

Ludicrous, monstrous, to think of Gemma as deformed. Tenderly and with an ache of longing, he recalled her beauty and their lovemaking. Then, closing the window sharply, he knew he wouldn't be going down to Eastbourne with Grace.

Bishop was remanded for a medical report. The head-shrinkers would get to work on him, Wexford thought. Maybe that would do some good, more likely it wouldn't. If he had had any faith in psychiatrists he would have recommended Burden to attend one. Still, their recent confrontation had done something to clear the air. Wexford felt the better for it and he hoped Burden did too. Now, at any rate, he was out on his own. Single-handed he must find the children's killer – or fall back on the Yard.

The events of the past twenty-four hours had distracted his mind from Mr and Mrs Rushworth. Now he considered them again. Rushworth was in the habit of wearing a duffel coat, Rushworth was suspected of molesting a child, but surely, if he had been the loiterer in the swings field, Mrs Mitchell would have recognised him as one of her neighbours? Moreover, at the time of John's disappearance, every man within a quarter-mile radius of Fontaine Road had been closely investigated, Rushworth included.

Wexford delved once more among the reports. On the afternoon of October 16th Rushworth claimed to have been in Sewingbury where he had a date to show a client over a house. The client, Wexford saw, hadn't turned up. Back in February Rushworth hadn't even been questioned. Why should he have been? Nothing pointed to a connection between him and Stella Rivers and no one knew then that he was the owner of the rented cottage in Mill Lane. At the time the ownership of that cottage had seemed irrelevant.

He wouldn't see Rushworth yet. First he needed enlightenment as to the man's character and veracity.

'To get away from this house!' Gemma said. 'Just to get away for a little while.' She put her arms round Burden's neck and clung to him. 'Where shall we go?'

'You decide.'

'I'd like London. You can lose yourself there, be just one in a lovely enormous crowd. And there are lights all night and things going on and . . .' She paused, biting her lip, perhaps at the look of horror on Burden's face. 'No, you'd hate it. We aren't much alike, are we, Mike?'

He didn't answer that. He wasn't going to admit it aloud. 'Why not somewhere on the coast?' he said.

'The sea?' She had been an actress, if not a very successful one, and she put all the loneliness and depth and vastness of the sea into those two words. He wondered why she had shivered. Then she said, 'I don't mind if you'd like to. But not to a big resort where you might see – well, families, people with – with children.'

'I thought of Eastover. It's November, so there won't be children.'

'All right.' She didn't point out to him that he had

196

asked her to decide. 'We'll go to Eastover.' Her lips trembled. 'It'll be fun,' she said.

'Everyone will think I've gone to Eastbourne with Grace and the children. I'd rather it was that way.'

'So that they can't get hold of you?' She nodded with a kind of sage innocence. 'I see. You remind me of Leonie. She always tells people she's going to one place when really she's going somewhere else so that she won't be badgered with letters and phone calls.'

'It wasn't that,' Burden said. 'It's just – well, I don't want anyone . . . Not until we're married, Gemma.'

She smiled, wide-eyed and uncomprehending. He saw that she really didn't understand him at all, his need to be respectable, to put a good face on things. They didn't speak the same language.

It was Wednesday afternoon, and Mrs Mitchell, that creature of routine, was cleaning her landing window. While she talked she clutched a pink duster in one hand and a bottle of pink cleaning fluid in the other and, because she refused to sit down, Wexford couldn't either.

'Of course I should have known if it was Mr Rushworth,' she said. 'Why, his own little boy, his Andrew, was playing there with the others. Besides, Mr Rushworth's quite a big man and the man I saw was little, very small-made. I told the other officer what little hands he had. Mr Rushworth wouldn't pick leaves.'

'How many children has he?'

'Four. There's Paul – he's fifteen – and two little girls and Andrew. I'm not saying they're my idea of good parents, mind. Those children are allowed to do just what they please, and Mrs Rushworth didn't take a blind bit of notice when I warned her about that man, but do a thing like that . . .! No, you've got the wrong end of the stick there.'

197

Perhaps he had. Wexford left Mrs Mitchell to her window-cleaning and crossed the swings field. The year was far too advanced now for any children to play there and there would be no more freak summers. The roundabout looked as if it had never spun on its scarlet axis and mould had begun to grow on the seesaw. Hardly a leaf remained on the trees, oak and ash and sycamore, which grew between the field and Mill Lane. He touched the lower branches and fancied that here and there he could see where a twig had been snapped off. Then, in a more ungainly fashion, he was sure, than the leaf-picker and his young companion, he scrambled down the bank.

Briskly he walked the length of the lane, telling himself it was as much for his health's sake as for duty. He hadn't expected to find anyone at home in the rented cottage but Harry Wild's friend was off work with a cold. Leaving again after a quarter of an hour, Wexford was afraid his visit had only served to raise the man's temperature, so heated had he been on the subject of Rushworth, a far from ideal landlord. Unless the tenant's account was exaggerated, it appeared that the whole Rushworth family was in the habit of entering the cottage, helping themselves to garden produce and occasionally removing small pieces of furniture for which they substituted pencilled notes of explanation. They had retained a key of their own and the tenant paid so low a rent that he was afraid to expostulate. At any rate, Wexford now knew the identity of the boy who had been seen leaving the cottage that February afternoon. Beyond a doubt, it had been Paul Rushworth.

The day had been dull and overcast and now evening was closing in, although it was scarcely five. Wexford felt a first few drops of rain. On just such a day and at much this time Stella had followed the road he was taking, quickening her steps perhaps, wishing she had more to protect her than a thin riding jacket. Or had she even come so far back towards Stowerton? Had her journey – and her life – taken her no further than the cottage he had just left?

He had immersed himself so much in Stella, mentally transmuting his own elderly, male and stout body into the slight form of a twelve-year-old girl, that when he heard the sounds ahead of him he stepped back on to the grass verge and listened with a kind of hope.

The sounds were of horse's hooves. A horse was coming round the bend in the lane.

He was Stella, not old Reg Wexford. He was alone and a bit frightened and it was beginning to rain, but Swan was coming . . . On a *horse*? One horse for two people? Why not in a car?

The horse and its rider came into sight. Wexford shook himself back into himself and called out. 'Good afternoon, Mrs Fenn.'

The riding instructress reined in the big grey. 'Isn't he lovely?' she said. 'I wish he was mine, but I've got to take him back to Miss Williams at Equita. We've had such a nice afternoon out, haven't we, Silver?' She patted the animal's neck. 'You haven't – er – caught anyone yet? The man who killed poor Stella Swan?'

Wexford shook his head.

'Stella *Rivers*, I should say. I don't know why I find it so confusing. After all, I've got two names myself and half my friends call me Margaret and half by my second name. I ought not to get mixed up. Must be getting old.'

Wexford felt no inclination for gallantry and simply asked if she had ever seen Rushworth in the grounds of Saltram House.

199

'Bob Rushworth? Now you come to mention it, he and his wife were up here a lot last winter and she actually asked me if I thought it would be all right for them to take one of the statues away with them. The one that was lying down in the grass, you know.'

'You said nothing about this before.'

'Well, of *course* not,' said Mrs Fenn, bending over to coo into the horse's ear. 'I *know* the Rushworths, I've known them for years. Paul calls me auntie. I suppose they wanted the statue for their garden. It's not my place to say whether you can have it or you can't, I said.' She edged herself more comfortably into the saddle. 'If you'll excuse me I must be on my way. Silver's very highly bred and he gets nervous when it's dark.' The horse lifted its head and emitted a loud whinny of agreement. 'Never mind, darling,' said Mrs Fenn. 'Soon be home with Mother.'

Wexford went on. The rain was falling thinly but steadily. He passed Saltram Lodge and entered that part of the lane which was most thickly overshadowed by trees. They thinned out after two or three hundred yards to disclose the celebrated view of the great house.

The parkland looked grey and the house itself, looming through mist, a black skeleton with empty eye-sockets. Wexford was glad he had never known the place or been in the habit of visiting it. To him it had become a graveyard.

Chapter 20

He hadn't been able to bring himself to book a double room for Mr and Mrs Burden. One day Gemma would be Mrs Burden and then it would be different. In the meantime the name was Jean's. Jean held the title like a champion whose honours cannot be taken from her by death.

Their hotel was Eastover village pub which had been extended since the war to accommodate half a dozen guests, and they had been given rooms side by side, both overlooking the wide grey sea. It was too cold for bathing, but there are always children on beaches. While Gemma unpacked, Burden watched the children, five of them, brought down there to play by their parents. The tide was far out and the beach a silvery ochre, the sand packed too tight and flattened too firmly by the sea to show footprints from this distance. The man and the woman walked far apart from each other, seeming entirely detached. Married for many years, Burden supposed – the eldest girl looked at least twelve – they had no need of contact or of reassurance. The children, running from one to the other, then wheeling towards the sea, were evidence enough of love. He saw the parents, separated now by a wide drift of shells and pebbles, glance casually at each other and in that glance he read a secret language of mutual trust and hope and profound understanding.

One day it would be like that for him and Gemma.

They would bring their children, his and *theirs*, to such a beach as this and walk with them between the water and the sky and remember their nights and days and look forward to the night. He turned quickly to tell her what he was thinking but suddenly it came to him that he mustn't tell her, he couldn't because to do so would be to draw her attention to the children.

'What is it, Mike?'

'Nothing. I only wanted to say that I love you.'

He closed the window and drew the curtains, but in the half-dark he could still see the children. He took her in his arms and closed his eyes and still he could see them. Then he made love to her violently and passionately to exorcise the children and, in particular, the little fair-haired boy whom he had never seen but who was more real to him than those he had watched on the seashore.

The weekenders' cottage was very ancient, built before the Civil War, before the departure of the *Mayflower*, perhaps even before the last of the Tudors. Rushworth's was newer, though still old, belonging, Wexford decided, to the same period as that of Saltram House and its lodge, about 1750. In Burden's absence he was spending much of his time in Mill Lane, viewing the three little houses, sometimes entering their gardens and walking thoughtfully around them.

Once he walked from Rushworth's cottage to the fountains at Saltram House and back again, timing himself. It took him half an hour. Then he did it again, pausing this time to play-act the lifting of the cistern slab and the insertion of a body. Forty minutes.

He drove to Sewingbury and saw the woman who had a date to meet Rushworth on that October afternoon and heard from her that she had been unable to keep the appointment. What of that other afternoon in February?

One evening he made his way to Fontaine Road in search of the Crantocks and on an impulse knocked first at number 61. He had nothing to say to Mrs Lawrence, no good news, but he was curious to see this forlorn woman people said was beautiful and he knew from past experience that his very presence, stolid and fatherly, could sometimes be a comfort. No one answered his knock and this time he sensed quite a different atmosphere from that he had felt outside Bishop's door. Nobody answered because there was nobody there to hear.

For some moments he stood thoughtfully in the quiet street, and then, discomfited now for personal reasons, he went next door to the Crantocks.

'If you wanted Gemma,' said Mrs Crantock, 'she's away, gone down to the South Coast for the weekend.'

'I really want to talk to you and your husband. About a man called Rushworth and your daughter.'

'Oh, that? Your inspector kindly saw her home. We *were* grateful. Mind you, there was nothing in it. I know they say Mr Rushworth chases the girls, but I expect that's just gossip, and they don't mean *little* girls. My daughter's only fourteen.'

Crantock came into the hall to see who had called. He recognised Wexford immediately and shook hands. 'As a matter of fact,' he said, 'Rushworth came round the next day to apologise. He said he'd only called out to Janet because he'd heard we'd got a piano we wanted to get rid of.' Crantock grinned and turned up his eyes. 'I told him *sell*, not get rid of, so, of course, he wasn't interested.'

'Silly of Janet, really,' said his wife, 'to have got so worked up.'

'I don't know.' Crantock had stopped smiling. 'We're all on edge, especially kids who are old enough to understand.' He looked deep into Wexford's eyes. 'And people with kids,' he added.

Wexford walked into Chiltern Avenue by way of the shrub-shadowed alley. There he had to use his torch and as he went he thought, not by any means for the first time, on his great good fortune in having been born a man, and a big man at that, instead of a woman. Only in daylight and fine weather could a woman have walked there without fear, without turning her head and feeling her heart-beats quicken. No wonder Janet Crantock had been frightened. And then he thought of John Lawrence whose youth had given him a woman's vulnerability and who would never grow up to be a man.

In the evenings when the tide was far out they walked along the sands in the dark or sat on the rocks at the entrance to a cave they had found. The rain held off, but it was November and cold at night. The first time they went there they wore thick coats but the heavy clothing separated and isolated them, so after that Burden brought the car rug. They cocooned themselves in it, their bodies pressed together, their hands tightly clasped, the thick woollen folds enclosing them and keeping out the salty sea wind. When he was alone with her in the darkness on the seashore he was very happy.

Even at this time of the year Eastbourne would be crowded and she was afraid of people. So they avoided the big resort and even the next village, Chine Warren. Gemma had visited the place before and wanted to walk there, but Burden prevented her. It was from there, he believed, that the children came. He tried all the time to keep children out of her sight. Sometimes, pitying her for her sorrow yet jealous of the cause of it, he found himself wishing a modern Pied Piper would come and whistle away all the little children of Sussex so that they might not be there to laugh and play and torment her and deprive him of joy.

'Would it be a quick death, the sea?' she said.

He shivered, watching the running tide. 'I don't know. Nobody who has died in it has ever been able to tell us.'

'I think it would be quick.' Her voice was a child's, gravely considering. 'Cold and clean and quick.'

In the afternoons Burden made love to her – he had never been more conscious of and more satisfied with his manhood than when he saw how his love comforted her – and afterwards, while she slept, he walked down to the shore or over the cliff to Chine Warren. There was still a little warmth left in the sunshine and the children came to build sandcastles. He had discovered that they were not a family, the couple not husband and wife, but that four of the children belonged to the man and the other one to the woman. How teasing and deceptive were first impressions! He looked back now with self-disgust on his romancing, his sentimental notion that this pair, known to each other perhaps only by sight, had an idyllic marriage. Illusion and disillusion, he reflected, what life is and what we think it is. Why, from this distance he couldn't even tell if the solitary child were a boy or a girl, for it was capped and trousered and booted like all the children.

The woman kept stooping down to collect shells and once she stumbled. When she stood up again he noticed that she dragged her leg and he wondered if he should go down the seaweedy steps and cross the sands to offer her his help. But perhaps that would mean bringing her back to the hotel while he fetched his car, and the sound of the child's voice would awaken Gemma . . .

They rounded the foot of the cliff, going towards Chine Warren. Receding fast, the tide seemed to be drawing the sea back into the heart of the red sunset, a November sunset which is the most lovely of the whole year.

Now the great wide sweep of beach was deserted, but its young visitors had left evidence behind them. As sure as he could be that he was unobserved, Burden walked down the steps, pretending to stroll casually. The two sandcastles stood proudly erect, as if confident of their endurance until the sea conquered them, rushing them away when it returned at midnight. He hesitated, the rational sensible man momentarily intervening, and then he kicked over their turrets and stamped on their battlements until the sand they were made of was as flat as the surrounding shore.

Once more the beach belonged to him and Gemma. John or his deputies, his representatives, should not take her away from him. He was a man and any day a match for a lost dead child.

Rushworth came to the door in his duffel coat.

'Oh, it's you,' he said. 'I was just going to take the dog out.'

'Postpone it for half an hour, will you?'

Not very willingly, Rushworth took off his coat, hung up the lead and led Wexford into a living room amid the cries of the disappointed terrier. Two teenage children were watching television, a girl of about eight sat at the table doing a jigsaw puzzle, and on the floor, lying on his stomach, was the most junior member of the family, Andrew, who had been John Lawrence's friend.

'I'd like to talk to you alone,' said Wexford.

It was a biggish house with what Rushworth, in one of his house agent's blurbs, would perhaps have described as three reception rooms. That evening none was fit for the reception of anyone except possibly a second-hand-furniture dealer. The Rushworths were apparently acquisitive creatures, snappers up of anything they could get for nothing, and Wexford, seating himself in this morning room-cum-study-cum-library, observed a set of Dickens he had surely last seen in Pomfret Grange before the Rogerses sold out and two stone urns whose design seemed very much in keeping with the other garden ornaments of Saltram House.

'I've racked my brains and I can't tell you another thing about the fellows in that search party.'

'I've not come about that,' said Wexford. 'Did you pinch those urns from Saltram House?'

' "Pinch" is a bit strong,' said Rushworth, turning red. 'They were lying about and no one wanted them.'

'You had your eye on one of the statues too, didn't you?'

'What's this got to do with John Lawrence?'

Wexford shrugged. 'I don't know. It might have something to do with Stella Rivers. To put it in a nutshell, I'm here to know where you were and what you were doing on February 25th.'

'How can I remember that far back? I know what it is, it's Margaret Fenn putting you up to all this. Just because I complained my girl wasn't doing as well as she should at her riding lessons.' Rushworth opened the door and shouted, 'Eileen!'

When she wasn't at work, typing specifications for her husband, Mrs Rushworth managed this sprawling household single-handed and it showed. She looked dowdy and harassed and her skirt hem was coming down at the back. Perhaps there was some foundation in the gossip that her husband chased the girls.

'Where were you that Thursday?' she enquired of him. 'In the office, I suppose. I know where I was. I got it all sorted out in my mind when there was all that fuss about Stella Rivers being missing. It was half-term and I'd taken Andrew to work with me. He came with me in the car to pick Linda up from Equita and – oh, yes – Paul – that's my eldest – he came too and dropped off at the cottage. There was a little table there we thought we might as well have here. But we didn't see Stella. I didn't even know her by sight.'

'Your husband was in the office when you got back?'

'Oh, yes. He waited for me to get back before he went out in the car.'

'What kind of a car, Mr Rushworth?'

'Jaguar. Maroon colour. Your people have already been all over my car on account of its being a Jaguar and a kind of red colour. Look, we didn't know Stella Rivers. As far as we know, we'd never even seen her. Until she disappeared I'd only heard of her through Margaret always going on about how marvellous she was on a horse.'

Wexford favoured them with a hard, unsympathetic stare. He was thinking deeply, fitting in puzzle pieces, casting aside irrelevancies.

'You,' he said to Rushworth, 'were at work when Stella disappeared. When John disappeared you were in Sewingbury waiting for a client who never turned up.' He turned to Mrs Rushworth. 'You were at work when John disappeared. When Stella vanished you were driving back from Equita along Mill Lane. Did you pass anyone?'

'Nobody,' said Mrs Rushworth firmly. 'Paul was still in the cottage. I know that – he'd put a light on –

and, well, I'd better be quite frank with you. He'd actually been in Margaret Fenn's place too. I'm sure he had because the front door was open, just a little bit ajar. I know he shouldn't, though she does always leave her back door unlocked and when he was little she used to say he could let himself in and see her whenever he liked. Of course, it's different now he's so old, and I've told him again and again ...'

'Never mind,' Wexford said suddenly. 'It doesn't matter.'

'If you wanted to talk to Paul ... I mean, if it would clear the air ... ?'

'I don't want to see him.' Wexford got up abruptly. He didn't want to see anyone at all. He knew the answer. It had begun to come to him when Rushworth called out to his wife and now nothing remained but to sit down somewhere in utter silence and work it all out.

Chapter 21

'Our last day,' said Burden. 'Where would you like to go? Shall we have a quiet drive somewhere and lunch in a pub?'

'I don't mind. Anything you say.' She took his hand, held it against her face for a moment, and burst out, as if she had kept the words inside her, burning and corroding for many hours, 'I've got a dreadful feeling, a sort of premonition, that when we get back we'll hear that they've found him.'

'John?'

'And – and the man who killed him,' she whispered.

'They'd let us know.'

'They don't know where we are, Mike. No one knows.'

Slowly and evenly he said, 'It will be better for you when you know it for sure. Terrible pain is better than terrible anxiety.' But was it? Was it better for him to know that Jean was dead than to fear she would die? Terrible anxiety always contains terrible hope. 'Better for you,' he said firmly. 'And then, when it's behind you, you can start your new life.'

'Let's go,' she said. 'Let's go out.'

It was Saturday and still no one had been charged.

'There's an uneasy sort of lull about this place,' said Harry Wild to Camb. 'Quite a contrast to all the activity of yore.'

'My what?' said Camb.

'Your nothing. *Yore*. Days gone by.'

'No good asking me. Nobody ever tells me anything.'

'Life,' said Wild, 'is passing us by, old man. Trouble with us is we've not been ambitious. We've been content to sport with Amaryllis in the shade.'

Camb looked shocked. 'Speak for yourself,' he said, and then, softening, 'Shall I see if there's any tea going?'

Late in the afternoon Dr Crocker breezed into Wexford's office. 'Very quiet, aren't we? I hope that means you'll be free for golf in the morning.'

'Don't feel like golf,' said Wexford. 'Can't, anyway.'

'Surely you're not going to Colchester *again*?'

'I've been. I went this morning. Scott's dead.'

The doctor pranced over to the window and opened it. 'You need some fresh air in here. Who's Scott?'

'You ought to know. He was your patient. He had a stroke and now he's had another. Want to hear about it?'

'Why would I? People are always having strokes. I've just come from an old boy down in Charteris Road who's had one. Why would I want to know about this Scott?' He came closer to Wexford and bent critically over him. 'Reg?' he said. 'Are you all right? My God, I'm more concerned that you *shouldn't* have one. You look rotten.'

'It *is* rotten. But not for me. For me it's just a problem.' Wexford got up suddenly. 'Let's go down the Olive.'

There was no one else in the lush, rather over-decorated cocktail bar.

'I'd like a double Scotch.'

'And you shall have one,' said Crocker. 'For once I'll go so far as to prescribe it.'

Briefly Wexford thought of that other humbler hostelry where Monkey and Mr Casaubon had both disgusted him and whetted his appetite. He pushed them from his mind as the doctor returned with their drinks.

'Thanks. I wish your tablets came in such a palatable form. Cheers.'

'Good health,' said Crocker meaningfully.

Wexford leaned back against the red-velvet upholstery of the settle. 'All the time,' he began, 'I thought it must be Swan, although there didn't seem to be any motive. And then, when I got all that stuff from Monkey and Mr Casaubon and the more accurate stuff about the inquest, I thought I could see a motive, simply that Swan got rid of people who got in his way. That would imply madness, of course. So what? The world is full of ordinary people with lunacy underlying their ordinariness. Look at Bishop.'

'What inquest?' Crocker asked.

Wexford explained. 'But I was looking at it from the wrong way round,' he said, 'and it took me a long time to look at it the right way.'

'Let's have the right way, then.'

'First things first. When a child disappears one of the first things we consider is that he or she was picked up by a car. Another disservice done to the world by the inventor of the internal-combustion engine, or did kids once get abducted in carriages? But I mustn't digress. Now we knew it was very unlikely Stella accepted a lift in a car because she had *already refused the lift we knew had been offered to her.* Therefore it was probable that she was either met and taken somewhere by someone she knew, such as her mother, her stepfather or Mrs Fenn, or that she went into one of the houses in Mill Lane.'

The doctor sipped his sherry austerely. 'There are only three,' he said.

'Four, if you count Saltram House. Swan had no real alibi. He could have ridden to Mill Lane, taken Stella into the grounds of Saltram House on some pretext, and killed her. Mrs Swan had no alibi. Contrary to my former belief, she *can* drive. She could have driven to Mill Lane. Monstrous as it is to think of a woman killing her own child, I had to consider Rosalind Swan. She worships her husband obsessively. Was it possible, in her mind, that Stella, who also worshipped Swan – little girls seem to – would in a few years' time grow into a rival?'

'And Mrs Fenn?'

'Tidying up at Equita, she *said*. We had only her word for it. But even my inventive mind, twisted mind, if you like, couldn't see a motive there. Finally, I dismissed all those theories and considered the four houses.' Wexford lowered his voice slightly as a man and a girl entered the bar. 'Stella left Equita at twenty-five minutes to five. The first house she passed was the weekenders' cottage, but it was a Thursday and the cottage was empty. Besides, it dated from about 1550.'

Crocker looked astonished. 'What's that got to do with it?'

'You'll see in a minute. She went on and it began to rain. At twenty to five the Forby bank manager stopped and offered her a lift. She refused. For once it would have been wise for a child to have accepted a lift from a strange man.' The newcomers had found seats by a far window and Wexford resumed his normal voice. 'The next cottage she came to is owned, though not occupied, by a man called Robert Rushworth who lives in Chiltern Avenue. Now

Rushworth interested me very much. He knew John Lawrence, he wears a duffel coat, he has been suspected, perhaps with foundation, perhaps not, of molesting a child. His wife, though warned by Mrs Mitchell that a man had been seen observing the children in the swings field, did not inform the police. On the afternoon of February 25th he could have been in Mill Lane. His wife and his eldest son certainly were. All the family were in the habit of going into their cottage just when it pleased them – and Mrs Rushworth's Christian name is Eileen.'

The doctor stared blankly. 'I don't follow any of this. So what if her name is Eileen?'

'Last Sunday,' Wexford went on, 'I went down to Colchester to see Mr and Mrs Scott, the parents of Bridget Scott. At that time I had no suspicion at all of Rushworth. I simply had a forlorn hope that one or both of the Scotts might be able to give me a little more insight into the character of Ivor Swan. But Scott, as you know, is – was, I should say – a very sick man.'

'*I* should know?'

'Of course you should know,' said Wexford severely. 'Really, you're very slow.' Having for once the whip hand over his friend was cheering Wexford up. It was a pleasant change to see Crocker at a disadvantage. 'I was afraid to question Scott. I was uncertain what might be the effect of alarming him. Besides, for my purposes, it seemed adequate to work on his wife. She told me nothing which increased my knowledge of Swan, but, unwittingly, she gave me four pieces of information that helped me solve this case.' He cleared his throat. 'Firstly, she told me that she and her husband had been in the habit of staying for holidays with a relative who lived near Kingsmarkham and that they had stayed there for the last time last winter; secondly, that the relative lived in an eighteenth-century house; thirdly, that in March, *a fortnight after he had been taken ill*, her husband was a very sick man indeed; fourthly, that the relative's name was Eileen. Now, sometime in March might well be a fortnight after February 25th.' He paused significantly for all this to sink in.

The doctor put his head on one side. At last he said, 'I'm beginning to get this clear. My God, you'd hardly believe it, but people are a funny lot. It was with the Rushworths that the Scotts were staying, Eileen Rushworth was the relative. Scott somehow induced Rushworth to make away with Stella in revenge for what Swan had done to his own child. Offered him money, maybe. What a ghastly thing!'

Wexford sighed. It was at times like this that he most missed Burden, or Burden as he used to be. 'I think we'll have another drink,' he said. 'My round.'

'You don't have to act as if I was a complete fool,' said the doctor huffily. 'I'm not trained to make this sort of diagnosis.' As Wexford got up, he snapped vindictively, 'Orange juice for you, that's an order.'

With a glass of lager, not orange juice, before him, Wexford said, 'You're worse than Dr Watson, you are. And while we're on the subject, though I've the utmost respect for Sir Arthur, life isn't much like Sherlock Holmes stories and I don't believe it ever was. People don't nurse revenge for years and years nor do they find it possible to bribe more or less respectable estate agents, fathers of families, into doing murder for them.'

'But you said,' Crocker retorted, 'that the Scotts were staying with the Rushworths in their cottage.'

'No, I didn't. Use your head. How could they have been staying in a house that was let to another tenant? All that made me consider that house was that it dated from about 1750. I had forgotten all about the Scotts' relative being called Eileen—it was only mentioned in passing—but when I heard Rushworth call his wife Eileen, then I knew. After that I only had to do some simple checking.'

'I am so entirely in the dark,' said Crocker, 'that I don't know what to say.'

For a moment Wexford savoured the experience of seeing the doctor at a loss. Then he said, 'Eileen is a fairly common name. Why should Mrs Rushworth be its only possessor in the district? At that point I remembered that someone else had told me she had two Christian names, was called by the first by half people she knew and by the second by the rest. I didn't care to enquire of her personally. I checked with Somerset House. And there I found that Mrs Margaret *Eileen* Fenn was the daughter of one James Collins and his wife Eileen Collins, *née* Scott.

'Beyond a doubt, it was with Mrs Fenn that the Scotts had been staying in February, at Saltram Lodge which is also an eighteenth-century house. They stayed with her, and on February 25th, after saying good-bye to Mrs Fenn before she left for work at Equita, they too left by taxi to catch the three-forty-five train from Stowerton to Victoria.'

Crocker held up his hand to halt Wexford. 'I remember now. Of course I do. It was poor old Scott who had that stroke on the platform. I happened to be in the station, booking a seat, and they sent for me. But it wasn't at a quarter to four, Reg. More like six o'clock.'

'Exactly. Mr and Mrs Scott didn't catch the three-forty-five. When they got to the station Scott realised they had left one of their suitcases behind at Mrs Fenn's. You ought to know that. It was you who told me.'

'So I did.'

'Scott was a strong, hale man at that time. Or so he

thought. There wasn't a taxi about—mind you I'm guessing this bit—and he decided to walk back to Mill Lane. It took him about three quarters of an hour. But that wouldn't have worried him. There wasn't another train that stopped at Stowerton till six-twenty-six. He had no difficulty in getting into the house, for Mrs Fenn always leaves her back door unlocked. Perhaps he made himself a cup of tea, perhaps he merely rested. We shall never know. We must now go back to Stella Rivers.'

'She called at Saltram Lodge?'

'Of course. It was the obvious place. She too knew about the unlocked back door and that Mrs Fenn, her friend and teacher, had a phone. It was raining, it was growing dark. She went into the kitchen and immediately encountered Scott.'

'And Scott recognised her?'

'As Stella Rivers. Not knowing what her correct name was, Mrs Fenn spoke of her sometimes as Rivers, sometimes as Swan. And she would have spoken of her to Scott, her uncle, and pointed her out, for she was proud of Stella.

'As soon as she had got over her surprise at finding someone in the house, Stella must have asked to use the phone. What words did she use? Something like this, I fancy: "I'd like to phone my father" – she referred to Swan as her father – "Mr Swan of Hall Farm. When he comes, we'll drive you back to Stowerton." Now Scott hated the very name of Swan. He had never forgotten and he had always dreaded a chance meeting with him. He must then have checked with Stella that it was Ivor Swan to whom she referred and then he realised that here he was, face to face with the daughter – or so he thought – of the man who had left his own child to die when she was at the same age as this child.'

Chapter 22

When they came back to Eastover from their drive the sun had set, leaving long fiery streaks to split the purple clouds and stain the sea with coppery gold. Burden pulled the car into an empty parking place on the cliff-top and they sat in silence, looking at the sea and the sky and at a solitary trawler, a little moving smudge on the horizon.

Gemma had withdrawn more and more into herself as the days had passed by and sometimes Burden felt that it was a shadow who walked with him, went out with him in the car and lay beside him at night. She hardly spoke. It was as if she had become bereavement incarnate or, worse than that, a dying woman. He knew she wanted to die, although she had not directly told him so. The night before he had found her lying in the bath in water that had grown cold, her eyes closed and her head slipping down into the water, and, although she denied it, he knew she had taken sleeping tablets half an hour before. And today, while they were on the downs, he had only just succeeded in preventing her from crossing the road in the path of an oncoming car.

Tomorrow they must go home. Within a month they would be married and before that he would have to apply for a transfer to one of the Metropolitan divisions. That meant finding new schools for the children, a new house. What kind of a house would he find in London for the price he would get for his

Sussex bungalow? But it must be done. The mean, indefensible thought that at any rate he would only have two children to support and not three, that in her state his wife would not vex him with riotous parties or fill the place with her friends, brought a blush of shame to his face.

He glanced tentatively at Gemma, but she was staring out to sea. Then he too followed her gaze and saw that the beach was no longer deserted. Quickly he started the car, reversed across the turf and turned towards the road that led inland. He didn't look at her again, but he knew that she was weeping, the tears falling unchecked down those thin pale cheeks.

'Scott's first thought,' said Wexford after a pause, 'was probably just to leave her to it, flee back the way he had come away from these Swans. They say murder victims – but this wasn't really murder – are self-selected. Did Stella point out that it was pouring with rain, that he could have a lift? Did she say, "I'll just phone. He'll be here in a quarter of an hour"? Scott remembered it all then. He had never forgotten it. He must stop her using that phone and he got hold of her. No doubt she cried out. How he must have hated her, thinking he knew what she meant to the man he hated. I think it was this which gave him strength and made him hold her too tight, press his strong old hands too hard about her neck ...'

The doctor said nothing, only staring the more intently at Wexford.

'It takes half an hour to walk from Rushworth's cottage to Saltram House and back again,' the chief inspector resumed. 'Less than that from Saltram Lodge. And Scott would have known about the fountains and the cisterns. He would have been interested in them. He was a plumbing engineer. He carried the dead child up to the Italian garden and put her in the cistern. Then he went back to the lodge and fetched his case. A passing motorist gave him a lift back to Stowerton. We may imagine what sort of a state he was in.'

'We know,' said Crocker quietly, 'he had a stroke.'

'Mrs Fenn knew nothing of it, nor did his wife. Last Wednesday he had another stroke and that killed him. I think – I'm afraid – that it was seeing me and guessing what I was that really killed him. His wife didn't understand the words he spoke to her before he died. She thought he was wandering in his mind. She told me what they were. "I held her too tight. I thought of my Bridget."'

'But what the hell are you going to do? You can't charge a dead man.'

'That's in Griswold's hands,' said Wexford. 'Some non-committal paragraph for the press, I suppose. The Swans have been told and Swan's uncle, Group Captain what's-his-name. Not that he'll need to pay up. We shan't be arresting anyone.'

The doctor looked thoughtful. 'You haven't said a word about John Lawrence.'

'Because I haven't a word to say,' said Wexford.

Their hotel had no rear entrance, so it was necessary to come at last out of the hinterland on to Eastover's little esplanade. Burden had been hoping with all his heart that by now, in the dusk, the beach would be empty of children, but the pair who had brought tears to Gemma's eyes were still there, the child that ran up and down at the water's edge and the woman who walked with him, trailing from one hand a long ribbon of seaweed. But for the slight limp, Burden wouldn't have recognised her, in her trousers and hooded coat, as the woman he had seen before, or indeed as a woman at all. Inanely, he tried to direct

Gemma's gaze inland towards a cottage she had seen a dozen times before.

She obeyed him – she was always acquiescent, anxious to please – but no sooner had she looked than she turned again to face the sea. Her arm was touching his and he felt her shiver.

'Stop the car,' she said.

'But there's nothing to see . . .'

'Stop the car!'

She never commanded. He had never heard her speak like that before. 'What, here?' he said. 'Let's get back. You'll only get cold.'

'Please stop the car, Mike.'

He couldn't blind her, shelter her, for ever. He parked the car behind a red Jaguar that was the only other vehicle on the sea front. Before he had switched off the ignition she had got the door open, slammed it behind her and was off down the steps.

It was absurd to remember what she had said about the sea, about a quick death, but he remembered it. He jumped from the car and followed her, striding at first, then running. Her bright hair, sunset red, streamed behind her. Their footsteps made a hard slapping sound on the sand and the woman turned to face them, standing stock still, the streamer of seaweed in her hand whirling suddenly in the wind like a dancer's scarf.

'Gemma! Gemma!' Burden called, but the wind took his words or else she was determined not to hear them. She seemed bent only on reaching the sea which curled and creamed at the child's feet. And now the child, who had been splashing in shallow foam to the top of his boots, also turned to stare, as children will when adults behave alarmingly.

She was going to throw herself into the sea. Ignoring the woman, Burden pounded after her and then he stopped suddenly as if, unseeing, he had flung himself against a solid wall. He was no more than ten feet from her. Wide-eyed, the child approached her. Without seeming to slacken her speed at all, without hesitation, she ran into the water and, in the water, fell on to her knees.

The little waves flowed over her feet, her legs, her dress. He saw it seep up, drenching her to the waist. He heard her cry out – miles away, he thought, that cry could have been heard – but he could not tell whether it brought him happiness or grief.

'John, John, my John!'

She threw out her arms and the child went into them. Still kneeling in the water, she held him in a close embrace, her mouth pressed hard against his bright golden hair.

Burden and the woman looked at each other without speaking. He knew at once who she was. That face had looked at him before from his daughter's scrapbook. But it was very ravaged now and very aged, the black hair under the hood chopped off raggedly as if, with the ruin of her career, she had submitted to and accelerated the ruin of her looks.

Her hands were tiny. It seemed that she collected specimens, botanical and marine, but now she dropped the ribbon of weed. Close to, Burden thought, no one could mistake her for a man – but at a distance? It occurred to him that from far away even a middle-aged woman might look like a youth if she were slight and had the litheness of a dancer.

What more natural than that she should want John, the child of her old lover who had never been able to give her a child? And she had been ill, mentally ill, he remembered. John would have gone with her, quite willingly, no doubt, recalling her as his father's friend, persuaded perhaps that his mother had temporarily committed him to her care.

And to the seaside. What child doesn't want to go to the seaside?

But something would happen now. As soon as she got over her first joy, Gemma would tear this woman to pieces. It wasn't as if this was the first outrage Leonie West had committed against her. Hadn't she, when Gemma was only a few months married, virtually stolen her husband from her? And now, a more monstrous iniquity, she had stolen her child.

He watched her rise slowly out of the water and, still keeping hold of John's hand, begin to cross the strip of sand that separated her from Leonie West. The dancer stood her ground, but she lifted her head with a kind of pathetic boldness and clenched the little hands Mrs Mitchell had seen picking leaves. Burden took a step forward and found his lost voice.

'Now listen, Gemma. The best thing is . . .'

What had he meant to say? That the best thing was for them all to keep calm, to discuss it rationally? He stared. Never would he have believed – had he ever really known her? – that she would do this, the best thing of all, the thing that, in his estimation, almost made a saint of her.

Her dress was soaked. Oddly, Burden thought of a picture he had once seen, an artist's impression of the sea giving up its dead. With a soft, tender glance at the boy, she dropped his hand and lifted Leonie West's instead. Speechless, the other woman looked at her, and then Gemma, hesitating only for a moment, took her into her arms.

Chapter 23

'It would never have worked, Mike. You know that as well as I do. I'm not conventional enough for you, not respectable, not good enough if you like.'

'I think you are too good for me,' said Burden.

'I did say once that John – if John was ever found I wouldn't marry you. I don't think you quite understood. It will be better for both of us if I do what we're planning and go and live with Leonie. She's so lonely, Mike, and I'm so dreadfully sorry for her. That way I can have London and my friends and she can have a share in John.'

They were sitting in the lounge of the hotel where they had stayed together. Burden thought she had never been so beautiful, her white skin glowing from her inner joy, her hair mantling her shoulders. And never so alien in the golden dress Leonie West had lent her because her own was ruined by salt water. Her face was sweeter and gentler than ever.

'But I love you,' he said.

'Dear Mike, are you sure you don't just love going to bed with me? Does that shock you?'

It did, but not so much, not nearly so much, as once it would have. She had taught him a multitude of things. She had given him his sentimental education.

'We can still be loving friends,' she said. 'You can come to me at Leonie's. You can meet all my friends.

We can sometimes go away together and I'll be so different now I am happy. You'll see.'

He did see. He almost shuddered. Go to her with her child there? Explain somehow to his own children that he had a – a mistress?

'It would never work,' he said clearly and firmly. 'I can see it wouldn't.'

She looked at him very tenderly. '"You'll court more women",' she said, half-singing, '"and I'll couch with more men ..."'

He knew his Shakespeare no better than he knew his Proust. They went out on to the sea front where Leonie West was waiting with John in her red car.

'Come and say hallo to him,' said Gemma.

But Burden shook his head. No doubt it was better this way, no doubt he would one day be grateful to the child who had robbed him of his happiness and his love. But not now, not yet. One does not say hallo to an enemy and a thief.

She lingered under the esplanade lights, turning towards him and then back again to where John was. Torn two ways, they called it, he thought, but there was little doubt who had won this tug of war. That light in her eyes had never been there when they looked at him, was not there now, died as soon as she ceased to face the car. She was parting from him not with regret, not with pain, but with *politeness*.

Always considerate, always ready to respect another person's conventions – for they were in a public place and people were passing – she held out her hand to him. He took it, and then, no longer caring for those passers-by, forgetting his cherished respectability, he pulled her to him there in the open street and kissed her for the last time.

When the red car had gone he leant on the rail and looked at the sea and knew that it was better this

225

way, knew too, because he had been through something like it before, that he would not go on wanting
to die.

Wexford was genial and sly and almost godlike.
'What a fortunate coincidence that you happened to
be in Eastbourne with Miss Woodville and happened
to go to Eastover and happened – Good God, what a
lot of happenings! – to meet Mrs Lawrence.' He
added more gravely, 'On the whole, you have done
well, Mike.'

Burden said nothing. He didn't think it necessary
to point out that it was Gemma who had found the
lost boy and not he.

Quietly, Wexford closed the door of his office and
for a few moments regarded Burden in silence. Then
he said, 'But I don't much care for coincidences or for
melodrama, come to that. I don't think they're in
your line, do you?'

'Perhaps not, sir.'

'Are you going to go on doing well, Mike? I have
to ask, I have to know. I have to know where to find
you when you're needed and, when I find you, that
you'll be your old self. Are you going to come back
and work with me and – well, to put it bluntly – pull
yourself together?'

Burden said slowly, remembering what he had
once said to Gemma, 'Work is the best thing, isn't it?'

'I think it is.'

'But it has to be real work, heart and soul in it, not
just coming in every day more or less automatically
and hoping everyone will admire you for being such
a martyr to duty. I've thought about it a lot, sir, I've
decided to count my blessings and . . .'

'That's fine,' Wexford cut off his words. 'Don't be
too sanctimonious about it, though, will you? That's
hard to live with. I can see you've changed and I'm

not going to enquire too closely into who or what has brought that change about. One good thing, I'm pretty sure I'm going to find that the quality of your mercy is a lot less strained than it used to be. And now let's go home.'

Half-way down the lift, he went on, 'You say Mrs Lawrence doesn't want this woman charged? That's all very well, but what about all our work, all the expenditure? Griswold will do his nut. He may insist on charging her. But if she's really a bit cuckoo . . . My God, one culprit dead and the other crazy!'

The lift opened, and there, inevitably, was Harry Wild.

'I have nothing for you,' Wexford said coldly.

'Nothing for me!' Wild said wrathfully to Camb. 'I know for a fact that . . .'

'There was quite a to-do in Pump Lane,' said Camb, opening his book. 'One police van and two fire engines arrived at five p.m. yesterday – Sunday, that was – to remove a cat from an elm tree . . .' Wild's infuriated glance cut him short. He cleared his throat and said soothingly, 'Let's see if there's any tea going.'

On the station forecourt Wexford said, 'I nearly forgot to tell you. Swan's uncle's going to pay out the reward.'

Burden stared. 'But it was offered for information leading to an arrest.'

'No, it wasn't. That's what I thought till I checked. It was offered for information leading to a *discovery*. The Group Captain's a just man, and not the sort of just man I mean when I talk about his nephew. That's two thousand smackers for Charly Catch, or would be if he wasn't a very sick old man.' Absently, Wexford felt in his pocket for his blood-pressure tablets. 'When Crocker arrived in Charteris Road last night there was a solicitor at his bedside and Monkey

227

keeping well in the background because a beneficiary can't also be a witness. I must work out sometime,' said the chief inspector, 'just how many king-size fags you could buy with all that boodle.'

'Are you all right, Mike?' said Grace. 'I mean, are you feeling all right? You've been home every night this week on the dot of six.'

Burden smiled. 'Let's say I've come to my senses. I find it a bit hard to put my feelings into words, but I suppose I've just realised how lucky I am to have my kids and what hell it would be to lose them.'

She didn't answer but went to the window and drew the curtains to shut out the night. With her back to him she said abruptly, 'I'm not going in for that nursing-home thing.'

'Now, look here . . .' He got up, went over to her and took her almost roughly by the arm. 'You're not to sacrifice yourself on my account. I won't have it.'

'My dear Mike!' Suddenly he saw that she was not troubled or conscience-stricken but happy. 'I'm not sacrificing myself. I . . .' She hesitated, remembering perhaps how in the past he would never talk to her, never speak of anything but the most mundane household arrangements.

'Tell me,' he said with a new fierce intensity.

She looked astonished. 'Well . . . Well, I met a man while we were in Eastbourne, a man I used to know years ago. I – I was in love with him. We quarrelled . . . Oh, it was so silly! And now – now he wants to begin again and come here and take me out and – and I think, Mike, I think . . .' She stopped and then said with the cold defiance he had taught her, 'You wouldn't be interested.'

'Oh, Grace,' he said, 'if only you knew!'

She was staring at him now as if he were a

stranger, but a stranger she had begun to like and would want to know better. 'Knew what?' she said.

For a moment he didn't answer. He was thinking that if only he had the sense to realise it now, he had found his listener, his one friend who would understand, because of her experience of many sides of life, the simple daily joy his marriage had been to him and understand too the blaze of glory, the little summer, he had found with Gemma.

'I want to talk too,' he said. 'I've got to tell someone. If I listen to you, will you listen to me?'

She nodded wonderingly. He thought how pretty she was, how like Jean, and that, because she was like Jean, she would make a wonderful wife for this man who loved her. And because there could now be no misunderstanding between them he hugged her briefly and rested his cheek against hers.

He felt her happiness in the warmth with which she returned the hug and it infected him, almost making him happy too. Would it last? Was he finally finding a sense of proportion? He couldn't tell, not yet. But his own boy and girl were safe, sleeping behind those closed doors, he could work again, and he had a friend who was waiting now, still tightly clasping his hands, to hear what he had to tell.

Grace led him back to the fire, sat down beside him and said, as if already she half understood, 'It'll be all right, Mike.' She leaned towards him, her face serious and intent. 'Let's talk,' she said.

RUTH RENDELL

SOME LIE AND SOME DIE

arrow books

To my son, Simon Rendell, who goes to festivals, and my cousin, Michael Richards, who wrote the song, this book is dedicated with love and gratitude.

Let-me-believe

I don't miss her smile or the flowers,
I don't eclipse distance or hours,
I don't kiss the wind or the showers,
I miss her, can't kiss her with lips that were ours.

So come by, come nigh,
  come try and tell why
  some sigh, some cry,
  some lie and some die.

Remember me and my life-without-life,
Come once more to be my wife,
Come today before I grieve,
Enter the web of let-me-believe.

So come by, come nigh, etc.

The house will be as if it were ours,
She'll fill the void with love-scented flowers,
She'll sit with me in the fast-fading light,
Then my dream will sift into night.

So come by, come nigh, etc.

Now she's gone in the harsh light of day,
When she'll return the night would not say,
And I am left to vision the time
When once more she'll come and be mine.

So come by, come nigh,
  come try and tell why
  some sigh, some cry,
  some lie and some die.

(Zeno Vedast's song from the 'Let-me-believe' L.P.
and the 'Sundays Album', issued by Galaphone Ltd
and obtainable from good record shops everywhere.)

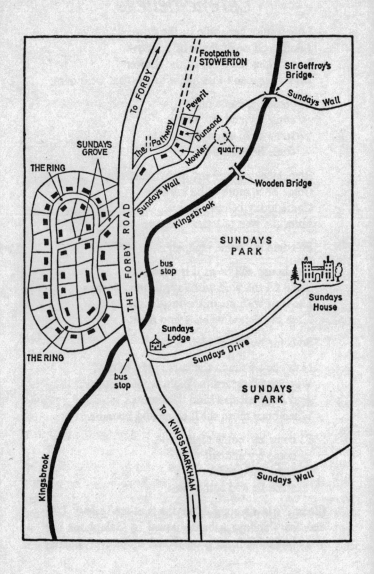

1

'But why here? Why do they have to come here? There must be thousands of places all over this country where they could go without doing anyone any harm. The Highlands for instance. Dartmoor. I don't see why they have to come here.'

Detective Inspector Michael Burden had made these remarks, or remarks very much like them, every day for the past month. But this time his voice held a note which had not been there before, a note of bitter bewilderment. The prospect had been bad enough. The reality was now unreeling itself some thirty feet below him in Kingsmarkham High Street and he opened the window to get a better—or a more devastating —look.

'There must be thousands of them, all coming up from Station Road. And this is only a small percentage when you consider how many more will be using other means of transport. It's an invasion. God, there's a dirty-looking great big one coming now. You know what it reminds me of? That poem my Pat was doing at school. Something about a pied piper. If "pied" means what I think it does, that customer's pied all right. You should see his coat.'

The only other occupant of the room had so far made no reply to this tirade. He was a big, heavy man, the inspector's senior by two decades, being at that time of life when people hesitated to describe him as middle-aged and considered 'elderly' as the more apt epithet. His face had never been handsome. Age and a very nearly total loss of hair had not

9

improved its pouchy outlines, but an expression that was not so much easy-going as tolerant of everything but intolerance, redeemed it and made it almost attractive. He was sitting at his rosewood desk, trying to compose a directive on crime prevention, and now, giving an impatient shake of his head, he threw down his pen.

'Anyone not in the know,' said Chief Inspector Wexford, 'would think you were talking about rats.' He pushed back his chair and got up. 'A plague of rats,' he said. 'Why can't you expand your mind a bit? They're only a bunch of kids come to enjoy themselves.'

'You'll tell a different tale when we get car-burning and shop-lifting and decent citizens beaten up and—and Hell's Angels.'

'Maybe. Wait till the time comes. Here, let me have a look.'

Burden shifted grudgingly from his point of vantage and allowed Wexford a few inches of window. It was early afternoon of a perfect summer's day, June the tenth. The High Street was busy as it always was on a Friday, cars pulling into and out of parking places, women pushing prams. Striped shop awnings were down to protect shoppers from an almost Mediterranean sun, and outside the Dragon workmen sat on benches drinking beer. But it was not these people who had attracted Burden's attention. They watched the influx as avidly as he and in some cases with as much hostility.

They were pouring across the road towards the bus stop by the Baptist church, a stream of boys and girls with packs on their backs and transistors swinging from their hands. Cars, which had pulled up at the zebra crossing to let them pass, hooted in protest, but they were as ineffectual as the waves of the Red Sea against the Children of Israel. On they came, not thousands perhaps, but a couple of hundred, laughing and jostling each other, singing. One of them, a boy in a tee-shirt printed with the face of Che Guevara, poked out his tongue at an angry motorist and raised two fingers.

10

Mostly they wore jeans. Not long since they had been at school—some still were—and they had protested hotly at the enforced wearing of uniforms. And yet now they had their own, voluntarily assumed, the uniform of denims and shirts, long hair and, in some cases, bare feet. But there were those among them making a total bid for freedom from conventional clothes, the girl in red bikini top and dirty ankle-length satin skirt, her companion sweating but happy in black leather. Towering above the rest walked the boy Burden had particularly singled out. He was a magnificent tall Negro whose hair was a burnished black bush and who had covered his bronze body from neck to ankles in a black and white pony-skin coat.

'And that's only the beginning, sir,' said Burden when he thought Wexford had had time enough to take it all in. 'They'll be coming all night and all tomorrow. Why are you looking like that? As if you'd—well, lost something?'

'I have. My youth. I'd like to be one of them. I'd like to be swinging along out there, off to the pop festival. Wouldn't *you*?'

'No, frankly, I wouldn't. I'm sure I never would have. Those young people are going to cause a lot of trouble, make a hell of a noise and ruin the weekend for all those unfortunate citizens who live on the Sundays estate. Heaven help them, that's all I can say.' Like most people who make that remark, Burden had a lot more to say and said it. 'My parents brought me up to be considerate of the feelings of others and I'm very glad they did. A trip to the local hop on a Saturday night, maybe, and a few drinks, but to take over God knows how many acres of parkland just to indulge my tastes at the expense of others! I wouldn't have wanted it. I'd have thought I hadn't achieved enough to deserve it.'

Wexford made the noise the Victorians wrote as 'Pshaw!' 'Just because you're so bloody virtuous it doesn't mean there aren't going to be any more cakes and ale. I suppose you'll stop that boy of yours going up there?'

'I've told him he can go to Sundays tomorrow evening for two hours just to hear this Zeno Vedast, but he's got to be in by eleven. I'm not having him camp there. He's only just fifteen. Zeno Vedast! That's not the name his godfathers and godmothers gave him at his baptism, you can bet your life. Jim Bloggs, more like. He comes from round here, they say. Thank God he didn't stay. I don't understand this craze for pop music. Why can't John play classical records?'

'Like his dad, eh? Sit at home getting a kick out of Mahler? Oh, come off it, Mike.'

Burden said sulkily, 'Well, I admit pop music's not my style. None of this is.'

'Your scene, Mike, your scene. Let's get the jargon right. We're pigs and fuzz as it is. We don't have to be square as well. Anyway, I'm sick of being an onlooker. Shall we get up there?'

'What, now? We'll have to be there tomorrow when the fighting and the burning starts.'

'I'm going now. You do as you like. Just one thing, Mike. Remember the words of another Puritan—"Bethink ye, bethink ye, in the bowels of Christ, that ye may be mistaken." '

Where the Regency mansion now stands a house called Sundays has stood since the Norman Conquest. Why Sundays? No one knows. Probably the name has nothing to do with the Sabbath Day; probably—and this is the general belief—it derives from the name of the man who built the first house, Sir Geffroy Beauvoir de Saint Dieu.

Once the Sundays lands extended from Kingsmarkham to Forby and beyond, but gradually fields and woodlands were sold off, and now the house has only a small garden and a park of a few acres. In the eyes of the preservationists Sundays is irretrievably spoilt. Its tall cedars remain and its avenue of hornbeams, the overgrown quarry is still untouched, but the Italian garden is gone, Martin Silk, the present owner, grows mushrooms in the orangery, and the view is ruined by the newly built Sundays estate.

The Forby road skirts the park and bisects the estate. It is along here that the Forby bus runs four times a day, halting at the Sundays request stop which is outside the park gates. Wexford and Burden pulled in to a lay-by and watched the first of the young pilgrims tumble out of the two-thirty bus and hump their baggage over to the gates. These were open and on the lodge steps stood Martin Silk with half a dozen helpers ready to examine tickets. Wexford got out of the car and read the poster which was pasted over one of the gates: *The Sundays Scene, June 11th and 12th, Zeno Vadast, Betti Ho, The Verb To Be, Greatheart, The Acid, Emmanuel Ellerman.* As the busload went through and passed into the hornbeam avenue, he went up to Silk.

'Everything O.K., Mr Silk?'

Silk was a small man in late middle age with shoulder-length grey hair and the figure—at any rate, until you looked closely or saw him walk—of a boy of twenty. He was rich, eccentric, one of those people who cannot bear to relinquish their youth. 'Of course it's O.K.,' Silk said abruptly. He had no time for his own contemporaries. 'Everything will be fine if we're left alone.'

He stepped aside, turning on a big smile, to take tickets from half a dozen boys whose slogan-painted Dormobile, pink, orange and purple, had come to a stop by the lodge.

'Welcome, friends, to Sundays. Pitch your tents where you like. First come, first served. You can park the truck up by the house.'

Burden, who had joined them, watched the Dormobile career rather wildly up the avenue, music braying from its open windows.

'I hope you know what you're doing,' he said dourly. 'Beats me why you want to do it.'

'I want to do it, Inspector, because I love young people. I

love their music. They've been hounded out of the Isle of Wight. No one wants them. I do. This festival is going to cost thousands and a good deal of it will come out of my pocket. I've had to sell another bit of land to raise money and people can say what they like about that.'

Burden said hotly, 'The preservationists will have plenty to say, Mr Silk. The older residents don't want all this new building. Planning permission can be rescinded. you know.'

Seeing Silk's face grow red with anger, Wexford intervened. 'We all hope the festival's going to be a success. I know I do. I'm told Betti Ho's arriving in her own helicopter tomorrow afternoon. Is that a fact?' When Silk, somewhat appeased, nodded, he went on: 'We want to keep the Hell's Angels out and try to keep trouble down to a minimum. Above all, we don't want violence, bikes set on fire and so on, the kind of thing they had at Weeley. I want to address the crowd before the concert starts, so maybe you'll allow me the use of your platform tomorrow evening. Shall we say six?'

'I don't mind as long as you don't antagonise people.' Silk greeted a group of girls, beaming on them, complimenting them on their ankle-length, vaguely Victorian gowns, approving the guitars which they wore slung from their shoulders. They giggled. At him, rather than with him, Wexford thought privately, but the encounter had the effect of putting Silk in a better temper. When the girls had wandered off into the park he said quite graciously to the policemen, 'D'you want to have a look round?'

'If you please,' said Wexford.

The encampment was to be sited on the left-hand side of the avenue where, under the limes and the cedars, a small herd of Friesians usually grazed. The cattle had been removed to pasture behind the house and the first of the tents were already up. In the midst of the park a stage had been erected, faced by arc-lamps. Wexford, who generally deplored armoured

14

fences, was glad that Sundays park was enclosed by a spiked wall to keep what Burden called 'undesirable elements' out. At only one point was the wall broken and this was at the side of the quarry, a deep semicircular fissure in the chalk at the Forby end. The two policemen walked up to the house, stood on the terrace and surveyed the scene.

A mobile shop selling soft drinks, crisps and chocolate had already been parked in the avenue, and a queue of hungry youth had formed alongside it. The stronger-minded were staking claims to desirable sites and banging in tent pegs. Through the gates came a thin but steady stream of new arrivals, on foot, in cars and on motor-cycles. Wexford jerked his head in the direction of the quarry and walked down the steps.

The lucky ones—those who had taken a day off work or missed a college lecture—had got there in the morning and established their camps. A boy in a Moroccan burnous was frying sausages over a calor-gas burner while his friends sat cross-legged beside him, entertaining him vocally and on a guitar. The Kingsbrook flows through Sundays park, dipping under the Forby Road and meandering between willows and alders close to the wall. It had already become a bathing place. Several campers were splashing about in the water, the girls in bras and panties, the boys in the black scants that serve as underpants or swimming trunks. Crossing the little wooden bridge, Burden looked the other way. He kept his eyes so determinedly averted that he almost fell over a couple who lay embraced in the long grass. Wexford laughed.

' "And thou," ' he said, ' "what needest with thy tribe's black tents who hast the red pavilion of my heart?" There's going to be a lot of that going on, Mike, so you'd best get used to it. Letts'll have to put a couple of men on that quarry if we don't want gate-crashers.'

'I don't know,' said Burden. 'You couldn't get a motor-bike in that way.' He added viciously: 'Personally, I couldn't care less who gets in free to Silk's bloody festival as long as they don't make trouble.'

On the Sundays side the chalk slope fell away unwalled; on the other it was rather feebly protected by broken chestnut paling and barbed wire. Beyond the paling, beyond a narrow strip of grass, the gardens of three houses in The Pathway were visible. Each had a tall new fence with its own gate. Wexford looked down into the quarry. It was about twenty feet deep, its sides overgrown with brambles and honeysuckle and wild roses. The roses were in full bloom, thousands of flat shell-pink blossoms showing against the dark shrubby growth and the golden blaze of gorse. Here and there rose the slim silver trunks of birches. In the quarry depths was a little natural lawn of turf scattered with harebells. One of the flowers seemed to spiral up into the air, and then Wexford saw it was not a flower at all but a butterfly, a Chalkhill Blue, harebell-coloured, azure-winged.

'Pity they had to build those houses. It rather spoils things, doesn't it?'

Burden nodded. 'These days,' he said, 'I sometimes think you have to go about with your eyes half-closed or a permanent crick in your neck.'

'It'll still be lovely at night, though, especially if there's a moon. I'm looking forward to hearing Betti Ho. She sings those anti-pollution ballads, and if there's anything we do agree on, Mike, it's stopping polution. You'll like Miss Ho. I must admit I want to hear this Vedast bloke do his stuff, too.'

'I get enough of him at home,' said Burden gloomily. 'John has his sickly love stuff churning out night and day.'

They turned back and walked along under the willows. A boy in the river splashed Wexford, wetting his trouser legs, and Burden shouted angrily at him, but Wexford only laughed.

2

'On the whole, they're behaving themselves very well.'

This remark was delivered by Inspector Burden on a note of incredulous astonishment as he and Wexford stood (in the words of Keats) on a little rounded hill, surveying from this eminence the *jeunesse dorée* beneath. It was Saturday night, late evening rather, the sky an inverted bowl of soft violet-blue in which the moon hung like a pearl, surrounded by bright galaxies. The light from these stars was as intense as it could be, but still insufficient, and the platform on which their own stars performed was dazzlingly illuminated, the clusters of arc-lamps like so many man-made moons.

The tents were empty, for their occupants sat or lay on the grass, blue now and pearling with dew, and the bright, bizarre clothes of this audience were muted by the moonlight, natural and artificial, to sombre tints of sapphire and smoke. And their hair was silvered, not by time but by night and the natural light of night-time. The calor-gas stoves had been extinguished, but some people had lit fires and from these arose slender spires, threads of blue melting into the deeper blue of the upper air. The whole encampment was blue-coloured, azure, jade where the parkland met the sky, tinted here and there like the plumage of a kingfisher, and the recumbent bodies of the *aficionados* were numberless dark blue shadows.

'How many, d'you reckon?' Wexford asked.

'Seventy or eighty thousand. They're not making much noise.'

17

'The moan of doves in immemorial elms
And murmuring of innumerable bees,'

quoted Wexford.

'Yes, maybe I shouldn't have thought of them as rats. They're more like bees, a swarm of bees.'

The soft buzz of conversation had broken out after Betti Ho had left the stage. Wexford couldn't sort out a single word from it, but from the concentrated intense atmosphere, the sense of total accord and quietly impassioned indignation, he knew they were speaking of the songs they had just heard and were agreeing with their sentiments.

The little Chinese girl, as pretty and delicate and clean as a flower, had sung of tides of filth, of poison, of encroaching doom. It had been strange to hear such things from such lips, strange in the clear purity of this night, and yet he knew, as they all knew, that the tides were there and the poison, the ugliness of waste and the squalor of indifference. She had been called back to sing once more their favourite, the ballad of the disappearing butterflies, and she had sung it through the blue plumes of their woodsmoke while the Kingsbrook chattered a soft accompaniment.

During the songs Burden had been seen to nod in vehement endorsement, but now he was darting quick glances here and there among the prone, murmuring crowd. At last he spotted his son with a group of other schoolboys, and he relaxed. But it was Wexford who noted the small additions John and his friends had made to their dress, the little tent they had put up, so that they would appear to conform with the crowd and not be stamped as mere local tyros, day boys and not experienced boarders.

Burden swatted at a gnat which had alighted on his wrist and at the same time caught sight of his watch.

'Vedast ought to be on soon,' he said. 'As soon as he's finished I'm going to collar John and send him straight home.'

'Spoilsport.'

The inspector was about to make a retort to this when the buzzing of the crowd suddenly increased in volume, rising to a roar of excited approval. People got up, stood, or moved nearer to the stage. The atmosphere seemed to grow tense.

'Here he comes,' said Wexford.

Zeno Vedast was announced by the disc jockey who was compèring the festival as one who needed no introduction, and when he advanced out of the shadows on to the platform the noise from the audience became one concentrated yell of joy. Rather different, Wexford thought wryly, from the chorus of 'Off, off, off . . . !' which had been their response to his own well-thought-out speech. He had been proud of that speech, tolerant and accommodating as it was, just a few words to assure them there would be no interference with their liberty, provided they behaved with restraint.

The police didn't want to spoil the festival, he had said, inserting a light joke; all they wanted was for the fans to be happy, to co-operate and not to annoy each other or the residents of Kingsmarkham. But it hadn't gone down at all well. He was a policeman and that was enough. 'Off, off, off,' they had shouted and 'Out, fuzz, out.' He hadn't been at all nervous but he had wondered what next. There hadn't been any next. Happily, law-abidingly, they were doing their own thing, listening to their own music in the blue and opalescent night.

Now they were roaring for Vedast and at him. The sound of their voices, their rhythmically clapping hands, their drumming feet, assailed him in a tide and seemed to wash over him as might a wave of floodwater. And he stood still in the white ambience, receiving the tide of tribute, his head bent, his bright hair hanging half over his face like a hood of silver cloth.

Then, suddenly, he flung back his head and held up one

19

hand. The roar died, the clamour softened to a patter, dwindled into silence. Out of the silence a girl's voice called, 'Zeno, we love you!' He smiled. Someone came up to the stage and handed him a bulbous stringed instrument. He struck a single, low, pulsating note from it, a note which had an esoteric meaning for the crowd, for a gentle sigh arose from it, a murmur of satisfaction. They knew what he was going to sing first, that single note had told them and, after a rustle of contentment, a ripple of happiness that seemed to travel through all eighty thousand of them, they settled down to listen to what that note had betokened.

'It's called "Let-me-believe",' whispered Burden. 'John's got it on an L.P.' He added rather gloomily: 'We know it better than the National Anthem in our house.'

'I don't know it,' said Wexford.

Vedast struck the single note again and began immediately to sing. The song was about love; about, as far as Wexford could gather, a girl going to her lover's or her husband's house and not loving him enough or something and things going wrong. A not unfamiliar theme. Vedast sang in a clear low voice, face deadpan, but they didn't let him get beyond the first line. They roared and drummed again; again he stood silent with head bent; again he lifted his head and struck the note. This time they let him complete it, interrupting only with a buzzing murmur of appreciation when his voice rose an octave for the second verse.

> 'Remember me and my life-without-life,
> Come once more to be my wife,
> Come today before I grieve,
> Enter the web of let-me-believe . . .'

The melody was that of a folk-song, catchy, tuneful, melancholy, as befitted the lyric and the tender beauty of the night. And the voice suited it utterly, an untrained, clear

20

tenor. Vedast seemed to have perfect pitch. His face was bony
with a big nose and wide mobile mouth, the skin pallid in the
moonlight, the eyes very pale in colour, perhaps a light hazel
or a glaucous green. The long, almost skeletal, fingers drew
not an accompaniment proper, not a tune, from the strings,
but a series of isolated vibrant notes that seemed to twang into
Wexford's brain and make his head swim.

> 'So come by, come nigh,
> come try and tell why
> some sigh, some cry,
> some lie and some die.'

When he had finished he waited for the tide to roar over
him again, and it came, pounding from and through the
crowd, a river of acclaim. He stood limply, bathing in the
applause, until three musicians joined him on the stage and
the first chords from their instruments cut into the tumult.
Vedast sang another ballad, this time about children at a fair,
and then another love-song. Although he hadn't gyrated or
thrown himself about, his chest, bare and bead-hung, glistened
with sweat. At the end of the third song he again stood almost
limply, sensitively, as if his whole heart and soul were exposed
to the audience, the clapping, the roaring, flagellating him.
Why then, Wexford wondered, did he feel that, for all the
man's intensity, his simplicity, his earnestness, the impression
he gave was not one of sincerity? Perhaps it was just that he
was getting old and cynical, inclined to suspect all entertainers
of having one eye on the publicity and the other on the money.

But he hadn't thought that of Betti Ho. He had preferred
her childlike bawling and her righteous anger. Still, he must be
wrong. To judge from the noise the crowd was making as
their idol left the stage, he was alone in his opinion, apart, of
course, from Burden, who had been determined from the start
to like nothing and who was already off in search of John.

'God, when I think of my own youth,' said Wexford as they strolled towards an open space where a van had arrived selling hot dogs. 'When I think of the prevalent attitude that it was somehow *wrong* to be young. We couldn't wait to be older so that we could compete with the old superior ruling people. They used to say, "You wouldn't understand at your age, you're too young." Now it's the young people who know everything, who make the fashions of speech and manners and clothes, and the old ones who are too old to understand.'

'Hum,' said Burden.

'We're two nations again now. Not so much the rich and the poor as the young and the old. Want a hot dog?'

'May as well.' Burden joined the queue, coldly disregarding the hostile glances he got, and bought two hot dogs from a boy in a striped apron. 'Thanks very much.'

'Thank *you*, dad,' said the boy.

Wexford laughed gleefully. 'You poor old dodderer,' he said. 'I hope your ancient teeth are up to eating this thing. How d'you like being my contemporary?' He pushed through the queue towards a stand selling soft drinks. 'Excuse me!'

'Mind who you're shoving, grandad,' said a girl.

Now it was Burden's turn to laugh. 'Contemporary? We're three nations, young, old and middle and always will be. Shall we go and look at the quarry?'

There was to be no more live music for an hour. People had got down to cooking or buying their evening meals in earnest now. A strong smell of frying rose and little wisps of smoke. Already boys and girls could be seen dressed in red and yellow tee-shirts, stamped with the words 'Sundays Scene' on chest and sleeves. The arc-lamps' range wasn't great enough to reach the river, but as the night deepened, the moon had grown very bright. No one was bathing in the clear shallow water, but bathers had left evidence behind them, trunks and bras and jeans spread over the parapet of the bridge to dry.

22

They walked round the rim of the quarry, brambles catching at their ankles, the tiny, newly formed berries of the wayfarer's tree occasionally tapping their faces, berries which felt like ice-cold glass beads.

The place seemed to be entirely empty, but on the estate side the barbed wire had been cut and broken down. The twisted metal gleamed bright silver in the moonlight. Neither Wexford nor Burden could remember if the wire had been like that yesterday. It didn't seem important. They strolled along, not speaking, enjoying the loveliness of the night, the scent of meadowsweet, the gentle, keening music coming from far away.

Suddenly a gate opened in the fence of the last house in The Pathway and a man came out. He was a tall man with a hard, handsome face and he looked cross.

'Are you by any chance running this'—he sought for an appropriate word—'this rave-up?'

'I beg your pardon?' said Wexford.

The man said rudely, 'You look too superannuated to be audience.'

'We're police officers. Is anything wrong?'

'*Wrong?* Yes, plenty's wrong. My name's Peveril. I live there.' He pointed back at the house whose garden gate he had come from. 'There's been an unholy racket going on for twenty-four hours now and the pace has hotted up revoltingly in the past three. I've been attempting to work, but that's quite impossible. What are you going to do about it?'

'Nothing, Mr Peveril, provided no one breaks the law.' Wexford put his head on one side. 'I can't hear anything at present, apart from a distant hum.'

'Then you must be going deaf. The trees muffle the noise down here. I don't know what use you think you're being here. You ought to hear it from my studio.'

'You were warned in plenty of time, sir. It'll all be over tomorrow. We did advise people who live near Sundays and

23

who felt apprehensive about the festival to notify us of their intention and go away for the weekend.'

'Yes, and have their homes broken into by teenage lay-abouts. Experience ought to have taught me not to expect decency from you people. You're not even in the thick of it.' Peveril went back into his garden and banged the gate.

'We ought to have asked him if he'd seen any interlopers,' said Burden, grinning.

'Everyone's an interloper to him.'

Wexford sniffed the air appreciatively. He lived in country air, he was used to it. For years he had never troubled to savour it, but he did now, not being sure how much longer it would last. The night was bringing its humidity, little mists lying low on the turf, wisps of whiteness drifting over the quarry walls. A hare started from a tangle of dog roses, stared at them briefly and fled across the wide silver meadow, gawky legs flying.

'Listen,' Wexford whispered. 'The nightingale . . .'

But Burden wasn't listening. He had stopped to glance into the brake from which the hare had come, had looked further down, done a double take, and turned, his face red.

'Look at that! It really is a bit much. Apart from being—well, disgusting, it happens to be against the law. This, after all, is a public place.'

The couple hadn't been visible from the Sundays side. They lay in a small declivity on the floor of the quarry where the lawn dipped to form a grassy basin about the size of a double bed. Burden had spoken in his normal voice, some twenty feet above their heads, but the sound hadn't disturbed the boy and girl, and Wexford recalled how Kinsey had said that in these circumstances a gun could be fired in the vicinity and the report pass unheard.

They were making love. They were both naked, eighteen or nineteen years old, and of an absolute physical perfection. Across the boy's long arched back the fern-like leaves of the

24

mountain ash which sheltered them scattered a lightly moving pattern of feathery black shadows. They made no sound at all. They were entirely engrossed in each other. And yet they seemed at the same time to be one with their surroundings, as if this setting had been made for them by some kindly god who had prepared it and waited yearningly for the lovers to come and make it complete.

The boy's hair was long, curly and golden, the girl's black and spread, her face cut crystal in the moonlight. Wexford watched them. He could not take his eyes away. There was nothing of voyeurism in the fascination they had for him and he felt no erotic stimulus. A cold atavistic chill invaded him, a kind of primeval awe. Bathed by the moonlight, enfolded by the violet night, they were Adam and Eve, Venus and Adonis, a man and woman alone at the beginning of the world. Silver flesh entwined, encanopied by an ever-moving, shivering embroidery of leaf shadows, they were so beautiful and their beauty so agonising, that Wexford felt enter into him that true panic, the pressure of procreating, urgent nature, that is the presence of the god.

He shivered. He whispered to Burden, as if parodying the other's words, 'Come away. This is a private place.'

They wouldn't have heard him if he had shouted, any more than they heard the sudden throb which thundered from the stage and then the thumping, yelling, screaming tumult as The Verb To Be broke into song.

3

There had been no trouble. A party of Hell's Angels had come to Sundays gates and been turned away. The walls were not high enough to keep them out but they kept out their bikes. A tent had caught fire. There was no question of arson. Someone had lit a fire too close to the canvas and Silk had housed the dispossessed owners in one of his spare bedrooms.

The singing went on most of the night, the keening swell, the thunderous roars, of it audible as far away as Forby, and calls from outraged residents—Peveril among them—came steadily into Kingsmarkham police station. By dawn all was silent and most people asleep. The fires had been stamped out and the arc-lamps switched off as the sun came up to shine on Sundays through a golden haze.

The day promised to be less hot, but it was still very warm, warm enough for the campers to bathe in the Kingsbrook and queue up afterwards for ice-cream. By noon the vendors of food and drink and souvenirs had parked their vans all the way up the avenue. The canned music and the music made by little amateur groups ceased and Emmanuel Ellerman opened the second day of the concert with his hit song, 'High Tide'. The mist which had lain close to the ground at dawn had risen to lie as a blanket of cloud through which the sun gleamed palely. It was sultry and the atmosphere made people breathless.

Burden's son John had been allowed to return and hear Zeno Vedast sing for the last time. He kept out of his father's way, embarrassed in this society to have a policeman for a

26

parent. Burden sniffed the air suspiciously as he and Wexford walked about the encampment.

'That smell is pot.'

'We've got enough to think about here without indulging in drug swoops,' said Wexford. 'The Chief Constable says to turn a blind eye unless we see anyone actually high and whooping about or jumping over the quarry because he's full of acid. I wish I could appreciate the noise those musicians are making but it's no good, I can't. I'm too bloody old. They've finished. I wonder who's next?'

'They all sound the same to me.' Burden kept looking for his son, fearing perhaps that he was being corrupted into taking drugs, making love or growing his hair. 'And they all look the same.'

'Do stop fretting about that boy of yours. That's not him you're looking at, anyway. I saw him go off to the hamburger stall just now. Hear that noise? That'll be Betti Ho's helicopter come to fetch her away.'

The bright yellow helicopter, like a gigantic insect in a horror film, hovered and spun and finally plopped into the field behind the house. The two policemen watched it come down and then joined the stream of people passing through the gate into the field. The Chinese singer wore a yellow dress —to match her aircraft?—and her black hair in a pigtail.

'What money she must get,' said Burden. 'I won't say *earn*.'

'She makes people think. She does a lot of good. I'd rather she had it than some of these politicians. There's your John, come to see the take-off. Now, don't go to him. Leave him alone. He's enjoying himself.'

'I wasn't going to. I'm not so daft I don't realise he doesn't want to know me here. There's Vedast. God, it's like the end of a state visit.'

Wexford didn't think it was much like that. A thousand or so of the fans had massed round the helicopter while Betti Ho stood in the midst of a circle of others, talking to Vedast who wore black jeans and whose chest was still bare. There was another girl with them and Vedast had his arm round her waist. Wexford moved closer to get a better look at her, for of all the striking, bizarre and strangely dressed people he had seen since Friday, she was the most fantastic.

She was nearly as tall as Vedast and good-looking in the flashy, highly coloured fashion of a beauty queen. It seemed to Wexford impossible that anyone could naturally possess so much hair, a frothy, bouffant mane of ice-blonde hair that bubbled all over her head and flowed nearly to her waist. Her figure was perfect. He told himself that it would need to be not to look ridiculous in skin-tight vest and hot pants of knitted string, principal-boy boots, thigh-high in gilt leather. From where he stood, twenty yards from her, he could see her eyelashes and see too that she wore tiny rainbow brilliants studded on to her eyelids.

'I wonder who that is?' he said to Burden.

'She's called Nell Tate,' said Burden surprisingly. 'Married to Vedast's road manager.'

'Looks as if she ought to be married to Vedast. How do *you* know, anyway?'

'How d'you think, sir? John told me. Sometimes I wish pop was an O Level subject, I can tell you.'

Wexford laughed. He could hardly take his eyes off the girl, and this was not because she attracted him or even because he admired her looks—he didn't. What intrigued him was contemplating for a moment the life her appearance advertised, a life and way of life utterly remote, he imagined, from anything he had ever known or, come to that, anything the majority of these fans had ever known. It was said that Vedast was a local boy made good. Where did she come from? What strange ladder had she climbed to find herself here and now the cynosure of so many eyes, embraced in public by the darling of the 'scene'?

Vedast withdrew his arm and kissed Betti Ho on both cheeks. It was the continental statesman's salute that has become the 'in' thing for a certain élite. Betti turned to Nell Tate and they too kissed. Then the Chinese girl climbed into her helicopter and the doors were closed..

'Things'll break up soon,' said Burden. 'What time is it?'

'Half four. The air's very heavy. Going to be a storm.'

'I wouldn't like to be in that thing in a storm.'

The aircraft buzzed and whirred and rose. Betti Ho leaned out and waved a yellow silk arm. The fans began to drift back towards Sundays park, drawn by the sound of amplified guitars. The Greatheart, a three-man group, had taken the stage. Burden, listening to them, began to show his first signs of approval since the beginning of the concert. The Greatheart made a speciality of singing parodies of wartime hits, but Burden didn't yet know they were parodies and a half-sentimental, half-suspicious smile twitched his lips.

Martin Silk was sitting on a camp-stool by the ashes of a dead fire talking to the boy in the magpie coat. It was too warm and humid to wear a jacket, let alone a fur coat, but the boy hadn't taken it off, as far as Wexford had noticed, since his arrival. Perhaps his dark bronze skin was accustomed to more tropical skies.

'Not a spot of trouble, you see,' said Silk, looking up.

'I wouldn't quite say that. There was that fire. Someone's reported a stolen bike and the bloke selling tee-shirts has had a hell of a lot pinched.'

'It's quite O.K. to nick things from *entrepreneurs*,' said the magpie boy in a mild, soft voice.

'In your philosophy, maybe. If and when it ever becomes the law of the land I'll go along with you.'

'It will, man, it will. Come the revolution.'

Wexford hadn't actually heard anyone speak seriously of the promised revolution as a foreseeable thing since he was himself a teenager in the early thirties. Apparently they were

29

still on the same old kick. 'But then,' he said, 'there won't be any *entrepreneurs*, will there?'

The magpie boy made no reply but merely smiled very kindly. 'Louis,' said Silk proudly, 'is reading philosophy at the University of the South. He has a remarkable political theory of his own. He is quite prepared to go to prison for his beliefs.'

'Well, he won't for his beliefs,' said Wexford. 'Not, that is, unless he breaches the peace with them.'

'Louis is the eldest son of a paramount chief. One day Louis Mbowele will be a name to be reckoned with in the emerging African states.'

'I shouldn't be at all surprised,' said Wexford sincerely. In his mind's eye he could see future headlines, blood, disaster, tyranny, and all well meant. 'Philosophy doctorate, political theory, British prison—he'll soon have all the qualifications. Good luck. Remember me when thou comest into thy kingdom.'

'Peace be with you,' said the African gravely.

Burden was standing with Superintendent Letts of the uniformed branch.

'Nearly all over, Reg,' said Letts.

'Yes. I don't want to be mean, but I'd like it soon to be over. All done and trouble-free.'

'Before the storm comes too. It'll be hell getting this lot off the park in a downpour.'

Above the roof of Sundays house the sky had deepened to indigo. And the house itself was bathed in livid light, that wan, spectral light that gleams under cloud canopies before a storm. The hornbeams in the avenue, stolid, conical trees, were too stocky to sway much in the rising breeze, but the low broom-like branches of the cedars had begun to sweep and sigh against the turf and, up by the house, the conifers shivered.

It was a hot wind, though, and when Zeno Vedast walked on to the stage he was still half-naked. He sang the 'Let-me-believe' ballad again to a silent crowd made tense by the stifling, thick air.

Wexford, who had once more wandered a little apart so that he was close by the scaffolding of the stage, found himself standing beside Nell Tate. Vedast was singing unaccompanied this time and she held his mandoline or ocarina or whatever it was. There was nothing exceptional in the fact that her eyes were fixed on the singer. So were seventy or eighty thousand other pairs of eyes. But whereas the rest showed enthusiasm, admiration, critical appreciation, hers were hungrily intense. Her gleaming mulberry-coloured lips were parted and she held her head slightly back in a yearning, swan-like curve. A little bored by the song, Wexford amused himself in watching her and then, suddenly, she turned and looked him full in the face.

He was shocked. Her expression was tragic, despairing, as if she had been and was for ever to be bitterly deprived of what she most wanted. Misery showed through the plastered biscuit make-up, the rosy blusher, the green and blue eyelid paint, and showed in spite of the absurd twinkling brilliants stuck about her eyes. He wondered why. She was older than he had thought at first but still only about twenty-eight. Was she in love with Vedast and unable to have him? That seemed improbable, for when Vedast had finished his first song he stepped over to the edge of the stage, squatted down and, in taking the stringed thing from Nell's hand, kissed her impulsively, but slowly and passionately, on the mouth. Vedast began singing again and now Wexford saw that she was looking calmer, the glittering lids closed briefly over her eyes.

'Is that the lot?' he asked, going back to Burden. 'I mean, is the concert over?'

Burden slipped unprotestingly into his role as pop expert, though a less likely or less enthusiastic authority could hardly have been found. 'Two more songs from The Greatheart,' he said, 'and then we can all go home. Some are going already. They only waited to hear the Naked Ape.'

'Fighting words, Mike, sacrilege. I thought he was rather good. There goes that pink and orange van. It's got graffiti all over it—did you see?—and someone's written on one of the doors "This truck also available in paperback".'

The tents were coming down. Gas burners and kettles and tins of instant coffee were being thrust into kit bags, and a barefoot girl wandered vaguely about looking among the heaps of litter for the shoes she had discarded twenty-four hours before. The future leader of an emerging African state had abandoned polemics for the more prosaic pursuit of rolling up his sleeping bag. Martin Silk strolled among them, smiling with regal benignity at his young guests and rather malicious triumph at Wexford.

'You can't help feeling sorry for those Greatheart people, singing their guts out to an audience who couldn't care less. They must know they only stayed for Vedast.'

Wexford's words went unheard. 'There they are,' said Burden, 'that girl and her boy friend, the ones we saw last night. Coming straight from the quarry. Well, their little honeymoon's over. And they've had a row by the look of them or been bitten by something. It's always said there are adders on Sundays land.'

'You'd like that, wouldn't you?' Wexford snapped. 'That'd be a suitable retribution for doing what comes naturally in the Garden of Eden.' The girl and the boy showed no sign of having quarrelled, nor did either of them seem disabled. They were holding hands and running like Olympic sprinters. In a dirty and tattered version of the tee-shirt-jeans uniform, their long hair wind-blown, they had lost their primeval beauty of the night before. The magic and the wonder was all gone. They were just an ordinary young couple running, breathless and—frightened. Wexford took a step in their direction, suddenly concerned.

They stopped dead in front of him. The girl's face was white, her breath laboured and choked. 'You're police, aren't you?' the boy said before Wexford could speak. 'Could you come, please? Come and see what...'

'In the quarry,' the girl said throatily. 'Oh, *please*. It was such a shock. There's a girl lying in the quarry and she's—she's dead. Ever so dead. Her face is—blood—horrible . . . Oh *God*!' She threw herself into the boy's arms and sobbed.

4

S he was screaming hysterically.

'You tell me,' Wexford said to the boy.

'We went to the quarry about ten minutes ago.' He talked jerkily, stammering. 'I—we—I'm with a party and Rosie's with a party and—and we shan't see each other again for a month. We wanted to be private but it's still daylight and we looked for somewhere we wouldn't be seen. Oh, Rosie, don't. Stop crying. Can't you *do something*?'

A crowd had gathered around them. Wexford spoke to a capable-looking girl. 'Take her into one of the tents and make some tea. Make it hot and strong. One of you others, find Mr Silk and see if he's got any brandy. Come along now. She'll tell you all about it. She'll want to.'

Rosie let forth a shriek. The other girl, justifying Wexford's faith in her, slapped one of the wet white cheeks. Rosie gagged and stared.

'That's better,' said Wexford. 'Into the tent with you. You'll be all right when you've had a hot drink.' He went back to the boy. 'What's your name?'

'Daniel. Daniel Somers.'

'You found a girl's body in the quarry?' Suddenly The Greatheart burst into song. 'God, I wish we could have a bit of hush. Where did you find it?'

'Under some bushes—well, sort of trees—on the side where the wire is.' Daniel shuddered, opening his eyes wide. 'There were—flies,' he said. 'Her face was all over blood and it was sort of dried and there were flies—*crawling*.'

'Come and show me.'

'Do I have to?'

'It won't take long,' Wexford said gently. 'You don't have to look at her again, only show us where she is.'

By now a fear that something had gone badly wrong had flurried the encampment on the side where they were standing, rumour 'stuffing the ears of men with false reports'. People came out of tents to stare, others raised themselves on one elbow from the ground, briefly deaf to The Greatheart. A low buzz of conversation broke out as boys and girls asked each other if this was the beginning of a drug swoop.

Daniel Somers, his face as white, his eyes as aghast as his girl friend's, seemed anxious now to get the whole thing over. He scrambled down the chalk slope and the policemen followed him in less gainly fashion. As yet there was nothing to see, nothing alarming. Under the louring grey sky, thick, purplish, not a blue rift showing, the quarry grass seemed a brighter, more livid green. Light, obliquely and strangely filtered under cloud rims, gave a vivid glow to the white faces of the wild roses and the silver undersides of birch leaves, lifting and shivering in the wind. On the little lawn the harebells shook like real bells ringing without sound.

Daniel hesitated a few feet from where a young birch grew out of a dense, man-high tangle of honeysuckle and dogwood. He shivered, himself near to hysteria.

'In there.' He pointed. 'I didn't touch her.'

Wexford nodded.

'You get back to Rosie now.'

The bushes had no thorns and were easily lifted. They surrounded the root of the tree like the fabric of a tent belling about its pole. Under them, half-curled around the root, lay the girl's body. It was somewhat in the position of a foetus, knees bent, arms folded so that the hands met under the chin.

Even Wexford's strong stomach lurched when he saw the face or what had been a face. It was a broken mass, encrusted

35

with black blood and blacker flies which swarmed and buzzed
sluggishly as the leafy covering was disturbed. Blood was in
the hair too, streaking the yellow, fibrous mass, matting it in
places into hard knots. And blood was probably on the dark
red dress, but its material, the colour of coagulated blood,
had absorbed and negatived it.

The Greatheart were still performing.

'A girl's been murdered,' Wexford said to Silk. 'You must
get this lot off the stage. Let me have a microphone.'

The crowd murmured angrily as the musicians broke off in
the middle of a song and retreated. The murmur grew more
menacing when Wexford appeared in their place. He held up
one hand. It had no effect.

'Quiet, please. I must have quiet.'

'Off, off, off!' they shouted.

All right. They could have it straight and see if that silenced
them. 'A girl has been murdered,' he said, pitching his voice
loud. 'Her body is in the quarry.' The voices died and he got
the silence he wanted. 'Thank you. We don't yet know who
she is. No one is to leave Sundays until I give permission.
Understood?' They said nothing. He felt a deep pity for them,
their festival spoiled, their eager young faces now cold and
shocked. 'If anyone has missed a member of their party,
a blonde girl in a red dress, will he or she please inform
me?'

Silk behaved rather as if Wexford himself had killed the
girl and put her in his quarry. 'Everything was going so well,'
he moaned. 'Why did this have to happen? You'll see, it'll be
another lever in the hands of the fuddy-duddies who want to
suppress all free activity and gag young people. You see if I'm
not right.' He gazed distractedly skywards at the grey massy
clouds which had rolled out of the west.

Wexford turned from him to speak to a boy who touched
his arm and said, 'There was a girl in our party who's dis-

appeared. No one's seen her since this morning. We thought she'd gone home. She wasn't enjoying herself much.'

'How was she dressed?'

The boy considered and said, 'Jeans, I think, and a green top.'

'Fair hair? Mauve tights and shoes?'

'God, no. She's dark and she wasn't wearing anything like that.'

'It isn't she,' said Wexford.

The rain was coming. He had a brief nightmarish vision of rain descending in torrents on the encampment, turning the trodden grass into seas of mud, beating on the fragile tents. And all the while, throughout the night certainly, he and every policeman he could get hold of would have to interrogate wet, unhappy and perhaps panicky teenagers.

The photographers had come. He saw their car bumping over the hard turf and stop at the wooden bridge. Once she had been photographed, he could move her and perhaps begin the business of identification. He felt a dash of cold water on his hand as the first drops of rain fell.

'I've been wondering if we could get them all into the house,' said Silk.

Eighty thousand people into one house? On the other hand, it was a big house . . .

'Not possible. Don't think of it.'

Behind him a girl cleared her throat to attract his attention. Two girls stood there, one of them holding a black velvet coat.

'Yes?' he said quickly.

'We haven't seen our friend since last night. She left her coat in the tent and just went off. We can't find her or her boy friend, and I thought—we thought . . .'

'That she might be the girl we found? Describe her, please.'

'She's eighteen. Very dark hair, very pretty. She's wearing black jeans. Oh, it isn't her, is it? She's called Rosie and her boy friend . . .'

'Is Daniel.' While the girl stared at him, round-eyed, marvelling at this omniscience, he said, 'Rosie's all right.' He pointed. 'She's over there, in that tent.'

'Thanks. God, we were really scared.'

How much more of this was there to be, he wondered, before he had to say yes, yes, it sounds like her? Then he saw Dr Crocker, lean, trim and energetic, stalking towards him. The police doctor wore a white raincoat and carried an umbrella as well as his bag.

'I've been away for the weekend, Reg, taking your people's advice. I thought I was going to keep clear of all this. What's it about?'

'Didn't they tell you?'

'No, only that I was wanted.'

'There's a dead girl in the quarry.'

'Is there, by God? One of *them*?' Crocker pointed vaguely into the crowd.

'I don't know. Come and see.'

The rain was falling lightly, intermittently, the way rain does after a drought and before a deluge, as if each drop was being squeezed painfully out. Three police cars had succeeded in negotiating the rough ground and were parked at the quarry edge. In the quarry itself the photographers had completed their work, the undergrowth had been cut away and a tarpaulin canopy erected to screen the body from view. In spite of this, a crowd of boys and girls squatted or lolled all round the quarry, speculating among themselves, their eyes wide.

'Get back to your tents, the lot of you,' Wexford said. 'You'll get wet and you won't see anything.' Slowly, they began to move. 'Come on now. Ghoulishness is for ignorant old people. Your generation is supposed to be above this sort of thing.'

That did it. One or two of them grinned sheepishly. By the time Wexford and the doctor had scrambled down on to the little lawn—the harebells trodden to a mush—the sightseers had dispersed. Crocker knelt by the body and examined it.

'She's been dead at least five days.'

Wexford felt himself relax with relief.

'She was dead before the festival started,' said Crocker, 'and she wasn't a teenager. I'd say at least twenty-seven, maybe thirty.'

Under the canopy the flies were thick and noisy. Wexford rolled the body on to its side, revealing a large handbag of mauve patent leather which lay beneath it. Handbag, shoes and tights matched each other and clashed with the dark red dress. He opened the bag, spilling the contents on to a sheet of plastic. An envelope addressed to Miss Dawn Stonor, 23 Philimede Gardens, London, S.W.5, fell out. There was a letter inside it addressed from Lower Road, Kingsmarkham:

Dear Dawn, I will be glad to see you Monday but I suppose it will be one of your flying visits and you won't condesend to stop the night. Granma has had one of her bad turns but is all right again now. I got the mauve slacks and blouse from the cleaners that you left there and you can take it away with you. They charged 65 p. which I will be glad of. See you Monday. Love, Mum.

He noted the illiteracies, the badly formed writing. Something else in the letter struck a chord in his mind, but he could think about that later. The main thing was that she had been easily and rapidly identified. 'Have the body removed,' he said to Sergeant Martin, 'and then I want the quarry searched.'

There was blood on his hand, fresh blood. How could that have come from a body five days dead? He looked again and saw that it hadn't. The blood was his own, flowing from a small wound near the base of his thumb.

'Broken glass everywhere,' he said wonderingly.

'Have you only just noticed?' Crocker gave a harsh, humourless laugh. 'You needn't bother to search for a weapon.'

They had come gaily and noisily, erupting from cars and trains and buses, arriving on a summer's day to hear music and bringing their own music with them. They left downcast, in silence, trudging through the rain. Most of them had had no more than a dozen hours of sleep throughout the weekend. Their faces were shocked and dirty and pale.

No one ran. There was no horseplay. They dismantled their wet tents, shouldered their baggage, leaving behind them greyish-white mountain ranges of rubbish. Moving towards the gates in long ragged files, they looked like refugees leaving a place of disaster. Daniel walked with Rosie, one arm embracing her, the other shouldering a rolled tent which bumped against his khaki pack. Louis Mbowele passed through the gates without looking up from the book he was reading. They chewed sweets, passed wine bottles from hand to hand in silence, indifferent in their saddened freemasonry as to who paid or who drank. Huddled together, they lit cigarettes, sheltering match flames from the downpour.

Lightning split the sky over Stowerton and the thunder rolled, grumbling in the west. From fast-travelling clouds, blue and black and roaring grey, the rain cascaded, sweeping people and their belongings into the avenue like so much debris buffeted by the tide. The cedars lifted their black arms, sleeved in spiky foliage, and slapped them, rattling, up and down on what had been turf. It was turf no longer. Thousand upon thousand of strong young feet had shaved the grass to stubble, to final scorched aridity. The rain fell on to acres of brown desert.

Someone had abandoned a torn tent, a red canvas tent that bounded in the wind like a huge drowning butterfly until it became waterlogged and collapsed against the footings of the stage. The river began to fill, carrying with it as it plunged under the Forby Road a bobbing flotsam of paper, cans, transistor batteries and lost shoes.

5

With the rain came a kind of false night, a streaming, early twilight. It drove everyone indoors, everyone, that is, but the departing young people who trudged through the downpour into Kingsmarkham. Soaked and shivering, the long processions came on towards the buses, towards the station. Some stayed behind on the Forby Road, hoping to hitch, doggedly resigned when cars passed without stopping, when motorists, put off by their draggled clothes and their long wet hair, rejected them.

They invaded the centre of the town, queueing for any bus that might come, forming dispirited lines that stretched the length of the High Street. A conglomeration of youth filled the centre, but the outskirts, the back streets, were deserted. In Lower Road where all the doors and windows were shut, every curtain drawn, rain drumming on rows of pavement-parked cars, it might have been the depths of winter. Only the roses in the front gardens of these squat red-brick council houses, the drooping foliage on cherry trees, showed that there should have been sunshine, that it was a June evening.

Number fifteen was a house just like its neighbours, a similar Dorothy Perkins trailing over the front door, its acid pink flowers clashing with ochreish red brick, similar white net curtains, draped crosswise like the bodice of a negligé, across its windows. A scaffolding of television aerials sprouted from its single chimney and juddered in the gale.

Wexford went slowly up the path. The rain was falling so heavily that he had to put up his umbrella even for this short

41

distance from the car to the front door. He hated having to question the bereaved, hated himself for intruding on their grief and for feeling, if not showing, impatience when memories overcame them and tears silenced them. He knew now that Dawn Stonor had had no father. It was a woman in the barren country of deep middle age, alone and perhaps utterly broken, he had to interview. He tapped softly on the door.

Detective Polly Davies let him in.

'How is she, Polly?'

'She's O.K., sir. There wasn't much love lost between mother and daughter, as far as I can see. Dawn hadn't lived at home for ten years.'

'Dreadful to feel relief at a lack of love . . . I'll talk to her now.'

Mrs Stonor had been driven to the mortuary and home again in a police car. Still wearing her coat, her red straw hat on the arm of her chair, she sat in the living room, drinking tea. She was a big, florid-faced woman of fifty-five with bad varicose veins, her swollen feet crushed into court shoes.

'Do you feel up to giving me some information, Mrs Stonor? I'm afraid this has been a bad shock for you.'

'What d'you want to know?' She spoke abruptly in a shrill, harsh voice. 'I can't tell you why she was in that quarry. Made a proper mess of her, didn't he?'

Wexford wasn't shocked. He knew that in most people there is something sado-masochistic, and even the newly-bereaved have an apparently ghoulish need to dwell with pleasurable horror on the injuries inflicted on dead relatives. Whether or not they express these feelings depends on their degree of cultivated repression rather than on grief.

'Who was "he", Mrs Stonor?'

She shrugged. 'Some man. There was always some man.'

'What did she do for a living?'

'Waitress in a club. Place called the Townsman up in

London, up West somewhere. I never went there.' Mrs Stonor gave him a lowering, aggressive look. 'It's for men. The girls get themselves up in daft costumes like bathing suits with skirts, showing off all they've got. "Disgusting!" I said to her. "Don't you tell me about it, I don't want to know." Her dad would have turned in his grave if he'd known what she did.'

'She came here on Monday?'

'That's right.' She took off her coat. He saw that she was heavily built, rigidly corseted. Her face was set in grim, peevish lines, and it was hard to tell whether it was more grim and peevish than usual. 'You wouldn't find a decent girl going to that quarry with a man,' she said. 'Had he done anything to her?'

The question was grotesque between people who had seen for themselves, but he knew what she meant. 'There was no sexual assault and intercourse hadn't taken place.'

She flushed darkly. He thought she was going to protest at his fairly blunt way of speaking but instead she rushed into an account of what he wanted to know. 'She came down by train, the one that gets in at half past eleven. I'd got her dinner for her, a bit of steak. She liked that.' The harsh voice wavered a little. 'She liked her bit of steak, did Dawn. Then we chatted a bit. We hadn't really got nothing in common any more.'

'Can you tell me what you talked about?'

'Nothing about *men*, if that's what you mean. She was fed-up on account of some little kid in the train had wiped his sticky fingers down her dress. It was a new dress, one of them minis, and it showed all her legs. I said she'd have to change it and she did.'

'She put on the dark red dress she was found in?'

'No, she never. That wasn't hers. I don't know where that come from. There was a mauve thing she had here as I'd fetched from the cleaners for her—they call them trouser suits —and she put that on. She was wearing mauve shoes so it looked all right. Well, like I said, we chatted a bit and she

43

went up to see her gran—that's my mother as lives with me—and then Dawn went off to catch the four-fifteen train. Left here just before four.'

Wexford looked thoughtful. 'You thought she was going straight back to London?'

'Of course I did. She said so. She said, I've got to be in the club by seven. She took the blue dress with her in a bag and she said she'd have to run not to miss her train.'

'Two more things, Mrs Stonor, and then I'll leave you in peace. I'd like you to describe the trouser suit, if you would.'

'Very showy, it was. More like pyjamas than something you'd wear in the street. There was slacks, sort of flared, and a kind of tunic. It was mauve nylon stuff with a bit of darker mauve round the sleeves and the bottom of the tunic. Dawn liked to dress flashy.'

'Have you a photograph of her?'

Mrs Stonor gave him a suspicious glare. 'What, got up in them clothes?'

'No. Any photograph.'

'There was a photo she sent me for Christmas. Funny idea giving your mum a photo of yourself for Christmas, I thought. You can have that if you like.'

The photograph, a studio portrait, was brought. It had never been framed and, from its pristine condition, Wexford supposed that it had never been shown with pride to Mrs Stonor's friends but kept since its arrival in a drawer. Dawn had been a heavy-featured, rather coarse-looking girl, who wore thick make-up. The blonde hair was piled into puffs and ringlets, a massy structure reminding him of the head-dresses of eighteenth-century belles or perhaps of actresses playing such parts. She wore a blue silk evening gown, very low-cut and showing a great deal of fleshy bosom and shoulder.

Mrs Stonor eyed it irritably, peevishly, and Wexford could see that it would have been a disappointing gift for a mother of her type. Dawn had been twenty-eight. To have met with maternal favour, the picture should have shown not only a daughter but grandchildren, a wedding ring on those stiffly posed fingers, and behind the group the outline of a semi-detached house, well kept-up and bought on a mortgage.

He felt a stirring of pity for this mother who was a mother no longer, a flash of sympathy which was dissipated at once when she said as he was leaving:

'About that trouser suit . . .'

'Yes?'

'It was more or less new. She only bought it back in the winter. I mean, I know a lady who'd give me five pounds for that.'

Wexford gave her a narrow glance. He tried not to show his distaste.

'We don't know what's become of it, Mrs Stonor. Perhaps the lady would like the shoes and the bag. You can have them in due course.'

The exodus continued. By now it was dark, a windswept, starless night, the rain falling relentlessly. Wexford drove back to the Sundays estate where, on both sides of the Forby road, police cars cruised along the streets or stood parked in lakes of trembling black water. Presently Burden found him and got into the car beside him.

'Well? Anything startling?'

'Nothing much, sir. Nobody remembers seeing a girl in a red dress down here during the week. But last Monday after-noon one woman from Sundays Grove, a Mrs Lorna Clarke, says she saw a blonde girl, answering Dawn's description, but wearing a . . .'

'Mauve trouser suit?'

'That's right! So it was her? I thought it must be from Mrs Clarke talking about mauve shoes and a mauve bag. Where did the red dress come from then?'

Wexford shook his head. 'It's beginning to look as if she

died on Monday. She left her mother's house just before four that afternoon. When and where did your Mrs Clarke see her?'

'She got off the five-twenty-five bus from Kingsmarkham. Mrs Clarke saw her get off the bus and cross the road towards The Pathway. A few minutes later someone else saw her in The Pathway.'

'Which backs on to the quarry. Go on.'

'There are only five houses in The Pathway, two bungalows and three proper houses. If you remember, they didn't do any more building down there. People made a fuss about it and the ministry reversed the decision to grant planning permission. She was next seen by a woman who lives in the last house.'

'Not the wife of that bloke who came out making a to-do on Saturday night?'

Burden nodded. 'A Mrs Peveril, sir. They're both at home all day. He's a graphic designer, works at home. His wife says she saw a blonde girl in mauve go down the road at five-thirty and enter the public footpath that goes across the fields to Stowerton. She gave a very detailed description of the trouser suit, the shoes and the bag. But, of course, I couldn't be sure it was Dawn. I couldn't understand her being dressed in mauve. Mrs Peveril says the girl was holding a brown carrier bag.'

'Mm-hm. It certainly was Dawn. She changed out of a blue dress into the mauve thing and it was obviously the blue one she was carrying in the bag. She seems to have gone in for a lot of clothes changing, doesn't she? I wonder why. No other help from The Pathway?'

'No one else saw her. Each of the bungalows has only one occupant and they were both out at the relevant time. Miss Mowler's a retired district nurse and she was out on Monday till eight. Dunsand—he's a lecturer at the University of the South, philosophy or something—didn't get home from work till after half past six. I can't find anyone else who saw her on

46

Monday or at any other time. My guess is she picked up some bloke and made a date to meet him between Sundays and Stowerton that evening.'

'Ye-es. I expect that's it. She left her mother at four and she must have caught the five-twelve bus. There are only two buses going to Forby in the afternoon, as you know. What did she do in that spare hour and ten minutes? We'll have to find out if anyone saw her in the High Street. There's the London angle too, but I've already got wheels moving there.'

'D'you want to see Mrs Peveril?'

'Not now, Mike. I doubt if we can make much progress tonight. I'll let them finish the house-to-house. They may get something more. She may have been seen later. I don't want to speculate at this stage.'

Burden left the car and, throwing his raincoat over his head, plunged off through the rain. Wexford turned the car, moving off in low gear through the torrents, the steady downpour, glancing once at Sundays where the last dispirited stragglers were leaving the park.

6

By the morning it had been established that Mrs Margaret Peveril of number five, The Pathway, was very probably the last person to have seen Dawn Stonor alive. On Monday, June sixth, Dawn had entered the pathfields at five-thirty and disappeared. By nine Wexford and Burden were back in The Pathway. By nine also an emergency interview room had been set up in the Baptist church hall where Sergeant Martin and a team of detectives waited to talk to anyone who might have seen Dawn on the previous Monday afternoon. The photograph had been blown up to poster size ready to jog memories, and another photograph prepared, this time of Polly Davies wearing a blonde wig and dressed in clothes resembling as nearly as possible Mrs Stonor's description of the mauve suit.

The rain had stopped during the night and the town and its environs looked washed, battered, wrung out to dry. All the summer warmth had gone with the storm, leaving a cloud-splashed sourly blue sky, a high sharp wind and mid-winter temperatures.

At Sundays Martin Silk was burning litter, the accumulated detritus of eighty thousand people's weekend. A row of fires blazed just behind the wall and the wind blew acrid white smoke in clouds over the Sundays estate, the Forby road and the barren brown plain of the park. Silk's little herd of Friesians had returned to their pasture. They stood in a huddle under the cedars, bewildered by the smoke.

The Pathway was shaped like an arm with bent elbow, its shoulder the junction with the Forby road, its wrist and hand

—or perhaps its one pointing finger—a footpath which ran through hilly meadows and copses to Stowerton. Three houses and two bungalows had been built along this arm, but in its crook there were only open fields. The bungalows were identical, rather large pink plastered bungalows with red tiled roofs and detached garages. They stood 'in their gardens', as estate agents put it, meaning that there are sections of garden at the sides as well as at front and back. Some twenty feet separated one from the other, and a further twenty feet down stood a two-storey house. Similar building materials had been used for this house and the two dwellings on the upper arm, red brick, white stone, cedarwood, but they varied in size and in design. All had sparse lawns and flower-beds planted with unhappy-looking annuals.

'The Peverils came in first,' said Burden. 'Their place was finished in January. Miss Mowler and Dunsand both moved in in March. He came from Myringham, Miss Mowler from the town here and the Peverils from Brighton. The Robinsons retired here from London, moving in in April, and the Streets came here from up north last month.'

'Do they all have garden gates opening on to that bit of land between them and the quarry?' asked Wexford.

'Only the Peverils and the two bungalows. There was going to be a path made at the back, but someone got the planning authority to veto that.'

'We'll go and have a word with your Mrs Peveril.'

She was a very nervous woman, breathless with nerves. Wexford thought she was in her late thirties. Her hair-style and her clothes were fussy but not in any of the current modes. She dressed evidently in a somewhat modified version of the style of her youth, full, longish skirt, stilt heels. He sized her up immediately as belonging to a distinct and not uncommon type, the sheltered and conservative woman who, childless and exclusively dependent on her husband for all emotional needs, tends to be suspicious of other men and of the outside world.

Such women will go to almost any lengths to preserve their security and their absolute domestic quietude, so Wexford was rather surprised that Mrs Peveril had volunteered any information about a murder victim.

'All that smoke,' she said querulously, leading them into an over-neat living room. 'Isn't it dreadful? I shan't be able to get my washing out for hours. It was bad enough having that ghastly racket over the weekend—I didn't get a wink of sleep. The noise was frightful. I'm not surprised someone got murdered.'

'The murder,' said Wexford, 'happened several days before the festival started.'

'Did it?' Mrs Peveril looked unconvinced. 'When I heard someone had been killed I said to my husband, they took too many of those drugs they all take and someone went too far. D'you mind not sitting on that cushion? I've just put a fresh cover on it.'

Wexford moved on to a leather-seated and apparently invulnerable chair. 'I believe you saw the girl?'

'Oh, yes, I saw her. There's no doubt about that.' She gave a short nervous laugh. 'I don't know many people round here except my friend on the other side of the estate, but I knew that girl wasn't local. The people round here don't dress like that.'

'What made you notice her?'

'If you're going to ask me a lot of questions I'd like my husband to be present. I'll just call him. He's working but he won't mind stopping for a bit. I might say—well, the wrong thing if he wasn't here. I'll just call him.'

Wexford shrugged. In a manner of speaking, the 'wrong' thing could easily be the thing he wanted her to say. But she had asked for her husband as some people ask for their lawyers and probably with less need. He saw no reason to refuse his permission and he got up, smiling pleasantly, when Peveril came in.

'You didn't see the girl yourself, Mr Peveril?'

'No, I was working.' Peveril was one of those men who talk about work and working as if labour belongs exclusively to them, as if it is an arduous, exacting cross they must bear, while the rest of the world make carefree holiday. 'I work a ten-hour day. Have to what with the cost of running this place. The first I heard of any girl was when my wife told me last night she'd given information to the police.' He glared at Burden. 'I was working when you lot came.'

'Perhaps we shouldn't keep you from your work now?'

'Oh, please don't go, Edward, please don't. You said I was silly to say what I said last night and now . . .'

'I can do with a short break,' said Peveril lugubriously. 'I've been at it since eight, thanks to being made totally idle by a weekend of uproar. I'm worn out.'

Comforted but still jumpy, his wife rushed into the middle of things. 'It's a matter of chance I was here at all. I nearly went to the pictures—my husband had seen the film in London and told me to go—but it was such a lovely afternoon. I just looked out of the window there and I saw her. I saw this girl walking up towards the footpath.'

'Describe her to me. In as much detail as you can, please.'

'She was about my height and she had a lot of dyed blonde hair cut in the shaggy way they all go in for.' Mrs Peveril twitched at her own over-permed, frizzy dark hair with an unsteady hand. 'And she was very heavily made-up, tarty. She had on this trouser suit, bright mauve—it hurt your eyes —with a darker mauve edging to it, and mauve patent shoes with high heels. Her handbag was mauve, a great big showy handbag with a gilt buckle, and she was carrying a brown carrier bag. I watched her because I wanted to tell my husband what a sight she was—he's very particular in his tastes, being a sort of artist—and I save up little things to tell him when he's finished work.'

'But you didn't tell him, Mrs Peveril?'

'I must have forgotten.' She was suddenly flurried. 'I wonder why I didn't tell you, Edward?'

The 'sort of artist' turned down the corners of his mouth. 'I expect I was too tired to listen. If you've finished with her I'll get back to the grindstone.'

'I've almost finished. Where did she go?'

'Across the field,' said Mrs Peveril promptly. 'That is, down the footpath, you know. I stayed at the window a long time but she didn't come back.'

She came to the door with them and watched them nervously as they got back into their car. Wexford's driver, glancing up innocently, received from her such a sharp look that he went red and turned away.

'Well, Mike, I don't quite know what to make of the Peverils, but she certainly saw the girl. Her description was too accurate to admit of anything else. Our best bet is to conclude that Dawn went across that field to meet a man. Where would she have met him?'

'In the open, I suppose. If she was going to meet him in Stowerton she'd have gone to Stowerton—the buses go every ten minutes between four and seven. There's no shelter between here and Stowerton except trees and the old pumping station.'

Wexford nodded. He knew the place Burden spoke of, a shed containing disused pumping equipment and standing in thick woodland on the banks of the Kingsbrook.

'We'll have it searched,' he said. 'That's quite an idea. Meanwhile, I'd like to see how things are progressing in the High Street.'

Things had progressed considerably. When Wexford entered the hall of the Baptist church, Martin had two people waiting to see him, each with information that was to complicate rather than simplify the case.

The first of these, an assistant from the Snowdrop Laundry

and Dry Cleaners in Kingsmarkham High Street, was a middle-aged cheerful woman who had known Dawn Stonor as a schoolgirl and since then had sometimes seen her on her rare visits to her mother.

'We sort of knew each other by sight really,' she said. 'She came in last Monday at about a quarter past four.'

'She was dressed in mauve?'

'That's right. A very smart trouser suit. I remember we cleaned it for her Easter time. When she came in on Monday I wasn't sure if she knew me, but I asked her how her mum was and her gran and she said all right. Well, she'd brought this blue frock in to be cleaned and she wanted to know if I could get it done express. She wanted to collect it the next morning. "We can just do it," I said, "seeing you've brought it before four-thirty." If they come in later than that, you see, they can't get their things back before the next afternoon.

' "I want to be on the ten-fifteen train tomorrow," she said, "so can I collect it at ten?" '

'She meant to collect it herself?' Wexford asked.

'Well, she said "I". She didn't say anything about her mum fetching it like she has in the past. No, she meant to get it herself. I said that'd be all right and I made out the slip for her. You can see our part of it if you like. I've got it here with me.'

Wexford thanked her and examined the slip, noting the name and the date.

'But she didn't collect it?'

'No. I had it all ready but she never came. I was going to pop up to her mum's with it this week and then I heard what had happened. Awful, isn't it? It made me go cold all over when I heard.'

Next Wexford saw the manager of the Luximart, a big new supermarket which stood between the Dragon and the Baptist church just beside the Forby bus stop. He was young, eager and helpful.

'The young lady came in here at half past four. We don't

get many customers late on a Monday on account of we don't sell meat on a Monday and the veg isn't fresh. Most people eat up the Sunday leftovers and shop on Tuesdays.

'She was almost my last customer and when she left she waited nearly half an hour for the Forby bus, the five-twelve. Stood outside here, she did. I cursed, I can tell you, because just after the bus had come and she'd got on it I was sweeping up in the shop and I found this slip from the cleaners.'

'May I see?'

'I was certain she'd dropped it. I was sure it hadn't been there before she came in and I was quite worried thinking maybe she'd have trouble collecting her cleaning. I reckoned she'd come back but she never did. Then when I saw your notices and heard the name . . .'

'You didn't know her?'

'Never saw her before,' said the manager, 'that I can recall.'

Wexford matched the two slips, the top and the carbon. *Miss Stonor*, he read, *15 Lower Road, Kingsmarkham. Blue dress, express, 46p.* 'Will you describe her, please?'

'Nice-looking blonde. Very smartly dressed in a sort of purple blouse and slacks. I don't know, I can't describe girls' clothes. I reckon she had a purple bag. I remember thinking . . .' The manager looked up ruefully and bit his lip. 'I remember thinking she was a smashing piece, but it seems awful saying that now she's dead.'

'What did she buy?'

'I knew you'd ask me that. I've been trying to think. I was at the check-out and she called me over to the deep freeze and asked me what the strawberry sundaes were like. They're sort of mousse things in cartons. I said I'd recommend them and she put two in the trolley. Wait, I'm trying to see it, sort of get a picture . . .'

Wexford nodded, saying nothing. He knew that this method, a kind of free association, was the best way. Let the man close his eyes, transport himself mentally back into the shop, stand

54

beside the girl, re-create the almost empty wire trolley . . .

'There was a can in the trolley.' He concentrated. 'I know what it was! Soup. Vichyssoise, the stuff you can have hot or cold. It's all coming back. She took a tin of chicken fillets off the shelf and tomatoes—yes, tomatoes in a pack. I think she bought bread, a cut loaf. She might have bought butter, I don't remember. I do remember she got a bottle of wine, though, because she had the cheapest line we do. Spanish beaujolais and some cigarettes. She hadn't a basket. I gave her a brown paper carrier.'

There was no one else to see. Wexford went back to the police station where he found Burden with the doctor. The wind rattled the windows and a thin rain spattered against the glass.

'She meant to spend the night here,' he said. 'She was going to call for that dress on Tuesday morning. And it was food she was carrying in that bag when Mrs Peveril saw her. Food for *two* people.'

'For her and her date,' said Burden.

'Then he wasn't a casual pick-up. A man she picked up would either not ask her to eat with him at all or else he'd invite her to some restaurant. You can't imagine a girl making a date with a stranger and that stranger saying, Bring a three-course meal with you and we'll have a picnic. She must have known him and known him well.' Wexford listed the items of food and said, 'What's the most interesting thing about that food, Mike?'

'It could have been eaten cold as it was or it could have been heated. In other words, it could have been bought especially to be eaten in the open air, or it could equally well have been heated—the soup and the chicken, that is—which means indoors, in a house.'

During this interchange the doctor, who had been sketching a duodenum on the back of Wexford's draft of the crime-prevention plans, looked up and said, 'It wasn't eaten at all.

I've got a provisional medical report prepared for you—
there'll be a more detailed one later from the experts, of course
—but the girl's stomach was empty. She hadn't eaten anything
for five or six hours. Maybe the boy friend ate the lot on his
own.'

'Or else food and wine and carrier bag are hidden somewhere with the mauve trouser suit.'

'Not the wine,' said Crocker. He stopped drawing and his
face was suddenly grim. 'The wine was used. Remember the
glass you found, Reg, the glass you cut your hand on? There
was glass embedded in her face and neck. Her dress was
stained with wine as well as blood. I don't think I'm being
unduly melodramatic when I say that her attacker went completely mad. Perhaps you and Mike will be able to find out
whatever it was she said or did to him. All I can say is that
something she did tipped him over the edge. He beat her to
death with that wine bottle. He beat her in such a frenzy that
the glass broke against the bones of her face.'

It was dark inside the little shed, half-filled as it was by
cumbersome, rusty machinery, and the men worked by the
light of lamps they had brought with them. Outside the pumping station the river rattled noisily and the wind slapped the
door monotonously against its rotted frame.

'If they came in here,' said Wexford at last, 'it was a very
brief visit. No blood, no crumbs, no cigarette ends.' He
touched his hair and brought away a handful of cobwebs.
'It's a filthy hole, not at all my idea of the sort of rendezvous
likely to entice a girl like Dawn Stonor, who, I take it, was
conscious of her appearance.' For a moment he watched the
men lifting up old sacks and searching through coils of rotted
rope. 'I wish to God I could understand why she put that red
dress on,' he said. 'I've a feeling that if I could I'd have the
key to the whole business.'

'Because she got dirty in here?' hazarded Burden.

'Doing what? Not eating, not smoking, not making love. Talking, maybe? Then where did the dress come from? She wasn't carrying it with her. Perhaps he was. I just don't think it's possible that in one day she got two garments soiled so as to be unwearable. The coincidence is too great, and it's beyond the bounds of credibility that he happened to have a dress with him ready for her to put on in case hers got dirty. And who was he?'

'We may get some help as far as that goes from the London end.'

'Let's hope so. Shall we go? All this dust is making me cough.'

What Burden termed help from the London end had come in while they were down by the river. It was not information, data, reported interviews, but help in actual human form. She was an attractive young woman, this girl who had shared a flat in Philimede Gardens, Earls Court, with Dawn Stonor. Wexford went into the interview room where they told him she was and found her drinking tea and chain-smoking, the ashtray on the table in front of her already choked with butts.

7

'My name's Joan Miall,' she said, shaking hands in a very forthright manner. 'An inspector came this morning and asked me a lot of questions. He said you'd want to see me and I thought I'd save you the trouble by coming to see you.' She was dark with a very pretty intelligent face and deep blue eyes. She looked about twenty-four. 'I still can't believe Dawn's dead. It seems so fantastic.'

'It's good of you to come, Miss Miall. I shall have a great deal to ask you so I think we'll go upstairs to my office where we can be more comfortable.'

In the lift she didn't speak but she lit another cigarette. Wexford understood that this heavy smoking was an antidote to shock. He approved her plain knee-length skirt and scarlet shirt, the healthy fine-boned face which, scarcely touched with make-up, was framed in shining hair, long and parted in the centre. Her hands were ringless, the nails short and lacquered pale pink. The pleasant, semi-living room appointments of his office seemed to set her more at ease. She relaxed, smiled and stubbed out her cigarette. 'I smoke too much.'

'Maybe,' he said. 'You were very fond of Dawn?'

She hesitated. 'I don't know really. I shared a flat with her for four years. We saw each other every day. We worked together. It was a shock.'

'You both worked at the Townsman Club?'

'Yes, that was where we met. We'd both been through a bit of a bad time. Dawn had been living with a man who was

58

almost pathologically jealous and I'd been sharing with my sister. My sister was terribly possessive. Dawn and I decided to take a flat together and we made a pact not to fuss each other and not to worry if the other one didn't always come home. That's why I wasn't worried. Not until Saturday. Then, I . . .'

'You're running on a bit, Miss Miall,' Wexford interrupted her. 'Tell me about last Monday first.'

The slight strain this called for demanded a fresh cigarette. She lit one, inhaled and leant back in her chair. 'Dawn had started a week's holiday the Saturday before, Saturday, June fourth. She couldn't make up her mind whether to go away or not. Her boy friend—he's called Paul Wickford and he keeps a garage near us—he wanted her to go touring in Devon with him, but she still hadn't decided by that Monday morning.'

'You expected her back on Monday evening?'

'Yes, in a way. She went off in the morning to catch the train for Kingsmarkham and she wasn't very cheerful. She never was when she was going to see her mother, they didn't get on. Dawn got on better with her grandmother.' Joan Miall paused and seemed to consider. 'Paul came round at about six, but when she hadn't come by seven he drove me to the club and then he went back to our flat to wait for her. Well, when she wasn't there on the Tuesday or the Wednesday and I didn't see anything of Paul, I thought they'd gone off to Devon together. We never left notes for each other, you see. We had this non-interference pact.'

'She told her mother she was working that night.'

Joan smiled slightly. 'I expect she did. That would just be an excuse to get away. Four or five hours in her mother's company would be as much as she could stand.' She stubbed out her cigarette, flicking ash fastidiously from her fingers. 'On Saturday—last Saturday, I mean—Paul appeared again. He hadn't been in Devon. His mother died that very Monday night and he'd had to go up north to the funeral and to see about things. He didn't know where Dawn was any more than I did.

'Then yesterday when we were both getting really worried— Dawn was due back at work tonight—the police came and told me what had happened.'

'Miss Miall, when Dawn was found she was wearing a dark red dress.' He noted her quick glance of surprise but ignored it for the moment. 'Now we have that dress here,' he said. 'It's rather badly stained. I'm going to ask you if you will be very brave and look at that dress. I warn you that you could find it upsetting. Will you look at it?'

She nodded.

'Yes, if you think it'll help. I can't remember Dawn ever wearing red. It wasn't her colour. But I'll look at it.'

The dress was made of a dark red rayon fabric with cap sleeves, a shaped waist and self belt. Because of its colour, the stains didn't show up except as a great stiff patch on the bodice.

The girl whitened and compressed her lips. 'May I touch it?' she said faintly.

'Yes.'

Rather tremulously, she fingered the neck opening and looked at the label. 'This is only a size twelve,' she said. 'Dawn was quite a big girl. She took a fourteen.'

'But she was wearing this dress.'

'It wasn't hers and it must have been quite a tight fit on her.' Abruptly she turned away and shivered. 'Look, perhaps you don't know much about fashion, but that dress is old, seven or eight years out of date, maybe more. Dawn was very fashion-conscious.'

Wexford led her back to his office. She sat down and the colour returned to her cheeks. He waited a little, marvelling at the friend's distress, the mother's indifference, and then he said, 'Miss Miall, will you try to give me a sort of character sketch of Dawn? What sort of girl she was, whom she knew and how she reacted to other people?'

'I'll try,' said Joan Miall.

'I don't want to give you the impression,' the girl began, 'that she wasn't a nice person. She was. But there were some—well, rather peculiar things about her.' She lifted her head and looked at him earnestly, almost aggressively.

'I'm not asking for a character *reference*, you know. And what you say will be between us. I shan't broadcast it about.'

'No, of course not. But she's dead and I have sort of old-fashioned ideas about not speaking ill of the dead. I expect you'll think that a doll who serves drinks in a club hasn't any right to get all upstage, sort of disapprove of other people's behaviour?'

Wexford didn't answer. He smiled gently and shook his head.

'Anyway,' she said, 'I didn't exactly disapprove of Dawn. It was just that—well, it's not always easy living with a compulsive liar. You don't know where you are with people like that. You don't know *them* and the relationship is sort of unreal. I know someone said that even a really bad liar tells more truth than lies, but you still can't tell what are lies and what truth, can you?'

It was on the tip of Wexford's tongue to ask what an intelligent girl like Joan Miall was doing at the Townsman Club, but he checked the impulse.

'So Dawn was a liar?' he said instead, reflecting that this wasn't going to make his task easier. He looked into the frank, clear eyes of the girl opposite him, a girl he was sure would be transparently truthful. 'What did she lie about?'

'Well, it was boasting and name-dropping really. She'd had an awful childhood. Her father used to knock her about, and her mother sort of knocked her about mentally. She'd tell her she was immoral and no good in one breath and then in the

61

next she'd say how she missed her and begged her to come home and marry and settle down. Mrs Stonor was always telling her they were—what was the phrase?—Oh, yes, "Just ordinary folk", and Dawn had no business giving herself airs. Then she'd say the work she did was no better than being a tart.

'It made her want to prove herself. Sorry if I'm talking like an amateur psychiatrist but I'm interested in that sort of thing. I tried to find out what made Dawn tick. When we first lived together I thought she really did know a lot of famous people. One day she brought a dog home and said she was going to look after it for a fortnight while its owner was away. She said the owner was a famous actor, a household word more or less. He's always on television.

'Then, after the dog had gone back, we were both in the club one night and this actor came in. Some member brought him as his guest. Of course I recognised him. He didn't even know Dawn. It wasn't that they'd quarrelled and weren't speaking. You could tell he just didn't know her.' Joan shrugged. She put her cigarettes into her bag and closed the bag decisively. 'She used to look through the evening paper and she'd spot a photograph of some well-known guy and say she'd worked with him or had an affair with him. I never said much. It embarrassed me. The biggest name she ever dropped was a singer, terribly famous. She said she'd known him for years and every so often they'd go out together. She *said*. A couple of weeks ago the phone rang and she answered it. She looked at me and covered up the mouthpiece and said it was him, but when she started talking to him she never said his name, just "Yes" and "No" and "That'd be lovely". She never actually called him Zeno. You can pretend a phone-caller is anyone, can't you? Your flatmate's not likely to go and listen on the extension.'

'Zeno?' said Wexford. 'D'you mean she claimed acquaintance with Zeno Vedast?'

62

'That's rather the word, "claimed". He never came to the flat. I never saw her with him. No, it was just the same as with the TV actor, name-dropping to impress, I'm afraid.'

'Miss Miall, was Dawn the sort of girl who might pick up a stranger and spend the night with him?'

She hesitated and then said impulsively, 'She might have. It sounds hateful but Dawn was very fond of money. She never had any money when she was a child, just a shilling a week or something ridiculous, and she was supposed to save half of that in a piggy bank you couldn't open. And her parents can't have been that poor—they both worked. I'm telling you this to explain why she might have picked someone up if she thought there was anything in it for her. When she first came to the club she was told like we all are that dating a customer means instant dismissal. The members know that but some of them try it on. Well, Dawn accepted an invitation from a member, in spite of the rule. He said if she'd go away for the weekend with him he'd buy her a fur coat. She did go and he gave her ten pounds. She never got the coat and I think she felt awfully humiliated because she never did that again. She liked admiration too and if a man wanted to sleep with her she thought . . . Oh, well, that it means a lot more than it does. Sometimes when she wasn't working she'd be away for a night and I think she was with a man. She couldn't bring him home, you see, in case Paul came round. But, as I told you, we didn't ask each other questions.'

'This Mr Wickford was a steady boy friend?'

She nodded. 'They'd been going out together for two years. I think she'd have married Paul in the end. The trouble seemed to be that he wasn't rich enough for her or famous or anything. He's about thirty-five, divorced, very nice. He was frightfully upset when he heard what had happened to her and the doctor had to give him sedatives. I'm sure she would have married him if she could only have grown out of all those ideas about knowing famous people. She was a very nice girl really, generous, good fun, always ready to help anyone out. It was just that she couldn't help telling lies . . .'

'One last thing. Miss Miall. Dawn brought food in Kingsmarkham last Monday afternoon, a tin of soup, tinned chicken and two strawberry mousse things in cartons. Is it possible she bought it to take home for lunch for the two of you on Tuesday?'

'Definitely not.'

'Why are you so sure?'

'For one thing—please don't think I don't like this place, it's a very nice town—but no one who lives—er, lived—where Dawn did would buy food here to take home. We're surrounded by delicatessen shops and big supermarkets. The other thing is, she wouldn't buy food for the two of us. I'm a bit of a faddist when it comes to food. Health-conscious. You wouldn't think so the way I smoke, would you?' She gave a slight laugh. 'I never eat food out of cans. Dawn knew that. We used to prepare our food quite separately unless one of us made a casserole or a salad. Dawn didn't care what she ate. She hated cooking and she used to say she ate to live.' Joan winced at the last word which had been used automatically, without thought. She lifted her eyes to Wexford and he saw that they shone with unshed tears. In a choking voice she said:

'She didn't live very long, did she?'

Michael Burden was a widower whose married life had been happy and who, as a result of this, tended to consider sexual relationships as ecstatically romantic or, when they were illicit, deeply sordid. But the solitary love affair he had had since his wife's death had slightly broadened his mind. He was now prepared to admit that unmarried people might love each other and consummate that love without degradation. Sometimes these newly enlightened views of his gave rise to romantic theories and it was one of these which he propounded to

Wexford as they drank their coffee together on Tuesday morning.

'We've agreed,' he began, 'that her killer can't have been a casual pick-up because of the food-shopping angle. And we know the food wasn't bought for her and the Miall girl. Therefore, she knew the man and knew him well enough to arrange with him that she'd buy their meal and meet him after he'd finished work. The time of the meeting—surely between five-thirty and six?—indicates it was to be after he'd finished work. Right?'

'Imagine so, Mike.'

'Well, sir, I've been wondering if she and this bloke had one of those long close friendships extending over years.'

'What long close friendships? What are you on about?'

'You know my sister-in-law Grace?' Wexford nodded impatiently. Of course he knew Grace, the sister of Burden's dead wife who had looked after Burden's children when they had first lost their mother and who he had later hoped would be the second Mrs Burden. That had come to nothing. Grace had married someone else and now had a baby of her own. 'I mention her,' said Burden, 'because it was her experience that gave me the idea. She and Terry knew each other off and on for years before they got married. There was always a sort of bond between them, although they didn't meet much and each of them had other—well, friends. Terry even got engaged to someone else.'

'You're suggesting this was the case with Dawn?'

'She lived here till she was eighteen. Suppose she knew this bloke when they were both very young and they had an affair and then they both left Kingsmarkham to work elsewhere. Or he stayed here and she went to London. What I'm suggesting is that they kept in touch and whenever she came home or he went to London they had one of these dates, secret dates necessarily because he was married and she was more or less engaged to Wickford. Frankly, I think this covers every

65

aspect of the case and deals with all the difficulties.'

Wexford stirred his coffee, looked longingly towards the sugar bowl and resisted the temptation to take another lump. 'It doesn't deal with that bloody red dress,' he said viciously.

'It does if they met in this chap's house. We'd have to admit the possibility of coincidence, that she stained the mauve outfit and then put on a dress belonging to this man's wife.'

'The wife being out presumably. She goes there, he lets her in. What happens to the mauve garment? They had no drinks for her to spill, ate nothing for her to drop, made no love to —er, crush it. (I put it like that, Mike, to save your delicate sensibilities.) Maybe the violence of his welcoming embrace creased it up and she was so dainty about her appearance that she rushed upstairs and slipped into one of her rival's ancient cast-offs. He was so upset about her thinking more of her clothes than of him that he upped and banged her with the bottle. Is that it?'

'It must have been something like that,' said Burden rather stiffly. Wexford was always pouring cold water on his flights of fancy and he never got used to it.

'Where was this house of assignation, then?'

'On the outskirts of Stowerton, the Forby side. She went by the fields because he was going to meet her there and take her back to his house. They arranged it that way just in case the wife changed her mind about going away.' He made a moue of distaste, sordidness temporarily conquering romance. 'Some people do go on like that, you know.'

'You seem to know, anyway. So all we have to do now is find a bloke living in a house on the north side of Stowerton who's known Dawn Stonor since they went to Sunday school together and whose wife was away Monday night. Oh, and find if the wife has missed a red dress.'

'You don't sound too enthusiastic, sir.'

'I'm not,' Wexford said frankly. 'The people you know may go on like that but the people I know don't. They act like *people*, not characters in a second feature film that's been thrown together for the sake of sensation rather than illustrating human nature. But since my mind is otherwise a blank, I reckon we'd better get asking Mrs Stonor who Dawn knew around Stowerton and who had a lifelong sentimental bond with her.'

8

'The folks round here,' said Mrs Stonor, 'weren't good enough for Dawn. She was a proper little snob, though what she'd got to be snobbish about I never will know.'

For all her frankly expressed unmaternal sentiments, Mrs Stonor was dressed in deepest black. She and the old woman who was with her, and who had been introduced as 'My mother, Mrs Peckham', had been sitting in semi-darkness, for the curtains were drawn. When the two policemen entered the room a light was switched on. Wexford noticed that a wall mirror had been covered by a black cloth.

'We think it possible,' he said, 'that Dawn went to meet an old friend on Monday night. I want you to try and remember the names of any boy friends she had before she left home or· any name she may have mentioned to you on her visits here.'

Instead of replying, Mrs Stonor addressed the old woman who was leaning forward avidly, clutching the two sticks that supported her when she walked. 'You can get off back to bed now, Mother. All this has got nothing to do with you. You've been up too long as it is.'

'I'm not tired,' said Mrs Peckham. She was very old, well over eighty. Her body was thin and tiny and her face simian, a maze of wrinkles. What sparse white hair she had was scragged on to the top of her head into a knot stuck full of pins. 'I don't want to go to bed, Phyllis. It's not often I have a bit of excitement.'

'Excitement! I like that. A nice way to talk when Dawn's

had her head bashed in by a maniac. Come along now. I'll take your arm up the stairs.'

A small devil in Wexford's head spoke for him. 'Mrs Peckham should stay. She may be able to help.' He said it more to irritate Mrs Stonor than because he thought her mother would be able to furnish them with information.

Mrs Peckham grinned with pleasure, showing a set of over-large false teeth. Reprieved, she helped herself to a sweet from the bag on a table beside her and began a ferocious crunching. Her daughter turned down the corners of her mouth and folded her hands.

'Can you think of anyone, Mrs Stonor?'

Still sulky from having her wishes baulked, Mrs Stonor said, 'Her dad never let her have boy friends. He wanted her to grow up respectable. We had a job with her as it was, always telling lies and staying out late. My husband tried every way we could think of to teach her the meaning of decency.'

'Tried his strap, mostly,' said Mrs Peckham. Protected by the presence of the policemen, she gave her daughter a triumphant and unpleasant grin. Wexford could see that she was one of those old pensioners who, dependent for all her needs on a hated child, was subservient, cringing, defiant or malicious as her fancy took her or circumstances demanded. When Mrs Stonor made no reply but only lifted her chin, her mother tried another dig. 'You and George ought never to have had no kids. Always smacking her and yelling at her. Knock one devil out and two in, that's what I say.'

Wexford cleared his throat. 'We don't seem to be getting very far. I can't believe Dawn never mentioned any man she was friendly with.'

'I never said she didn't. You'll get your stomach trouble again, Mother, if you don't leave them acid drops alone. The fact is, it was all lies with Dawn. I got so I let what she said go in one ear and out the other. I do know she had this man

69

Wickford on account of her bringing him down here for the day last year. They didn't stop long. Dawn could see what I thought about *him*. A divorced man, running a garage! That was the best she could do for herself.'

'There was no one else?' Burden asked coldly.

'I said I *don't know*. You're not going to tell me she got herself done in by some boy she was at school with, are you? That's all the local boys she knew.'

Mrs Peckham, having incompletely unwrapped her latest sweet, was removing shreds of paper from her mouth. 'There was Harold Goodbody,' she said.

'Don't be so stupid, Mother. As if Harold'd have anything to do with a girl like Dawn. Harold climbed too high for the likes of her.'

'Who is this man?' asked Wexford.

The sweet lodged in a wizened cheek pouch, the noisy sucking abated, Mrs Peckham heaved a heavy but not unhappy sigh. 'He was a lovely boy, was Harold. Him and his mum and dad used to live round here in the next street. I wasn't here then, I had my own cottage, but I used to see Harold when I had my job serving dinners at the school. Oh, he was a lad! Always one for a joke was Harold, April Fools all the year round for him. Him and Dawnie was pals from their first day at school. Then I come here to live with Phyllis and George and Dawnie'd bring him back to tea.'

'I never knew that,' said Mrs Stonor, bristling. 'George wouldn't have had that.'

'George wasn't here, was he? And you was working at that shop. I didn't see no harm in Dawnie bringing her friend home.' Mrs Peckham turned her back on her daughter and faced Wexford. 'Harold was a real freak to look at, all bones and his hair nearly as white as mine. I'd have boiled eggs all ready for the three of us, but when Dawnie and me started cracking ours we'd find just the empty shells. Harold'd brought a couple of empty shells to fool us. Ooh, he was

70

funny! He had a joke ink blot and a rubber spider. Made us scream, that spider did. One day I caught him playing with the phone. He'd rung this number and when the woman answered he said he was the engineers. He said to her there was an emergency. She was to pour boiling water down the receiver, leave it for ten minutes and then cut the lead with scissors. She was going to too, she believed him, but I put a stop to that, though I was laughing fit to die. Harold was a real scream.'

'Yes, I'm sure,' said Wexford. 'How old was he when all this fun and games was going on?'

'About fifteen.'

'And he still lives round here?'

'No, of course he don't. That Mr Silk from Sundays took him up and he left home and went to London when he was seventeen and got famous, didn't he?'

Wexford blinked. 'Famous? Harold Goodbody?'

Mrs Peckham wagged her gnarled hands impatiently. 'He changed his name when he got to be a singer. What did he call himself? Now I'm getting on I seem to forget everything. John Lennon, that was it.'

'I hardly think...' Wexford began.

Mrs Stonor, who had remained silent and scornful, opened her mouth and snapped, 'Zeno Vedast. He calls himself Zeno Vedast.'

'Dawn was at school with Zeno Vedast?' Wexford said blankly. So it hadn't been all boasting, vain name-dropping? Or some of it hadn't. 'They were friends?'

'You don't want to listen to Mother,' said Mrs Stonor. 'I daresay Dawn saw a bit of him when they were at school. She never saw him in London.'

'Oh, yes, she did, Phyllis. She told me so last Monday when she was home. She'd tell me things she'd never tell you. She knew you'd pour cold water on everything she did.'

71

'What did she say, Mrs Peckham?'

'She come into my room when I was in bed. You remember Hal, don't you, Gran? she says. We always called him Hal. Well, I went out to dinner with him Friday night, she said.'

'And you believed her?' Mrs Stonor gave the brittle laugh that is not a laugh at all. 'Harold Goodbody was in Manchester Friday night. I saw him myself on telly, I saw him live. She was just making up tales like she always did.'

Mrs Peckham scrunched indignantly. 'She got the night wrong, that's all. Poor little Dawnie.'

'Don't you be so stupid. He's a *famous* singer. Though what's so wonderful about his voice I never shall know. Richard Tauber, now that was a man who *had* a voice.'

Burden asked, 'Do his parents still live here?'

Mrs Stonor looked for a moment as if she was going to tell him not to be so stupid. She restrained herself and said sourly, 'When he got rich he bought them a great big detached place up near London. All right for some, isn't it? I've always been decent and brought my daughter up right and what did she ever do for me? I well remember Freda Goodbody going round to her neighbours to borrow a quarter of tea on account of Goodbody spending all his wages on the dogs. Harold never had more than one pair of shoes at a time and they was cast-offs from his cousin. "My darling boy" and "my precious Hal" she used to say but she used to give him baked beans for his Sunday dinner.'

Suddenly Mrs Peckham waxed appropriately biblical. ' "Better a dish of herbs where love is",' she said, ' "than a stalled ox and hatred therewith".' She took the last acid drop and sucked it noisily.

'There you are, sir,' said Burden when they were in the car. 'A lifelong friendship, like I said.'

'Well, not quite like you said, Mike. Zeno Vedast doesn't live in Stowerton, he has no wife, and I don't suppose he makes a habit of eating tinned food in fields with waitresses.

The odd thing is that she *did* know him. It seems to bear out what Joan Miall said that, in the nature of things, even a chronic liar must tell more truth than lies. We all know the story of the boy who cried wolf. Dawn Stonor was a lion-hunter. She cried lion and this time the lion was real. But we haven't a shred of evidence to connect Vedast with her last Monday. Very likely he was still in Manchester. All I can say at the moment is that it's intriguing, it's odd.'

'Surely you think we ought to see him?'

'Of course we must see him. We must see every man Dawn knew, unless he has a watertight alibi for that Monday night. We still don't know what Wickford was doing after seven.' The chief inspector tapped his driver's shoulder. 'Back to the station, please, Stephens.'

The man half-turned. He was young, rather shy, recently transferred from Brighton. He blushed when Wexford addressed him, rather as he had coloured under Mrs Peveril's stare.

'Did you want to say something to me?' Wexford asked gently.

'No, sir.'

'Back to the station, then. We can't sit here all day.'

By Wednesday Paul Wickford had been cleared of suspicion. After leaving Joan Miall at the Townsman Club in Hertford Street, he had gone into a pub in Shepherd Market where he had drunk one vodka and tonic before driving back to Earls Court. Waiting for him in his flat was his brother who brought the news of their mother's serious illness and asked Paul to drive with him immediately to Sheffield. Paul had then asked the tenant of the second floor flat to cancel his milk and papers and, if he happened to see Dawn Stonor, to tell her where he had gone. The two brothers had reached their mother's house in Sheffield soon after midnight, and by the following morning she was dead.

In spite of there being only thin evidence of Dawn's killer having lived on the outskirts of Stowerton, a house-to-house investigation had begun on Tuesday afternoon of the whole district. No one had seen Dawn; no one had seen a girl in mauve alone or with a man. Only two wives had been absent from home on the evening in question, one with her husband and one leaving him behind to mind their four children. No wife had been away for the whole night and no wife had missed a red dress. Wexford's men searched the fields for the trouser suit and the food. It was dreary work, for the rain fell heavily and there were fears that the river would flood.

Mrs Clarke and Mrs Peveril remained the only people who had seen Dawn after five-twenty, Mrs Peveril the last person —except her killer—to have seen her alive. Wexford concentrated on these two women, questioning them exhaustively, and it wasn't long before he found something odd in their evidence. It had not previously occurred to him that they might know each other, and it was only when, sitting in Mrs Clarke's living room, listening to her answer the phone, that the thought occurred to him.

'I can't talk now, Margaret. I'll ring you later. I hope Edward soon feels better.'

She didn't say who had been at the other end of the line. Why should she? She sat down with a bright, insincere smile. 'So sorry. You were saying?'

Wexford said sharply, 'Were you talking to Mrs Peveril?'

'How *could* you know? I was, as a matter of fact.'

'Then I imagine you are the one person she claims acquaintance with in this district?'

'Poor Margaret. She's so neurotic and she has an awful time with Edward. I suppose I am her only friend. She doesn't make friends easily.'

'Mrs Clarke, you were first questioned about Dawn Stonor last Sunday evening, I think? We questioned people on this side of the estate first.'

'Well, you ought to know that better than me.'

She looked a little offended, bored, but not at all frightened. Wexford considered carefully. Burden and Martin and Gates had begun their questions here at seven, not reaching The Pathway till nine. 'Did you phone Mrs Peveril on Sunday evening before nine?' Her glance became wary, defensive. 'I see you did. You told her you'd been questioned and, moreover, that you'd been able to help. It was only natural for you to talk to your friend about it. I expect you described the girl to her and told her which way you'd seen her go.'

'Is there anything wrong in that?'

'Discretion would have been wiser. Never mind. Describe Dawn Stonor to me again now, please.'

'But I've done it hundreds of times,' cried Mrs Clarke with exasperated exaggeration. 'I've told you over and over again.'

'Once more, for the last time.'

'I was coming along to get the bus into Kingsmarkham. I saw her get off the bus that went the other way. She crossed the road and went into The Pathway.' Mrs Clarke spoke slowly and deliberately as might a parent explaining for the dozenth time to a not very bright child the point of a simple story. 'She had fair hair, she was in her twenties, and she wore a lilac-coloured trouser suit and mauve shoes.'

'That was what you told Mrs Peveril?'

'Yes, and you and all your other people. I couldn't say any more because I don't know any more.'

'You didn't, for instance, notice her large mauve bag with a gilt buckle or that there was a darker edging to the suit?'

'No, I didn't. I didn't notice that and you saying it doesn't bring it back to me or anything. I'm sorry but I've told you everything I know.'

He shook his head, not in denial of her statement, but at his own bewilderment. At first, briefly, when she put the phone down he had suddenly been certain that Mrs Peveril had never seen Dawn at all, that the news from her friend had sparked off an urge for sensationalism, giving her an opportunity to make herself important. He remembered how, although she said she had taken careful note of the girl's appearance in order to tell her husband about her, she had never told him. But now he knew she must have seen her. How else could she, and she alone, have known of the bag and the purple border to the tunic?

9

Three houses that backed on to Sundays, three garden gates opening on to a narrow strip of land beyond which was the quarry. ... Each garden separated from its neighbours by high woven chestnut fencing, a strip of land overgrown with dense bushes and quite tall trees. Wexford thought how easy it would have been to carry a body out of one of those houses by night and drop it into the quarry. And yet, if Dawn had gone into one of those houses instead of across the fields, if Mrs Peveril had seen her do so and was a seeker after sensation, wouldn't these facts have made a far greater sensation?

'I thought you'd leave me alone after I'd told you the truth,' said Mrs Peveril fretfully. 'I shall be ill if you badger me. All right, Mrs Clarke did phone me. That doesn't mean I didn't see her too, does it? I saw her and I saw her walk across those fields.'

'She couldn't have gone into any of those houses, anyway, sir,' said Burden. 'Unless it was into Mrs Peveril's own house. In which case Mrs P. presumably wouldn't say she'd seen her at all. Dawn can't have gone into Dunsand's or Miss Mowler's. We've checked at Myringham, at the university, and Dunsand didn't leave there till six. He'd have been lucky to get home by six-thirty, more like twenty to seven. Miss Mowler was with her friend in Kingsmarkham till a quarter to eight.'

They went back to the police station and were about to enter the lift when a sharp draught of wind told Wexford that

the double doors to the entrance foyer had been swept un-
ceremoniously open. He turned round and saw an extraordinary figure. The man was immensely tall—far taller than
Wexford who topped six feet—with a bush of jet-black hair.
He wore an ankle-length pony-skin coat and carried a canvas
bag whose sopping wet contents had soaked the canvas and
were dripping on to the floor. Once inside, he paused, looked
about him confidently and was making for Sergeant Camb
who sat drinking tea behind his counter when Wexford inter-
cepted him.

'Mr Mbowele, I believe? We've met before.' Wexford put
out his hand which was immediately gripped in a huge copper-
coloured vice of bone-crushing fingers. 'What can I do for
you?'

The young African was extremely handsome. He had all
the glowing virile grace which has led clothes designers and
model agencies and photographers to take up the slogan—
'Black is beautiful'. Beaming at Wexford, his soft, dark eyes
alight, he withdrew his hand, dropped the sodden bag on to
the floor and undid the collar of his coat. Under it his chest
was bare, hung with a chain of small green stones.

'I don't altogether dig this rain, man,' he said, shaking
drops of water off his hair. 'You call this June?'

'I'm not responsible for the weather.' Wexford pointed to
the bag. 'And rain wasn't responsible for that unless the floods
have started.'

'I fished it out of the river,' said Louis Mbowele. 'Not here.
At Myringham. That's quite a river now, your little Kingsbrook, man. I go down the river every morning and walk. I
can think down there.' He stretched out his arms. It was easy
to imagine him striding by the full flowing river, his mind
equally in spate, his body brimming with vibrant energy. 'I
was thinking,' he said, 'about Wittgenstein's principle of
atomicity....'

'About *what*?'

'For an essay. It's not important. I looked in the river and I saw this purple silk thing . . .'

'Is that what's in the bag?'

'Didn't you get that? I knew what it was, man, I'd read the papers. I waded in and fished it out and put it in this bag—it's my girl friend's bag—and brought it here.'

'You shouldn't have touched it, Mr Mbowele.'

'Louis, man, Louis. We're all friends, aren't we? I've no prejudice against the fuzz. The fuzz have their place in a well-organised state. I'm no anarchist.'

Wexford sighed. 'You'd better come upstairs and bring the bag with you.'

In the office Louis made himself immediately at home by taking off the pony-skin coat and drying his hair on its lining. He sat on a chair like one who is more accustomed to sit on the floor, one long leg stuck out and the other hooked over the chair arm.

'Exactly where did you find this, Louis?'

'In the river between Mill Street and the college grounds. It'd been swept down from round here somewhere. Look, why freak out about it? If I'd left it there it'd be down by the sea somewhere now. Keep your cool, man.'

'I am not losing my cool,' said Wexford who couldn't help smiling. 'Was there anything else in the river?'

'Fish,' said Louis, grinning, 'and sticks and stones and a hell of a lot of water.'

It was pointless, anyway, to ask about the paper carrier of food. What carrier bag, what cardboard cartons, would survive ten days and fifteen miles of pounding in that swollen stream? The can and the jar would survive, of course. But only a miracle would have brought them to precisely the same spot in the river as the trouser suit when Louis Mbowele had found it. Maybe the Wittgenstein principle provided for that sort of coincidence, but Wexford decided not to pursue it. The bag and, to a lesser extent the coat, were soaking his carpet.

'Well, I'm very grateful to you. You've been most public-spirited.' Wexford risked his hand again and managed not to wince when the vice enclosed it. 'There's a bus goes to Myringham at ten past which you ought to be in time for.'

'I ought if I'm going to get to Len's tutorial.' He glanced at the window. It was pouring. 'Have you ever been to Marumi?'

'Marumi?'

'My country. Sometimes you get no rain there for three years. Man, is that country dry! You like the sun?'

'It makes a change,' said Wexford.

'You said I was to remember you when I came into my kingdom. It won't be a kingdom but I'll need fuzz and I could get along great with you if you got rid of your hang-ups. How does it grab you?'

'I'll be too old by that time, Louis.'

'Age,' said the philosopher, 'is just a state of mind.' He looked, Wexford thought, about twenty. 'It won't be that long, man, not long at all. Get yourself together. Think it over.'

From the window Wexford watched him cross the street, swinging the wet, empty bag. He chuckled. When Burden came into the room, he looked up from the mauve rags he was examining.

'Just been offered a job, Mike.'

'Doing what?'

'My own thing, man, my own thing. When the rain and boredom here freak me out I can go boss the fuzz in a sort of black Ruritania. Can you see me in epaulettes with a Mauser on each hip?'

'My God,' said Burden. He fingered the torn material fastidiously. 'Is that the missing suit?'

Wexford nodded. 'Down to the purple edging, as described by our accurate Mrs Peveril. Louis Mbowele found it in the river at Myringham. It had obviously been washed down there by the heavy rains.'

'From those fields?'

'From up there somewhere. She was killed up there. I'm as sure of that as I'm sure I'll never be the Maigret of Marumi.'

Wexford remembered Miss Mowler from when she had been a district nurse in Kingsmarkham. His wife had broken her ankle and Miss Mowler had called three times a week to bath her and keep an eye on the plaster cast. She greeted him like an old friend.

'Mrs Wexford not been climbing any more ladders, I hope? And how are your lovely girls? I saw Sheila on television last week. She's getting quite well known, isn't she? And amazingly good-looking.'

'You mean it's amazing with me for her dad?'

'Oh, Mr Wexford, you know I didn't mean that!' Miss Mowler blushed and looked very confused. She tried to cover her gaffe with a string of explanations, but Wexford laughed and cut her short.

'I've come to talk to you about this murder, Miss Mowler.'

'But I can't help you. I wasn't here.'

'No, but you were here later in the evening. If there was anything you noticed, any little oddity...'

'I really can't help you,' she said earnestly. 'I've only been here three months and I hardly even know my neighbours.'

'Tell me what you do know of them, of the Peverils especially.'

The hall of the bungalow was rather garishly decorated, black and gilt predominating. The black bitumastic flooring curved upwards at the edges to meet an astonishingly hideous wallpaper. Wexford was rather surprised that sprays of lipstick-red flowers, each petal a pear-shaped scarlet blot, with spiralling black stems and glossy golden leaves, should be to Miss Mowler's taste. He did not tell her so as she led him into the living room, but he must have looked it, for she plunged into characteristic excuses.

'Awful, isn't it? The builder finished both these bungalows

81

completely before he sold them. Dreadful taste. You see I've got blue birds and orange lilies on the walls in here. And Mr Dunsand's next door is exactly the same. I believe he's going to re-decorate completely in his holidays. But doing that is so expensive and arduous if you're a lone woman like I am. The trouble is it's very good-quality paper and completely washable. I don't know if the Peverils' is the same. I believe they were able to choose their own decorations, but I've never been in there.'

'Mrs Peveril is a strange woman.'

'A very neurotic one, I should think. I heard her quarrelling once in the garden with her husband. She was crying quite hysterically.'

'What were they quarrelling about, Miss Mowler?' Wexford asked.

'Well, she was accusing him of being unfaithful to her. I couldn't help overhearing.' Afraid of another digression in which a spate of excuses would be put forward, Wexford shook his head and smiled. 'Oh, well, it's different rather with a policeman, isn't it? It's not gossip. Mrs Peveril's talked to me in the street. I hardly know her but that doesn't stop her saying the most—well, intimate things. I do think it's a mistake for a man to work at home, don't you?'

'Why, Miss Mowler?'

'He and his wife never get away from each other. And if the wife's possessive and jealous she'll resent it and begin suspecting things if ever he does go out without her. Mrs Peveril seems to depend on her husband for every sort of support, and of course the poor man isn't adequate. Who is? I don't think he wanted to come here. She was the moving spirit behind that . . . Oh, I didn't mean to make a pun. She's the sort of woman who's always running away if you know what I mean.'

'Does she ever go out without her husband?'

'Oh dear, women like that can never appreciate that what's

sauce for the goose ought to be sauce for the gander. She certainly goes out to her dressmaking class every Monday evening and sometimes she has another evening out with Mrs Clarke.'

'I suppose you knew Dawn Stonor?'

Any allegation that she might have been acquainted with a murder victim might have been expected to evoke fulsome excuses from a woman of Miss Mowler's temperament. Instead, she set her mouth and looked affronted. 'Very selfish, flighty sort of girl. I know the family very well. Naturally, I look in on the grandmother, Mrs Peckham, from time to time. It would have made a world of difference to that old lady's life if Dawn had bothered to go home more often. But there you are, that's the young people of today all over. While I was still working I used to tell Dawn about it but she fired right up at me, said she couldn't stand the place or her mother. There was some nonsense about having had an unhappy childhood. They've all had unhappy childhoods, Mr Wexford, to account for every bit of bad behaviour.' She tossed her head. 'I haven't seen her for two or three years now and I can't say I'm sorry.'

It was such a change for Miss Mowler not to be able to say she was sorry that Wexford concluded Dawn's firing up must have riled her excessively. He thanked her and left. Dunsand's bungalow had the closed-up, discouraging look of a house that is seldom ocupied by day, all the windows shut, a milk bottle with a note stuck in it on the doorstep. He caught sight of Mrs Peveril, neatly overalled, watering a window box. She saw him, pretended she hadn't, and rushed indoors, slamming the front door.

She was a biggish woman, the victim of premature middle-aged spread, several stones heavier than Miss Mowler who was twenty-five years her senior. He hadn't really noticed that before. She wouldn't be a size twelve, more a sixteen. But a woman can put on a lot of weight in seven years, and Joan

Miall had said the dress was seven or eight years old . . .

He had himself driven to Lower Road and again he was aware of a fidgety unease on the part of young Stevens, his driver. These days the man seemed always on the point of saying something to him, of unburdening his soul perhaps. He would say 'Yes, sir' and 'No, sir', but there was no finality about these responses, rather a vague note of hesitation and often a preoccupied pause before the man turned away and started the car. Wexford tried asking him what was the matter but he was always answered by a respectful shake of the head, and he concluded that Stevens had some domestic trouble weighing on him that he longed to discuss but was too shy and too reticent to reveal.

Mrs Stonor was in her kitchen, ironing, her mother in a rocking chair beside her. It was a chair which squeaked each time it was moved and Mrs Peckham, who seemed in an even more maliciously cheerful frame of mind today, moved it constantly, taking delight in the noise it made—they say you cannot make a noise to annoy yourself—and munching Edinburgh rock.

'I never heard her mention no Peveril,' said Mrs Stonor, passing her iron across a pair of pink locknit knickers that could only have belonged to her mother yet were capacious enough to have contained the whole of that little, dried-up body. 'She was proud of *not* knowing anyone around here, called them provincials or some fine thing. There's ever such a nice woman as is manageress of the cleaners and she'd known Dawn all her life. Dawn had to pretend she'd never seen her before. What d'you think of that?'

Wexford had to keep his thoughts to himself. He was marvelling, not for the first time, at certain popular fallacies. That children naturally love their parents is a belief which has all but died away. The world still holds that parents love their children, love them automatically, through thick and thin, through disappointment and disillusion. He himself had until

84

recently believed that the loss of a child is the one insupportable grief. When would people come to understand that the death of a son or daughter, removing the need of a parent to put a good face on things, to lie to neighbours, to sustain a false image, can be a relief?

'If she had fallen in love with a local man,' he said carefully, 'perhaps these prejudices of hers wouldn't have counted for much.' He knew as he spoke that he was talking a foreign language to Mrs Stonor.

She seized upon the one point that meant anything to her. 'She wasn't capable of loving anyone.'

Mrs Peckham snorted. With surprising psychological insight, she said, 'Maybe she didn't know how. Kids don't know how if they don't get none theirselves. Same thing with dogs.' She passed Wexford the bag of rock and grinned grimly when he took a piece. 'And monkeys,' she added. 'I read that in me *Reader's Digest*.'

'We're wondering, Mrs Stonor, if she went into a man's house.' With any other bereaved mother he would have softened his words; with this one any tact seemed a superfluous sentimentality. 'We think she may have had an assignation with a local man while his wife was away.'

'I wouldn't put it past her. She hadn't got no morals. But she wouldn't go to a fellow's house—even I can see that. That's stupid. She'd got a flat of her own, hadn't she? Them girls was only too ready to make themselves scarce if the other one was up to any funny business.' It was atrociously put, but it was unanswerable. 'Dawn didn't even have the decency to hide any of that from me,' Mrs Stonor said fiercely. 'She told me she'd been with men in that way. She called it being honest and leading her own life. As if she knew the meaning of honesty! I'd have died before I'd have told such things to my mother.'

A shrieking cackle came from Mrs Peckham. 'You'd nothing to tell, Phyllis. You aren't 'uman.'

'Don't be so stupid, Mother. The sergeant don't want you poking your nose in all the time, and it's time you had your rest. You've been fancying yourself ever since that young man come to see you this morning, buttering you up like I don't know what.'

Amused at his sudden demotion two rungs down the ladder, Wexford, who had risen to go, gave the older woman a conspiratorial half-smile. 'A grandson, Mrs Peckham?'

'No, I never had no kids but Phyllis. More's the pity.' She said it not as if she pined for a replica of Mrs Stonor but perhaps for her antithesis. 'Mind you, he was like a grandson in a way, was Hal.'

'Will you do as I ask, Mother, and get off to bed?'

'I'm going, Phyllis. I'm on me way.' An awareness that, after all, she depended for her bed and board on her daughter's good graces briefly softened Mrs Peckham's asperity, but not for long. She heaved herself up, clutching her sweets. 'You've got it in for poor Hal just because he wasn't all over you like he was me. He kissed me,' she said proudly.

'Mrs Peckham, am I right in thinking that Zeno Vedast has been here to see you? Do you mean while the festival was on? You didn't tell me that before.'

She propped herself on her walking aid, hunching her thin shoulders. 'He come this morning,' she said. 'Looking out for a house for hisself round here, one of them big places as we used to call gentlemen's houses. Ooh, he's very grand in his ideas, is Hal. He's got a whole suite to hisself at that big hotel in the Forest, but he wasn't too proud to come and see old Granny Peckham and say how cut up he was about poor Dawnie. He come in a big gold car and he kissed me and brought me a two-pound box of Black Magic.' Her eyes gleamed greedily at the thought of the chocolates, waiting for her perhaps in her bedroom. She sighed contentedly. 'I'll get off for me lay-down now,' she said.

10

The Burden children were old enough now to come home to an empty house and get their own tea, but more often they went straight from school to the house of their Aunt Grace, and in the holidays Pat Burden spent most of her time there, playing with the baby. Her brother led the marauding life of a teenage boy, wandering with a small gang of contemporaries in the fields, fishing in the Kingsbrook or playing the jukebox at the Carousel café. Burden knew very well that his son's life would have differed very little from this pattern even if there had been a mother at the bungalow in Tabard Road. He understood that a girl child needs an adult female on whom to model herself and he knew that she had that in Grace. But he worried incessantly about his children. Would John become a delinquent if he were out after nine in the evening? Would Pat carry a trauma through life because at the age of thirteen she was occasionally expected to open a tin or make tea? Did he give them too much pocket money or not enough? Ought he, for their sakes, to marry again? Innocent of any, he was loaded down with guilt.

He went to absurd lengths to ensure that neither of them had to do any work they would not have done had his wife lived. For this reason he was always taking them out to meals or rushing home with packages of expensive frozen food. Pat must never walk the half-mile from Grace's house to Tabard Road. He would have let her walk it without a thought if Jean had lived. But motherless children had to be fetched in father's car. He suffered agonies of frustration and recrimination if he was busy on a case and Pat had to wait an hour or even be abandoned to her aunt for an evening.

Wexford knew this. Whereas he would never excuse Burden from essential work on these grounds, he regretfully gave up the practice of detaining the inspector after hours to sit with him in the Olive and Dove and thrash out some current problem. Burden was worse than useless as a participant in these discussions. His eyes were always on the clock. Every drink he had was 'one for the road', and from time to time he would start from his seat and express the worry uppermost in his mind. Had John come in yet?

But old habits die hard. Wexford preferred the atmosphere in the Olive to the adolescent-ruled, untidy living room of the bungalow. He felt guilty when Pat was prevented from doing her ballet exercises and John had to turn off the record player, but he had to talk to Burden sometimes, discuss things with him outside hours. As he came to the door that evening, he heard the pom-pom, the roar and the whine of pop music before he rang the bell.

Burden was in his shirt sleeves, a plastic apron round his waist. He took this off hurriedly when he saw who his caller was. 'Just finishing the dishes,' he said. 'I'll nip out for some beer, shall I?'

'No need. I've brought it. What did you think I'd got in the bag? More treasures from the river? Who's the vocalist, John?'

'Zeno Vedast,' said John reverently. He looked at his father. 'I suppose I'll have to turn it off now.'

'Not on my account,' said Wexford. 'I rather like his voice.'

Vedast wasn't singing any of the festival songs but an older hit which had for so long been number one in the charts that even Wexford had heard it. Once or twice he had heard himself humming the melody. It was a gentle folk song about a country wedding.

'Dad's going to buy me the Sundays album for my birthday.'

'That'll set you back a bit, Mike.'

'Six quid,' said Burden gloomily.

'I wonder if any of these songs will live? We tend to forget that some of the greatest songs were pop in their day. After *The Marriage of Figaro* was first performed in the seventeeneighties, they say Mozart heard the errand boys whistling *Non piu andrai* in the streets of Vienna. And it's still popular.'

'Oh, yes?' said Burden politely and uncomprehendingly. 'You can turn it off now, John. Mr Wexford didn't come round here to talk about Zeno Vedast or Goodbody or whatever his name is.'

'That's just what I did come for.' Wexford went into the kitchen and picked up a tea towel. He began polishing glasses, resisting Burden's efforts to stop him. 'I've a feeling that before we go any further we ought to see Dawn's lion, the lion who roars like any sucking dove.'

'Wherever he may be at this moment.'

'That's no problem, Mike. He's here. Or, at any rate, he's at the Cheriton Forest Hotel.' Wexford drank the half-pint Burden had poured out for him and told the inspector about his talk with Mrs Peckham. 'I don't know that it means much. He may make a point of visiting old ladies rather on the lines of a parliamentary candidate nursing babies. Never neglect any opportunity of currying favour and influencing people. Or he may be an ordinary nice bloke who wanted to condole with the dead girl's grandma. It certainly doesn't mean he'd seen Dawn recently.'

John put his head round the door. 'I'm going out, Dad.'

Burden began to flap. 'Where? Why? What d'you want to go out now for?'

'Only down the Carousel.'

Wexford said smoothly, 'That's fine, John, because we're going out too. Your father won't be back till ten-thirty, so you'd better have the key. You're bound to be in before him, aren't you?'

Burden handed over the key in meek stupefaction and John took it as if it were something precious and wonderful. When the boy had gone—rapidly before there could be any changes of heart—Burden said suspiciously, 'You talked to him exactly as if he were grown-up.'

'Don't have any more beer, Mike. I want you to drive us.'

'To Cheriton Forest, I suppose?'

'Mm-hm. Vedast's dining in tonight. I checked.' Wexford looked at his watch. 'He ought to have just about finished his dinner.'

'Oh God. I don't know. Pat's at Grace's. John . . .'

'The boy's glad you're going out. It was a relief. Couldn't you see that? You won't go out for his sake. D'you want him to get so he can't go out for yours?'

'I sometimes think human relationships are impossible. Communication's impossible.'

'And you're a fool,' said Wexford, but he said it affectionately.

Cheriton Forest, a large fir plantation, lies some two miles to the south of Kingsmarkham. It is intersected by a number of sandy rides and one metalled road on which, in a big heathy clearing, is situated the Cheriton Forest Hotel.

This is a newer and far more fashionable hotel than the Olive and Dove in Kingsmarkham. The original building, put up in the thirties, is supposed to be a copy of a Tudor manor house. But there are too many beams and studs, the plaster is too white and the beams too black, the woodwork a decoration rather than an integral part of the structure. And the whole thing which might have mellowed with time has been vulgarised by a vast glass cocktail bar and by rows of motel bungalows added on in the late sixties.

When Wexford and Burden arrived at the hotel it was still

broad daylight, a dull summer evening, windy and cool. The wind stirred the forest trees, ruffling them against a pale sky where grey clouds, rimmed in the west with pink, moved, gathered, lost their shapes, torn by the wind.

On a Saturday night the forecourt would by this time have been crammed with cars and the cocktail bar full of people. But this was mid-week. Through a mullioned window a few sedate diners could be seen at tables, waiters moving unhurriedly with trays. This dining-room window was closed as were all the others in the building except one on the floor above, a pair of french windows giving on to a balcony which was quite out of keeping with the design of the hotel. The wind sent these diamond-paned glass doors banging shut and bursting open again, and from time to time it caught the velvet curtains, beating them, making them toss like washing on a line.

There was plenty of room in the parking bays for the half-dozen vehicles which stood there. Only one was on the forecourt proper, a golden Rolls-Royce parked askew, the silver gable of its grid nosing into a flower-bed and crushing geranium blossoms.

Wexford stared at this car from the windows of his own which Burden was steering, with rule-abiding propriety, into a vacant bay. He had heard of the fashion of covering the bodywork of cars in a furry coating to seem like skin or coarse velvet, but he had never yet seen this done in use, except in glossy advertisements. The Rolls wore a skin of pale golden fur, the vibrant sand colour of a lion's pelt which gleamed softly and richly, and on its bonnet, just above the grid, was attached a statuette of a plunging lion that seemed to be made of solid gold.

'This beast-of-prey motif keeps cropping up,' he said. He approached the car to get a closer look and as he did so the driver's door opened and a girl got out. It was Nell Tate.

'Good evening,' he said. 'We've met before.'

'I don't think so. I don't remember.' It was the voice of a person accustomed to defending a celebrity from intrusive fans.

'At the festival.' Wexford introduced himself and Burden. 'I'd like a word with Mr Vedast.'

Nell Tate looked seriously alarmed. 'You can't see Zeno. He's resting. He's probably asleep. We're all trying to get a quiet evening. I only came down to get something out of the car.'

She looked as if she were in need of rest. Beautifully dressed in a long clinging gown of silver lace under which she obviously wore nothing at all, heavy platinum ornaments at neck and wrists, she had a look of hag-ridden exhaustion. Under the silver and purple paint, her left eye was very swollen, the white of it bloodshot between puffy, painful lids. Studying it covertly, Wexford thought that considerable courage must have been needed to stick false lashes on to that bruised membrane.

'There's no hurry,' he said smoothly. 'We'll wait. Are you in the motel?'

'Oh, no.' She had a false poise that was growing brittle. 'We've got what they call the Elizabethan suite. Can you give me some idea what it's about?'

'Dawn Stonor. Tell him we want to talk to him about Dawn Stonor.'

She didn't even go through the pretence of looking bewildered or asking who this was. 'I'll tell him. Couldn't you come back tomorrow?'

'I think we'll wait,' said Wexford. He and Burden followed her into the foyer of the hotel, a porter having sprung forward to open the door for her. Observing the way she swept past the man, her head going up and her shoulders wriggling, passing him without a word or a nod, Wexford hardened his heart. 'We'll give you a quarter of an hour and then we'll come up.'

She made for the lift. The spurned porter, not at all put out, watched her admiringly. Once in the lift, before the doors closed on her, she appeared multiplied three times by the mirrors which lined its walls. Four blonde girls in silver, four bruised eyes, glared at Wexford and then the doors closed and she was whisked upwards.

'Lovely,' said the porter feelingly.

'What are they doing here?'

'Mr Vedast's here to purchase a country property, sir.'

Anyone else, thought Wexford, would have just bought a house. He fished for a couple of coins and found only a fifty-pence piece. 'Any luck, yet?'

'Thank you very much, sir. They go out looking every day, sir, him and Mr and Mrs Tate. We've had a few fans outside but they didn't have no joy on account of Mr Vedast takes all his meals in his suite.'

'She was scared stiff when you said who we were,' said Burden when the porter had gone out of earshot.

'I know, but that may be only that she's afraid of having him disturbed. I wonder if it was he who gave her that black eye?'

'More likely her husband, poor devil. That's a *ménage à trois* if ever there was one. D'you think there are two bedrooms or only one in that suite?'

'For a self-avowed puritan, Mike, you take a very lubricious interest in these things. Here you are, get your nose into *Nova* and you can pass me *The Field*.'

For fifteen minutes they leafed through the glossy periodicals provided in the Shakespeare Lounge. A very old couple came in and switched on the television. When they were satisfied that it was glowing with colour and braying forth cricket scores, they ignored it and began to read novels. A Dalmatian entered, wandered about and fell into a despairing heap in front of the cold electric heater.

'Right, time's up,' said Wexford. 'Now for the lion's den.'

11

The suite was on the first floor. They were admitted not by Nell but by a small dark man of about thirty who introduced himself as Godfrey Tate and who favoured them with a narrow smile. There was something spare and economical about him from his longish thin black hair and dab of moustache to his tiny feet in lace-up boots. He wore tube-like black slacks, a very tight skimpy black shirt, and the air of one who rations his movements, his speech and his manners to the starkest barrenness social usage permits.

'Zeno can spare you ten minutes.'

They were in a small entrance hall filled with flowers, displays of roses, sweet peas and stephanotis, whose perfume hung cloyingly on the air. Burden knocked a rosebud out of a vase and cursed softly. The living room was large and not at all Elizabethan, being done up in the style of a provincial casino with panels of pink mirror on the walls, niches containing more flowers in gilt urns, and french windows, hung with velvet and opening on to a balcony. In here the atmosphere was not stuffy or soporific. All the doors were open, showing a bathroom whose floor was cluttered with wet towels, and the interiors of two bedrooms, one containing a huge double bed and the other two singles. All had been occupied until recently as the tumbled bedclothes showed, but as to who had occupied which and with whom it was impossible to tell. Both bedrooms, like the living room, were littered all over with discarded clothes, magazines, records, and suitcases spilling out their contents. A lusty gale blew through the open windows,

94

shaking the flowers and making the curtains billow and thrash.

Nell Tate looked blue with cold, her arms spiky with goose-flesh. Not so her companion, who, bare-chested, sat at a table by the window eating roast duck with the enthusiasm of one who has been brought up on baked beans.

'Good evening, Mr Vedast. I'm sorry to disturb your dinner.'

Vedast didn't get up, but his hairless, polished-looking face, all bones and almost Slavonic planes, split into a wide grin. 'Hallo. Good evening. Have some coffee.' His voice had no affectations. It was still what it must have always been, the local mixture of Sussex burr and mild cockney. 'Make them send up more coffee, Nello, and take all this away.' He made a sweeping gesture with his arm, indicating the two other plates on which the food had only been picked at, the covered dishes, the basket of melba toast. 'Phone down now. Go on.' No one had touched the cream trifle. Vedast took the whole bowl and set it in his lap.

'Maybe they'd rather have a drink,' said Godfrey Tate.

'You mean *you* would, Goffo. Didn't you know they're not allowed to drink on duty?' Spooning up trifle, Vedast grinned at Wexford. He had an ugly attractive face, *joli laid*, very white and oddly bare. His eyes were a light, clear brown that sometimes looked yellow. 'The trouble with Nello and Goffo,' he said, 'is that they never read. They're not informed. Get on with your phoning and drinking, dears.'

Like discontented slaves, the Tates did his bidding. Tate took an almost empty bottle of brandy from a pseudo Louis Quinze cabinet and tipped what remained of it into a glass. He stood drinking it and watching his wife darkly while she phoned down for more coffee. Vedast laughed.

'Why don't you sit down? Not too cold in here, is it?' He put out his hand to Nell and beckoned her, pursing his lips into a whistle shape. She came up to him eagerly, too eagerly.

She was trembling with cold. It was all she could do to stop her teeth from chattering. 'Fresh air is good for Nello and Goffo. If I didn't look after their health they'd be like two little broiler chickens, shut up all day in hot hutches. I think we'll do our house-hunting on foot tomorrow, Nello.'

'Then you can count me out,' said Tate.

'Must we? You won't mind if Nello comes with me, will you?' Emaciated, starved-looking, Vedast finished the dessert which had been intended for three people. 'Perhaps our visitors can tell us of all sorts of lovely houses going spare round here?'

'We aren't house agents, Mr Vedast,' said Burden, 'and we've come to ask you questions, not answer them.'

The coffee arrived before Vedast could reply to this. Tate took one look at it, swallowed his drink and searched in the cupboard for a fresh bottle of brandy. While his wife poured coffee, he found a bottle tucked away at the back and quite full though already opened. A liberal measure in his glass, he took a long deep draught.

Immediately he was convulsed, choking and clapping one hand over his mouth.

'Christ!' A dribble of liquid came out through his fingers. 'That's not brandy! What the hell is it?'

Vedast laughed, his head on one side. 'Meths and cold tea, Goffo. Just a little experiment to see if you could tell the difference.' Nell giggled, squeezed close against Vedast's side. 'I poured the brandy down the loo. Best place for it.'

Tate said nothing. He went into the bathroom and slammed the door.

'Poor little man! Never mind, we'll take him out to dinner tomorrow at that lovely place in Pomfret. Kiss, Nello? That's right. No hard feelings because I like playing tricks on your old man? How is your coffee, Chief Inspector?'

'Well, it *is* coffee, Mr Vedast. Apparently one runs a risk drinking in your establishment.'

'I wouldn't dare doctor your coffee. I've a great respect for the law.'

'Good,' said Wexford drily. 'I hope you've enough respect to tell me what was your relationship with Dawn Stonor.'

For a moment Vedast was silent but he didn't seem disturbed. He was waiting while Nell poured cream into his cup and then added four lumps of sugar.

'Thank you, Nello darling. Now you run away and paint something. Your poor eye, for instance.'

'Do I have to?' said Nell like a child who has been told she must go to the dentist.

'Of course you do when Zeno says so. The quicker you go the sooner it will all be over. Run along.'

She ran along. She wasn't a child but a grown woman, shivering with cold and with a black eye. Vedast smiled indulgently. He walked to the bathroom door and paused, listening to Tate running taps and brushing his teeth. Then he came back, kicking shut the door of the drinks cabinet as he passed it, and stretched himself out full-length on the pink velvet sofa.

'You wanted to ask me about Dawnie,' he said. 'I suppose you've been talking to Mummy Stonor or even Granny Peckham?'

'They say you were at school with Dawn.'

'So I was. So were ever such a lot of other people. Why pick on me?'

'Mr Vedast,' said Wexford heavily, 'Dawn told her flatmate that you and she had remained friends since you left school, and she told her grandmother that you took her out to dinner on the Friday before she died. We know that can't have been true since you were in Manchester that day, but we'd like to know how well you knew Dawn and when you last saw her.'

Vedast took a lump of sugar and sucked it. He seemed completely relaxed, one leg casually crossed over the other.

Still in their raincoats, Wexford and Burden were not even comfortably warm, but Vedast, almost naked, showed no sign of being affected by the cold damp wind. The golden hairs on his chest lay flat under the light gold chain which hung against them.

'When we both lived here,' he said, 'she was my girl friend.'

'You mean you were lovers?'

Vedast nodded, smiling pleasantly. 'I was her first lover. We were sixteen. Rather moving, don't you think? Martin Silk discovered me and all sorts of exciting things happened to me which wouldn't interest you at all. Dawnie and I lost touch. I didn't see her again till this year.'

'Where did you see her?'

'In the Townsman Club,' said Vedast promptly. 'Nello and Goffo and I went there as guests of a friend of mine, and there was Dawnie serving drinks. My poor little Dawnie in a yellow satin corset and tights! I nearly laughed but that would have been unkind. She came and sat down at our table and we had a long chat about old times. She even remembered what I like to drink, orange juice with sugar in it.'

'Did you communicate with her after that?'

'Just once.' Vedast spoke very lightly, very easily, his fingers playing with the gold chain. 'Nello and Goffo had gone away to see Goffo's mum and I was rather lonely, all on my own and sad, you know.' He smiled, the unspoilt star, the poor little rich boy. 'Dawnie had written down her phone number for me at the club. Nello didn't like that a bit, you can imagine. I thought, why not give Dawnie a ring?'

'And did you?'

'Of course I did.' Now Vedast's smile was apologetic, a little rueful, the smile of the unspoilt star who longs for the companions of his humbler days to treat him as the simple country boy he really is at heart. 'But it's very off-putting, isn't it, when people sort of swamp you? D'you know what I mean? When they're terribly enthusiastic, sort of fawning?'

'You mean you got bored?' said Burden bluntly.

'It sounds unkind, put that way. Let's say I thought it better not to revive something which was dead and gone. Sorry, that wasn't very tactful. What I mean is I choked Dawnie off. I said it would be lovely if we could meet again sometime, but I was so busy at present.'

'When did this telephone conversation take place, Mr Vedast?'

'Three or four weeks ago. It was just a little chat, leading to nothing. Fancy Dawnie telling Granny Peckham we'd met! Nello and Goffo could tell you when it was they went away.' He fixed his cat's eyes, yellowish, narrow, on Wexford, opening them very wide suddenly, and again they had a sharp sly glint. 'And they'll tell you where I was on June sixth. I know that'll be the next thing you'll ask.'

'Where were you, Mr Vedast?'

'At my house in Duvette Gardens, South Kensington. Nello and Goffo and I were all there. We came back from Manchester during the Sunday night and just lazed about and slept all that Monday. Here's Goffo, all clean and purified. He'll tell you.'

Godfrey Tate had emerged from the bathroom, blank-faced, contained, wary, but showing no grudge against Vedast for the humiliating trick to which the singer had subjected him.

'Who's taking my name in vain?' he said with an almost pathetically unsuccessful attempt at jocularity.

'Tell the officers where I was on June sixth, Goffo.'

'With me and Nell.' He responded so promptly, so glibly, that it was evident the stating of this alibi had been rehearsed. 'We were all together in Duvette Gardens all day and all night. Nell can tell you the same. Nell!'

Wexford was sure she had been listening behind the door, for she exclaimed when her husband opened it as if she had been knocked backwards.

'Of course we were all there,' she said. She had covered her-

99

self with a long coat but she was still cold and she moved towards the window as if to close it. When Vedast, still smiling, shook his head, she sat down obediently, huddled in the coat, and at a glance from him, said, 'We didn't go out all day. We were exhausted after Manchester.' One hand went up to the sore eye, hovered and fell again into her lap.

'And now,' said the singer, 'tell the officers when you went off on your trip to see Goffo's mum.'

If Tate had had a tail, Wexford thought, he would at this point have wagged it. Rather like a performing dog who loves yet fears his master and who is utterly hypnotised by him, he sat up, raised his head eagerly.

'About a month ago, wasn't it?' prompted Vedast.

'We went on May twenty-second,' said Nell, 'and . . .'

'Came back on Wednesday, the twenty-fifth,' her husband ended for her.

Vedast looked pleased. For a moment it looked as if he would pat his dogs on their heads, but instead he smiled at Tate and blew a kiss at Tate's wife. 'You see, Chief Inspector? We lead a very quiet life. I didn't kill Dawnie out of passion, Goffo didn't kill her because I told him to—though I'm sure he would have done if I had—and Nello didn't kill her out of jealousy. So we can't help you. We've got masses of stuff from agents to look through tonight, so may we get on with our house-hunting?'

'Yes, Mr Vedast, you may, but I can't promise I shan't want to see you again.'

Vedast sprang to his feet in one supple movement. 'No, don't promise. I should love to see you again. We've had such a nice talk. We don't see many people, we have to be so careful.' Wexford's hand was cordially shaken. 'See them out, Goffo, and lock up the car.'

'I wish you good hunting, Mr Vedast,' said Wexford.

John Burden was at home and already in bed, having left a

note for his father to tell him that Pat would be staying the night with her aunt. The key had been left under a flower-pot, which shocked the policeman in Burden while the father showed a fatuous pride in his son's forethought. He removed the Vedast L.P. from the turntable and closed the record player.

'One of these songs,' he said, 'is called "Whistle and I'll come to you, my love".'

'Very appropriate.' Wexford glanced at the record sleeve. 'He must have written that for the Tates' theme song.'

'My God, yes. Why do they put up with it?'

'She for love, he for money. Both for the reflected glory. He hit the nail right on the head when he said "Goffo" would have killed Dawn if he'd told him to. They'd do anything for him. "Being your slave, what should I do but tend upon the hours and times of your desire?" It's not just love and money and glory, but the power of the man's personality. It's sinister, it's most unpleasant. In a set-up of this kind that alibi goes for nothing. An alibi supported by slaves is no alibi. The Romans in their heyday were very chary about admitting slaves' evidence.'

Burden chuckled. 'I daresay you're right, Caesar. How did he know he needed an alibi for the sixth of June, anyway? We didn't tell him.'

'Mrs Stonor or Mrs Peckham may have told him. There was something about it in the papers, about our thinking that the probable date of her death. I don't really suppose he's involved at all. He likes playing with us, that's all. He likes sailing near the wind. Above all, he enjoys frightening the others.' Wexford added in the words of the Duke of Wellington: ' "By God, he frightens me!" '

12

The interior decorations of Leonard Dunsand's bungalow were precisely the same as those of Miss Mowler's. Identical red spotted paper covered the hall walls, identical birds and lilies pained the eye in the living room. But Miss Mowler, for all her genteel shudders at the builder's bad taste, had shown little more judgment in her own and had filled the place with garish furniture and mass-produced pictures. Dunsand's drab pieces, brown leather smoking-room chairs, late Victorian tables and, above all, shelf upon shelf of scholarly books, looked absurdly incongruous here. Little shrivelled cacti, lifeless greenish-brown pin-cushions, stood in pots on the window-sills. There was nothing in the hall but a bare mahogany table and no carpet on the floor. It was the typical home of the celibate intellectual, uncharacteristic only in that it was as clean as Mrs Peveril's and that, on a table in the living room, lay a stack of holiday brochures, their covers even more vividly coloured than the wallpaper.

Dunsand, who had just come home from work, asked them to sit down in a colourless but cultivated voice. He seemed about forty with thinning mousey hair and rubbery face whose features were too puffy for that tight mouth. Thick glasses distorted his eyes, making them appear protuberant. He wore an immaculate, extremely conventional dark suit, white shirt and dark tie. Neither obstructive nor ingratiating, he repeated what he had already told Burden, that he had reached home at about six-forty on June sixth and had noticed no unusual happenings in The Pathway during that evening.

'I prepared myself a meal,' he said, 'and then I did some housework. This place is very ugly inside but I see no reason why it should also be dirty.'

'Did you see anything of your neighbours?'

'I saw Mrs Peveril go down the road at half past seven. I understand she attends an evening class in some sort of handicraft.'

'You didn't go out yourself? It was a fine evening.'

'Was it?' said Dunsand politely. 'No, I didn't go out.'

'Are you on friendly terms with your neighbours, Mr Dunsand?'

'Oh, yes, very.'

'You go into their houses, for instance? They visit you?'

'No. I think I misunderstood you. I simply mean we nod to each other and say a word if we meet in the street.'

Wexford sighed to himself. He found Dunsand depressing and he pitied his students. Philosophy, he knew—although he knew little about it—is not all ethics, witty syllogisms, anecdotes about Pythagoras, but logic, abstruse mathematics, points and instants, epistemological premisses. Imagine this one holding forth for a couple of hours on Wittgenstein!

'So you can tell us nothing of Mr and Mrs Peveril's way of life, their habits, who calls on them and so on?'

'No, nothing.' Dunsand spoke in the same drab level voice, but Wexford fancied that for a brief moment he had caught a certain animation in the man's eye, a sign of life, a flash perhaps of pain. It was gone, the magnified eyes were still and staring. 'I think I can say, Chief Inspector, that I know nothing of any private life but my own.'

'And that is ... ?' Wexford said hesitantly.

'What you see.' Dunsand cleared his throat. 'Beginning to rain again,' he said. 'If you don't want to ask me anything else I'll go and put my car away.'

'Do you ever go to London, Mr Peveril?'

'Of course I do in connection with my work.' Peveril put a

gloomy and irritable emphasis on the last word. He had once more been fetched from his studio and his fingers were actually inky. Wexford couldn't help feeling that the ink had been put there deliberately just as the man's hair had been purposely shaken and made to stand up in awry spikes. 'I go up occasionally, once a fortnight, once a month.'

'And stay overnight?'

'I have done.'

'When did you last go?'

'Oh God, it would have been June first, I think. I didn't stay.' Peveril glanced towards the closed door which excluded his wife. 'Scenes,' he said stiffly, 'are made if I venture to spend a night away from the matrimonial nest.' Misanthropic, his whole manner showing how distasteful he found this probing, he nevertheless was unable to resist making frank disclosures. 'You'd imagine that a woman who has everything soft and easy for her, never earned a penny since she found someone to keep her, wouldn't deny the breadwinner a few hours of freedom. But there it is. If I go to London I have to phone her when I get there and leave a number for her to call me whenever she fancies, that means about three times in one evening.'

Wexford shrugged. It was not an uncommon type of marriage that Peveril had described; he was only one of many who had elected to make the dreariest and the longest journey with a jealous foe. But why talk about it? Because it would induce his interrogator to believe that such surveillance kept him from other women? Wexford almost smiled at such naivety. He knew that good-looking, dissatisfied men of Peveril's stamp, childless men long out of love with their wives, could be Houdini-like in the facility with which they escaped from domestic bonds. He left the subject.

'Your wife went to an evening class on that Monday evening,' he said. 'Would you mind telling me what your movements were?'

104

'I *moved* into my studio to work and I didn't *move* out of it until my wife got back at eleven.'

'There are no buses at that time of night. She didn't take your car?'

An edge of contempt to his voice, Peveril said, 'She can't drive. She walked into Kingsmarkham and some woman gave her a lift back.'

'You didn't think of driving her, then? It was a fine evening and it isn't far.'

'Damn it all!' said Peveril, his ready temper rising. 'Why the hell should I drive her to some daft hen party where they don't learn a bloody thing? It's not as if she was going to work, going to bring in some much-needed money.' He added sullenly, 'I usually do drive her, as a matter of fact.'

'Why didn't you that night?'

'The worm turned,' said Peveril. 'That's why not. Now I'd appreciate it if you'd let me get on with my work.'

It was on the red dress that Wexford concentrated that Friday. He called a semi-informal conference consisting of himself, Burden, Dr Crocker, Sergeant Martin and Detective Polly Davies. They sat in his office, their chairs in a circle, with the dress laid on his desk. Then Wexford decided that for them all to get a better view of it while they talked, the best thing would be to hang it from the ceiling. A hanger was produced by Polly, and dress and hanger suspended from the lead of Wexford's central light.

Laboratory experts had subjected it to a thorough examination. They had found that it was made of synthetic fibre and that it had been frequently worn probably by the same person, a brown-haired, fair-skinned Caucasian. There were no sweat stains in the armpits. In the fibre had been found traces of an unidentified perfume, talcum powder, anti-perspirant and carbon tetrachloride, a cleaning fluid. Other researches showed the dress to have been manufactured some eight or nine years previously at a North London factory for distribution by a small fashion house that dealt in medium-priced clothes. It might have been bought in London, Manchester, Birmingham or a host of other towns and cities in the British Isles. No Kingsmarkham store had ever stocked the garments from this fashion house, but they were, and had for a long time been, obtainable in Brighton.

The dress itself was a dark purplish red, darker than magenta and bluer than burgundy. It had a plain round neck, three-quarter-length sleeves, a fitted waist with self belt and a skirt designed just to show the wearer's knees. This indicated that it had been bought for a woman about five feet seven inches tall, a woman who was also, but not exceptionally, slim, for it was a size twelve. On Dawn Stonor it had been a tight fit and an unfashionable length for this or any other epoch.

'Comments, please,' said Wexford. 'You first, Polly. You look as if you've got something to say.'

'Well, sir, I was just thinking that she must have looked really grotty in it.' Polly was a lively, black-haired young woman who habitually dressed in the 'dolly' mode, mini-skirts, natty waistcoats and velvet baker-boy caps. Her way of painting her mouth strawberry red and blotching two red dabs on her cheeks made her look less intelligent than she was. Now she saw from Wexford's frown that her imprecise epithet had displeased him and she corrected herself hurriedly. 'I mean, it wouldn't have suited her and she'd have looked dowdy and awful. A real freak. I know that sounds unkind—of course she looked dreadful when she was found—but what I'm trying to say is that she must have looked dreadful from the moment she put it on.'

'You'd say, would you, that the dress itself is unattractive as a garment? I'm asking you particularly, Polly, because you're a woman and more likely to see these things than we are.'

'It's so hard to say, sir, when something's gone out of date. I suppose with jewellery and so forth it might have looked all right on a dark person it fitted well. It wouldn't have looked good on Dawn because she had sort of reddish-blonde hair and she must have absolutely bulged out of it. I can't think she'd ever have put it on from *choice*. And another thing, sir, you said I'm more likely to notice these things than you are, but—well, just for an experiment, could you all say what you think of it as, say, a dress you'd like your wives to wear?'

'Anything you say. Doctor?'

Crocker uncrossed his elegant legs and put his head on one side. 'It's a bit difficult,' he began, 'to separate it from the unpleasant associations it has, but I'll try. It's rather *dull*. Let me say that if my wife wore it I'd feel she wasn't letting me down in any way. I wouldn't mind who saw her in it. It's got what I believe they call an "uncluttered line" and it would show off a woman's figure in a discreet kind of way. On the other hand, supposing I was the sort of man who took other women out, I don't think I'd feel any too thrilled if my girl friend turned up to a date wearing it because it wouldn't be—well, adventurous enough.'

'Mike?'

Burden had no wife, but he had come to terms with his condition. He was able to talk of wives now without inner pain or outward embarrassment. 'I agree with the doctor that it's rather distasteful to imagine anyone close to you wearing it because of the circumstances and so on associated with it. When I make myself look at it as I might look at a dress in a shop window I'd say I rather like it. No doubt, I've no idea of fashion, but I'd call it smart. If I were—er, a married man I'd like to see my wife in it.'

'Sergeant?'

'It's a smart dress, sir,' said Martin eagerly. 'My wife's got a dress rather like it and that sort of shade. I bought it for her

107

last Christmas, chose it myself, come to that. My daughter—she's twenty-two—she says she wouldn't be seen dead in it, but you know these young girls—beg your pardon, Polly. That's a nice, smart dress, sir, or was.'

'Now for me,' said Wexford. 'I like it. It looks comfortable and practical for everyday wear. One would feel pleasantly uxorious and somehow secure sitting down in the evening with a woman in that dress. And I think it would be becoming on the right person. As the doctor says, it follows the natural lines of a woman's figure. It's not daring or dramatic or embarrassing. It's conservative. There you are, Polly. What do you make of all that?'

Polly laughed. 'It tells me more about all you than the dress,' she said pertly. 'But what it does tell me is that it's a *man's* dress, sir. I mean, it's the sort of thing a man would choose because it's figure-flattering and plain and somehow, as you said, secure. Dr Crocker said he wouldn't want to see his girl friend in it. Doesn't all this mean it's a *wife's* dress chosen by a *husband* partly because he subconsciously realises it shows she's a good little married lady and any other man seeing her in it will know she's not made of girl-friend stuff?'

'Perhaps it does,' said Wexford thoughtfully. The window was open and the dress swayed and swivelled in the breeze. Find the owner, he thought, and then I have all I need to know. 'That's intelligent of you, Polly, but where does it get us? You've convinced me it was owned at one time by a married woman who bought it to please her husband. We already know Dawn didn't own it. Its owner might have sent it to a jumble sale, given it to her cleaner or taken it to the Oxfam shop.'

'We could check with the Oxfam people here, sir.'

'Yes, Sergeant, that must be done. I believe you said, Mike, that Mrs Peveril denies ownership?'

'She may be lying. When it was shown to her I thought she

was going to faint. With that stain on it it isn't a particularly attractive object and there are, as we've said, the associations. But she reacted to it very strongly. On the other hand, we know she's a nervy and hysterical woman. It could be a natural reaction.'

'Have you talked to Mrs Clarke again?'

'She says her friend had some sort of mental breakdown last year and lost a lot of weight, so it hardly looks as if she was ever slim enough to wear the dress. But Mrs Clarke has only known her four years.'

'Eight years ago,' Wexford said thoughtfully, 'the Peverils might still have been on romantic terms. He might have been choosing clothes for her that were particularly to his taste. But I agree with you that the question of size makes that unlikely. Well, I won't detain you any longer. It's a massive plan I've got in mind, but I think it's the only course to take. Somehow or other we're going to have to question every woman in Kingsmarkham and Stowerton between the ages of thirty and sixty, show them the dress and get reactions. Ask each one if it's hers or, if not, whether she's ever seen anyone else wearing it.'

His announcement was received with groans by all but the doctor, who left quickly, declaring that his presence was needed at the infirmary.

13

The response to Wexford's appeal was enormous and immediate. Women queued up outside the Baptist church hall to view the dress as they might have queued on the first day of a significant sale. Public-spirited? Wexford thought their enthusiasm sprang more from a need to seem for a little while important. People like to be caught up in the whirlwind of something sensational and they like it even more if, instead of being part of a crowd, each can for a brief moment be an individual, noticed, attended to, taken seriously. They like to leave their names and addresses, see themselves recorded. He supposed they also liked to feast their eyes on the relic of a violent act. Was it so bad if they did? Was it what the young festival visitors would have called sick? Or was it rather evidence of a strong human vitality, the curiosity that wants to see everything, know everything, be in the swim, that when refined and made scholarly, is the prerogative of the historian and the archaeologist?

He had long ago ceased to allow hope to triumph over experience. He didn't suppose that some woman would come forward and say her husband had unexpectedly and inexplicably borrowed the dress from her that Monday evening. Nor did he anticipate any dramatic scene in the hall, a wife screaming or falling into a faint because she recognised the dress and realised simultaneously what recognition implied. No woman harbouring a guilty secret would come there voluntarily. But he did hope for something. Someone would say she had seen the garment on a friend or an acquaintance; someone would admit to having possessed it and then to have given it away or sold it.

No one did. All Friday afternoon they filed along the wooden passage that smelt of hymn books and Boy Scouts, passed into the grim brown hall to sit on the Women's Fellowship chairs and stare at the posters for coffee mornings and social evenings. Then, one by one, they went behind the screens where Martin and Polly had the dress laid out on a trestle table. One by one they came out with the baulked, rather irritable, look on their faces of do-gooders whom ill-luck had robbed of the chance to be more than negatively helpful.

'I suppose,' said Burden, 'that she could have been picked up by a man in a car. A prearranged pick-up, of course. He might have come from anywhere.'

'In that case, why take a bus to Sundays and walk across the fields? Mrs Peveril says she saw her go into those fields and her description is so accurate that I think we must believe her. Dawn may have been early for her date—that was the only bus as we've said before—gone into the fields to sit down and wait, and then doubled back. But if she did that, she didn't go far back.'

'What makes you say that?'

'Four people saw her between the time she left her mother's house and the time she went into those fields, five-thirty. We've not been able to find anyone who saw her *after* five-thirty, though God knows we've made enough appeals and questioned enough people. Therefore it's almost certain she went into some house somewhere just after five-thirty.'

Burden frowned. 'On the Sundays estate, you mean?'

'To put it more narrowly than that, in The Pathway. The body was in the quarry, Mike. It was carried or dragged to the quarry, not transported in a car. You know what a job it was to get our own cars down there. When the gates to the drive are locked no car could get in.' Wexford glanced at his watch.

'It's five-thirty and the Olive's open. Can't we leave Martin to carry on with this and adjourn for a drink? I'd rather talk all this out sitting down over a pint.'

Burden's brow creased further and he bit his lip. 'What about Pat? She'll have to get her own tea. She'll have to walk to her dancing lesson. John'll be all alone.'

In a tone that is usually described as patient but which, in fact indicates an extreme degree of controlled exasperation, Wexford said, 'He is six feet tall. He is fifteen. By the time he was that age my old dad had been out at work eighteen months. Why can't he escort his sister to her dancing class? Taking it for granted, of course, that if she walks three hundred yards alone on a bright summer evening, she's bound to be set on by kidnappers.'

'I'll phone them,' said Burden with a shamefaced grin.

The saloon bar of the Olive and Dove was almost empty, a little gloomy and uninviting as deserted low-ceilinged places always are when the sun shines brightly outside. Wexford carried their drinks into the garden where wooden tables and chairs were arranged under an arbour. Vines and clematises made a leafy roof over their heads. It was the home-going hour, the time when the peace and the quiet of this spot was usually shattered by the sound of brakes and shifting gears as traffic poured over the Kingsbrook bridge.

Today all man-made noise was drowned by the chatter of the swollen river running beside the terraced garden. It was a steady low roar, constant and unchanging, but like all natural sound it was neither tedious to the ear nor a hindrance to conversation. It was soothing. It spoke of timeless forces, pure and untameable, which in a world of ugliness and violence resisted man's indifferent soiling of the earth. Listening to it, sitting in silence, Wexford thought of that ugliness, the scheme of things in which a girl could be beaten to death, thrown into a bower which had been made and used for love, thrown like garbage.

He shivered. He could never quite get used to it, the appalling things that happened, the waste, the pointlessness. But now he had to think of practical matters, of why and how this particular ugliness had taken place, and when Burden came to the table he said:

'You've talked to the occupants of the other two houses in The Pathway and I haven't. Would you say we could exclude them?'

'The Streets are a married couple with four children, all of whom were at home with their parents the whole evening. None of them saw Dawn. Mrs Street saw Miss Mowler come home at eight o'clock. Apart from that, none of them saw any of their neighbours that evening. They heard nothing and they remained in the front of the house from about six till about ten. Mrs Street's kitchen is in the front.

'The Robinsons are elderly. He's bedridden and they have a fiercely respectable old housekeeper. Mr Robinson's bedroom overlooks Sundays but not the quarry. His wife spent the evening with him in his bedroom as she always does and went to her own room at nine-thirty. She saw and heard nothing. The housekeeper saw Dunsand come home at twenty to seven and Miss Mowler at eight. She didn't see the Peverils and she herself went to bed at ten.'

Wexford nodded. 'How about Silk?'

'Up in London from June sixth to June eighth, making last-minute festival arrangements. Says he left Sundays at about seven on the evening of the sixth.'

'Can anyone corroborate that?'

'His wife and his two grown-up children are in Italy. They've been there since the end of May and they aren't back yet. Silk says they always go abroad for two months in the summer, but it looks to me as if they aren't as keen as he on the pop scene.'

'And it's his quarry,' said Wexford thoughtfully. 'If anybody had easy access to it, he did. I imagine he's often in

London, too. I don't suppose he was at school with Dawn, was he?'

'Hardly, sir,' said Burden. 'He's as old as you.' He added generously: 'And looks a good deal more.'

Wexford laughed. 'I won't bother to grow my hair, then. It doesn't seem likely that Dawn would have played around with him, and if she had done she'd have gone straight up to the house, surely, not tried to sneak round by a back way. There was no wife at Sundays for her to hide from.'

'And no possible reason for her to bring a picnic.'

'No, I think we can exclude Silk on the grounds of age and general ineligibility. That leaves us with the Peverils, Dunsand and Miss Mowler. But Peveril wasn't alone in his house at five-thirty and Miss Mowler and Dunsand weren't even at home. And yet who but the occupants of one of those three houses could have put Dawn's body in the quarry without being seen?'

Burden glanced surreptitiously at his watch, shifting uneasily. 'Then we're saying she doubled back, sir, and was admitted to one of those houses. Somebody let her in. Not Dunsand or Miss Mowler. Peveril or Mrs Peveril, then? That must mean the Peverils are in it up to their necks. In that case, why does Mrs Peveril say she saw the girl at all? Why say anything?'

'Possibly because she isn't up to her neck in it at all. Because she *did* see Dawn go into those fields and didn't know of any connection between the girl she saw and her husband. Dawn caught that bus because it was the only bus she could catch. She loitered in the fields for two hours—remember how warm and sunny it was—and returned to Peveril's house *after* Mrs Peveril had left for her class. D'you want another drink?'

'Oh, no,' said Burden quickly. 'Good heavens, no.'

'Then we may as well get back to your place. I can't stand this watch-watching.'

Outside the Baptist church the queues had lengthened.

Housewives departing to prepare evening meals had been replaced by working women released from shops and offices.

'Better get something special for the children's dinner,' said conscientious Burden. 'The Luximart stays open late on Fridays. You eating with us?'

'No, thanks. My wife'll have something for me at eight.'

They went into the shop where they were immediately recognised by the manager. He insisted on pointing out to them personally items precisely similar to those Dawn had bought from the six tomatoes in a plastic-covered tray to the bottle of cheap wine. The shop was full and the manager spoke loudly as if anxious to cash in on and reap the benefits of a particularly ghoulish form of advertising.

'Tomatoes as purchased by our very own murder victim,' said Wexford disgustedly.

Burden avoided them studiously and averted his eyes from the row of strawberry mousses. 'You forgot the food in your theory,' he whispered. 'Peveril would have already eaten. His wife would have given him his dinner before she went out.' Regardless of expense, he selected three packages of *bœuf bourguignon* from the frozen-food trough. 'She meant to stay overnight too. You forgot that. Or was Peveril going to hide her in his studio when his wife got home at eleven?'

'Everything all right, sir?' said the manager. 'How about a bottle of wine to go with that?'

'No, thanks.' Burden paid and they left, their progress watched by a dozen pairs of curious eyes. The sun was still bright, the wind brisk. Martin was fixing a fresh, larger, poster of Dawn's picture to the church-hall door.

'Anything yet?' asked Wexford.

'We've had five hundred women pass through here, sir, and not one of them able to give us a bit of help.'

'Keep on at it tomorrow.'

They walked the length of the High Street and turned left into Tabard Road. Burden's step always quickened at this point. Once he had made himself aware that no fire engines or ambulances thronged the street outside his bungalow he relaxed and his breathing became more even.

'Was Peveril going to keep her hidden all night?' he said. 'Or, failing that, maybe she got into Dunsand's place through the larder window. There's an idea for you. Poor old Dunsand who has to fend for himself like me, living on frozen food he buys on his way home, no doubt. Miss Mowler must have actually known her—district nurses know everybody. Perhaps Dawn hid in her garden until eight o'clock, keeping herself from boredom by trying on a dress she found hanging in the shed?'

'I'm the one who asks the derisive questions, not you, remember? All this reversing our roles throws me off balance.' Wexford raised his eyebrows at the three bicycles leaning against the Burdens' gate and the moped parked at the kerb. 'Doesn't look as if your boy's moping in solitude,' he said. 'Good thing he's been prudent and shut the windows.'

The six teenagers who were gyrating energetically in Burden's living room stopped abashed when the policemen came in, and Pat, standing by the record player, pressed the 'reject' lever. Vedast's line, 'Come once more and be my wife', groaned away on a dying fall, the last word a melancholy moan.

'Having your dancing lesson at home tonight, my dear?' said Wexford, smiling.

The two Burden children began to make hasty excuses while their friends made for the door with the silent speed that looks like treachery but is in fact the loyalty of those accustomed to parental censure and who know it is better faced without an audience. Wexford didn't think they ought to have to apologise for innocently enjoying themselves and he interrupted Burden's half-hearted reproaches.

'Play it again, will you, Pat?'

Expertly she found the right track on the L.P. without

116

having to check with the sleeve and lowered the pick-up arm delicately.

'I don't like you doing that,' said John. 'You'll scratch it.'

'I won't. I'm more careful with records than you are. So there!' The Burden children were usually at loggerheads and seldom missed an opportunity to rile each other. 'It's a horrible song, anyway. All sloppy love stuff. Folk music ought to have some point to it and Zeno Vedast's hasn't any point at all.'

'What d'you mean by "point", Pat?'

'Well, be anti-war, Mr Wexford, or for everybody loving each other not just one stupid girl. Or anti-ugliness and mess like Betti Ho. Zeno Vedast's songs are all for him, all for self.'

Wexford listened interestedly to this but Burden said sourly, 'Everybody loving each other! You can talk.' He sniffed. 'I don't hold with all this putting the world right.'

'Then you shouldn't be a policeman,' said Wexford. 'Play it, Pat.'

The song started with a little grinding scratch which made John frown and purse his lips. Then Vedast's strings twanged and the clear, unaffected voice began to sing:

> 'I don't miss her smile or the flowers,
> I don't eclipse distance or hours . . .'

'He writes his own songs?' Wexford whispered.

'Oh, yes, always,' said John reverently. 'This one's two years old but it's his best.'

'Boring!' Pat ducked behind the player to avoid her brother's wrath.

It wasn't boring. Listening to the slight, delicate story which the verses and the chorus told, Wexford had a strong sense that the singer was relating a true experience.

Suddenly the backing grew loud and Vedast's voice bitter, keening:

'Now she's gone in the harsh light of day,
When she'll return the night would not say,
And I am left to vision the time
When once more she'll come and be mine.

So come by, come nigh,
    come try and tell why
    some sigh, some cry,
    some lie and some di-i-ie.'

Burden broke the silence which followed. 'I'm going to get
this food heated up.' He went into the kitchen but Wexford
lingered.

'Does he ever write joke songs, John?'

'*Joke* songs?'

'Yes—I mean, well, they're hardly in the same class, but
Haydn and Mozart sometimes wrote jokes into their music.
If you're a joker in private life, joking often comes into your
work as well. D'you know the Surprise Symphony?'

Pat said, 'We did it at school. There's a sort of soft gentle
bit and then a big boom that makes you jump.'

Wexford nodded. 'I wondered if Vedast...'

'Some of them are a bit like that,' said John. 'Sudden loud
bits or a funny change of key. And all his songs are supposed
to be somebody's story or to have a special meaning for a
friend.' He added eagerly: 'I'll play you some more, shall I?'

'Not now.' Burden came back to lay the table. Pat tried to
take the knives and forks out of his hand, but the daughter
who had been admonished for showing insufficient love must
not be allowed to show it now by helping her father. He kept
his hold on the cutlery and shook his head with rather a mar-
tyred air. 'Ready in five minutes. You'd better wash your
hands and sit up at the table.'

Wexford followed him into the kitchen.

'I've learnt some interesting facts about our slave-driver. I wonder how long he's staying in this neck of the woods?'

'John says indefinitely. You don't really think he had anything to do with all this?'

Wexford shrugged. 'He intrigues me. I can't do what Scott advises and stop mine ear against the singer. His song is beginning to haunt me. I think I'll buy a single of it tomorrow.'

Burden switched off the oven. 'We might play it over and over in your office,' he said sarcastically. 'Get a couple of the W.P.C.s in and dance. Have ourselves a rave-up. There won't be anything else to do if no one's identified that dress.'

'There will be for me,' said Wexford, taking his leave. 'I'm going to London to have another talk with Joan Miall.'

14

Wexford bought a local paper to read in the train. The *Kingsmarkham Courier* came out on a Friday and Dawn's body had been found on the previous Monday, so that news was stale even by local standards. Harry Wild, the chief reporter, had made what he could of it by giving headline publicity to Wexford's appeals in connection with the red dress, but by far the greater part of the front page was devoted to Zeno Vedast. A large photograph, taken by a not very expert *Courier* staff man, showed the singer and the Tates leaning against the bonnet of the golden Rolls. Nell was smiling serenely, one hand caressing the lion ornament. Wild had married his two lead stories by including in his caption to the picture a frank confession from Vedast that he had been at school with Dawn Stonor. Reading it, Wexford felt even more convinced that Vedast could not be involved in Dawn's death, that he had nothing to hide. But why then was he staying on in Cheriton Forest, staying even though, as the caption stated, he had found and started negotiations for the house he intended to buy? Could it be that he was staying to see the case through, to await the outcome?

Joan Miall's flat was on the second floor of a tall shabby house between the Earls Court Road and Warwick Road. It wasn't a shabby flat, but smartly and even adventurously decorated, the ceilings painted in bold dark colours to reduce their height. A close observer could tell that the furniture was mostly secondhand, but the girls had re-covered the armchairs, put new pictures in old frames and filled the shelves with brightly jacketed paperbacks. There were a great many plants, fresh and green from recent watering.

She received him without pomp, without preparation. She wore red trousers, a red spotted smock and no make-up. A big old vacuum cleaner, cast off perhaps by some more affluent relative, was plugged in just inside the front door. He had heard its whine die away when he rang the bell.

She was expecting him and she put on a kettle to make coffee. 'I miss Dawn,' she said. 'Especially round about lunchtime. We were almost always together then. I keep expecting to hear her call out from her bedroom that she's dying for a cup of coffee. Oh, "dying"—the expressions one uses! But she often said she was dying. Dying of boredom, dying for a drink.'

'I know so little about her. If I knew more, I might know how and why. You see, Miss Miall, there are two kinds of murder victim, those who are killed by a stranger for gain or for some obscure pathological reason, and those who are killed by someone who is not a stranger, someone who might be or have been a friend. It is in those cases that it's invaluable to know as much as may be known about the character and the tastes and the peculiarities of the victim.'

'Yes, I do see. Of course I do.' She paused, frowning. 'But people are little worlds, aren't they? There's so much in everyone, depths and layers, strange countries if we're talking about worlds. I might just be showing you the wrong country.'

It took her a little while to get the coffee. She was a faddist, he remembered. He heard and smelt her grinding coffee beans —nothing pre-ground out of a packet for her—and when she came in with the tray he saw that the coffee was in an earthenware jug. But as soon as she sat down she lit a cigarette and she sighed with a kind of relief as she exhaled. It recalled to him her words about the strange countries in each person's make-up. She hadn't mentioned the inconsistencies which those who delve into character must encounter as bafflingly as the unknown.

'Did you both work every night at the Townsman?' he began.

'It's more complicated than that. We do lunches as well. Members can lunch between twelve and three, so we either work an eleven till five shift or one from seven at night to two in the morning. If you do the night shift, you can be sure you won't have to do the lunchtime one next day, but otherwise it's rather haphazard. We get two full days off a week, not necessarily Saturday and Sunday, of course. Dawn and I often worked the same shift, but just as often we didn't. There were lots and lots of times when she was alone here seeing people and getting calls I knew nothing about.'

'You knew about the one particular call you told me of.'

'Yes,' she said, 'I've thought a lot about that since then, trying to sort it all out, and I've remembered all sorts of things I didn't tell you. But the things I've remembered aren't helpful. They really only prove it *wasn't* Zeno Vedast who phoned her.'

'I'd like to hear them just the same.'

'I forgot to tell you that his name came up long before the phone call. It must have been in March or April. Of course, we'd see him on TV or read about him in the papers and she'd say she'd known him for years, but she never actually spoke of him as a friend she *saw*. Then one morning—I think it was the end of March—she said he'd been in the club the night before. I hadn't been working that night and, frankly, I didn't believe her. I knew he wasn't a member. I asked one of the other girls and she said Zeno Vedast had been in and had sort of chatted Dawn up a bit. I still wasn't convinced and I'm not now—about the friendship, I mean. We get a lot of celebrities in the club and they do chat us up. That's what we're there for.'

'When did the phone call come, Miss Miall?'

'It was a Monday.' She frowned, concentrating. 'Dawn had had the day off, I'd been working the lunchtime shift. Let me see—it wasn't the last Monday in May. I think it must have been May twenty-third, about half past eight in the evening. We were sitting in here by ourselves, watching television. The phone rang and Dawn answered it. She said hallo and then something like, "How super of you to phone me." She covered up the mouthpiece and whispered to me to turn down the TV. Then she said, "It's Zeno Vedast." I was embarrassed. I thought she must be in a really neurotic state if she was prepared to fantasise that far.'

Wexford accepted a second cup of coffee. 'Miss Miall, suppose I told you that Vedast did recognise her in the club, that it was he who phoned that night, what would you say to that?'

'That I knew her and you didn't,' the girl said obstinately. 'He was in the club all right. I know that. He talked to her. A maharajah talked to me for half an hour one night but that doesn't make us lifelong friends. I'll tell you why I'm sure it wasn't Zeno Vedast who phoned. When some celebrity really took notice of Dawn—a film star paying her attention at the club, say—she'd be full of it for days. When it was just make-believe—or let-me-believe like in his song—when she saw someone she said she knew in a photograph or on the TV, she'd comment on it, sort of reminisce a bit, and then forget all about it. After that phone call she wasn't a bit elated. She just said, "I told you I knew him," and then she was quite gloomy, the way she was after she'd had a nasty letter from her mother or some man had stood her up.'

'Who did you think had phoned her then?'

'Some new man she'd met,' Joan Miall said firmly. 'Someone who was attracted to her but who wasn't rich enough or well known enough to be worth bragging about.' A shade of sadness crossed her pretty face. 'Dawn was getting a bit old for our kind of work and she didn't wear well. I know that

123

sounds ridiculous. She was only twenty-eight. But it bothered her a lot, knowing she'd be past it in a couple of years. She'd have had to get a different job or—marry Paul. She was desperate to make everyone believe she was as attractive as ever and to her way of thinking you measure attractiveness by the number of successful men who want to take you out.'

Wexford sighed. When you are twenty-five, thirty seems old. That was all right, that was natural. But surely when you are forty, thirty ought to seem young? It sickened him that this girl and her dead friend had moved in a world where to a man of fifty a girl of twenty-eight was getting 'past it'.

'This new man,' he said, 'you've no foundation for believing in his existence? Nothing to make you think he existed but a phone call which I tell you Vedast himself made?'

'Yes, I have. She went out with him the following week.'

'Miss Miall,' Wexford said rather severely, 'you should have told me of this before. Is this one of the "unhelpful" things you've remembered?'

'One of the things that prove it wasn't Vedast, yes. But I don't know his name. I don't even know if he wasn't another of Dawn's dreams.'

There was a framed photograph on the mantelpiece, an enlarged snapshot of a dark young man and a girl on a beach somewhere. Wexford picked up the picture and scrutinised it.

'That's Paul,' said Joan Miall.

It took him a few moments to realise that the girl was Dawn. In shorts and a shirt, her hair wind-blown, she looked quite different from the painted, overdressed creature whose portrait on posters was stuck up all over Kingsmarkham like a cabaret star's publicity. At last, he thought, she had achieved a kind of fame. Though posthumously, she had got herself into the public eye. But she looked happier in the snapshot. No, happy wasn't the right word—content, rather, tranquil, and perhaps just a tiny bit bored?

There had been no ecstasy, no excitement, in being on a beach with her ordinary fiancé. Mrs Stonor had seen to that. By belittling her daughter, by comparing her unfavourably to others, by denying her love, she had so warped her personality that everyday affection meant nothing to her. Dawn understood love only when it came from and was directed to money and success, the love of a man who would make her rich and get her name in the papers. Well, some man had got her name in the papers ...

'Go on, Miss Miall,' said Wexford, laying the photograph down.

'The day I'm going to tell you about was June first. It was a Wednesday and it was Paul's birthday.'

The date meant something to Wexford. He nodded, listening alertly.

'On the Tuesday, the day before, Dawn and I had both had our day off. She went out in the afternoon and bought the blue dress, the one she wore to go and see her mother. I remember I asked her if she'd bought it to take away on holiday with Paul. Well, she said she couldn't make up her mind whether she was going away with Paul or not but she wouldn't say why not, only that it might be boring. They hadn't quarrelled. Paul spent the evening with us and stayed the night with Dawn. They seemed very happy.'

'Let's come to June first.'

'Paul went off to work before we were up. He was going to come back for a birthday lunch Dawn was giving him and then take the afternoon off. Dawn and I were both due to work the evening shift. She went out to buy food for lunch, steak and salad—I insisted on fresh stuff—and after she came back, while she was laying the table, the phone rang. I answered it and a man's voice asked to speak to Dawn. I didn't ask who it was and he didn't say. I gave the phone to Dawn and I didn't stay to hear what she said. I went on with preparing the lunch. She came back into the kitchen and she was very flushed and excited-looking but a bit—well, narked too. I'm explaining this badly but I do remember just what she was like. She was excited and yet she was upset. I could see she didn't want to say who had rung her so I didn't ask.'

'Did you ever find out?'

'No, I didn't. But there's more to come. Paul was expected at half past one. By about a quarter to twelve everything was ready for lunch. We just had to grill the steaks when Paul came. Dawn was already dressed and made-up, but at twelve she went away and changed and when she came out of her bedroom she was wearing her new dress and she'd done her hair on top of her head and put on a lot more eye make-up. In fact, she'd overdone the whole thing and she was wearing far too much perfume. I was sitting in here reading a magazine. She came in and said, "I've got to go out for an hour or so. If Paul gets here before I'm back you can tell him some tale. Say I forgot the wine or something." Well, as I said, we didn't ask each other questions. I wasn't too thrilled about lying to Paul. The wine was already on the table so I couldn't say that. I just hoped she wouldn't be long.'

'Was she?' Wexford asked.

'She went out at sometime between twelve and half past. Paul was a bit late. He got here at twenty to two and still she wasn't back. I told him she had some last-minute shopping, but I could see he was hurt. After all, it was his birthday and they were more or less engaged.'

'When did she come back?'

'Ten past three. I remember the time exactly because when she came in I realised she must have been in a pub and they close at three. She'd had too much to drink, anyway. Her face was all puffy and her speech wasn't quite clear. Paul's a very good-tempered bloke but he was nearly doing his nut by this time.'

'Where did she say she'd been?'

'She said she'd met a girl who used to work in the club and

was now a model—poor Dawn could never resist the fame and glamour bit—and they'd gone into a pub and forgotten the time talking.'

'You didn't believe her?'

'Of course I didn't. Later on, after Paul had gone Dawn wrote to her mother to say she'd go and see her on the following Monday.'

'You didn't connect the pub visit with the letter?'

'I didn't at the time,' the girl said thoughtfully, 'but I do now. You see, it was very unlike Dawn to make up her mind about anything to do with her mother on the spur of the moment. She knew she had to go to Kingsmarkham sometimes but usually she'd start sort of arguing with herself about it weeks beforehand. You know, saying she'd have to go but she didn't want to and maybe she could let it ride for a few more weeks. Then she'd write a letter and tear it up and sort of swear about it. It'd take her weeks to get a letter actually written and posted. But it didn't this time. She sat down and dashed it off.'

Wexford said, 'Did she ever mention what happened on June first again?'

She nodded, looking unhappy. 'On the Saturday, the first day of her holiday. She said, "What would you think of a bloke who said he was dying to see you and the best date he could fix up was a few drinks in a pub at lunchtime?" She went to that mirror over there and put her face right close up to it, staring at herself and pulling at the skin under her eyes. "If you were really crazy about a man," she said, "you wouldn't care, would you? You'd just want his company. You wouldn't worry if he was too scared or too mean to take you to a hotel for the night." I didn't really know whether she was referring to me or herself. I thought she might be talking about me because my boy friend is poor. Then Paul came and took her out and I gathered she meant to go away on holiday with him.'

Joan Miall sighed. She reached for a fresh cigarette but the packet was empty. The air in the room was blue with hanging smoke. Wexford thanked her and went away. In the Earls Court Road he went into a record shop and bought a single of 'Let-me-believe'.

15

The red dress was back in Wexford's office. Several thousand women had looked at it, handled it, backed away from the dark stain; not one had recognised it. It lay on the rosewood surface, on the wood whose colour matched it, an old shabby dress, folded, soiled, keeping its secret as implacably as ever.

Wexford touched it, glanced again at the label and at the whitish talc marks around the neckline. Dawn had worn it but she had never owned it. She had found it in Kingsmarkham and for some unfathomable reason had put it on, she who had been fashion-conscious and who was already dressed in garments which matched her shoes and her bag. She had found it in Kingsmarkham, but, unless deception had been practised, no Kingsmarkham or Stowerton woman had ever owned it. A woman never forgets any dress she has owned, not even if fifty years have elapsed between her discarding of it and her being confronted with it again, much less if only seven or eight years have passed.

Burden came into the office, glanced at Wexford, glared at the dress as if to say, Why bother with it? Why let it keep confusing us, holding us up? Aloud he said, 'How did you get on with the Miall girl?'

'It looks as if Dawn had another man friend. Mike, I'm wondering if it could have been Peveril. He was in London on June first, and on that day Dawn met a man for a drink. She went out to meet someone in an underhand way when she had a pretty pressing engagement at home. Now that date took place only five days before the day she died.'

'Go on,' said Burden, interested.

'Dawn was in Kingsmarkham at Easter. The Peverils were already living in The Pathway at Easter. Suppose Peveril picked her up somewhere in Kingsmarkham, had a drink with her, got her to give him her phone number?'

'Didn't he ever phone her?'

'According to Joan Miall, Dawn had a rather mysterious phone call from a man on Monday, May twenty-third. That could have been Peveril. His wife goes out on Monday evenings and that would have given him his opportunity.'

'Sounds promising.'

'Unfortunately, it isn't. We know Zeno Vedast phoned Dawn about that time. He says he did, and Dawn told Joan Miall it was he as soon as she answered the phone. Joan didn't believe her because afterwards she wasn't elated or excited. But, on his own admission, Vedast put her off with vague promises. Dawn wasn't a fool. She could tell he was bored and that rocked her so much that she couldn't even bring herself to brag about knowing him any more or weave any of her usual fantasies. Therefore, I think we must conclude that it was Vedast who phoned her that night and that Vedast had no further communication with her. He's out of it. But that doesn't mean Peveril didn't phone her. He could easily have done so on some occasion when Joan wasn't there.

'During the weekend following her pub date, the weekend preceding her death, she gave Joan to understand that she was embarking on an affair with a man too mean or too scared to take her to an hotel. That description would fit Edward Peveril, a man who owned a house from which his wife would be absent for several hours on a Monday evening; Edward Peveril who came out to us while we were at the festival and tried to distract our attention from the quarry as soon as he knew who we were; Edward Peveril who no longer cares for his wife and who, on Miss Mowler's evidence, is occasionally unfaithful to her.'

Burden pondered. 'What do you think happened that night, then?'

'Whatever happened, Mrs Peveril must know of it.'

'You don't mean connived at it, sir?'

'Not beforehand, certainly. She may have been suspicious beforehand. Don't forget that she told us it was a matter of chance that she was in the house at all at five-thirty. Her *husband* had tried to persuade her to go to a film in Kingsmarkham that afternoon and stay on for her evening class. Why didn't she do that? Because she was suspicious of his motives? Confident that he could persuade her, he asked Dawn to bring with her a meal for the two of them. But Mrs Peveril didn't go out. She saw Dawn at five-thirty, the actual time of the appointment, *and Dawn saw her*. Therefore, carrying her bag of food, she waited in those fields until she saw Margaret Peveril go out.

'Dawn was then admitted by Peveril. She began to prepare the food, changing into an old dress Peveril gave her so as not to spoil the mauve thing. Before the meal was ready, she asked Peveril if it would be all right for her to stay the night as he, knowing this couldn't be but using any inducements to get Dawn to come, had previously promised. When he told her that idea was off, they quarrelled, she threatening to stay and confront his wife. He killed her in a panic.'

Burden said, 'But when Mrs Peveril came home he threw himself on her mercy. She was needed to help him clean up and dispose of the body.'

'I don't know, Mike. I haven't great confidence in this theory. Why did Mrs Peveril mention having seen the girl at all if it's true? I can't get a warrant on this evidence but tomorrow I'm going to ask Peveril's permission to search. Tomorrow's Sunday and it's your day off.'

'Oh, I'll come,' said Burden.

'No. Have your Sunday with the kids. If we find anything I'll let you know at once.'

Wexford allowed his glance to fall once more on the dress, caught now in a ray of evening sunshine which touched it like a stage spotlight. He tried to imagine Margaret Peveril slender, rejuvenated, but he could only see her as she was, bigger and fleshier than Dawn, a woman whose whole build showed that she could never, since her teens, have worn that dress. He shrugged.

He didn't attempt to get a search warrant. With Martin and three constables, he went to The Pathway in the morning, a misty, cool morning such as heralds a fine day. The sunshine hung like a sheet of gold satin under a fine tulle veil.

Muttering and pleading that his work would be disturbed, Peveril agreed without much protest to his house being searched. Wexford was disappointed. He had expected the man to put up a front of aggressive opposition. They lifted the fitted carpets, scrutinised skirting boards, examined the hems of curtains. Mrs Peveril watched them, biting her nails. This ultimate desecration of her home had driven her into a kind of fugue, a total withdrawal into apathy and silence. Her husband sat in his studio, surrounded by men crawling on the floor and peering under cabinets; he doodled on his drawing board, making meaningless sketches which could not, under any circumstances, have been saleable.

Miss Mowler, returning home from church, came up to Wexford at the gate and asked if the men would like tea. Wexford refused. He noticed, not for the first time, how the churchgoing woman who might more conveniently carry a prayer book in her handbag, always holds it ostentatiously in her hands, an outward and visible sign of spiritual superiority. Dunsand was mowing his lawn, emptying the cuttings into a spruce little green wheelbarrow. Wexford went back into the house. Presently he looked out of the window and, to his astonishment, saw Louis Mbowele approaching, his coat swinging open to allow the soft summer air to fan his brown, bead-hung chest. Louis went into Dunsand's garden, the mowing was abandoned and the two men entered the bungalow. Not so very astonishing, after all. Wexford remembered that Louis was a philosophy student at Myringham where Dunsand taught philosophy.

'How are you doing?' he said to Martin.

'She wasn't killed here, sir. Unless it was in the bathroom. I reckon you could stick a pig in that bathroom and not leave a trace.'

'We may as well get out then. This is supposed to be a day of rest and I'm going home.'

'Just one thing, sir. Young Stevens asked me if you'd see him before he goes off duty. He's at the station. He mentioned it last night but what with all this it went out of my head. He's got something on his mind but he won't tell me what.'

The house was restored to order. Wexford apologised sparingly to Mrs Peveril.

'I told you she didn't come here,' she said with a cowed resentful look. 'I told you she went right away from here. She went across the fields.'

Wexford got into the car beside Martin. 'I wish she wouldn't keep saying that, you know, gratuitously, as it were.' He slammed the door. Martin listened politely as he was obliged to do, his mind on his Sunday dinner which would probably be spoilt by now, anyway. 'Why does she say it if it isn't true?' said Wexford.

'Maybe it is true, sir.'

'Then why didn't anyone else see her after five-thirty? Think of all those blokes coming home for their dinners at Sundays and in Stowerton around six. They'd have seen her. She was the kind of girl men notice.'

The mention of dinner made Sergeant Martin even more

133

obtuse than usual. 'Maybe she sat in the fields for hours, sir, sat there till it was dark.'

'Oh God!' Wexford roared. 'If she was going to have to hang about for hours she'd have stayed at her mother's or if that was unbearable, gone to the pictures in Kingsmarkham.'

'But the last bus, sir?'

'It's less than a mile, man. She was a strong healthy girl. Wouldn't she have walked it later rather than sit about in a field?'

'Then Mrs Peveril never saw her.'

'Oh, yes, she did. She observed her closely, every detail of her appearance.'

The car drew up and the two men got out, Martin to depart for a long and well-deserved dinner, Wexford to see Stevens who was already waiting for him in his office. The shy and inarticulate young policeman stood to attention rigidly which made Wexford even crosser and also made him want to laugh. He told the man to sit down and Stevens did so, less at ease in a chair than stiffly on his feet.

Wexford didn't laugh. He said quite gently, 'We do have a welfare officer, Stevens, if the men have some domestic or private problem that's interfering with their work.'

'But it's work that's interfering with my work, sir,' Stevens stuttered.

'I don't know what you mean.'

The man swallowed. 'Sir.' He stopped. He said it again. 'Sir,' and then, rushing, the words tumbling out, 'Mrs Peveril, sir, I've wanted to tell you for days. I didn't think it was for me to put myself forward. I didn't know what to do.'

'If you know something about Mrs Peveril that I ought to know, you must tell me at once. You know that, Stevens. Now come on, pull yourself together.'

'Sir, I was transferred here from Brighton last year.' He waited for Wexford's nod of encouragement which came with brisk impatience. 'There was a bank robbery, sir, last summer.

134

Mrs Peveril saw the raid and she—she came to the police voluntarily to give evidence. The superintendent interviewed her a lot, sir, and she had to try to identify the villains. We never caught them.'

'You recognised her? Her name? Her face?'

'Her face, sir, and then when I heard her name I remembered. She knew me too. She was very hysterical, sir, a bad witness, kept saying it was all making her ill. I've had it on my conscience all week and then I kept thinking, well, so what? She didn't hold up the bank clerk. And then it got so I thought—well, I had to tell you, sir.'

'Stevens,' sighed Wexford, 'you've got a lot to learn. Never mind, you've told me at last. Go away and have your dinner. I'll check all this with Brighton.'

He began to have an inkling of what had happened. But he must check before going back to The Pathway. There wasn't going to be any Sunday dinner for him.

The Peverils were just finishing theirs. It struck Wexford that this was the first time he had encountered Peveril not working or coming straight from his work or fidgeting to get back to it.

'What is it this time?' he said, looking up from roast beef and Yorkshire pudding.

'I'm sorry to disturb your lunch, Mr Peveril. I want to talk to your wife.'

Peveril promptly picked up his plate, tucked his napkin into the neck of his sweater and, having paused to grab the mustard pot, was making for the door to his studio.

'Don't leave me, Edward!' said his wife in the thin, high-pitched voice which, if it were louder, would be a scream. 'You never give me any support, you never have done. I shall be ill again. I can't bear being questioned. I'm frightened.'

'You're always bloody frightened. Don't hang on me.' He pushed her away. 'Can't you see I've got a plate in my hand?'

135

'Edward, can't you see, he's going to make me say who did it! He's going to make me pick someone out!'

'Mrs Peveril, sit down. Please sit down. I'd be glad if you wouldn't go away, sir. I don't think it's for me to interfere between husband and wife but, if I may say so, Mrs Peveril might not be quite so frightened if you'd try to give her the support she wants. Please, sir, do as I ask.'

Wexford's tone had been very stern and commanding. It was effective. Bullies crumple fast when sharply admonished, and Peveril, though he moved no closer to his wife and did not look at her, sat down, put his plate on the edge of the table and folded his arms sullenly. Mrs Peveril crept towards him and hesitated, biting her thumbnail. She gave Wexford the half-sly, half-desperate look of the hysteric who is trying to preserve intact the thickly packed layers of neurosis.

'Now will you both listen quietly to what I have to say?' He waited. Neither spoke. 'Mrs Peveril, let me tell you what I think happened. In Brighton you witnessed a bank robbery.' Her eyes opened wide. She gave a little chattering murmur. 'That was a most upsetting experience for you, but you very properly came forward to give information to the police. You were a key witness. Naturally, the police questioned you exhaustively. You fancied yourself badgered and you became frightened, ill perhaps with fright, both from the constant visits of the police and from a notion that some revenge might be taken against you for the information you had given. You moved here to get away from that. Am I right?'

Mrs Peveril said nothing. Her husband, who never missed a cue, said, 'Sure, you're right. Never mind where I had my roots, my contacts, my ideal studio. Madam wanted to run away so we ran away.'

'Please, Mr Peveril.' Wexford turned to the woman, sensing that he must be very careful, very gentle. Her stillness, the compulsive nail biting, the hard set furrows in her face, were ominous. 'You had only been here a few months when you realised, because of what you had seen, that you might soon be involved in another and perhaps even more disturbing criminal case. Mrs Peveril, we know you saw Dawn Stonor on Monday, June sixth. You gave an accurate description of her, more precise than any other we have. I suggest to you—please don't be alarmed—that you either admitted her to this house or saw her enter another house. You told us you saw her cross the fields because you believed that would be the surest way to draw our attention, the attention you find so frightening, away from you and your own neighbourhood.'

It might have been all right. She took her hand from her mouth and bit her lip. She made a little preparatory murmur. It would have been all right if Peveril hadn't started to his feet and shouted at her, 'Christ, is that true? You bloody fool! I thought there was something fishy, I knew it. You told lies to the police and nearly landed me right in it. My God!'

She began to scream. 'I never saw her at all! I never saw her!' A slap on the face would have been effective. Instead, her husband began shaking her so that the screams came out in stifled strangled gasps. She crumpled and fell on the floor. Peveril took a step backwards, white-faced.

'Get Miss Mowler,' snapped Wexford.

By the time he returned with the nurse, Mrs Peveril was lying back in a chair, moaning softly. Miss Mowler gave her a bracing, toothy smile.

'We'll get you to bed, dear, and then I'll make you a nice strong cup of tea.'

Mrs Peveril cringed away from her. 'Go away. I don't want you. I want Edward '

'All right, dear. Just as you like. Edward can get you to bed while I make the tea.'

At the use of his Christian name Peveril frowned ferociously, but he gave an arm to his wife and helped her up the stairs. Miss Mowler bustled about, removing plates of congealing food, boiling a kettle, hunting for aspirins. A little thin woman, she was quick in her movements and efficient. She talked all the time she worked, apologising for non-existent faults. What a pity she hadn't been on the spot when 'it' happened. If only she had been in her garden, for instance. How unfortunate that, what with one thing and another, she had had to wash her hands and take off her overall before accompanying Mr Peveril to the house. Wexford said very little. He was thinking that he would be lucky to get any more out of Mrs Peveril that day.

The tea was taken up. Peveril didn't reappear. Wexford followed Miss Mowler back into her own bungalow where newspapers were spread over the hall carpet and a kind of late spring cleaning seemed to be in progress.

'I spilt a cup of cocoa down the wall. It's a blessing this paper's washable. I don't know what you must think of me, washing walls on a Sunday afternoon.'

'The better the day, the better the deed,' said Wexford politely. 'I want to have another look at the quarry, Miss Mowler. May I make my way there through your garden?'

He was permitted to do so but only after he had refused pressing offers of tea and coffee, sherry, a sandwich. Miss Mowler, having been assured that he didn't need her to accompany him down the path and open the gate for him, returned to her work. He let himself out of the garden and into the narrow no man's land that separated the estate from Sundays.

16

Heavy rains had fallen and now the sun had returned as bright and hot as ever. But it was too soon yet for new grass to show, too soon for even the beginnings of the green carpet which by autumn would once more cover the desert plain which Sundays park had become. Wexford sat down on the edge of the quarry. Here nature was winning, for the flowers and shrubs, the delicate yet lush herbage of June, had been assailed by only half a dozen trampling feet. New roses, new harebells, were opening to replace the crushed blossoms. He looked at the broken wire, the wall, the three gates, but they told him nothing more, and gradually the scented air, sun-warmed and soft, drove thoughts of the case from his mind. A butterfly, a Clouded Yellow, drifted languidly past him and alighted on a rose, its petals paler and creamier than the buttercup-coloured wings. Not so many butterflies these days as when he was a child, not so many as when even his daughters were children. Under his breath he caught himself humming a tune. At first he thought it was that song of Vedast's which stuck in his mind and irritated him. Then he realised it wasn't that one but a ballad of Betti Ho's in which she prophesied that her children would never see a butterfly except in a museum. The Clouded Yellow took to the air again, hovering, floating ...

'You're trespassing!'

Wexford started to his feet, shaking himself out of his dream.

'You're trespassing,' said Silk again, half-serious, half-peevishly ironic. 'I don't see why I should always have the fuzz trampling over my land.'

Looking up into the irritable white face and the smiling black one, Wexford said, 'I'm not trampling. I was sitting and thinking. What are you two up to? Planning another festival?'

'No, we're going to try and get a commune going here during the university vacation. Louis and I and his girl friend and about half a dozen others. Louis wants to see how it works out with a view to operating a kibbutz system in Marumi.'

'Really?' said Wexford blankly. He didn't see how gathering together a house party in a fully-equipped and furnished mansion could be a rehearsal for kibbutzim in an equatorial state, but he didn't say so. 'Well, I think I'll trample off now.'

'So will I,' said Louis unexpectedly. He gave his radiant grin and patted Silk on the grey head which reached just to his shoulder. 'Peace be with you.'

They skirted the Peverils' fence and emerged at the head of The Pathway. Mrs Peveril's bedroom curtains were drawn. Dunsand was pulling puny little weeds out of his flowerless borders. Beside Miss Mowler's car a bucket of soapy water stood unattended. It was hot, sunny, a radiant day. The English do not relax in deck-chairs in their front gardens and, apart from the crouching figure of the philosophy lecturer, the place was deserted. Louis waved graciously to him.

'Want a lift into Kingsmarkham?'

'Thanks,' Louis said. 'That way I might get the three-thirty bus to Myringham.'

Wexford's car was a fair-sized one, but no car except perhaps Vedast's Rolls would have been roomy enough to accommodate Louis Mbowele comfortably. Laughing, he hunched himself inside the folds of his pony-skin and slid the passenger seat back to its fullest extent.

Wexford said, 'When you get to the top of wherever it is you're going, are you going to *make* them live in communes?'

'It's the only way of life, man.'

'And force them to be equal and dictate the pattern of their houses and the subjects of their study and operate a censorship and forbid other political parties?'

'For a time, for a time. It's necessary. They have to learn. When they see it all works and the new generation's grown up and we have peace and full bellies, then we can start to relax. It's necessary to make them do what they aren't just too crazy to do right now. So you have to make them for their own good.'

'Do you know a saying of James Boswell? "We have no right to make people happy against their will"?'

Louis nodded, smiling no longer.

'I know it, man, and I know the connection in which it was said. The slave trade. The traders excused themselves on the ground that my people would be happier on plantations than in jungles. This is different. This is for real. And it's only for a time.'

'Oh, Louis,' said Wexford, turning into the Forby road, 'that's what they all say.'

They drove into Kingsmarkham in silence. The heat of the day, his failure to get anywhere, enervated Wexford. There seemed nothing else to do with his afternoon but go home, eat his stale lunch, maybe sleep. Then, as they approached the place where the Myringham bus stopped, he became aware of the long silence and wondered if he had offended the young African. Louis looked as if he would have a hearty appetite, and the Olive and Dove did a good Sunday lunch. . . .

'Have you eaten?' he said.

'Sure. I cadged some bread and cheese off Len.'

'Mr Dunsand? Why did you have to cadge? Isn't he very hospitable?'

Louis grinned. Evidently, he hadn't been offended, only sleepy from the sun. 'He's a recluse,' he said. 'He finds it hard to communicate. Still, I took him out to lunch a while back in

141

Myringham—last Wednesday fortnight it was—so I guess he owed me a meal. I asked him to join our commune but he's not together enough for that.'

'Strange. You'd think a lecturer in philosophy would . . .'

'Have found the way? Found himself?' Louis leapt out of the car and strode round to open Wexford's door. 'That's a popular misconception, man. It's living—a broad spectrum of living—that teaches you how to live, not philosophy. Philosophy teaches you how to *think*.'

The bus was late. Louis, scorning to join the queue, sat down on the steps of the Snowdrop Cleaners, and Wexford, leaving the car at the kerb, followed him.

'How do you get on with him?'

Louis considered. The dozen or so people in the queue bestowed upon him glances of intense, if repressed, curiosity. Few black-skinned men and women had penetrated to this country town, and to them his coat, his beads and the green silk scarf he wore round his head—although no more than fashionable 'gear' for black and white alike—perhaps appeared as tribal paraphernalia. He returned their looks with the gracious smile of a prince, a tawny Rasselas, and said to Wexford:

'He's all right as a teacher, he knows his subject. But he doesn't seem to like people. You see, he's afraid of them.'

'What else is there to be afraid of?' asked Wexford to whom this idea, in all its truth, had come suddenly as if out of the air. 'Except, maybe, thunderstorms, floods, what insurance companies call Acts of God. If you say you're afraid of bombs or war, it's people who make the bombs and the war.'

'You're right. But, oh, man, there are a lot of people and they are frightening. And it's worse when one of the people you're frightened of is yourself.' Louis gazed into the heart of the afternoon sun. 'Someone told me he was better when his wife lived with him. He used to go away on holidays then, the Majorca bit, the Costa Brava scramble. He doesn't do anything now but read and paint the house and mow the lawn. But you can't picture him married to *her*, can you?' Louis got up, thrust out his hand. 'Here's the bus.'

'Picture her? I don't know her. Do you?'

Extending one huge furry arm to support her, Louis helped a fragile-looking old lady on to the bus platform. In the manner of one whose girlhood dreams have at last been realised and who has fallen into the hands of a sheikh, she blushed, giggled and almost panicked. The other passengers stared and whispered.

'Come along now,' said the driver. 'We haven't got all day.'

Louis grinned. Head and shoulders above the rest, he gave his fare, looking over a diminutive woman's hat at Wexford.

'I don't know her. Old Silk told me who she was at the festival, pointed her out while Zeno Vedast was singing. Man, you stood next to her.'

'I did?'

The bus started.

'Peace be with you,' Louis shouted.

'And with you,' said Wexford.

The golden car wasn't there. Perhaps it had been silly of him to think it would be. On such a fine afternoon they would all have gone out to see the house Vedast was buying. On the almost bare forecourt, blanched ashen pale by hard sunlight, his own car looked forlorn. The Cheriton Forest Hotel seemed asleep. But the porter who had admired Nell Tate was awake. He sat in the deserted hall, reading the *Sunday Express* and smoking a cigarette which he stubbed out quickly when Wexford appeared.

'I'm afraid not, sir,' he said in answer to the chief inspector's enquiry. 'Mr Vedast and Mrs Tate went out in Mr Vedast's car after lunch.'

'You don't know when they'll be back?'

Memories of fifty-pence pieces easily earned stirred in the

porter's mind. He was obviously reluctant to deny Wexford anything. 'Mr Tate took his coffee out into the garden, sir. Would you care for me to . . . ?'

'No, I'll find him myself.'

'As you like sir,' said the man, philosophically contemplating the smaller coin his efforts had won him.

Wexford strolled round the gabled, studded, mullioned and heavily rose-hung building. There was nobody about. Birds sang sleepily in the deciduous trees which bordered the fir plantations. He reached the back and saw the elderly couple with whom he had shared the Shakespeare Lounge snoring in long chairs on the terrace. A gravel path wound between rose-beds to a small round lawn in the middle of which was an umbrella with a table and chair under it. A man sat in the chair, his back to the terrace. The porter, a tactful servant, had described Tate as taking his coffee in the garden and there was certainly a diminutive cup on the table beside him. But what Tate was taking was brandy. An eager hand had just grasped the bottle of Courvoisier and was about to tip a further measure into the already half-full glass.

'Good afternoon, Mr Tate.'

If Wexford had hoped to make Tate jump he was disappointed. The man didn't get up. He filled his glass, replaced the bottle top and said, 'Hallo. Have a drink.'

Wexford remembered that he was driving, that he had had no lunch, and he refused. 'I'd like to talk to you. D'you mind if I fetch myself a chair?'

'No,' said Tate economically.

Wexford fetched himself a deck-chair and drew it under the umbrella's shade. Tate didn't say anything. His face quite blank, he contemplated the view of the hilly forest, lying black and furry-looking, and a smooth blue sky. He wasn't in the least drunk. Alcoholics never get drunk. Wexford thought that this was probably Tate's misfortune, that he had drunk so much and drunk so chronically that, perpetually intoxicated, he could never now enjoy the felicity of what most people call intoxication. His skin was a rough greyish red, his eyeballs veined with red, their rims vermilion and moist. And yet he was a young man still, unlined, thin, not bad-looking, his hair untouched by grey.

'Mr Tate, I really wanted to talk to your wife.'

'She's gone out with Zeno to see the new house.'

As he had thought. 'So Mr Vedast found one to his liking?' Tate agreed that this was so. He sipped his brandy. 'It's called Cheriton Hall.'

'Ah, yes. I think I know it. On the Pomfret side of the forest. Will you all live there?'

'We go where Zeno goes.'

Guessing, hoping, very much in the dark, Wexford essayed, 'Your wife won't find it awkward living so comparatively close to her ex-husband?'

The unhealthy colour in Tate's face deepened, the grey overpowering the red. He made no answer but he fixed on Wexford a truculent and rather puzzled stare.

'I'm right in thinking your wife was once married to Mr Dunsand?' Tate shrugged. The shrug implied an indifference to Wexford's opinions rather than a doubt as to their veracity. 'For the past week,' Wexford went on, 'I've been trying to discover a connection between Dawn Stonor and some resident of the Sundays estate, especially of The Pathway. Until now I've been unable to succeed.'

'Small world,' said Tate uneasily.

'Is it? I think it's an enormous world. I think it's extraordinary that Dawn should have last been seen alive in The Pathway where Mrs Tate's ex-husband lives. I think it particularly odd now that I know Dawn was once a close friend of Zeno Vedast who is now a—er, close friend of your wife's. And yet I'm to dismiss it as being due to the smallness of the world.'

Tate shrugged again. 'Zeno and Nell and me were all in

145

Duvette Gardens that night you're talking about.' He put Vedast's name before his wife's, Wexford noticed. 'We were all together and that guy Silk looked in about ten to talk about the festival.' Morosely, he said, 'We've never been near that place.'

'Surely you were when you were at the festival, very near? Didn't your wife point Mr Dunsand's house out to you?'

It was a trap and the slow-witted Tate fell into it. 'She said, that's Len's house, yes.'

Wexford pounced. 'So she knew it? He'd only lived there a matter of weeks but she knew it. Not by the street name and the number. She knew it by the look of it!'

'I shouldn't like to have your job, meddling in people's private affairs.'

'And I shouldn't like to have yours, Mr Tate,' said Wexford crisply. He leant across the table, forcing the other man to look at him. 'Whose wife is she, yours or that singer you fawn on? Yours or the man who divorced her? What sort of a set-up are you running here? Or do you do just what you're told, lie, pimp, connive at obstructing the police, anything he and she tell you?'

There was too little of one kind of spirit in Tate and too much of the other for him to react violently to these insults. He passed a hand across bleary eyes as if his head ached and said in a sour cowed voice, 'Christ, how you do go on! Never you mind my wife. I can deal with her.'

'By blacking her eye?'

'She told you? I bet she didn't tell you why.'

'I think it was because you found out she'd been seeing Dunsand. At the festival when she pointed out his house you put two and two together. You didn't mind about Vedast, that was different. Maybe you found she'd got a key to his house so you had it out with her and blacked her eye.'

Tate half-smiled. It was the smile of one who is accustomed to subservience to a superior intellect, a smile of grudging

146

admiration. He took something out of his trouser pocket and laid it on the table. A key.

'I found it in her handbag. It'll be safer with you. She might get it away from me and use it again.' He got up abruptly, took his bottle and walked very carefully and steadily up the terrace steps and into the hotel.

Wexford pocketed the key. He tiptoed past the old couple, made his way through a cool and shadowy corridor to the front entrance. Then, seeing the golden car had arrived, he slipped back into the porch and waited.

Nell and Zeno Vedast got out. The swelling had gone down from the girl's eye and her painted face was almost serene. Her hair, freshly washed, was a yellow cloud but the bright light showed darker roots. Vedast, wearing jeans and a thin embroidered waistcoat, took a springy stride towards Wexford's car and stood contemplating it, smiling, his head on one side. His face wore very much the expression Wexford had seen there just before Tate drank the doctored liquor, and he heard him say:

'That parking ticket we got, shall we put it on his windscreen?'

'What's the point?' said Nell.

'Fun is the point, Nello darling. A joke. He'll twig it in two seconds but think how mad he'll be first. Go and get it, Nello. It's on the back seat.'

She opened the rear door of the Rolls. Hypnotised by him, obedient as ever, she gave him the ticket. But as he was lifting one of the wipers she broke out:

'I'm sick of jokes. Why can't we grow up, do things for real? I hate always playing games.'

'Do you really, Nello? You are a funny girl.' Vedast clipped the ticket under the wiper and laughed. He shook back his hair and his yellow eyes glowed. 'I don't believe you. I think you liked all that funny dressing up and pretending to be good and making cosy little plans.' He took her hand, kissed her cheek lightly. 'That's why we get on so well, dear, you and me with our little fantasies. Shall we go and rouse Goffo from his Sunday stupor?'

She nodded, clutching his arm. They went off towards the rose garden. When they had disappeared around the side of the hotel Wexford emerged thoughtfully. Having a strong objection to the scattering of litter, he placed the parking ticket under the paws of the golden lion and then he drove away.

17

Some little good had come out of Mrs Peveril's hysterical breakdown. The information she was now willing to give was imparted too late to be of much use—Wexford knew it already, or most of it—but her despair had shocked her husband into anxiety for her.

He said soberly, 'You were pretty decent, very patient actually. I never realised what a bad state she'd got herself into. Will she have to appear in court?'

'I don't know, Mr Peveril. I still don't quite know what she did see. I must have a final word with her.'

'If she does have to I'll be there. She won't mind so much if I'm with her. The fact is I've been too wrapped up in my work. I let her face all that business in Brighton alone and it was too much for her. When this is over I'm going to scrape up the cash and take her away for a good holiday.'

The uxoriousness wouldn't last, Wexford knew that. Such a *volte-face* often takes place at crises in a marriage but it is only in romances that it becomes a permanency.

And Peveril revealed just how ephemeral it was when, as they went upstairs to see his wife, he muttered, 'You have to bloody wet-nurse some women all their lives, don't you? If I'm not wanted for the next half-hour I may as well catch up on a spot of work.'

Mrs Peveril, wan-looking but calm, sat up in bed wrapped in a jaded broderie anglais dressing gown.

'It was like you said,' she admitted. 'I wanted to make you all think she'd gone a long, long way from here. I wanted to

149

be left in peace. When I first saw her I meant to tell Edward what I'd seen but I didn't because he gets cross with me if I gossip. He says he works for me all day and all I've got to do with myself is look out of the window and tell stories about the neighbours.' She sighed heavily. 'Then when Mrs Clarke phoned me on that Sunday night and said you were coming round asking, I thought I'd say she'd gone into the fields. If I'd said she'd gone next door you'd never have left me alone. I thought saying I hadn't seen her at all would be perjury.'

Wexford shook his head. It was quite useless to point out to her that what she had said was equally perjury.

'You saw her go next door to Mr Dunsand's? At what time?'

'At half past five. I did say,' said Mrs Peveril, eagerly attempting to retrieve her integrity, 'I saw her at five-thirty. I watched her. I saw her go into the porch and someone must have let her in because she never came out again.' Prevarication at an end now, Mrs Peveril was cheerfully burning her boats, gabbling out belated information. Wexford knew she was speaking the truth. 'I was very interested. You see, I couldn't think who she could be. Mr Dunsand never has any visitors except sometimes his students.'

'Never?' Wexford asked quickly.

She said ingenuously, 'Oh, no, I should have noticed. I spend a lot of time at my window when Edward's in his studio and you can see everything these light evenings, can't you? That's why I was so *intrigued* by this girl.' Fear touched her afresh and the wan look returned. 'You'll protect me, won't you? I mean, when I've been to the court and said how Mr Dunsand did it you won't let me come to any harm?'

'When you have been to the court and told the truth, Mrs Peveril,' Wexford corrected her, 'we'll see that you're quite safe.'

With a passing, thoughtful glance at Dunsand's bungalow,

its windows closed against the midsummer evening, Wexford drove to Tabard Road. He found Burden and the children in the garden and for once there was no music playing. Burden was too respectable and had far too much social conscience to allow record players or transistors out of doors. The boy and girl sat at a wicker table, arguing and making some pretence of doing their homework. John, who was always pleased to see the chief inspector whom he regarded as an ally and friend of oppressed youth, fetched him a chair and said:

'Could you give me a bit of help, Mr Wexford? I've got to do an essay on the French Revolution, and Dad's no use. He's not educated.'

'Really!' spluttered Burden. 'Don't be so rude.'

His son ignored him. 'I've left my book at school and I can't remember the new names the Convention gave to the months. I'll have to know them and I thought . . .'

'I'll try.' Wexford hesitated. 'We're in *Messidor* now, that's June. You're supposed to start with September. Let's see . . . *Vendemiaire, Brumaire, Frimaire; Nivose, Pluviose, Ventose;* then *Germinal* like Zola's book, *Floreal* and *Prairial; Messidor, Thermidor* and—wait . . .'

'*Fructidor!*' exclaimed John.

Wexford chuckled. 'You might care to know the contemporary and rather scathing English translation: Wheezy, Sneezy, Freezy; Slippy, Drippy, Nippy; Showery, Flowery, Bowery; Wheaty, Heaty, Sweety. There, you can put that in your essay and maybe you'll get an A.' He cut short the boy's thanks and said, 'One good turn deserves another. Now I want a bit of help from you.'

'*Me?*'

'Mm-hm. About Zeno Vedast. Or, more precisely, about Godfrey Tate. You must know something about him. You told your father who his wife was.'

'I read about it,' John said, 'in the *Musical Express.* Anything about Zeno's news, you see.' He put down his pen and

151

flashed a look of triumph at his father. 'What d'you want to know, Mr Wexford?'

'Anything about Zeno. What you read.'

'Zeno ran her over in his car . . .'

'He *what* . . . ?'

'It was like this. He went to Myringham to give a concert—it was sponsored by that Mr Silk, Silk Enterprises—and there was a big crowd outside the theatre afterwards and she got in front of his car and got hurt. It said in the paper that Silk Enterprises paid for a private room in the hospital for her and sent her flowers and fruit and things. I expect Zeno thought that would be good publicity, don't you? It was about two years ago, maybe three. Dad,' said John resentfully, 'won't let me save copies of old magazines. He says it's hoarding. She was married to someone else then. I think he was called Dunn, something like Dunn.'

'Go on.'

'When she got married again it was in the papers because Zeno was at the wedding and Mr Silk. I expect she'd rather have married Zeno.'

'I daresay she would, John, but he wouldn't have her so she took the next best thing. Catch as catch can.'

'Good heavens,' said Burden crossly, 'must you fill him up with these cynical views of life?'

Wexford winked indiscreetly at the boy and for the time being said no more. He was thinking of the bald story he had been told and, more particularly, of the gaps in it which only an older person with experience of life could fill. Nell was still young. She must have been very young when she first married Dunsand. He wondered what had led to that ill-assorted marriage, what had made her choose the reserved, repressed lecturer for a husband. An unhappy home life like Dawn Stonor's? The need to escape from some dreary backwater? If this were so, it must have been a case of out of the frying pan into the fire. He pictured her among the faculty wives, decades her senior, the long evenings at home with Dunsand; the leather chairs, Wittgenstein, the lawn-mowing ... Still a teenager at heart, she must have longed for younger people, for music, for excitement. And yet there was in her the stuff that makes a slave. Had she also been Dunsand's slave? Perhaps. But she had escaped—into a glamorous, eventful, luxurious life that was nonetheless slavery. About two years ago, at the time the song was written.

> 'So come by, come nigh,
> come try and tell why
> some sigh, some cry,
> some lie and some die.'

He had sung it aloud and the others were staring at him. Pat giggled.

John said, 'Very groovey, Mr Wexford.'

In the same parlance Wexford said, 'I shouldn't make much bread that way, John. Apart from not being able to sing, I don't have the figure for it.' He raised his heavy body out of the chair and said rather sharply to the inspector, 'Come into the house.'

'First thing tomorrow,' Wexford said, 'I want you to swear out a warrant to search Dunsand's house.'

'What, another fruitless search?'

'Maybe it won't be fruitless.'

Burden took Pat's ballet shoes off the seat of one chair and John's tennis racket off another. 'On what evidence, for God's sake?'

'If Mrs Peveril has any value as a witness at all, Dawn Stonor went to Dunsand's house. She was last seen going to his house and she was never seen coming out of it, never seen again. I would calculate that it's a shorter distance from his back fence to the quarry than from any other back fence. She was killed in that house, Mike.'

'Will you ask Dunsand's consent first?'

'Yes, but he'll refuse. At least, I think so. I shall also ask him not to go to work tomorrow. They come down this week, so he can't have anything very pressing to do.'

Burden looked bewildered. 'You were just as sure it happened in Peveril's house, sir. Are you saying she knew Dunsand, that it was Dunsand she met in that pub on June first?'

'No. I know it wasn't. Dunsand was in Myringham on June first. Louis Mbowele told me that.'

'And Dunsand can't have let her in on that Monday. He wasn't there at five-thirty. We're as certain as can be she didn't know Dunsand. Can you imagine him picking a girl up, asking her to come to his house?'

'You must remember that Dunsand isn't the only person who could have let her in. Nell Tate had a key.'

'She used to go and see her ex-husband?' Burden asked doubtfully.

'I should think not,' Wexford rejoined slowly. 'Mrs Peveril would have seen her if she hàd been and Mrs Peveril never saw her. Perhaps he sent her the key in the hope that she would visit him. The fact remains that she had a key and she could have been in Dunsand's house by five-thirty. Did you ever check on that Duvette Gardens alibi?'

Burden looked a little offended. He was conscientious, proud of his thoroughness. 'Of course I did. Although, there didn't seem much point when you got so interested in Peveril. I got the Met. on it.'

'And?'

'Vedast's car was stuck outside all day and all night, gathering his usual parking tickets. Nobody seems to have a clue whether they were inside the house. One of them may not have been. We just can't tell.'

Wexford nodded. 'The Tates would lie themselves black in the face to protect their master and he'd lie to protect his little ones. I think he cares a good deal more for "Goffo" than for "Nello", though, don't you? I wish I could see a motive. One might suggest that Nell was jealous of Dawn's relationship with Zeno Vedast, only there wasn't a relationship any more. Vedast might have had a date to meet Dawn somewhere in the neighbourhood and Nell found out about it and lured her into the house to kill her. D'you fancy that idea?'

'Of course I don't.'

'Tate might have fallen in love with Dawn when they met at the Townsman Club and got the key from his wife to use Dunsand's house for a love nest. Then Vedast killed her to prevent her spoiling their jolly little *tria juncta in uno*. Does that suit you better?'

'Well, I suppose anything's possible with people of their sort.'

'Sure it is. Nell arranged to meet Dawn there because she had Dunsand's loneliness on her conscience. She thought Dawn might make him a suitable second wife—no less suitable than his first, at any rate—but when Dawn had confessed that Vedast had phoned her, shown interest in her, Nell got into a rage. She would, of course, have instructed Dawn to bring with her a second-hand red dress because Dunsand likes second-hand clothes, red is his favourite colour, and he prefers dresses to be a tight fit.'

Burden said distantly, 'I don't see the point of all this, sir. Aren't you rather arguing with yourself? It's you who want to search the place, not I.'

'I expect I am, Mike,' said Wexford. 'I haven't an idea how it happened, but two things I'm certain of. We shall find traces of blood in Dunsand's house tomorrow, and Dunsand will confess to having killed Dawn Stonor from the chivalrous motive of protecting his former and still much-loved wife. It's going to be a heavy day so I think I'll be off home now.'

18

While they ransacked the bungalow, Wexford sat with Dunsand in the sombre living room. The search warrant had been shown to him and he had read it carefully, scrupulously, in total silence. He lifted his shoulders, nodded and followed Wexford into the living room, pausing at the window to pick a dead flower off one of the dehydrated cacti. Then he sat down and began to leaf through one of the travel brochures in the manner of a patient in a doctor's waiting room. The light fell on his glasses, turning them into gleaming opaque ovals. His eyes were invisible, his thick mouth closed and set, so that his whole face was expressionless. But as he turned the pages and came to one on which some words had been pencilled in the margin, there came suddenly a tightening of those rubbery cheek muscles that was like a wince.

'Your wife had a key to this house, Mr Dunsand.'

He looked up. 'Yes. I sent it to her. But she's my wife no longer.'

'I beg your pardon. We believe she or a friend of hers was here on June sixth.'

'No,' he said. 'Oh, no.'

Wexford thought he had closed his eyes, although he could not be sure. He was aware of a terrible stillness in the room, a profound silence, which the movements in the hall and overhead accentuated rather than disturbed. Dunsand was not in the least like Godfrey Tate to look at or in manner, yet they shared this strange reticence. Both Nell Tate's husbands possessed the rare quality of being able to answer a searching

156

question with a straight yes or no. Had she chosen them for this or had she made them so? Had she chosen them at all? The man Wexford could be sure she had chosen was chatty, verbose, an extrovert whom some would call charming.

He tried again. 'Do you ever see your former wife?'

'No.'

'Never, Mr Dunsand?'

'Not now. I shall never see her again now.'

'You're aware that she's staying at the Cheriton Forest Hotel?'

'Yes. I saw it in the paper, a picture of her with a lot of flowers. She used to fill the house with flowers.' He glanced at the moribund cacti and then he picked up his brochure again. Underneath it on the pile was a pamphlet advertising dishwashers and another for garden equipment. 'I'd rather not talk any more now, if you don't mind.' He added curiously, 'I'm not obliged to say anything, am I?'

Wexford left him and went into one of the bedrooms. Bryant, Gates and Loring were crawling about, examining the carpet.

'Are there any women's clothes in the wardrobes?'

'No, sir, and there's no blood. We've done the whole place. This is the last room. We've even been up in the loft.'

'I heard you. Contents of the refrigerator?'

'It's empty. He's been defrosting it. He's very houseproud, sir. If you're thinking of that food she bought, the dustbins have been emptied twice since June sixth.'

Aghast, suddenly weary, Wexford said, 'I *know* she was killed here!'

'The hall floor's bitumastic, sir, the kind of stuff that's poured on as liquid and then left to set. There are no joins. I suppose we could get it taken up. We could have the tiles off the bathroom walls.'

Wexford went back into the room where Dunsand was. He

cleared his throat and then found he was at a loss for words. His eyes met not Dunsand's own but the thick baffling glass which shielded them. Dunsand got up and handed him two identical keys.

'One of these,' he said in a calm, neutral voice, 'is mine. The other I sent to my former wife and she returned it to me by post.' Wexford looked at the keys, the first of which was scraped and scarred from daily use, the second scarcely marked. 'Mrs Tate,' said Dunsand with awful precision, 'was never here. I should like to make a point of that.' Things were happening, Wexford thought, at least to some extent according to the pattern he had forecast. Dunsand swallowed, looked down at the floor. 'I found the girl here when I got home on June sixth. She must have got in by a window. The kitchen fanlight had been left unfastened. I encountered her as soon as I let myself in. She was giving the place what I think thieves call a "going over". We struggled and I—killed her. I hit her with a bottle of wine she had left on the hall table.'

'Mr Dunsand . . .' Wexford began almost despairingly.

'No, wait. Let me finish. She had brought some things with her, apart from the wine, some shopping in a bag and some clothes. Perhaps she thought my house was empty and she meant to camp there—"squat" is the word, isn't it? After it got dark I put her body in the quarry and the other things into the river under the bridge. Then I washed the floor and the walls.' Staring at Wexford, he said abruptly, 'Aren't you going to caution me? Shouldn't there be witnesses to take all this down?'

'This confession—you insist on making it?'

'Of course. It's true. I killed her. I knew it was only a matter of time before you arrested me.' He took off his glasses and rubbed them against his sleeve. His naked eyes were frightening. There was something terrible yet indefinable in their depths, a light that told perhaps of passion, of single-minded fanaticism under that flaccid exterior. He was used to teaching, to instructing. Now, in a teacher's voice, he proceeded to direct Wexford.

'The proper thing, I think, will be for me to go to the police station and make a statement.' He put on his glasses, wiped a beading of sweat from above his left eyebrow. 'I could go in my own car or accompany you if you think that wiser. I'm quite ready.'

'Well, you were right,' said Burden in grudging admiration.

'Only up to a point. We didn't find a trace of blood.'

'He must be a nut or a saint, taking that on himself to shield a woman like Nell Tate.' Burden began to pace the office, growing vehement. 'That statement he made, it doesn't even remotely fit the facts. For one thing, Dawn was let into the house. She did't go round the back. And for another, why should she suppose Dunsand's house to have been empty—I mean, unoccupied? If she had, she wouldn't have camped there on her own. She had a home to go to. Can you see Dunsand beating a woman to death because he suspected her of breaking into his house? Crocker said her killer was mad with rage, in a frenzy. That phlegmatic character in a frenzy?'

'He and Tate,' said Wexford, 'are apparently both phlegmatic characters. They are still waters which not only run deep but which may have turbulent undercurrents. Strange, isn't it? Dunsand hasn't asked for a lawyer, hasn't put up the least resistance. He's behaved almost fatalistically. That woman breaks the men she doesn't want but can't scratch the surface of the man she does want.'

Burden shook his head impatiently. 'What do we do now? What next?'

'Go back to Dunsand's place, I suppose. Have another look round and experiment with those keys a bit.'

Bright noon in The Pathway, the hottest day yet of a summer that promised to be all halcyon. The sun had brought into blossom tiny pink flowers on the plants in Miss Mowler's garden. In the meadows in the crook of the arm-shaped road they were cutting hay, cropping flowers far more lush and vigorous than those man had planted. The crude pink of Dunsand's bungalow was blanched to a rosy pallor by the hard hot light.

Wexford went up to the front door and tried Dunsand's keys. Both worked. The third key, the one Tate had given him, looked different, and by now he was sure it wouldn't move the lock. It didn't.

'It's a much older key than the others,' said Burden. 'What's Tate playing at?'

'Let's go inside.'

The whole house had been searched, but for evidence of a crime, not for clues to a life. Wexford remembered how Dunsand had planned to redecorate the place. He held on to that, certain it must have some significance. In a week's time perhaps that ugly wallpaper, those wriggling black stems, those golden flowers, would have been removed. Dunsand would have stripped it down, replaced it. But Dunsand had confessed...

Reticently, disliking the job, he went into the living room where the cacti were, where Dunsand had sat, blindly studying his brochures, and opened the desk. He found no letters, only bills; no marriage certificate, no album of photographs. But in a small drawer under the roll-top he discovered Dunsand's address book, a brown leather-covered book very sparing of entries. A London phone number was recorded under the letter T, just a number followed by a dash and the name Helen. Wexford noted the code and thought it might probably be Vedast's. He looked under S and under D but found no reference to Dawn Stonor.

It was at this point that it occurred to him how she, the dead, she whose death was the cause of this enquiry, had for some days past seemed to fade from its screen. It was as if she, as a real person, a personality, had lost her importance, and that he was searching for the answer to some other puzzle in the ramifications of which her death had been almost incidental. And he saw her—vividly but briefly—as a pawn, a used creature, her life blundering across other, brighter lives, falling through folly and vanity into death.

But the vision went, leaving him no wiser, and he thrust his hands once more into the pigeon-holes of the desk. A bunch of photographs came to light at last. They were in an envelope stuffed into a slot at the side of the roll-top interior, and they were mostly snapshots of Dunsand, much younger, with people who were evidently his parents, but underneath them were two much larger shots which Wexford took to the window. The strong light showed him first a wedding photograph, Dunsand still young, Dunsand smiling down without reserve at his bride in her badly fitting wedding dress, her veil wind-blown, young bony hands clutching a tight posy of rosebuds. Unless he had been twice married, the bride must be Nell. Time and art had changed her so much in the intervening years—eight? Ten?—since the picture was taken as to make her scarcely recognisable as its subject. Her hair was dark, cropped short, her face fresh and childlike. But it was she. The big yearning eyes were unchanged and the short upper lip, showing even in those days its petulant curl.

He brought out the other photograph, the last one, from under it. Nell again, Nell fractionally older, her hair still short and feathery, her skin apparently innocent of make-up. The portrait was coloured, tinted in the shades of old china, rose and sepia and ice-blue and plum red. Nell's new wedding ring gleamed brassily against the dull red stuff of her dress, and on the simple bodice, just below the round neckline, hung a pearl drop on a gold chain.

Wexford went ponderously out into the hall.

19

On all-fours Burden was examining the floor and the hideous shiny wallpaper with its pattern of little gold flowers and tiny, regularly recurring crimson leaves, wallpaper which met a floor that curved up to join it without any intervening skirting board.

'Get up, Mike. It's useless. We've done all that already.'

'One must do something,' said Burden irritably. He got up and brushed his hands against each other. 'What's the matter? You've found something!'

'This.'

'It's the dress! But who's the girl?'

'Nell Tate.'

Burden stared incredulously at the portrait. Then he put it beside the wedding picture, nodded, looked up at the chief inspector. 'I like her better how she was,' he said quietly.

'So would most men, but maybe she doesn't know that.' Wexford slipped the two photographs back into the envelope. 'Mike, I've a curious feeling I'm losing touch with Dawn Stonor, that she's fading away from me and I'm coming to grips with something stranger, something almost more terrible than her actual death. There must be many murder victims,' he said slowly, 'who meet their deaths without knowing in the least why they are to die.'

'Most of them, I should think. Victims of poisoners, old shopkeepers who know the till's empty, all children.'

'She wasn't a child,' said Wexford. 'Perhaps your list isn't

162

completely comprehensive. I don't know, Mike. I'm only dreaming, not really getting anywhere. This is a gloomy place, isn't it? The windows are huge and yet the light doesn't seem to get in. Of course, it's an illusion, it's something to do with the dulling, deadening influence of the man's personality.'

They moved back into the living room where the books frowned on the blue birds and the orange lilies that covered the walls.

Burden said, 'We're getting too dreamlike for me. I'd be happier if I could understand about the keys, if I could see how Dawn got in here.'

'Someone let her in. Someone asked her to come and that someone was here to let her in when she arrived at five-thirty. Not Dunsand.'

'But he cleared up the mess. He was left to dispose of the body he found when he got home.'

'I suppose so. You talk about mess, Mike. What mess? Where is it? Where are the traces of it? Is this killer the one killer we've ever come across who can commit a crime as bloody as this one and leave no blood? I don't believe it.'

'This place will have to be taken apart,' Burden said, crossing the passage and entering the bathroom. 'If it was done without leaving any apparent trace it must have been done in here.' He looked at the gleaming taps, the spotless bath and basin. The sunlight showed no film of dust on glass, no fingermarks on mirrors.

Wexford nodded. 'Yes,' he said, 'the tiles off, the pipes out. And if that yields nothing, the same with the kitchen.'

'Dunsand may crack. He may tell us what at the moment he's doing his utmost to conceal.'

'If he has anything to conceal.'

'Come on, sir. He must know more than he's told us. He must know why his wife would kill an unknown girl in his house, how it happened, the circumstances. He must know that.'

'I wonder?' said Wexford. 'Does he know any more than that his wife—the woman he still thinks of as his wife—may be in danger? I believe he knows very little, Mike, as little of the whole of it as the girl who died.'

Wexford stared up at the ceiling, scanned the smooth glossy walls. The whole place smelt soapy, too clean.

'Mind you don't trip,' said Burden. 'Your shoelace is undone. It's no good looking up there. It's no use looking at all. If she was killed here, someone worked a miracle of butchery.'

Wexford stooped down to re-tie the lace. A bright circle of gold, a little sunbeam refracted through a pane, had lighted on the wall beside his left leg. He stared at the trembling illumination. The gold flowers occurred on the paper in vertical lines about two inches apart, a thin black stripe dividing each line from the next, and the red leaves, pear-shaped, were printed in clusters of three between each flower. Flower, cluster, flower, followed each other immaculately and evenly to meet the bitumastic ridge. There were signs of faint blurring on the pattern, the result perhaps of washing the paper, but nothing had been obliterated. Three leaves, flower, three leaves ...

'Mike,' he said in a strange voice, 'your sight's better than mine. Have a look at this.'

'I looked before and you stopped me. It's been washed. So what?'

'You were looking for signs of washing, maybe for a missing bit of the pattern. Look again.'

Impatiently Burden got to his knees. He concentrated on the puddle of light.

'Not a missing leaf,' said Wexford. 'In the lowest cluster there aren't three leaves but four.'

They squatted down side by side and examined the hall paper.

'You see,' Wexford said excitedly, 'in this one and this one, in all of them, there are three little pear-shaped leaves like the leaves in a fleur-de-lis. But in the one we're looking at there's a fourth leaf under the centre one.'

'And it's not quite the same colour. It's darker, it's browner.'

'It's blood,' said Wexford, and he added wonderingly, 'One little spot of blood.'

'Shall I . . . ?'

'No, don't touch it. The experts can come here, get their sample themselves. It's too precious for us to mess about with. Mike, d'you realise that's the one real piece of evidence we've got?'

'If it's blood, if it's hers.'

'I know it's hers. It has to be.'

They went outside where the sun blazed on the road, melting tar and creating, where concrete ended and fields began, a mirage like a veil of shimmering water. The car was oven-hot inside, its seats burning to the touch. Burden rolled down his window and drove in his shirt sleeves.

'Now to check the key,' said Wexford.

'Which one, sir? The one that didn't fit?'

'Yes. I think we'll find a door that it will open.' Sweating profusely, Wexford pulled down the eyeshade across the windscreen. 'But that's a simple job, a job for Martin.'

'I'm not with you,' said Burden, falling into line behind the bus that, with its load of Sundays estate passengers, made its way along the sunny road to Kingsmarkham. 'I haven't a clue what particular door you expect it to unlock.'

Wexford smiled. 'A lot of doors are beginning to unlock inside my head, Mike, but this one, this actual door, is in Myringham. It's the door to the house Dunsand lived in before he moved here.'

The afternoon wore on and the heat seemed to mount, reaching the eighties by four o'clock. Wexford shut himself up in his office, the windows open, the blinds down. He sat alone, waiting, thinking, and then, on the principle that it is better to shut away a problem whose answer continually eludes one, to exclude it and return to it later, he resumed work on that crime-prevention directive which had lain unattended since before the festival.

The reports began to come in. The blood was human and of Dawn Stonor's group. The key which Tate had given him in the hotel garden opened the door of Leonard Dunsand's former home in Myringham. But at Sundays, where questioning of housewives had continued all the afternoon, no one had been found to say that she had ever seen Nell Tate, much less observed her call at Dunsand's house.

The five-twelve bus stopped outside the Baptist church. Wexford watched the passengers get on it. A girl came out of the Luximart, carrying a brown paper bag. She wasn't wearing mauve, she wasn't in the least like Dawn, and she was going to her new house at Sundays, not to her death. Wexford phoned the Cheriton Forest Hotel. Yes, Mr Vedast was still there. Mr Vedast planned to leave that evening. The receptionist couldn't say any more, perhaps, if Wexford was the press, she had said too much already...

He turned the sheets of the crime-prevention directive face downwards. He returned to his problem as the day began to cool and the sun's rays slanted. At seven he went across the road to the Carousel café where he found Burden and his children eating steak and salad while Emmanuel Ellerman's hit song 'High Tide' brayed at them from wall speakers.

'Pity you've eaten,' said Wexford. 'I was going to take you out to dinner at the Cheriton Forest.' He ordered a sandwich. 'We shall have to be content to take our coffee with Zeno Vedast instead.'

'I don't suppose...' began John wistfully.

'I'm afraid you can't come, John. This is a serious visit, an official visit.'

'Pat and I were going to hang about in the High Street to see him pass through. He's going back to London tonight.'

'I don't think he'll be going just yet,' said Wexford.

20

The receptionist put a call through to the Elizabethan Suite. 'Mr Vedast says will you wait, please? Mr Vedast is engaged at present.' She was young, the right age to be among Vedast's adorers. 'If you'd care to go into the Shakespeare Lounge, it's over there on the ...'

'We know the way,' said Wexford.

There was no one in the lounge but the dog. It got up when they came in, stared at them morosely, then collapsed again some two yards from where it had previously been lying.

'I'm in the dark,' said Burden, impatiently rejecting the magazines Wexford passed to him. 'I think you ought to tell me why we're here.'

'Why are we ever anywhere?' Wexford sighed. 'To ask, to deduce, to conclude and to catch. Only it's a little different this time.'

'Oh, riddles, philosophy. What I want to know is ...'

'Wait.'

Godfrey Tate had come very quietly into the room, Godfrey Tate in his usual dapper black that made his torso look as thin as a teenager's and his limbs spidery.

'Zeno's got that guy Silk with him,' he said, without greeting, without preamble. 'He says to ask you what you want.'

Wexford said quietly, 'I want to tell him what I think of him.'

Tate was bemused with drink, not 'high' on alcohol, but low, dulled, cut off, almost somnambulistic. 'Do I tell him that?'

'Mr Tate, it's a matter of indifference to me what you tell him. Why is Silk here?'

'He'd heard Dunsand's been arrested. He came to tell Nell.'

'And now you're celebrating?'

Tate blinked at him. He turned, shuffled towards the door.

'See you,' said Wexford, looking at his watch, 'in ten minutes.'

But before the ten minutes were up—minutes in which Burden had picked up magazine after magazine, discarding them all, and Wexford had sat still, watching the hall—Martin Silk emerged from the lift. Long hair on the elderly makes its wearer look like a nineteenth-century statesman, but in Silk's case the resemblance ended at his neck. He wore a white tee-shirt with a bunch of grapes appliqued on the chest. As he passed the reception desk he swaggered like a proud adolescent, thrusting his hips forward, but as he neared the lounge door he began to scuttle, an old man getting away from trouble.

'Mr Silk!'

Silk stopped and forced a broad smile, creasing his face into a thousand wrinkles, enclosing his eyes in cracked parchment skin.

'I hope we haven't driven you away,' said Wexford. 'You're welcome to stay as far as we're concerned.'

Sidling into the lounge, Silk perched himself on the arm of a chair. His knee joint cracked as he swung one leg.

'Merely a social call,' he said. 'I dropped by to tell Zeno there's quite a crowd waiting in Kingsmarkham to give him a send-off. Of course,' he added spuriously, 'I shall be seeing a lot of him now he's bought this lush pad.'

'But you've always seen a lot of him, haven't you, Mr Silk? One might say that you've been a sort of . . .' Wexford glanced meaningly at the shaggy grey hair, '. . . a sort of *éminence grise* in his life. Or are you another slave?'

'I don't know what you mean.'

'But for you he'd still be Harold Goodbody and he never would have met Nell Dunsand.'

Silk stared at him. 'I acted for the best. We can't know what tragedies may hang on our small actions. I gave to youth a musical genius. If Dunsand freaked out, if certain people were—well, expendable...'

'Is that how you see it? Mr Silk, you interfere too much. You organise too much. Be warned, and don't interfere with Louis Mbowele. You might cause a war this time.'

'Really, I think you're twisted, sick. You're not together. Who is, at your age?' He sneered. 'The hung-up generation.'

'If I belong to it,' Wexford retorted, 'so do you. We're the same age. Only I know it, I accept it. You don't. I accept that all the sport is stale and all the wheels run down. And when I consider what some people call sport, I'm not all that sorry.'

At Wexford's words, particularly the reminder of his true age, a look of real pain crossed Silk's face. Mirrors show us what we want to see, but sometimes we look into living, human mirrors and then, briefly, the fantasising has to stop. Wexford was fat, Silk skinny, the one in a crumpled old suit, the other in tee-shirt and jeans, but they were both sixty. The mirror comparison lay in their shared age, the shared weariness of muscle and bone, and painfully Silk saw it.

He said shrilly, 'What are you doing here?'

'Talking to you at the moment. Now we're going upstairs to talk to your genius.'

'But you've got Dunsand. Zeno wasn't even there. I was with Zeno and the Tates in Kensington. You've got Dunsand under lock and key!'

'What an old-fashioned expression!' Wexford mocked. 'Can't you find a more trendy way of putting it? Come on, Mike, we've wasted enough time.'

They walked up. Silk stood at the foot of the staircase watching them, hesitating, torn perhaps between a fear of his protégé coming to harm and an even greater fear of more cruel jibes levelled at him concerning his age.

Wexford said, 'He knows nothing about it. He knows less even than Dunsand.' He smiled obscurely, tapped on the door of the Elizabethan Suite.

They were packing. At last they were going home. His face an even duskier red than usual, Tate was on his knees, trying to fasten an overfull suitcase, while Vedast sat cross-legged on top of a lacquer cabinet watching him. Wordlessly, Nell led them through the labyrinth of piled luggage and mountains of frippery, magazines and records.

Dead flowers, smelling foetid, were heaped on the balcony. Fresh flowers had arrived that day, perhaps that afternoon, roses, lilies, carnations, and they were dying too. No one had bothered to put them in water.

Nell was as carefully dressed and made-up as usual, but her exertions in the heat had given her an air of dishevelment, for it was still hot, the evening air windless, the sun a smouldering crimson knot over the forest. She scowled at the policemen, met Vedast's cool gaze, and turned immediately to look at herself in one of the mirrors. Vedast gave a light laugh.

'Fasten that case, Goffo. Get a move on, dears. Why don't you go and order some coffee, Nello?' He swayed his body towards Wexford. 'That will give her a chance to repair her poor face,' he said as if she wasn't there.

Burden, who had followed the chief inspector's example and cleared a seat for himself, said gruffly, 'No coffee for us.'

'Just as you like.' Vedast flicked his fingers at Nell, who, still in front of the mirror, was apathetically fidgeting with her hair while watching the policemen in the glass. She sprang round as if those snapping fingers had actually touched her, fetched his orange juice and handed it to him with a pleading look. He removed a lump of ice and licked it. 'How glum you all look!' he said, surveying the four faces. 'You're frightening my little ones, Chief Inspector. Why don't we take it as read. I know what happened and so, presumably, do you —now. It *did* take you a long time. But you can't prove it. So why don't we just congratulate each other like clever cats and mice and you pop off home?'

Wexford quoted softly, ' "What need we fear who knows it when none can call our power to account?" '

The Tates looked at him uncomprehendingly, Nell edging closer to Vedast, who said, 'Macbeth. I sometimes think of changing over to the legitimate theatre. I've had no end of offers.' He swallowed what remained of his ice cube. 'But I don't want to start now, thank you so much. We're none of us feeling quite strong enough for drama.'

'You mean you've had enough of it? You've made your tragedy and now you're exhausted? The function of tragedy, as I'm sure you know, Mr Vedast, is to purge with pity and terror, and that's what I'm going to try to do to you—or some of you. So sit down, Mr Tate, and you too, Mrs Tate, and listen to me.'

Both Nell and her husband looked doubtfully at Vedast for instructions. He nodded lightly.

'Do what the man says, dears.'

Nell flounced on to the sofa, tipping off a heap of dirty clothes and what seemed to be a stack of fan letters. A full glass in his hand, a hand which trembled, Tate crept towards her.

She made a slight movement of rejection, turning her shoulder and at the same time spreading out her thick, stiffly embroidered skirts so that there was no room for her husband to sit beside her. He gave her a bitter look, a look of dark reproach, from under swollen veined eyelids. Clasping his drink as if it were a protective talisman, he perched himself on the sofa arm.

The singer watched them, amused that they had obeyed so easily. A law unto himself, he got down from the cabinet and lounged against the open french window. With the setting of the sun, a light breeze had begun to blow. It fanned his hair, lifting it into a golden aureole. Outside the blue of the sky was deepening to violet, feathered with flamingo red. The frosty orange glass glowed in his hand like a lamp. He stood as if he were about to sing, his chin lifted, his hips thrust forward, quite still, utterly relaxed.

'A tragedy,' said Wexford, 'in two parts.'

'It concerns,' he began, 'two people who by their looks and the power of their personalities were able to command obsessive love. You, Mr Vedast, and you, Mrs Tate. I'm not flattering you. Anyone may become the object of such love and, in my experience, those who do are usually shallow, narcissistic and self-centred.'

Nell said shrilly, 'Are you going to let him talk to me like that, Godfrey?'

Hunched up, nursing his glass, Tate gave her a black look. He said nothing. The breeze chilled him, making the dark hairs on his wrists stand erect.

'The need to love like this lies in the characters of the lovers who fasten generally on the first desirable person who comes in their way, fasten and, if they can, hold on. Unfortunately, the beloved objects trade on this and use it for their own ends, for cruelty and victimisation. Just in case Mrs Tate is under any misapprehension as to whom I mean when I speak of the man who loves her obsessively, in case she should be so obtuse as to suppose I mean Mr Vedast, I'll tell her now that I refer to her first husband, Leonard Dunsand. A foolish, clever, learned, dull and conventional little man who has loved her since she was eighteen when he married her.'

One of those people who will bear any insult provided it carries with it a hint of flattery, Nell apparently couldn't resist preening herself at this. She crossed her long and very shapely legs and gave a sidelong glance in Vedast's direction.

Vedast stroked the string of beads he wore, running them through his fingers.

Wexford went on: 'Who is probably the only man sufficiently capable of self-delusion to love her sincerely, the only man who ever will.' He waited for some reaction from Nell's present husband. Tate reacted characteristically, behaving as he always did in crises or threatened crises. Without getting up, he reached for the brandy bottle. 'If you are in a position to be thankful for anything, Mr Tate, be thankful that you are more sophisticated and have eyes to see. Pity you've clouded them so much with that stuff.'

'I can look after myself,' said Tate in a low voice.

'I never saw a man less capable of doing so, unless it is Mr Dunsand.'

'I'll look after Goffo.' Vedast turned idly, smiling, cooling his hands on the glass, caressing it. 'Do tell us who's in love with me. I'm dying to know.'

'Thousands, I imagine. The one in particular I speak of is dead. She was dying for you too often and at last she really died. You were her first lover. That's supposed to have some profound effect on a woman and, whether it's true or not, it had a profound effect on Dawn Stonor. I wonder how much of that story Mr and Mrs Tate know?' While Vedast resumed his scanning of the sky in which a few pale stars had appeared, Wexford leant towards the Tates. 'They were at school together, Dawn and a boy called Harold Goodbody, a boy who went to tea with his girl friend's grandmother because he only had baked beans at home; Harold Goodbody who wore his cousin's cast-off shoes and whose father spent the housekeeping on dog racing; Harold Goodbody who played April Fool tricks to amuse his friends, who doubtless carried young Dawn's satchel for her. A rustic idyll, wasn't it? Dawn Stonor and her first love, Harold Goodbody.'

'I would prefer you not to call me that,' said Vedast, and for the first time Wexford heard an edge of temper to his voice.

'You'd prefer me to go away, but I shan't do that,' Wexford flashed back. 'You said you were dying to hear and you shall hear.' He leaned back, pleased at the unease his words had provoked in Nell, pleased by Tate's cringing. 'You left your friend,' he said to Vedast, 'and went to London. For you the idyll was over. Soon afterwards she went to London too, but by then you were beyond her reach. And yet she never forgot you. She told her friends and she pretended, perhaps to herself as well as to her friends, that you had always remained lovers and between you was some enduring bond.' Wexford glanced at Burden and inclined his head, giving the inspector honour for this idea which at first he had ridiculed. 'In fact,' he went on, 'nearly a decade passed by before you saw each other again. In that time you had become very famous, many exciting things had happened to you. Very little had happened to her. She was a waitress in a club and she remained a waitress.

'It was a pity you ever went into that club. If you hadn't, Dawn might at this moment be making wedding plans with her fiancé. Why did you go?'

Vedast shrugged. 'This bloke asked us. We hadn't anything better to do.'

'You could hardly have done worse.'

'I didn't kill her. I never touched her.'

Wexford turned towards the Tates, to Godfrey Tate whose bloodshot eyes were wide open and staring.

21

'I shall now go back,' said the chief inspector, 'to one of your exciting happenings, although I don't believe you'll regard it as a highspot when you come to write your memoirs. I refer to your meeting with Mrs Tate, and to describe that I must return to the other love story.'

A glance from Vedast was enough to make Nell get up and switch on the rose-shaded lamps. She moved stiffly, tripping over the red grip and cursing. Vedast gave her his empty glass and she refilled it. He took it without thanks like a duke receiving the drink he has ordered from a parlourmaid.

'Ice, Nello,' he said.

She spooned two cubes out of a pool of water in a bowl on the cabinet. Tate was crouched over his brandy, gazing into the golden liquid. The rosy light played on him, muting the harsh blackness of his hair. Nell gave Vedast his glass again, keeping her hands clasped round it so that his fingers would brush hers as he took it. They brushed them as a stranger's might without lingering. She seemed desperate to stay beside him, to remain with him on the cool, darkening balcony whose rail, reddened by the setting sun, was now a black filagree trellis behind the mound of dead blossoms.

'Go away, Nello. You fidget me.'

She hung her head, crept just inside the window and dropped on to an upright chair, her arms hanging limply by her sides.

'That's right, Mrs Tate, sit where I can see you. You're a very good-looking woman, but you've changed a good deal

176

since you were a bride for the first time. For one thing, you've tinted your hair. I don't suppose you ever wear dark red these days, do you?

'Mr Dunsand liked your short dark hair. He liked you in simple, wifely dresses. I understand from what information was gathered today in Myringham that you were known as a quiet little thing, a good cook, fond of flowers, of home-making, but inclined to be bored with the society you moved in. They were all so much older than you, those faculty wives, weren't they? You would have preferred the company of your husband's students. Those coffee mornings, those empty after-noons, were very dull for you. But they were nothing to the evenings when, after you had prepared the kind of meal Mr Dunsand liked, you had to sit for hours alone with him, the record player switched off, and plan together your annual holiday, plan your budget, decide what new equipment or furniture you could afford that year.

'To Mr Dunsand it was the very essence of contentment. I expect you played your part well. Women like you, born sycophants, usually do, and all the time they wait quietly for the means of escape. Your chance came when Zeno Vedast, your idol, gave a concert in Myringham. I don't suppose Mr Dunsand wanted you to go to that concert. The idea of his wife, the wife who depended on him utterly for her support, disporting herself among a bunch of teenagers at a pop con-cert, can hardly have appealed to him. No, he couldn't have liked to think of you raving among his own students, but you went. If you hadn't gone, Dawn Stonor would be alive today, making wedding plans with her fiancé.

'I don't think you threw yourself under Mr Vedast's car deliberately—you wouldn't have the courage—let's say it was an unconscious urge you couldn't control or resist.

'Mr Vedast had put you in a private room at the hospital. How you must have prayed for Mr Vedast himself to appear with the grapes and the chocolates! You didn't know him.

177

You don't know him now. He sent his minion, and it was any port in a storm for you, Mrs Tate. But you're not unique, don't think it. Many a master in the past has married a likely wench off to his servant so that he can have the enjoying of her without any of the trouble.'

'You've no right to insult me!' Nell flared. She waited for her husband to defend her. When he said nothing, while Vedast smiled and sipped his orange juice, she said, 'Why shouldn't I have left my husband? Why shouldn't I have got married again? I'm not the only one. I was sick to death of living with Len.'

Vedast turned. He said smoothly, 'Like the judges say, this isn't a court of morals, Mr Wexford.'

'Oh, but it is. It must be because it can't be a court of justice.'

'In that case . . .' Nell got up. 'In that case, I'm going. Let's go, Zeno. He can't keep us here.'

'Do as you like, Nello.' Vedast gave her a sly sidelong glance. She couldn't do as she liked. She never had been able to. 'You go if you want,' he said in the voice, usual with him, that was both gentle and unkind. 'I'm staying. I'm fascinated. How about you, Goffo, are you going to take your wife away or stay and support your old mate?'

'Mr Tate stays,' said Burden sharply.

Wexford just glanced at him, raising his eyebrows. 'Let us have an intermission,' he said. 'An interval to relax in. If my voice were better, I'd offer to sing you a song, but in this company . . .' He hesitated, then said, 'You all know the song. It was written at the time of Mrs Tate's second marriage. It would be ingenuous of me to suppose it doesn't illustrate a true story, render someone's real suffering. That's why it was written. Poets,' he said, 'are said to make little songs out of their great sorrows. You . . .' His eyes went to the window, '. . . amused yourself and feathered your luxurious nest by making a song out of someone else's'

178

Vedast jerked round. He came into the room, his yellow eyes sharp and narrow.

'I'll sing it,' he said. 'There's nothing wrong with my voice.'

Wexford nodded. He could tell what Burden was thinking, that his son, that any fan at the festival, would have given a week's wages, a month's grant, a term's pocket money, to have been in their shoes. Vedast, who could command thousands for one concert, was going to sing in private for them. He felt a little sick.

In the pale rosy light, the soft kind light, Vedast looked very young, a teenager himself. He stood in a corner of the room, resting his bare elbows on a shelf from which rose-buds hung, young, fresh rose-buds dead before they opened from dehydration. He waited in the silence of the evening, the silence of the forest which surrounded them. The first word came loud like a note vibrating from a string, then the clear, light voice dropped a little, filling the room with sweet bitterness.

Nell watched the singer adoringly, tapping in time to the tune throughout the first verse, the first chorus. Wexford frowned at her and she tossed her head, flinging herself back petulantly against a cushion. His sickness was passing. He listened to the words as if he had never heard them before, as if he had never fully understood the depth of their meaning.

> 'Remember me and my life-without-life,
> Come once more to be my wife,
> Come today before I grieve,
> Enter the web of let-me-believe.
>
> So come by, come nigh,
> come try and tell why
> some sigh, some cry,
> some lie and some die . . .'

There was no applause. Vedast dropped his head. Then he flung it back, shaking his hair.

'Thank you,' said Wexford crisply. 'It's all in that song, isn't it? All Mr Dunsand's sorrow is there. He pleaded with you, I imagine, not to break with him entirely, not to leave him utterly without life, to let him believe sometimes, very occasionally, that you were still his wife. And you repeated these conversations to Mr Vedast, giving him such a good idea for a song.'

Tate looked up, frowning, a trickle of brandy coursing down his chin. He wiped his mouth on his sleeve.

'Why did you agree to what Mr Dunsand asked?'

'I didn't want to hurt him too much,' Nell muttered.

A dull, humourless laugh escaped from Burden and it was echoed, surprisingly, by Tate. Wexford didn't laugh. 'Mrs Tate, is that you talking? *You?* When have you ever minded whom you hurt, you who are an expert treader on other people's dreams? If you won't tell me why, I shall have to guess.'

'It was to nark me,' Tate interrupted.

'But you didn't know until after the festival,' Wexford said quickly.

Bewildered, Tate said, 'That's true. She'd been seeing him two or three times a year, going to his house and bloody well sleeping with him. I blacked her eye for her.'

'So you told me. And you gave me a key. Only it wasn't the key to Mr Dunsand's house in The Pathway. It opens the front door of his former home in Myringham. Mrs Tate had never been to The Pathway house. She knew it only because Mr Dunsand described it to her over the phone as the middle house of the three. But he sent her a key, intending that she should keep up the custom of the Myringham days.'

Tate said slowly:

'What custom? What are you on about.'

'I believe you, Mr Tate, when you say you knew nothing of

180

these visits of your wife's until after the festival when, frightened of what she had done but not frightened enough to confess everything, she told you she had been seeing her first husband. I believe you are entirely innocent of this crime, in no way an accessory. You had been kept in the dark as you are, I daresay, about many things.' Tate shrugged awkwardly. The level of golden liquor in the bottle was going steadily down. He poured himself some more in silence. 'Nor do I think you would have been a party to any of this had you known about it,' said Wexford.

'Mr Vedast wasn't in the dark. He knew. Mrs Tate told him she had promised these—shall I say loans?—loans of herself to Mr Dunsand. And so I come back to why. Why did she do it? You're not a very happy woman, are you, Mrs Tate? Apparently you have everything you wanted, but only apparently. I think that very soon after your second marriage you saw what you had got, luxury and excitement, yes, but at what a price. Another not very inspiring husband—forgive me, Mr Tate—though a complaisant one, a condescending master, kind when you were obedient. So you agreed to Mr Dunsand's request for the sake of the contrast. Those few evenings, those nights, you spent with him, showed you that what you had was at least preferable to your former married life. After a night in Myringham you could go back to London, to Europe, to Bermuda, your loins girded, as it were, with the memory of the alternative.'

'Is that true, Nello? I never knew that.'

'I'm glad to be able to tell you something you don't know, Mr Vedast. But you knew of the part she played while she was there, didn't you? I'm sure Mrs Tate told you all the details, the props, the costume required, shall I say? I'm sure she told you of the setting of the little play they enacted two or three times a year, the activities, following always the same pattern, in which the actors indulged, marriage *à la mode*

181

Dunsand. Indeed, I know she did. Had she not, you wouldn't have been able to play your—your practical joke.'

Nell said, 'I want a drink, Godfrey.'

'Get it yourself.'

She did so, clattering the bottle neck against the glass, spilling vermouth on to the pale embroidery on her white linen skirt. It made a red stain like blood.

Wexford said, 'I expect you thought all this very amusing, Mr Vedast, until there was a threat of the performance of this play interfering with your own plans. About a month ago Mrs Tate told you that she would be paying her first visit to Mr Dunsand's new home on the afternoon of Monday, June sixth. But that didn't suit you, for you and Mr and Mrs Tate would only just have returned from Manchester where you had a concert engagement.'

Tate shook his head. 'No, that's not right,' he said. 'He meant to stay over till the Monday. It was me said at the last moment it'd be too tiring for him.'

'Ah.' Wexford sighed. 'Even better—or worse. When Mrs Tate first confided in you, you intended that she and you and Mr Tate would all be away from the South on June sixth.' He looked at Nell, at the red stain on her dress which she had not attempted to remove, at the red colour that burned her face. 'Why didn't you just change the date of your appointment with your first husband, Mrs Tate? Surely you could have put it off for a few days?'

For a moment she looked as if she were searching in her mind for an excuse. She put out a trembling hand to Vedast who ignored her, who smiled, his head on one side.

'Because that would have "hurt" Mr Dunsand?' Wexford went on relentlessly. 'Or did you do what you always do, obeyed Mr Vedast?'

In a small, thin voice, she said, 'I left it to Zeno.'

'You left it to Zeno. He was to get in touch with Mr Dunsand, was he? He, a world-famous singer, a pop idol, was to phone Mr Dunsand and tell him you couldn't make it but would, say, Wednesday do instead?'

She was near to tears. She held her hands crushed together so that the peeling nails dug into the flesh. 'You know it wasn't like that. You know you're just tormenting me.'

'Not everyone is as zealous as you, Mrs Tate, about the feelings of others. Not everyone is as anxious as you to go through life without doing hurt. But it's true that I know what happened.' Wexford got up and walked over to Vedast who had taken up a Yoga position, a half-Lotus, on the floor by the open window. He stood over the singer, looking down, his own grey eyes meeting the amber ones.

'No, Mr Vedast,' he said. 'To a person of your temperament it was far more amusing to keep the date, changing not the day but the female protagonist.'

Tate broke the silence.

'What d'you mean? I don't follow you. Female whatsit, what does it mean?'

Wexford came over to him. He spoke gently. 'It means, Mr Tate, that your employer saw a way of getting Mrs Tate out of her appointment, and perhaps all further similar appointments, and at the same time of playing one of his favourite jokes.

'He decided to send a substitute for your wife to The Pathway. First, I suspect, he thought of sending a call girl. But why go to all that trouble when he could send Dawn Stonor whose acquaintance he had renewed some weeks before and whom he had telephoned on May twenty-third?'

183

22

Wexford sat down in the centre of the room. 'I don't know why you phoned Dawn last night,' he went on, addressing himself directly to Vedast. 'I think your motive was akin to Mrs Tate's motive for visiting her former husband. Probably at the Townsman Club you contrasted Dawn's humble situation with your successful one, remembering how you came from similar beginnings, how you had had even chances of money, fame, glory—but you had achieved them and she had not.

'On May twenty-third Mr and Mrs Tate were away. You were bored. Perhaps you even felt insecure. Why not phone Dawn, do a little slumming, so that afterwards you might have the pleasure of appreciating what you are and what you might have been? I daresay that phone conversation had the desired effect on you. You were quickly tired of her eagerness and you rang off, having vaguely suggested you see each other "sometime" but not, in fact, ever intending to see her again.

'During that week, I believe, Mrs Tate told you of the visit she planned to make to Mr Dunsand's new house. On the phone you had already, I think, boasted to Dawn of the house you were yourself thinking of buying near Kingsmarkham. Why not play a joke, the biggest joke of your career?'

'My thought processes,' said Vedast, 'don't work quite like that. Stop hovering, Nello. Go and sit down somewhere.'

The only spot in the room where she wanted to be was at his side. She looked at the sofa where her husband sat hunched, at the two occupied chairs, at the empty chairs which were either near her husband or near the policemen. And like an insect with bright antennae, bright wings, she fluttered desperately, hovered, as Vedast had put it, finally alighting—her heels were high, her shoes platformed—on another spot of carpet as near to him as she had been when he had shooed her away. The insect had come back to the flame.

Wexford had paused when the interruption came but, apart from hesitating briefly, he took no notice of her.

'The first of June,' he said to Vedast, 'was the birthday of the man Dawn was very probably going to marry, the man she would have married if you had left her alone. She was at home, waiting for him to come to lunch. You didn't know that. Would you have cared if you had? You phoned her in the morning and asked her to meet you for a drink.' Burden stirred in his chair, his eyebrows lifting. 'She wasn't very elated about it. Perhaps she realised that a man like you, a man as rich as you are, who could afford without noticing it the most expensive restaurant in London, only takes a girl for drinks in a pub if he despises her, if he thinks she isn't worth any more. But she dressed carefully for you just the same; changing out of the clothes that were good enough for an ordinary fiancé.

'And later, when the excitement of that lunchtime date had begun to recede, she asked herself—and her flatmate—if she *was* despised, if that was the reason why you were only prepared to have a hole-in-corner, *sub rosa* affair with her, hiding her in a house no one knew you had bought instead of taking her to an hotel.

'In that pub, between one o'clock and three, you asked her, after some preliminary flattery and flirtation, no doubt, to spend the night of the following Monday with you in your new house. Of course, she agreed. She would be on holiday. She could go and see her mother and then go on to The Pathway. That she and Dunsand were *people* with feelings never entered your head, did it? You were as careless of his as of hers. That Mrs Tate was in the habit of preparing for him on these occasions a special meal of his favourite food, of bringing good wine and beautiful flowers—to fill the void?—didn't trouble you at all. You told Dawn anything would do, just some quick picnic food for you and her to share. Any old wine, the cheapest she could get.

'She must go there first, you told her, and you gave her the key Mr Dunsand had sent to Mrs Tate and which Mrs Tate had given you. No responsibility, Mrs Tate? You left it all to Zeno?' Wexford turned back to Vedast. 'You'd be along around half past six. As soon as she was in the house she was to go upstairs where she would find a red dress.

'Now this dress had been laid out on the bed by Mr Dunsand. During his married life this dress of Mrs Tate's had been his favourite. When she wore it, sat down to dinner with him, listened to his account of his day and gave him account of hers, he could fancy himself protected from the "harsh light of day" and back safe and happy with his wife.

'Dawn knew nothing of this. She was told nothing of this. You asked her to wear this dress because it belonged to a fashion current when you were still together, still lovers, and you told her it would recall to you that past time.'

Looking ill, the colour all gone from his face, leaving a swarthy pallor, Tate lurched to his feet. He edged round the sofa and said to Vedast, 'Is that true?'

'We didn't mean any harm.'

'No harm? Christ . . . You did that and *she* knew it. God, I feel like I've never known either of you, never seen you before . . .'

'Godfrey . . .' Nell put out a feeble hand. 'I didn't do anything. I only told him—well, you know.'

'Have another drink, Goffo,' Vedast drawled.

'I don't want any more.' Tate made this remark in a thick but wondering voice. He swung on Wexford. 'Go on, then. What happened? Tell me the rest. Him . . .' He pointed at

Vedast as if reluctant to use his name. 'Him and her, they were with me that evening. Honest, they were. They can't have killed her.'

'Who kills, Mr Tate, the one who holds the knife, the one who says "stab!" or the one who sends the victim to the appointed place? Which of the three Fates is responsible for our destinies, she who spins the thread, she who cuts it or she who merely holds the scissors?' Wexford could tell from Tate's puzzled, vacant expression that all this was going over his head. 'Maybe Mr Dunsand could tell us. He's the philosopher.' Glancing at Burden, hoping there would be no actual exclamation of shock, he said, 'He killed her, of course. He's admitted it. He isn't the kind of man to prevaricate for long. Only chivalry made him tell a few lies to avoid any involvement of . . .' Scornful eyes came to rest on Nell, '. . . of his beloved former wife.'

Wexford went on carefully, 'As to what he did, I'll tell you. He came home, longing, of course, for the evening and the night ahead. He let himself in with his own key at twenty to seven. By that time Dawn must have been feeling uneasy. There were many things to make her uneasy, the modest size of the place, the austere furnishings, the superabundance of learned books. And the dress—a dress that was too small for her, unbecoming, too tight. Of course she felt uneasy. Of course, when she heard a key in the lock, she came out of the living room shyly, not speaking, just standing there.

'Instead of Vedast, she saw a little middle-aged stranger. Instead of his wife, Dunsand saw—what? What, Mrs Tate?'

'Dawn Stonor,' she said in a small, sullen voice.

'Oh, no. She didn't exist for him. He never even knew her name. He saw his wife, yet not his wife, a girl of his wife's age but bigger, coarser, with even more make-up, with brassier hair, yet wearing his wife's dress, his favourite dress.

'Perhaps he didn't believe in the reality of this sight. Even to a better-balanced man than Dunsand, what he saw looming

187

in the little hall would have seemed a hallucination. To him it wasn't just a travesty of his wife but a kind of succubus sent by something which existed in his clever sick mind to torment him. He wanted to destroy what he saw and he simply did so, attacking the hallucinatory shape with the first weapon that came to hand, the wine bottle his visitant had left on the hall table.'

Vedast got up, lifted his head sharply as he had lifted it at the festival, shook back his lion's mane. 'How was I to know things would go that way?' He held out his glass. 'Get me some more of that stuff, will you, Goffo.'

Tate said, 'Not me. Get your own bloody drink.'

'Temper, temper.' The golden eyebrows went up, the teeth showed in what was perhaps a smile.

'Can't you do anything to him?' Tate said to Wexford. 'He killed her. He's the real killer.'

'I know it, Mr Tate, but no, I can't do anything to him. What should be done to him? He is as sick as Mr Dunsand, a megalomaniac who lives on fantasies.'

'Don't give me that balls. He ought to be shot. Hanging'd be too good for him.'

' "Heaven hath no rage like love to hatred turned" . . . You are not obliged to associate with them, Mr Tate. You need not, just because you also married her, copy her first husband and be chivalrous.'

'Too bloody right, I needn't.' Shock had brought Tate complete cold sobriety. On his knees, he flung armfuls of garments into the red grip, seized it and a smaller suitcase. 'I'm going, I'm quitting.' He got up, said to Vedast, 'You owe me a hundred quid. You can send it care of my mum's. *She* knows the address.'

'You can't go,' said Vedast and at last he wasn't playing. His voice had lost its lightness. 'We've been together for eight years. What'll I do without you?'

188

'Cut your bloody throat, but cut hers first.' Tate held out his hand to Wexford. 'I used to call you lot pigs,' he said, 'and maybe I will again. But, thanks, you've done me a good turn. If you've done nothing else you've got me away from them. I might even stop drinking now.' Then he used the first cultivated, literate phrase Wexford had ever heard from his lips but, even as he said it, the chief inspector knew he had learnt it parrot fashion from the 'scene' with which he had been associated. 'They'd have destroyed me utterly.'

'I really think they would, Mr Tate.'

When he had gone, slamming the suite door, the slave who remained seized Vedast's arm and said, 'Good riddance. I just feel relief, don't you?'

Vedast made no reply. He picked up the phone sullenly, asked for a porter. Immediately Nell, taking her cue, bundled heaps of clothes into cases, bags, carriers. Wexford and Burden, ready to leave, helpless, impotent, watched her. The cases were all packed in five minutes. Vedast stood at the window, his expression inscrutable. He looked over the balcony rail once, perhaps at the departing Tate. The porter came in, took two cases in his hands, one under his arm. Nell flung a white coat round her shoulders.

'I take it we shan't be wanted any more?'

'You will be wanted at Mr Dunsand's trial. Before that, statements will have to be taken from you.'

'Me?' said Vedast. 'I can't appear in court. It will be ghastly bad publicity. Why did Goffo have to go like that? Goffo could have coped.'

'I'll cope,' said Nell fondly. 'Let's go now, shall we? It's nearly midnight. Let's get going.'

He pushed her away. 'I'm going,' he said. 'I'm going by myself. You can get a taxi to whatever station there is in this hole.'

'But we've got the car!'

Petulantly, like a little boy, he said, 'It's my car. *I'm* going in it. You'd better face it, Nello, you're no use to me without Godfrey. He looked after me and then—then you came along.' His face cleared a little. 'You were a nice bit of decoration,' he said.

The flesh of her face seemed to sag. Her lip curled up, her eyes widened, stretching the skin, wrinkling it. 'You can't mean it, Zeno. Zeno, don't leave me! I've worshipped you since I was twenty. I've never thought of any man but you.'

'No, dear, I know. You just married them.'

As the porter returned to fetch the remaining luggage, Vedast tried to unhook her hands from his shoulders. 'Nello, do as I say. Let go of me. I'm going to pay the bill and then I'm going.' He went up to Wexford, the bantering tone quelled by what he had to say and by the presence of the inquisitive porter. 'I suppose we can keep all this quiet?' One of the long, lean hands sketched a gesture towards a jeans pocket. 'I imagine...'

'Mr Vedast, we are leaving.'

'I'll come down with you.'

'Zeno!' Nell screamed. 'Zeno, I love you!'

The two policemen had moved a pace or two away from the singer, moved distastefully. Nell flung herself upon Vedast. Her coat fell from her shoulders. She clung to his neck, pushing her fingers through the golden hair, pressing her body against him.

'Where am I to go? What am I to do?'

Struggling, pushing her, he said, 'You can go to Godfrey's mum. Go where you like, only get off me. Get off! Christ, Dawn Stonor'd have been a better bet than you. Get off!'

They grappled together like wrestlers, Nell screaming and clinging. Vedast was strong and muscular but not quite strong enough. He kicked and punched, grabbing at her hair, tearing it. They toppled and rolled on the floor among the dead flowers, the empty bottles, knocking over and breaking into fragments the orange-juice glass.

'Let's go,' said Wexford laconically.

In the corridor bedroom doors had been cautiously opened and sleepy people stared out. On the stairs the policemen passed four or five of the hotel night staff running up, alarmed by the screams, the thumps on the floorboards. Lights began to come on as the somnolent hotel woke to life.

The night was as clear, as softly violet-blue as the night of the festival, but now the moon was waning. And there were no ballads to be heard here, no plangent note from a string plucked with controlled power. Wexford could still hear Vedast's voice, though, raised now in a high-pitched lunatic scream, a sound none of his fans would have recognised. Instead of that vibrant twang came the crash of flying furniture; instead of melody, Nell's hysterical sobbing, and instead of applause, the manager gravely and quite ineffectively begging his guests to stop.

'Perhaps they'll kill each other,' said Burden as they passed the furred golden car.

'Perhaps they will. Who cares?' Wexford sighed. 'Vedast won't like it in court. Will it have any effect on his career?'

Once again Burden was being appealed to as the expert on such matters. 'I doubt it,' he said, starting the car. 'These singers, they're always appearing in court on drug offences. Did you ever hear of their records selling less well afterwards?'

'Drugs are one thing. Provided you don't deal in them, drugs harm no one but yourself. But there's a big thing among young people at the moment for loving your neighbour, for not hurting—above all, for keeping in mind that people are people. I don't think they'll be too pleased when they know their idol forgot or, rather, neglected to care for that fact.'

'Poor old Dunsand. What of him?'

'His career will be ruined, but it won't be prison for him. Mental hospital for years? Is that much better? It was a succubus he killed. Unfortunately for him, we know succubi don't exist—they're flesh and blood.'

191

A single light showed in Burden's bungalow. In an armchair in the living room John lay asleep, his hair tousled, a half-empty glass of milk beside him. The indicator light on the record player still glowed red.

'God, I forgot the kids! I was so carried away I forgot them.' Burden stooped tenderly over his son, but the boy didn't stir. 'He waited up for me,' he said wonderingly.

Wexford smiled rather sadly. 'Poor John. Somehow I don't think he'll get the Sundays album for his birthday now.'

'He certainly won't.' Burden took a stride to the record player, his face flushing with anger when he saw what lay on the turntable. Savagely, he seized 'Let-me-believe' in both hands and seemed about to twist it, to bend it double, when Wexford laid a gentle, warning hand on his arm.

'No, Mike,' he said. 'Don't do that. Leave it to John and— and all of them. Let them be his judges.'